Rethinking Peter Weiss

German Life and Civilization

Jost Hermand
General Editor

Advisory Board

Helen Fehervary
Ohio State University

Peter Uwe Hohendahl
Cornell University

Robert C. Holub
University of California at Berkeley

Klaus Scherpe
Humboldt University, Berlin

Frank Trommler
University of Pennsylvania

Vol. 32

PETER LANG
New York • Washington, D.C./Baltimore • Boston • Bern
Frankfurt am Main • Berlin • Brussels • Vienna • Canterbury

Rethinking Peter Weiss

Edited by
Jost Hermand
& Marc Silberman

PETER LANG
New York • Washington, D.C./Baltimore • Boston • Bern
Frankfurt am Main • Berlin • Brussels • Vienna • Canterbury

Library of Congress Cataloging-in-Publication Data

Rethinking Peter Weiss / edited by Jost Hermand and Marc Silberman.
p. cm. — (German life and civilization; vol. 32)
"...revised versions of lectures originally presented
on November 6–7, 1998, at the University of Wisconsin"—Pref.
Includes bibliographical references.
1. Weiss, Peter, 1916– —Criticism and interpretation.
I. Hermand, Jost. II. Silberman, Marc. III. Series.
PT2685.E5Z8468 832'.914—dc21 99-37419
ISBN 0-8204-4851-6
ISSN 0899-9899

Die Deutsche Bibliothek-CIP-Einheitsaufnahme

Rethinking Peter Weiss / ed. by Jost Hermand and Marc Silberman.
–New York; Washington, D.C./Baltimore; Boston; Bern;
Frankfurt am Main; Berlin; Brussels; Vienna; Canterbury: Lang.
(German life and civilization; Vol. 32)
ISBN 0-8204-4851-6

Contents

Preface

It is impossible to escape the impression that the painter, film maker, essayist, novelist, and dramatist Peter Weiss has abruptly been forgotten, both by general audiences and literary scholars. While this abruptness itself might be a legitimate matter of investigation in a symptomatic reading of how literary tastes change and how the writing of literary history is connected to larger social and political agendas, we want recall the fact that Peter Weiss enjoyed during the 1970s and 1980s a reputation as one of the foremost European authors, a writer who emerged from the tradition of heady modernism among the French surrealists to struggle with the defeats and shocks of exile, World War II, the Holocaust, and cold-war conflicts as a politically engaged and morally authoritative voice of reason. With the end of the cold war, there was a sudden flurry of interest in Weiss. The *Peter Weiss Jahrbuch,* with editors centered at the universities of Essen and Hannover, came into existence and in the meantime has published seven impressive volumes. Independently of that endeavor a scholarly "Peter Weiss Gesellschaft" was established with a regular newsletter and a commitment to stage occasional conferences that focus on issues relevant to his creative work. Weiss was born in 1916 in a suburb of Potsdam called Nowawes, and with the fall of the Berlin Wall this place suddenly became accessible to Westerners. On the initiative of the Peter Weiss Gesellschaft an official marker was soon placed at the house there where Weiss had grown up.

Since then, however, the interest in Peter Weiss has receded again. His publishing house, Suhrkamp Verlag, is neither reprinting nor reissuing his works, and the plans on the part of Maisonneuve Press (Washington, D.C.) to publish the three-volume novel, *The Aesthetics of Resistance*, in English translation by Joachim Neugroschel, is proceeding, if at all, with great tardiness. Weiss's plays are hardly produced any longer on German or international stages except for an occasional revival of *Die Ermittlung* (The Investigation), while the formerly steady stream of articles, book chapters, and dissertations on his work has diminished in the past five years. It seems that Weiss's substantial oeuvre has become a casualty of the cold war's end, of the collapse of socialism, of the "end of history" at the beginning of a new millenium—as some would call it. This in itself strikes us as a valid reason to reconsider Peter Weiss, to face the challenge of rethinking the work of a writer and artist who was a committed socialist and utopian thinker at a time when these very categories have been fundamentally called into question.

But there is an additional reason, and that is the growing distance from the writer's most celebrated successes. We are referring to the span of time, for example, since his 1964 drama about the French revolution known by the short title *Marat/Sade*, the one that launched him internationally through Peter Brook's incredible London production that was subsequently filmed and distributed around the world; we are referring to the critical and controversial reception in the mid-sixties of *Die Ermittlung*, his documentary drama about the Frankfurt Auschwitz trial, as well as to his other political documentary plays of the sixties; and we are referring to his challenging masterpiece *Die Ästhetik des Widerstands,* published shortly before his death during the years 1975 to 1982, a work that spawned a mini-industry of readers' guides, university seminars, and conference lectures in the early 1980s.

Searching for the traces of this reception, for the ways in which Weiss himself intervened vis-à-vis the public echo of his writings as well as the ways in which his work was instrumentalized for specific interests, deserves careful attention. His role as an outsider, as a victim of the Third Reich's racial policies against the Jews, and as an exile living in Sweden who refused to align himself too closely with either East or West Germany was in some sense a unique position. His voice possessed a critical authority that resonated in different registers **within** a Germany divided into two parts, each with its respective ghosts of the past, and **beyond** Germany in a world that was skeptically interested in gauging how Germans were going to be integrated into the postwar situation. Retrospectively it also becomes clear that Peter Weiss was a writer whose critical acclaim emerged at a time when strategies for combining political and moral issues with innovative aesthetic forms dominated cultural discourse. His contribution in this context was important, perhaps exemplary. Yet, as the discourse changes so do judgments. Thus, we find ourselves asking: is there more to Peter

Weiss's work than the historically constrained parameters have allowed us to recognize?

The contributions in this volume, all revised versions of lectures originally presented on November 6-7, 1998, at the University of Wisconsin, suggest that indeed there are new questions to ask and astonishing responses awaiting us. The intense exchange that arose in this forum would not have been possible without the concentrated efforts of our guest speakers and moderators, who included Klaus L. Berghahn (University of Wisconsin, Madison), Susan Brantly (University of Wisconsin, Madison), Robert Cohen (New York University), Katja Garloff (Reed College, Oregon), Julia Hell (University of Michigan, Ann Arbor), Alexander Honold (Freie Universität Berlin), Helga Kraft (University of Illinois, Chicago), Roswitha Mueller (University of Wisconsin, Milwaukee), Yvonne Spielmann (Universität Siegen), James D. Steakley (University of Wisconsin, Madison), Jochen Vogt (Universität Essen), and a graduate student collective consisting of Jennifer Jenkins, Michella Lang, and Cordelia Scharpf.

The Workshop organizers wish to acknowledge here the timely advice on the part of Julia Hell and Robert Cohen during the initial planning stages for the conference; and above all we are indebted to the institutional partners that financially supported the Workshop project: the Anonymous Fund of the University of Wisconsin, which made it possible to cover travel and expenses of the out-of-town guests, the Swedish Institute in Stockholm, which generously provided a selection of Weiss's films, the University of Wisconsin Cinematheque for screening them, and the William F. Vilas Trust, which made possible the publication of this volume. Finally, without the usual cheerful, professional assistance of Joan Leffler, the German Department Coordinator, none of this would have been possible.

Madison, March 1999 The Editors

Katja Garloff

Cosmopolitan Leftovers and Experimental Prose: Peter Weiss's *Das Gespräch der drei Gehenden*

Recent criticism on Peter Weiss that discusses the role of exile and displacement in his work frequently invokes the opposition between two kinds of border crossings, namely that of the self-expansive cosmopolitan versus that of the victimized exile. In her analysis of representations of the Third World in postwar German literature, Arlene Teraoka recognizes that Weiss's interest in colonialism and its aftermath derived from his belated confrontation with the horrors of Auschwitz and interprets his political commitment of the 1960s as a reversal of his political passivity during the Second World War. Her conclusion that his political engagement with the victims of colonialism served primarily to mitigate his own sense of guilt, recalls contemporary critiques of cosmopolitanism as an endless expansion of the self through projection. In contrast, Alfons Söllner emphasizes in *Peter Weiss und die Deutschen* Weiss's own victimization during the Third Reich and reads his early, pre-1953 work as an aesthetically and politically intricate expression of his "exile after exile." Weiss's abiding exclusion after 1945 from the cultural sphere of Germany, the country that had forced him into exile, singularly positioned him to lend a voice to the victims of Holocaust. The following essay aims to go beyond the dichotomy between self-assertive cosmopolitanism and catastrophic exile by showing that both operate in Weiss's texts in a productive tension that marks his work as *diasporic*.

Weiss's cosmopolitan vision is perhaps most forcefully articulated at the end of his semi-autobiographical novel *Fluchtpunkt* (1962), which describes the life of a refugee and artist in Stockholm from 1940 to 1947. In this work the narrator's development of a cosmopolitan view is predicated upon a radical break with his refugee past during a trip to Paris. Upon his arrival he first experiences intense feelings of isolation and non-belonging before recuperating his original language and adopting a cosmopolitan identity.

> Die Freiheit war noch vorhanden, doch ich hatte Boden in ihr gewonnen, sie war keine Leere mehr, in der ich im Alptraum der Anonymität lag und in der alle Beziehungen ihren Sinn verloren, es war eine Freiheit, in der ich jedem Ding seinen Namen geben konnte. ... Und die Sprache, die sich jetzt einstellte, war die Sprache, die ich am Anfang meines Lebens gelernt hatte, die natürliche Sprache, die mein Werkzeug war, die nur noch mir selbst gehörte, und mit dem Land, in dem ich aufgewachsen war, nichts mehr zu tun hatte. Diese Sprache war gegenwärtig, wann immer ich wollte und wo immer ich mich befand. Ich konnte in Paris leben oder in Stockholm, in London oder New York, und ich trug die Sprache bei mir, im leichtesten Gepäck. In diesem Augenblick war der Krieg überwunden, und die Jahre der Flucht waren überlebt ... An diesem Abend, im Fühjahr 1947, auf dem Seinedamm in Paris, im Alter von dreißig Jahren, sah ich, daß ich teilhaben konnte an einem Austausch von Gedanken, der ringsum stattfand, an kein Land gebunden (196f.).

This concluding vision of *Fluchtpunkt* resonates with traditional notions of cosmopolitanism, particularly with the German Enlightenment tradition of *Weltbürgertum*, in that it links the cosmopolitan outlook to gestures of self-location.[1] For although cosmopolitanism denotes a tolerant openness toward other cultures, a cosmopolitan lifestyle is usually contingent upon a secure position within a particular culture, or at least commensurable with the alignment to a particular culture. This safe anchoring in a native culture reverberates, for example, in Goethe's well known concept of a future world literature, which would be "eine allgemeine Weltliteratur, worin uns Deutschen eine ehrenvolle Rolle vorbehalten ist. Alle Nationen schauen sich nach uns um, sie loben, sie tadeln, nehmen auf und verwerfen ..." (Goethe 361). And while cosmopolitanism figures as a regulative, never completely realized principle of human history in Kant's "Idee zu einer allgemeinen Geschichte in weltbürgerlicher Absicht," its more pragmatic meaning in *Zum ewigen Frieden* betrays a similar centrist tendency. *Weltbürgerrecht* is there defined as the stranger's right to fair treatment in a foreign country, a right Kant never fully disentangles from the rights of an individual within a national constitution, the *Staatsbürgerrecht* (213f.) Cosmopolitan and national identities are thus not mutually exclusive but rather interdependent: someone who has a safe place within a national constitution, or in a national culture, is also more likely to find a safe place anywhere in the world. The tolerant, world-embracing view of the cosmopolitan emerges out of his being anchored somewhere.

In *Fluchtpunkt* this stabilization of the subject's position as a precondition for the expansion of its circle of concern, transpires in a number of ways. Most importantly, it is a particular place name— Paris—that signifies cosmopolitan freedom and that tears down the barriers separating the narrator from the international community. By evoking Paris, he inscribes a *Fluchtpunkt* in the technical sense of the word, that is, a point that defines the perspective of a painting and thus renders it coherent and meaningful: Paris is the vanishing point which gives meaning to the narrator's erratic wanderings. Textually, this painting technique also translates into visual descriptions that fix and accentuate the narrator's location through the play of light against the city scape, such as: "Ich stand still, sah die Boote vorbeifahren, sah den Abglanz der gesunkenen Sonne auf der Spitze des Eiffelturms ..." (195). A similar doubleness of localization and de-localization marks the narrator's recuperation of his native language. Freeing this language from its geographical and historical boundedness, he at the same time reclaims it as a place of symbolic origin.

Despite the novel's optimistic ending the narrator's self-chosen *Weltbürgertum* remains tenuous, not only because the abruptness and imposed teleology of the final scene give it a contrived character, but also because the signs of persecution engraved upon the bodies of other Jewish refugees continue to haunt the narrator's sense of freedom. In the novel the connection between Jewishness and exile is established through a number of subtle textual strategies, for example, through the description of the narrator's gaze falling on an old Jewish cemetery at the moment when he becomes painfully aware of his own restlessness and inability to stay with a woman for any significant length of time (44). Most importantly, the narrator arrives at his vision of self-chosen exile only by separating himself from two other exiles who are associated with Jewishness. These are his father, whose self-hatred and fruitless pursuit of assimilation reveal deep-seated anxieties and ineluctable homelessness, and the painter Anatol, whose driven, Ahasveros-like demeanor marks a similarly discomforting, unchosen exile. In both cases, the emphatic visualization of physical markers of exile—the father's circumcised penis and what we may call Anatol's "mark of Cain"—distances the narrator from these figures.[2] The development of the cosmopolitan view, which establishes exile as site of subjective empowerment, is thus constantly undermined by other forms of exiles, forms of exile that result from persecution and that are most prominently embodied by Jewish figures.

These other modes of exile constitute a kind of catastrophic remainder that cannot be integrated into the positive model of cosmopolitanism, a split that returns in various ways in Weiss's work from the 1960s on.[3] In another place I have shown that this tension produces the specific critical potential of Weiss's texts, which narrate the violent rupture between the subject and its place of origin for an imagined German audience. Weiss's use of distance as a hermeneutic device manifests itself, for example, in the ethnographic perspective of *Bericht über Einrichtungen und Gebräuche in den Siedlungen der Grauhäute* and in the hyper-objective mode of *Die Ermittlung*. I have further proposed that concepts of diaspora developed in recent years in conjunction with postcolonial criticism be used to analyze the cultural productivity of what I would call the "cosmopolitan leftover." In what follows, I wish to compound this argument by showing that Weiss not only directs the diasporic imagination critically against Germany but that he also, in *Das Gespräch der drei Gehenden* (1963), envisions the emergence of a community of refugees out of historical trauma.

I

At this juncture, a brief consideration of the analytic benefits of the term "diaspora" is necessary. In scholarship on Jewish history an attempt has been made to distinguish between imposed and self-chosen exile, the latter being designated by the term diaspora. These more positive connotations of diaspora reverberate in adaptations of the term by postcolonial critics, who have redefined diaspora not merely as a place of dwelling but as enunciative position and mode of articulation. Stuart Hall, for instance, uses the term diaspora to describe a form of cultural identity which, although mentally bound to a lost place of origin, recognizes the insurmountable distance between this imaginary spatial center and the lived experience of postcolonial migrants. According to him it is the gap between "here" and "there," and the refusal to cover this gap through nostalgia and idealization of the lost home, that makes diasporic discourse intrinsically utopian and capable of producing new places from which to speak. The acceptance of an irreparable rupture between the subject and its place of origin, Hall further suggests, prevents the hypostatization of this place as pure origin while guarding against any form of ethnocentric absolutism that would preclude an engagement with the dynamic and hybrid reality of cultural identities. In view of mass displacements that elude a clear distinction between imposed and self-chosen exile, critics like Hall thus replace the criterion of willingness with that of cultural productivity.

One aspect of this productivity is the conception of diaspora as an alternative form of community. This notion draws on the traditional semantics of diaspora, which signifies the state of dispersal as well as the group of the dispersed, whereas exile connotes a more solitary state of separation. Of particular interest in this context is Paul Gilroy who, in his analysis of the interrelations between black cultures on both sides of the Atlantic, furnishes concepts of diasporic collective identity that he traces back to Judaic traditions. I would suggest that we can reimport some of his insights for an analysis of German Jewish diaspora culture after the Holocaust. Gilroy himself lays the grounds for this reverse borrowing when he points out the analogy between racial slavery and industrial genocide, both of which are distinctively modern phenomena that undermine modernity's promise of emancipation and historical progress. Both testify to the "complicity of rationality and ethnocidal terror" (213) that characterizes, for example, racial science and modern eugenics.

We may add that the absence of a shared religion and genealogy, which Gilroy identifies as a feature that distinguishes the predicament of blacks from that of Jews, also characterizes the situation of post-Holocaust German Jews, many of whom came, like Peter Weiss, from a mixed or assimilated background and felt bound to other Jews at best through the experience of exile and persecution. A distinct diaspora consciousness—defined for the moment as the attachment to another place that shapes the experience of one's present place of dwelling—was a constitutive element of Jewish group identity in premodern Europe, yet largely disappeared in the German-speaking countries during the nineteenth century process of emancipation and acculturation.[4] The displacement of German Jews in the wake of the Second World War and the Holocaust destabilized the notion of a shared and localizable origin even more radically, creating a renewed and doubled diaspora consciousness that involved a profoundly negative attachment to the home that had turned into a site of genocide.

It is here that Gilroy is most helpful in formulating a concept of diasporas as fragile communities emerging from historical trauma. An important factor in the constitution of such communities are cultural practices that draw audiences momentarily into groups. Of course, Benedict Anderson's *Imagined Communities* and other recent works on national identity have shown that national communities, too, rely on cultural forms to create social cohesion, but the need to fashion communities is more obvious in the diaspora because of the erosion of commonality in a history of dispersal and suffering. It is for this reason that the phatic aspect of diaspora cultural expressions, that is, their capacity to initiate and sustain contact between human beings, takes on such crucial significance. This capacity is more immediately tangible in the musical performances Gilroy describes, but it is also intrinsic to the literary forms deployed by black modernists. Their experimental, radically unfinished forms of writing have the power to interpellate readers, while the narratives of exile and journeying take on a mnemonic function, "directing the consciousness of the group back to significant, nodal points in its common history and its social memory" (198).

Diaspora figures in Gilroy as a form of transnational connectedness that is devoid of the homogenizing and self-assertive tendencies of nationalism and ethnocentrism and that incorporates and renders productive a state of vulnerability. Central to this concept is the redefinition of tradition not as a static archive of past cultural forms but a process of intra-group communication across temporal and spatial boundaries. Commenting upon the circulation and transmutation of musical forms across the black Atlantic as well as on the elliptic invocations of African origins in this music, Gilroy writes that "it may make sense to try and reserve the idea of tradition for the nameless, evasive, minimal qualities that make these diaspora conversations possible. This would involve keeping the term as a way to speak about the apparently magical processes of connectedness that arise as much from the transformation of Africa by diaspora cultures as from the affiliation of diaspora cultures to Africa and the traces of Africa that those diaspora cultures enclose" (199). Gilroy thus furnishes a model of intra-group communication that reflects the heterogeneity and constant remaking of this group and that hinges upon a moment of misrecognition, undiminishable distance, and historical rupture. Diaspora cultural expressions constitute hybrid communities, not only because they are inevitably entangled with the surrounding majority cultures, but also because they destabilize the idea of a localizable origin while establishing new—imagined, tenuous—grounds of collective identity.[5]

II

The idea of a diasporic interconnectedness created through an interpellation of audiences has to be qualified, of course, when considering Peter Weiss. If diaspora writing always addresses at least two different audiences—namely the diasporic group and the majority culture to which it relates—it is the confrontational encounter with the latter which preoccupied Weiss's mind during the early 1960s. Elsewhere I have shown in more detail that Weiss's belated recognition as a German language writer around 1960, commonly treated as his literary breakthrough, was accompanied by feelings of ambivalence and a renewed sense of his separateness from Germany and German culture.[6] In 1962, Weiss was invited for the first time to a meeting of the *Gruppe 47* and recited from the text which I will analyze below, *Das Gespräch der drei Gehenden*. Given his ambivalent feelings about that group in particular, Weiss's choice of a text that meditates on the experience of flight and persecution probably was a distancing gesture rather than an offer for dialog. It is therefore all the more interesting that *Das Gespräch der drei Gehenden* projects a vision of a subterranean, transitory, tenuous communication between the dispersed. As I will show, this experimental prose text can be read as a conversation between three refugees across broken story lines, a faltering dialog between atomized exiles whose fragmentary speech never reaches an interlocutor without distortion. It takes place in a space that is itself fragmented, despite the appearance of a harbor in the background. In this text the absence of a consistent and stable narrative center entails a creation of transitory centers, purely fictitious grounds of encounter where the threads of different stories converge occasionally. In short, I propose to read *Das Gespräch* as an allegory of a community of refugees, whose accidental encounter, mingling voices, and evasive moments of contact recall the hybrid and unstable diasporic communities described by Gilroy.

Formally, *Das Gespräch* is a montage of short descriptions and narratives, vaguely allocated in the introductory scene to the voices of "Abel, Babel und Cabel" (7). If I refer below to "speakers," it has to be kept in mind that they are never identifiable as persons and that their voices sometimes merge and affect each other's. There is, nonetheless, enough continuity between the different segments that we can attribute most of them to one of three speakers whom I will simply call A, B, and C.[7] These three figures have met accidentally and are now telling each other various stories and incidents of their lives. "Sie gingen und sahen sich um und sahen was sich zeigte, und sie sprachen darüber und über anderes was sich früher gezeigt hatte" (7). And this, "was sich früher gezeigt hatte," consists for at least two of the speakers mostly of flight, persecution, and hiding. Frequently, their discourse starts with a deictic gesture, with one of them pointing to a place or an object and elaborating on the events associated with it. Or the rhythm of the walk itself dictates the stream of memories:

> Und wenn ich unsere Schritte im Kies höre, hier in dieser Stille hinter den Mauern, dann ist das andere wieder da, das nie zu einem Abschluß kam, und da liege ich immer noch, im Sand, vor einem offenen Schober, und kann ein Stück an Stacheldrähten entlangkriechen, in einer eng begrenzten, von Bäumen durchwachsenen Anlage. Wenn ich dort bin gibt es kein Herauskommen, ich kann es nur zeitweise vergessen, da sage ich mir, ich bin wach, ich lebe noch, und dann ist es wieder da, dann steht es wieder bevor, und ich zermartere mich mit Gedanken, auf welche Weise es geschehen wird, mit dem Strick, dem Beil, den Geschossen... (47).

The experimental character of the text manifests itself in its spatial logic, a critical adaptation of the *nouveau roman* style. Like the *nouveau roman*, *Das Gespräch* is descriptive in a way that ultimately dissolves the temporal and spatial coherence of narrative. Certain scenes and places recur several times, yet are cast into different times and circumstances, which makes their very existence questionable. The bridge where the three walkers initially meet, for example, figures as a variable in a number of different narratives, with one voice depicting it being built the night before and another voice claiming it as the site of a grotesque incident that happened long ago (8, 10f.). This style, far from being an end in itself, mimetically reproduces the perspective of refugees who experience space as fragmented, as a net of hiding places and intersections on nomadic routes. The nomadic nature of the figures is first hinted at by the name of the second speaker—"Babel"—and becomes more evident in their various stories of flight and attempted return. The image of the harbor that underlies most of the text also suggests this kind of perspective. A nodal point of traffic and communication, but also a place of ongoing transformations where newly erected buildings stand next to ruins and piles of debris, the harbor is a site where different times and different places interconnect (26f., 60, 102ff.).

The reconstruction of the refugee's perspective in *Das Gespräch* incorporates the fleeting character of his experience into the very process of narration. One effect of this is that narrated space fails to constitute a stable background for a set of events; the harbor, the bridge, and the street are transient effects of enunciation rather than chronotopes. As Mikhail Bakhtin defines them, chronotopes are categories of cultural systems that relate time and space in a narrative, thus establishing a realm of human action; they are relatively stable units that precede the individual literary text and prefigure its meaning. In *Das Gespräch*, however, the lengthy topographical descriptions of the harbor continuously construct and de-construct a spatio-temporal unit, rather than organizing the refugee's experience into a unity of signification.

The spatial logic of this text is best described in Michel de Certeau's terms as a continuous transformation of place into space, that is, as an infusion of human agency and movement into an otherwise stable configuration of positions.[8] The distinction between place and space corresponds to that between the map, which is a static depiction of immobile objects, and the itinerary, which is a description of space traversed and "practiced" by human agents. The spatialization of place creates a multitude of possibilities while obfuscating geometrical order and spatial transparency. The multiple paths of pedestrians, who appropriate urban places through everyday activities such as walking and window shopping, for example, transform the ordered space of architectural planning into the *"opaque and blind* mobility characteristic of the bustling city" (93). City walking thus presents a view from below, devoid of panoramic overview but in close proximity to concrete localities and events.

Similarly, the speakers in *Das Gespräch* retrieve through walking what Weiss once called in his *Notizbücher* a topological memory, that is a memory dispersed into the contingent particulars of a street without end or beginning: "Topologisches Gedächtnis. Die Straße. Das Wiedererkennen des zurückgelegten Weges. Unzählige kleine Merkmale, ein Kratzer, ein Loch, ein Riß, hier geschah dies, dort jenes" (*Notizbücher* 108). In *Das Gespräch* such a topological memory is relayed through the numerous deictic locutions, which disseminate memories while establishing tentative nodal points between past and present. It further becomes clear that the speakers' attendance to the concrete sites of experience reflects the fragmentation of this experience: "Als ich müde war legte ich mich hin, wo ich gerade war, in der Nähe des Wassers, auf eine glattgewalzte Straßenfläche, mit Bruchstellen, Speichelfladen, Pferdeäpfeln" (41f.). The picaresque chronotope of the street could subsume these contingencies of the refugee's life once again under the logic of sequentiality. But the particular, even contrasting, narrative uses each speaker makes of the spatial images of bridge, harbor, and street are analogous to the city walker's mobilization of localized objects for diverse, sometimes incommensurable, itineraries. In short, rather than containing the dispersion of time and space into formal coherence, the style of *Das Gespräch der drei Gehenden* redoubles dispersion.

III

What kind of conversation can take place in such a text, between these three walkers? In what follows, I suggest that it is a conversation much like the diaspora conversations described by Gilroy, one that accommodates the experience of historical trauma and an irreducible distance between interlocutors. As we have seen above, the bridge, the traditional metaphor for encounter and dialog, becomes a variable in two different narratives contesting each other. Indeed, if the text relates a conversation, it is one in which mutual understanding is at best an effect of chance: "Wenn einer sprach schwiegen die beiden andern und hörten zu oder sahen sich um und hörten auf anderes, und wenn der eine zuende gesprochen hatte, sprach der zweite, und dann der dritte, und die beiden andern hörten zu oder dachten an anderes" (7). This casual indifference pointedly describes the character of the conversation in which a speaker would occasionally continue the speech of the previous speaker in an associative manner, but more often would simply ignore it and relate something he sees or continue an earlier tale.

The fictitious character of these tales is emphasized through the conspicuous use of the ferryman motif, which is associated with free-floating imagination in such German expressions as "Seemannsgarn spinnen." Throughout *Das Gespräch* speaker A relates anecdotes of a ferryman and his six sons whose fantastic physiques and live styles are reminiscent of tall tales. The speaker's implication that the ferryman's discourse is fuzzy and that he may not have understood him properly, enhances the impression of stories constantly being made up, while the interspersed fairy tale motives emphasize the fantastic character of these stories.[9] The dialog that emerges in *Das Gespräch* is an indirect one: as the speakers tell their stories in an often grotesque manner in which lies and truths become inseparable, they sometimes merge, or affect each other, with one voice picking up the thread of another voice's tale, spinning it on and changing it.

One might be tempted to read *Das Gespräch der drei Gehenden* as a rather playful account of three travelers who improvise stories to deceive and outdo each other—"Seemannsgeschichten," in short—were it not for some instances in which the ordeal of exile surfaces with unexpected intensity. One of these instances deserves particular attention, since it reiterates a scene that appears in several of Weiss's writings. This scene, which appears, for example, in the final pages of *Fluchtpunkt* quoted above, depicts the exile's life as a drama of language lost and reclaimed. More precisely, the exile who has been ousted from his native language first regresses into a child's lallation and then reappropriates his language in an act of self-empowerment which enables him to free language from its historical and geographical boundedness. The exile's language dilemma is most pointedly captured in Weiss's address "Laokoon oder Über die Grenzen der Sprache," in which language appears as the very agent of persecution and expulsion. I have said before that the experience of an irreparable rupture between the subject and its place of origin, which returns as the rupture between the subject and its language, constitutes a central trauma of German Jewish exiles after the Holocaust. I would also suggest that the emphatic cosmopolitan vision at the end of *Fluchtpunkt* functions as a screen memory that covers up the traumatic core of the refugee's experience.

Das Gespräch der drei Gehenden approaches this traumatic core through a process of fictionalization and defictionalization and suspends trauma in a new form of collectivity. A series of three episodes in which someone hides under a pile of lumber near the railway bridge and observes the city culminates in a scene of language lost and reclaimed that recalls the narrator's experience in *Fluchtpunkt*, but offers a decisively different view on it. The first of these scenes is narrated by speaker C, who relates personal experience, the second is told by speaker A, who renders the fantastic and possibly misremembered stories of the ferryman, and the third is again told by speaker C. While the first scene relates a relatively harmless episode in speaker C's life (59-61), the second one recounts how the fourth son of the ferryman, Jom, spent the latter part of his life under a pile of packing paper and corrugated board, composing nonsense rhymes with a pencil discarded by a carpenter. These rhymes recall the lallation of the insane Hölderlin—Jom's odes and hymns and the carpenter's pencil evoke this figure—but also avant-garde artistic practices in which word sequences are generated through random letter variations. Jom seems to deploy here a modernist technique of writing, one that employs chance and improvisation and foregrounds sound and rhythm at the expense of semantics: "Er, der des Sprechens nicht fähig ist, läßt diese Laute ertönen, sie klingen wie Salbe Malbe halbe kalbe balde Walde falte kalte halte Spalte, und so weiter, die Worte sind beliebig zu ersetzen" (76). The fact that the speaker later states that he is not sure about the veracity of this scene, that Jom might rather be a successful writer sitting in an expensive apartment and composing polished sentences on a typewriter (76), underscores the hypothetical nature of the speaker's description.

The last time this scenario recurs, it is deprived of its playful grotesqueness and transformed into images of threat and horror. One of these images even evokes a mass grave:

... und da sah ich schon, daß dieser Raum angefüllt war mit Mengen von gleichartigen beweglichen Stücken, großen Füßen, Händen, Rümpfen oder Hälsen, alle behaart und verschorft, manche mit stumm aufklappenden Mündern, es waren auch Reihen von Zähnen, mit Fleischfasern daran, und halbe Ohren, in deren Blutkruste es von Gold blinkte, und Finger, mit eingefaßten Steinen, und dies alles regte sich unter mir, und es war mir darum zu tun, herauszufinden, was dies für ein Tümpel, für eine Grube war ... (106f.).

And a few pages further down, the wasting away of the speaker's speech gets metaphorically linked to the decomposition of bodies in the mass grave:

... und jetzt soll ich Zeugnis ablegen, Rechenschaft geben für ein Leben, mit all diesen zurückgelegten Wegen, diesen geöffneten und geschlossenen Türen, mit all diesen Bewegungen und Berührungen, mit diesen Worten, dieser Flut von Worten, die ausgesprochen und vernommen worden waren, zu keinem andern Nutzen, als zu versickern, zu verschwimmen, zu zerrinnen (109).

In Weiss's *Rekonvaleszenz* a similar metaphorical association is made, perhaps unwittingly, between the destruction of the exile writer's work and the burning of the Jews in the death camps.[10]

In the third hiding scene of *Das Gespräch* word cascades similar to those of Jom spring from the refugee's desire to bear witness to what he sees, a desire that is frustrated by his complete lack of understanding. In contrast to the babbling Jom, this speaker uses not only adjectives and nouns but also verbs, thus creating rudimentary propositional clauses.

These are nonetheless still produced through a rather mechanical rhyming technique: "Mit ungeheurer Anstrengung versuchte ich mir dies zu erklären, ich dachte mir dazu ein weißes Blatt Papier, dessen Leere sich völlig ausfüllen ließ mit Worten, und ich hörte mich lallen, lallen allen ballen fallen hallen schallen, Samen kamen Namen lahmen mahnen Bahnen, Lasten Masten faßten, hasten tasten paßten ..." (108). If I am right in reading this scene as the expression of an exile's struggle with his language, we can say that he deploys here a mimetic mode of defense: overwhelmed by the hostility of language and unable to experience language as meaningful, he mimes the senseless spluttering of words in order not to be reduced to a mere object of linguistic violence. As the speaker imagines himself mechanically filling blank paper with words, the size of the sheet defines the measure of his speech. And yet, by organizing his linguistic material through the systematic deployment of chance, he also becomes, like a writer of concrete poetry, an agent in the automated production of words.[11]

In a way this is a self-reflexive scene that discloses the principles of the text of *Das Gespräch* itself, whose main figures are alphabetical ciphers rather than psychologically developed characters. In fact, the names of the speakers as well as those of the ferryman's sons are generated through the systematic exchange of letters, respectively vowels: Abel, Babel, Cabel, and Jam, Jem, Jim, Jom, Jum, Jym. Whereas the names of the first two speakers relate mimetically to the themes of flight and persecution—Abel is an archetypal victim and Babel the most salient symbol of dispersion—the third name evinces the text's somewhat mindless adherence to the alphabetical sequence of letters. Even if we read the "Cabel" as a "Kabel," signifying connectedness in a world of electronic media, this letter substitution draws our attention to the ruling of the alphabet. That is, both speaker C and the author of the text surrender their linguistic creativity to an external order that ignores semantics but also provides a minimal form of resistance against the amorphous dispersal of the exile's writing. My point is that, if this scene is about a refugee's struggle with language, it arrives at a rather modest resolution, one that neither results from an act of self-empowerment nor entails a sovereign mastery over language. Rather, it is effected by the circulation and transmutation of speech fragments across the distances that never cease to separate the speakers from each other. A closer examination of the wording of the three segments shows how word sequences are repeated, conflated, and distorted while circulating among the speakers.[12] While establishing this new form of collectivity, *Das Gespräch* revokes the teleology of self articulated in *Fluchtpunkt*. The poetic license to fashion life stories whose fictitious character remains exposed replaces here the subject's freedom from geographical and historical boundedness invoked in *Fluchtpunkt*.

In summary, the accidental encounter among refugees in *Das Gespräch* creates a vision of the possibilities of exile quite different from cosmopolitanism. The text as a whole presents a conversation between atomized exiles, a conversation that is devoid of the grand gesture of the *Weltbürger* who speaks to the whole world owing to his stable position in one culture. This conversation, like the diaspora conversations described by Gilroy, renders productive a state of vulnerability: from the experience of persecution and hiding, the possibility of meeting in transitory spaces and fashioning transitory life stories emerges. The experimental style of *Das Gespräch* is instrumental in creating this possibility. This same style, however, also indicates the limited applicability of Gilroy's model to the writing of a post-Holocaust German Jewish writer like Peter Weiss. The absence of referential markers and the radical fragmentation of narrative space in *Das Gespräch* suggest that not even the image of a shared geographical origin is available for its speakers. It further seems questionable that the collectivity established through the mingling of their voices extends beyond the text to include its readers, an impression that is supported by Weiss's ambivalent reaction to his reception in Germany. In the post-Holocaust era Weiss's diasporic writing articulates not the existence of an alternative form of community, but instead its hypothetical conjecture in view of its factual absence.

Notes

1   Weiss himself invokes this tradition in interviews and letters from the
    1960s, in which he refers to himself as a "Weltbürger." See, for instance,
    his letter to Marcel Reich-Ranicki from October 3, 1995. Weiss argues
    there that his identity as a "Weltbürger" allows him to regard German
    problems within a universalizing framework: "Indem ich nicht an
    Deutschland gebunden bin, sehe ich es geographisch nur als kleinen
    Bestandteil der Erdkontinente, und in der Auseinandersetzung die dort,
    ständig neu aufflammend und sich immer mehr erweiternd stattfindet, geht
    es um andere Dinge als um die Selbstzufriedenheit, von der die offizielle
    westdeutsche Politik geprägt ist" (Peter Weiss-Archiv, Stiftung Archiv der
    Akademie der Künste, Berlin, 76/86/2172-1). For Weiss's self-labeling as a
    "Weltbürger," see further below in the letter (76/86/2172-2).

2   See the portrayal of Anatol: "Seine Stirn war bis zur Mitte des Schädels kahl,
    und auf ihrer Höhe zeichnete sich im scharfen Licht der Glühbirne, die von
    der Decke herabhing, eine kreisrunde Vertiefung ab" (33). See also the
    visualization of the father's circumcised penis, the (hidden) mark of his
    Jewishness: "Auch die verwirrten Worte meines Vaters wurden mir
    verständlich, mit denen er das Unglück verfluchte, das ihn auf die Flucht und
    in die Heimatlosigkeit getrieben hatte. Ich sah ihn an einem Sonntagmorgen,
    als ich im Badezimmer stand und mich rasierte, und er nicht wagte, nackt in
    das eingelaufene Bad zu steigen, und deshalb die Hose seines Schlafanzuges
    anbehielt. Ich sah ihn im warmen Wasser liegen, von der Hose umflossen,
    die mir sein Geschlecht verbarg, das beschnitten war, und das er mir nie
    gezeigt hatte" (53).

3   In *Die Ästhetik des Widerstands* this dichotomy receives an interesting new
    accent. Exile figures there both as a positive hermeneutic stance and as the
    sign of a catastrophe eluding the narrator's attempts at rationalization. As
    the novel critically reconstructs the antifascist struggle from its spatial
    margins, those who are "exiled" (in Sweden) from the centers of political
    resistance prove to be most perceptive of its contradictions and failures. At
    the same time another, negative form of exile surfaces when the narrator's
    mother identifies with the stream of Jewish refugees fleeing from Germany.
    As the mother gradually turns into a silent allegory of the plight of these
    racially persecuted victims, their catastrophic exile becomes marked as both
    Jewish and female.

4   This generalization brackets such related issues as the rise of Zionism and
    the persistence of religious belief, particularly in some parts of the

Habsburg Empire. Furthermore, the process of emancipation clearly remained incomplete, situating Jews rather uneasily within German-speaking cultures. However problematic such integration into new "fatherlands" was, it nonetheless represented a significant shift from the earlier bond to a distant homeland.

5   Another term to be considered in this context is "vernacular cosmopolitanism," developed by Homi Bhabha in "Unsatisfied: Notes on Vernacular Cosmopolitanism." For both Bhabha and Gilroy, transnational solidarity is based not on the empathy of the strong with the weak, but on the vulnerability of the dislocated and suffering, and both emphasize the dynamic and hybrid character of transnational identities. I prefer, however, the term "diaspora" because it captures better than "vernacular cosmopolitanism" the sense of interconnectedness among members of a particular group—even if this group shares nothing but historical suffering. Bhabha is interested in the generalizable critical potential of minority discourse rather than its power to constitute particular diasporic groups. See in particular his seminal article "Dissemi-Nation: Time, Narrative and the Margins of the Modern Nation." Drawing on Jacques Derrida's analysis of supplementary logic, Bhabha argues there that the supplementary function of minority discourse—which he somewhat interchangeably labels diasporic, cosmopolitan, marginalized, etc.—exposes the foundational split within the national community.

6   See Garloff 54f., 59f. An important source for Weiss's reaction to his reception in Germany are his *Notizbücher 1960-1971*. He recorded there, for instance, scraps of Nazi language he overheard on German streets during a reading tour (227) and outbreaks of persecution fears he suffered during the 1964 meeting of the *Gruppe 47* in Sigtuna (293). He even imagines the returning exile as a belated victim of Nazi persecution: "Der Besuch des Emigranten in Deutschl.—Er stirbt daran, wird also verspätet doch noch ermordet —" (226).

7   Helmut Lüttmann suggests a plausible sequence of the speakers (footnote 7, p. 133).

8   "A place (*lieu*) is the order (of whatever kind) in accord with which elements are distributed in relationships of coexistence... A place is thus an instantaneous configuration of positions. It implies an indication of stability. A space exists when one takes into consideration vectors of direction, velocities, and time variables. Thus space is composed of intersections of mobile elements" (de Certeau 117).

9   See, for instance, the following qualifications made by speaker A: "wenn

ich ihn nicht mißverstand" (17) and "Aus den Andeutungen des Fährmanns ging hervor" (75). The ferryman's stories, which speaker A relates, frequently feature fairytale figures like witches and dwarfs, and the other two speakers also evoke fairytale motives (e.g., the number seven, 116).

10   See the wording Weiss uses to describe his early writing attempts in exile: "doch auch in diesem Fragmentarischen, in diesen zerknitterten Zeugnissen einer krankhaften Einsamkeit, kann ich nicht unbrauchbaren Abfall sehn, nur wert, in den Verbrennungsofen zu fallen" (125). The combination of "Verbrennung" and "Ofen" is unusual and occurs, to my knowledge, only in references to the crematoria at Auschwitz.

11   The discrepancy between meaningful language and traumatic experience becomes even more tangible when the narrator, shortly thereafter, uses narrative structures to render his experiences. Interspersed with qualifications and hesitations, these structures are indicative of his failing attempt to verbalize unspeakable horror: "und *ich wollte mir meine Lage vereinfachen*, nun ja, dachte ich, ich bin von meiner Frau weggerissen worden, und meine Kinder hat man an der Wand zerschlagen, *wahrscheinlich* hat man mich in ein Gefängnis geschmissen und dann, *wie üblich*, in ein Massengrab" (109, my emphasis). In other words, while developing increasingly complex semantic units, the narrator exposes their stereotypical character and ultimate inadequacy.

12   See, for example, the three descriptions of the hide-out. First, speaker A conflates the words of the ferryman he remembers—perhaps misremembers—with those of C, which he has just heard, and then C uses the words he heard from A to recast the original scene: "Hier hatte ich mein Versteck, in den Ufergegenden des Stroms ..., *unter einem Bretterhaufen* hatte ich es mir wohnlich eingerichtet, und durch die Ritzen sah ich die Züge auf dem Bahndamm vorbeifahren, ich sah, wie die Schlepper ... unter der Eisenbahnbrücke hindurchfuhren" (58). "Aus den Andeutungen des Fährmanns ging hervor, daß er irgendwo *zwischen Packpaier und Wellpappe in den Gerümpelhaufen* hinter Eisenbahnbrücke haust" (75). "... da lag ich *unter Brettern und aufgeweichter Pappe* am Rand des Stroms, vor der Eisenbahnbrücke, und sah die nächtlichen Erscheinungen und die Erscheinungen bei Tag, und was sich zeigte war unerklärlich" (106). All emphases are mine.

Works Cited

Anderson, Benedict. *Imagined Communities: Reflections on the Origins and Spread of Nationalism*. Revised Edition (London 1991).

Bakhtin, Mikhail M. "Forms of Time and of the Chronotope in the Novel." In: *The Dialogic Imagination*. Michael Holquist, ed. Caryl Emerson and Michael Holquist, trans. (Austin 1981), p. 84-258.

Bhabha, Homi. "Dissemi-Nation: Time, Narrative and the Margins of the Modern Nation." In: *The Location of Culture* (London 1994), p. 139-170.

———. "Unsatisfied: Notes on Vernacular Cosmopolitanism." In: *Text and Nation: Cross-Disciplinary Essays on Cultural and National Identities*. Laura García-Moreno and Peter C. Pfeiffer, eds. (Columbia 1996), p. 191-207.

De Certeau, Michel. *The Practice of Everyday Life*. Steven Rendall, trans. (Berkeley 1984).

Garloff, Katja. "Peter Weiss's Entry into the German Public Sphere: On Diaspora, Language, and the Uses of Distance." In: *Colloquia Germanica* 30.1 (1997), p. 47-70.

Gilroy, Paul. *The Black Atlantic: Modernity and Double Consciousness*. (Cambridge, Mass 1993).

Goethe, Johann Wolfgang. *Werke*. Hamburger Ausgabe. Vol. 12 (München 1981).

Hall, Stuart. "Cultural Identity and Diaspora." In: *Identity: Community, Culture, Difference*. Jonathan Rutherford, ed. (London 1990), p. 222-37.

Kant, Immanuel. "Ideen zu einer allgemeinen Geschichte in weltbürgerlicher Absicht." In: *Werkausgabe*. Vol. XI (Frankfurt a.M. 1993), p. 33-50.

———. "Zum ewigen Frieden." In: *Werkausgabe*. Vol. XI, p. 193-251.

Lüttmann, Helmut. *Die Prosawerke von Peter Weiss* (Hamburg 1972).

Söllner, Alfons. *Peter Weiss und die Deutschen: Die Entstehung einer politischen Ästhetik wider die Verdrängung* (Opladen 1988).

Teraoka, Arlene A. *East, West, and Others: The Third World in Postwar German Literature* (Lincoln, Nebraska 1996).

Weiss, Peter. *Das Gespräch der drei Gehenden*. Frankfurt a.M. 1963.

———. *Die Ästhetik des Widerstands* (Frankfurt a.M. 1988).

———. *Fluchtpunkt* (Frankfurt a.M. 1965).

———. "Laokoon oder über die Grenzen der Sprache." In: *Rapporte* (Frankfurt a.M. 1968), p. 170-87.

———. *Notizbücher 1960-1971* (Frankfurt a.M. 1982).

———. *Rekonvaleszenz* (Frankfurt a.M. 1991).

Julia Hell

From Laokoon to Ge:
Resistance to Jewish Authorship in Peter Weiss's *Ästhetik des Widerstands*

> Weil ich tot bin—deshalb hört man mich nicht.
> Peter Weiss, *Notizbücher*, 1962.

In the cultural sphere of post-unification Germany, Peter Weiss is not a presence. He was, however, a presence during the brief transitional period from one Germany to another: dealing with their anxieties aroused by unification, East German intellectuals included excerpts from Weiss's *Ästhetik des Widerstands* in their series of public readings at the Berlin Akademie der Künste in 1989. Here, Weiss figured next to Canetti and other authors firmly located in the antifascist tradition. 1989 also saw the founding of the Peter Weiss Gesellschaft. And in 1992, Martin Rector, Jochen Vogt, and other academics from the former West founded the *Peter Weiss Jahrbuch*. The introduction to their first issue celebrates Weiss as an "eigensinnigen Linken" whose oeuvre, the editors maintain, always calls for the transgression of boundaries—political as well as aesthetic boundaries.[1] Clearly, the founders of both the Weiss society and the journal were hoping to initiate a process of re-thinking the project of the German left after the Cold War, and they were hoping that Weiss, one of the most controversial figures of the left, would serve as a sort of cultural rallying point.

Weiss's work never achieved this public resonance in the new Germany, however. Like Grass, Wolf, or Böll, Weiss was suddenly relegated to Germany's postwar literature, a literature whose concern with the Nazi past was deemed outdated. In the mid-90s, we were suddenly confronted with another revival, the enthusiastic celebration of a rather unlikely pair, the East German Heiner Müller and the West German Ernst Jünger.[2] There also was the revival of Uwe Johnson, whose *Jahrestage*, a memory project on the scale of Weiss's *Ästhetik*, fits much better into the current social democratic revival, on the one hand, and the "ostalgic" longing to re-discover one's East German past, on the other.

There is no Peter Weiss revival at the end of the 90s. After its seventh issue, the *Peter Weiss Jahrbuch* is now struggling to survive; Suhrkamp, Weiss's publisher, is no longer interested in financing a re-edition of Weiss's works; and in the canon debate conducted by *Die Zeit* in 1997, Weiss is not even mentioned. The situation in the U.S. is, however, different. In the context of Holocaust studies, Weiss is slowly emerging as one of the most important German authors. This American reception is lively, albeit rather controversial. For example, James Young in *Writing and Rewriting the Holocaust* or Alvin H. Rosenfeld in *A Double Dying: Reflections on Holocaust Literature*, discuss *Die Ermittlung* (*The Investigation*). The arguments are familiar from the German context of the 1960s: the word "Jew" does not appear in the text, Young argues, and Weiss's Marxist framework ultimately leads him to downplay the importance of antisemitism.[3] In *The Yale Companion to Jewish Writing and Thought in German Culture* Weiss appears as *the* Jewish author of the immediate postwar period. While the section on the period between 1945 to 1966 has one entry on Paul Celan, Hanna Arendt, Adorno, or Manes Sperber, to name but a few, it has two entries on Weiss (actually he is the only author represented twice). Thus, while the volume's editors, Sander Gilman and Jack Zipes, question in their introduction to the volume the very meaning of Jewish writing in German, of what it means to be a Jewish author, they celebrate Weiss as the Jewish author of the period which they call "The Return of Outside Voices."[4] Finally, there is Katja Garloff's brilliant dissertation on Weiss, Celan, and Sachs in which she discusses the post-war oeuvre of these three authors as expressions of a diasporic consciousness. Garloff uses this term with the connotations it has acquired in the debates on postcolonial culture. Like Celan and Sachs, Garloff argues, Weiss dealt with the enduring displacement that he experienced after 1945 by trying to "render livable and productive an irreparable rupture between the subject and its place of origin."[5] Like the editors of the *Peter Weiss Jahrbuch*—and like many other post-89 critics—Garloff thus foregrounds Weiss's "Unzugehörigkeit," his non-belonging, yet she discusses it in terms of post-Holocaust exile. Garloff knows that discussing Weiss with Celan and Sachs poses certain problems: "With 'Jewish,' I include a writer like Peter Weiss, who neither identified himself as a Jew in any positive way (religious, ethnic, etc.) nor would be regarded as one by Jewish religious laws (his mother was non-Jewish). Nonetheless, his sense of self was, at least temporarily, shaped by the knowledge of having been persecuted as a Jew."[6]

One of Garloff's main goals is to shift the debate about Weiss away from the familiar periodization of his work around the author's politicization in the early 1960s. That is, for a long time, German critics discussed Peter Weiss's work in terms of a fundamental break between the early and the late Weiss, between the subjectivist surrealist and the politicized artist. This is a familiar reading, a myth to which Weiss himself contributed. Starting with Jochen Vogt's monograph on Weiss in 1987, another story emerged.[7] This new story foregrounds continuity. Critics such as Vogt, but also Alfons Söllner, Robert Cohen, and now Garloff, emphasize Weiss's preoccupation with his own past: the fact that he was persecuted as a Jew and forced into exile, the fact that he was banished from his "natural" language, to use Weiss's own words.[8] These critics also point to Weiss's "Ästhetik wider die Verdrängung."[9] With this phrase Söllner captures Weiss's effort to write against the repression of the Nazi past in both East and West Germany.

Weiss himself called his work in 1965: "[M]ein Beitrag zur deutschen Vergangenheits-Bewältigung."[10] 1965 is the year in which Weiss's *Ermittlung* premiered in both Germanies, the year after he visited Auschwitz and published "Meine Ortschaft," and, finally, the year in which he delivered his acceptance speech for the Lessing Prize, "Laokoon oder Über die Grenzen der Sprache." 1965 is also the year in which Weiss's work to come to terms with his own past, to engage in his own form of "Vergangenheits-Bewältigung," reached both its moment of greatest density and a sudden halt with the publication of "10 Arbeitspunkte eines Autors in einer geteilten Welt."

In this article I propose to further explore Weiss's relationship to his Jewishness, or rather the fact of his having been persecuted as a Jew with respect to *Die Ästhetik des Widerstands*. I will, however, first concentrate on a set of earlier texts: "Laokoon oder Über die Grenzen der Sprache" and "Meine Ortschaft," both texts written almost simultaneously in 1964/65, and *Fluchtpunkt*, his novel from 1962.

I

In Book Three of *Die Ästhetik des Widerstands* Heilmann writes to the narrator: "[W]ir können nicht leben, ohne uns ein Bild von uns zu machen."[11] Heilmann is, of course, writing about the image of Herakles. I focus first, however, on two other images that constitute the very core of "Laokoon oder Über die Grenzen der Sprache." Most Weiss readers are familiar with the first image, the sculpture of Laokoon and his sons, which Weiss introduces with the following words: "Laokoon und seine Söhne, von Schlangen umwunden, verharren in den … Krümmungen ihres Gefangenseins."[12] Let's forget for a moment the controversy staged in this text between painting and writing in order to concentrate on the contrast that Weiss creates between the oldest son, on the one hand, and Laokoon and his youngest son, on the other: "Laokoon und sein jüngster Sohn … bilden nur noch ein Monument über ihren eigenen Untergang. Nie mehr geben sie einen Laut von sich. Der ältere Sohn aber gehört noch einer belebten Welt an, er bricht sich aus dem Statuarischen heraus, um … Bericht zu erstatten (L/180-81)." Later the author will explicitly identify with this older son: "Er war Laokoons ältester Sohn" (L/183).

In this acceptance speech Weiss also confronts us with another image, the image of himself as Laokoon's younger son, one could argue. I will quote this passage at length because I consider this one of the central images that Weiss has created of himself, a haunting portrait that captures the author's traumatic experience of persecution and his exile after exile:

> Für ihn, dem es die Stimme verschlagen hatte, bestand zeitweise nur die Erstarrung. Die Bilder, die vor ihm auftauchten waren reglos und spiegelten seine Ohnmacht. Er war an seine Vergangenheit gebunden und vermochte nicht, sich mit den Wörtern einer Sprache von ihr zu befreien.
> Er lag auf seinem Bett und brachte kaum die Kraft auf, die Hand nach Block und Stift auszustrecken, um etwas von den Erscheinungen festzuhalten. Der Untergang, in dem er sich befand, war totaler, als es frühere Katastrophen

gewesen waren, die einem Beobachter noch einen Fußbreit Boden gönnten, von dem aus sich die Ereignisse betrachten und besingen ließen. Zwar war der Leib des Liegenden noch nicht zerschlagen und ausgeblutet, die Wände um ihn waren noch nicht niedergebrannt, doch war er, wie alle anderen auch, der Gewalt ausgeliefert, die sich über alles Lebende hermachte.

Erst jetzt, Jahre nach seinem Austritt aus der natürlichen Sprache, erkannte er die Reichweite des Bruchs. Der Gedanke, daß es einmal möglich sein könnte, zu denen zurückzukehren, die die Sprache noch besaßen und mit dieser Sprache trieben, was ihnen beliebte, war noch nicht da. Er mußte lernen, sich in der neuen Sprache anzusiedeln, oder er mußte in der Sprachlosigkeit untergehn (L/181).

What does Weiss let us read in this passage? First and foremost, it is a passage about a moment in the speaker's past where language was lost and nothing remained but images. Which images? Arrested, frozen images that reflect nothing but the subject's powerlessness—the glaring, blinding images, I would argue, that Weiss had seen seven years earlier:

Dann, im Frühjahr 1945, sah ich den Endpunkt der Entwicklung ... Auf der blendend hellen Bildfläche sah ich die Stätten, für die ich bestimmt gewesen war, die Gestalten zu denen ich hätte gehören sollen ... Wir saßen in der Geborgenheit eines dunklen Saals und sahen, was bisher unvorstellbar gewesen war ...

Dort, vor uns, zwischen den Leichenbergen, kauerten die Gestalten der äußersten Erniedrigung . . Knochenbündel, blind füreinander, in einem Schattenreich ...

Zu wem gehörte ich jetzt, als Lebender, als Überlebender, gehörte ich wirklich zu jenen, die mich anstarrten mit ihren übergroßen Augen, und die ich längst verraten hatte, gehörte ich nicht eher zu den Mördern und Henkern (FP/135-36).

This is an excerpt from *Fluchtpunkt* that tells us what rendered Laokoon's youngest son mute and where the images originated that still hold him captive.

And yet, as I mentioned above, through the shift from the image of the younger to the older son, Laokoon expresses the hope that words might have the power to liberate Laokoon's younger son from these very images. Indeed, in this speech the restoration of language and the possibility of a new identity are inextricably linked: "So wie er seiner selbst nicht sicher war, war er auch der alten Sprache nicht mehr sicher.

Gleichzeitig mit dem Versuch, sich wiederzuentdecken und neu zu bewerten, mußte auch diese Sprache wieder neu errichtet werden" (L/186-87). This new language, the speaker tells us, is a language "die nirgendwo mehr einen festen Wohnsitz hat," it is a mere tool. Readers familiar with *Fluchtpunkt* will immediately recall the ecstatic moment in Paris with which the novel ends:

> Die Freiheit war absolut, ich konnte mich darin wiederfinden, ich konnte mich darin verlieren …
> Und die Sprache, die sich jetzt einstellte, war die Sprache, die ich am Anfang meines Lebens gelernt hatte, die natürliche Sprache, die mein Werkzeug war, die nur noch mir selbst gehörte, und mit dem Land, in dem ich aufgewachsen war, nichts mehr zu tun hatte (FP/196).

Thus, what Laokoon tells its German audience is a story of liberation from a trauma that they, or their fathers inflicted on the speaker. Like *Fluchtpunkt*, it asserts the re-appropriation of German by the one who was expelled from that language.

This is also a story of images, or rather the story of the supersession of the image of the oldest by that of the youngest son. In Laokoon, I would thus argue, we witness a process of identification away from Laokoon's younger to his older son, from the one who was rendered mute to the one who will bear witness. "Laokoon oder Über die Grenzen der Sprache" thus argues for language against image, yet at the same time it produces a set of images that will remain both defining and definitive.

But it is important not to forget that Laokoon formulates this new identity, which rests on the notion of language as a mere tool without history, in terms of a mere possibility: "Aber die Möglichkeit entsteht, daß er mit der Sprache, die ihm zur Arbeit dient und die nirgendwo mehr einen festen Wohnsitz hat, überall in der Freiheit zu Hause sei" (L/187). In her reading of *Fluchtpunkt*, Katja Garloff has most convincingly traced the fragility of this construction of language and identity "outside" of Weiss's past of persecution and exile.[13] In this essay I will argue the following: with *Rekonvaleszenz*, and later *Die Ästhetik des Widerstands* Weiss will once again confront the issue of this past of persecution and exile, the issue of his German past. He will once again try to find "einen Fußbreit Boden ... von dem aus sich die Ereignisse betrachten und besingen [lassen]." And what we will find in both *Rekonvaleszenz* and *Die Ästhetik* is the persistence of one particular image, the image of Laokoon's younger son. This image will never disappear, it will continue to cast a shadow over the image of the older son, complicating once more the story of liberation told first in *Fluchtpunkt* and then in "Laokoon."

Before I proceed, I would like to make two structural points about Weiss's Laokoon speech that pertain to the particular speaking position of this text, the absence of the speaker's "Ich," or "I." Weiss speaks about himself as "[e]r, von dem hier die Rede ist." He only uses the first person at the end, and then only once: "[d]er Schreibende aber, von dessen Erfahrungen ich hier spreche" (L/174 and 185). How should we read this odd construction? First, I would propose to read the absence of the "I" as an act of distancing, something akin to a polite but rather firm refusal to enter into direct dialogue with the German audience. Second, I would argue that this specific form of discourse fundamentally transforms the structural conditions of the acceptance speech itself: rather than having the author—and his works—judged by the audience, it is the author who pronounces judgment upon himself, thereby excluding the audience, rendering it, so to speak, mute. And while the speaker refuses to address his audience through an implicit "you," the one whose image is offered to the gaze of the audience does not return this gaze. We see him, Laokoon's youngest son, blinded by the images and anticipating his destruction. In fact, what we witness in this passage is someone on the verge of identifying with the victims of the Holocaust, someone living under the threat of being "zerschlagen und ausgeblutet." Like the concentration camp survivors whom Weiss saw on screen in 1945, this figure does not return the onlookers' gaze; he is lost in a stream of images. This scene is clearly deployed for the gaze of the audience. One could even say that it is deployed to exhibit the damage wrought by the country to which its audience belongs. Yet this gaze is not returned.

One last point: discussing fantasy, or, more specifically, the phantasmatic scene of masochism, Slavoj Žižek points to its staged nature, to the fact that the masochist participates in this scene, that he or she remains in control at all times, maintains a distance.[14] We find, I would argue, the same structural elements in this text in the very ways in which it offers the unbearable image of the younger son petrified by the fear of his body not yet bloody, not yet beaten. Thus, this image anticipates the reality of the masochist fantasy from "Meine Ortschaft," another text from 1965: "Nur wenn er selbst von seinem Tisch gestoßen und gefesselt wird, wenn er getreten und gepeitscht wird, weiß er, was dies ist."[15] Unlike the narrator of "Laokoon," the narrator of "Meine Ortschaft" speaks in the first person. However, in the text's very last paragraph, which contains this fantasy of being tortured, the "I" changes to a "he." In both cases the split of the subject into "I" and "he" suggests with the issue of maintaining control over the staging of the masochistic fantasy.

To summarize briefly the main points before considering *Rekonvaleszenz*: first, the connection between language and identity constitutes a connection between the subject's language and the images that he creates of himself; second, the creation of a story of liberation proceeds through the liberation from one image into the other, the move from the younger to the older son, from the mute, the voiceless survivor frozen in the act of identification with the Jewish victims to the one who will raise his voice to bear witness.

Pointing to Weiss's "10 Arbeitspunkte eines Autors in der geteilten Welt," Karl Heinz Götze argues: "[Mit Laokoon] trieb Weiss geradezu programmatisch der Sprache die Bilder aus, von denen seine Prosa bisher gelebt hatte."[16] This statement needs to be modified. While the aesthetic program of "Laokoon" might be adequately described in these terms ("der Sprache die Bilder austreiben"), my reading emphasizes a counter-logic running through this speech, namely the subject's engagement in his imaginary, the very production of images of the self. I agree, however, with Götze's observation that Weiss's writing between 1966 and 1970 is characterized by the repression of these images.[17] I also share Götze's view that *Rekonvaleszenz*, the journal written in 1970, rehabilitates this inner world of obsessional images as the very precondition for writing after the Shoah.[18] In the very first line of his journal, Weiss tells the reader that the privileging of "äußere Vorkommnisse" over his dreams and the tracing of his inner monologues led to an "unüberwindbare[r] Widerstand."[19] For Weiss, *Rekonvaleszenz* thus represents an exercise through which he seeks to overcome his writing block. He characterizes this block as his sudden inability to continue writing in the mode of the documentary plays that followed upon his "10 Arbeitspunkte." This form of "objective" writing based on "Exzerpte, Zeitungsausschnitte, Bibliotheken," he now knows, repressed what he calls his "persönliche Problematik" (R/7).

Reflecting on his journal, however, Weiss observes at the end of 1970 that the text is marked by a rather striking contradiction: "In diesem Journal ... überwiegen die Eindrücke der sozialen, politischen Welt, obgleich meine Absicht war ... eher die versteckten nächtlichen Bilder zum Ausdruck zu bringen, eher einer Stimme Gehör zu schaffen, die von den rationalen Erwägungen beiseite gedrängt worden war" (R/178). Although Weiss then wonders whether he made a mistake by sliding back into the familiar terrain of politics, he nevertheless quickly reaffirms this return to politics as inevitable: "mein Weg in konkrete politische Zusammenhänge ... in parteiliche Entscheidungen entstand in den frühesten Regionen" (R/178). Yet, this moment of closure is again rather tenuous. Just a few pages later he comments: "Das Dilemma, daß es an sich kein Finale gibt, und daß ich mich bereits im Übergang zu einer neuen Variation befinde, kenne ich von allen Stücken und Prosaarbeiten her ... Fast ausnahmslos wird das was ich eigentlich dem Publikum als ein Credo vorstellen sollte, zu einer Notlösung" (R/184). Yet the author did turn away from dreams and inner monologues, from this entire traumatic complex that he tries to capture with the rather laconic phrase "meine persönliche Problematik" (R/7).

What produced the departure from the original project? *Rekonvaleszenz* collects a series of dreams that mostly deal with desire, intense and forbidden desires. However, towards the end, the dreams slowly start to fade from the text.[20] One of the very last dreams deals with memories of the author's family. The entry under November 29, 1970, begins *in medias res*, with images "aus den frühesten Ablagerungen." These images originate in Bremen and reflect buildings that did not survive the war. Weiss then tells us about his visit to Bremen in 1947. After this visit he knows that any attempt to retrace the origin of these images "in reality" would be an absurd attempt to deny

death. From the memories of Bremen the narrator then turns to a series
of photographs that show him with his parents. The last picture, taken
after the family's emigration and before his parents' death, suddenly
makes him realize that nothing can be repaired, nothing can be restored.
Weiss then ends the entry with the following reflection:

> Oft geht es mir beim Schreiben, beim Heraufbeschwören von Einzelheiten,
> beim Umkreisen größerer Zusammenhänge, um die Wiederherstellung von
> etwas Verlorenem, das vielleicht noch vorhanden war, als meine Eltern mit mir
> vorm Gartentor in Nowawes standen, das mich aber schon in der Grünenstraße,
> wenige Jahre später, in jenen Hinterhalt getrieben hatte, aus dessen
> Efeudschungel ich ängstlich ... spähte (R/165).

This particular entry, I would argue, causes the text to veer away
from dreams and the images they produce and back to the discourse on
politics. Its focus on the narrator's family, its evocation of forced
emigration, of death, and of loss is at the very root of the return to
politics. But even more decisive is the re-emergence of the image of the
author as victim, the image of someone driven into "jenen Hinterhalt ...
aus dessen Efeudschungel ich ängstlich ... spähte." A similar movement,
I will argue, underlies *Die Ästhetik des Widerstands*. The novel
develops a specific form of political discourse as resistance to images
which stage the identification with the victims of the Holocaust. In *Die
Ästhetik des Widerstands* this identification with the Jewish victims is
represented as a feminine act, and this very femininity becomes a site of
struggle.

II

Rekonvaleszenz is, then, the product of a crisis that forced Weiss to
acknowledge the power of his German past. During the writing of the
novel Weiss faced another crisis. In his notebooks he formulates this as
a crisis that revolves around his position as an author honored in
Germany: he does not want to become Germany's "Renommier-Jude"—
and this applies to both Germanies. In the middle of his reflections on
the Dehler Prize in 1977, Weiss notes in his diaries: "Hasse dieses
Deutschland, das ich so lange verdrängt hatte, bis es mir abhanden

gekommen war. Angehört hatte ich diesem Deutschland ohnedies nie, war dort nur umhergezogen als Mitglied einer Familie mit Ausländerpaß" (NBII/641). This time Weiss's reaction is more radical. He decides not to write an acceptance speech at all—after much agonizing, one should add. Weiss realizes that, essentially, he has nothing new to add to his "Laokoon" speech. He would have to speak again about his experience of persecution and exile, about his difficulties of writing in German.[21] Once more he expresses his ambivalence about this language: "Die Hemmung, mich dieser Sprache zu bedienen" (NBII/645). We should remember that these reflections were written in 1977, i.e., in the middle of writing *Die Ästhetik des Widerstands*. In a gesture of distancing, he writes: "Mein Judentum war ein halbes—(mein Deutschtum nicht mal)" (NBII/644). And he finally puts an end to this agonizing process: "in dieser Lage das Notwendigste die Besinnung, die Selbsterkenntnis u in den Besitz einer eignen Vergangenheit zu kommen" (NBII/649). *Die Ästhetik des Widerstands*, he decides, will be his acceptance speech.

In all of Weiss's texts, the Jewish figure is the father, not only in *Abschied von den Eltern* and *Fluchtpunkt* but also in his notebooks, in "Meine Ortschaft," and in *Die Besiegten*. This latter text contains a scene of the father in a concentration camp: "Mein Vater starb im Steinbruch, als die Peitschen knallten … Mein Vater liebte die Menschen und er sah sie in endlosen Reihen den großen Öfen entgegenziehen, durch deren Schornsteine der süßliche Geruch von verbranntem Menschenfleisch auf ihn herabfuhr." The last sentence of this passage reads: "Die Welt ging unter im Vater, während der Sohn verloren außerhalb der Mauern stand."[22] Being Jewish thus means a male lineage, a relationship of father to son.

In *Die Ästhetik des Widerstands* the Jewish figure is the mother. Or, more precisely, the mother declares herself to be a Jew, she is identified as Jewish by the son, and, finally, dies in identification with the Jewish victims of the Holocaust. Thus, we read at the end of volume One: "Während sie mich ins Haus zog, sagte sie mir, daß sie, nachdem man sie ihres dunklen Haares wegen einige Male als Jüdin bezeichnet hatte, sich nun selbst zur Jüdin erklärt hatte" (ÄDWI/189). Later on, at the end of an apocalyptic dream, the narrator finds himself next to his mother:

"neben mir, auf der Seite, das Gesicht in die Hand gestützt, lag meine Mutter und sah mich an." Still dreaming, the narrator remembers that they are on a journey to Berlin where they will join the narrator's father. The core segment of this dream reads as follows:

> [E]twas stimmte nicht, ich wußte nicht, wo meine Mutter verblieben war, eben noch hatte sie mich an der Hand gehalten ... eine schreckliche Ungewißheit kam auf, wo ich sie verloren haben mochte, vielleicht war sie verschleppt worden, ich hörte nur ein Geschrei und Jammern, Menschen eilten vorbei, es klirrte, als wären Scheiben zertrümmert worden, die Menge trieb eine Frau vor sich her, man hatte ihr ein Schild um den Hals gehängt, mit der Aufschrift Jidd, in jüdischen Lettern, vielleicht war es meine Mutter (ÄDWII/76; emphasis mine).

This dream obviously works with oedipal material, it also obviously thematizes an archaic fear of losing the mother. But I want to foreground once again the mother's identification as Jewish, albeit a rather tenuous identification: "Vielleicht war es meine Mutter."

In Weiss's notebooks we find another version of this passage which locates the fantasy scenario in Paris:[23]

> Meine Mutter war verschwunden, eine schreckliche Ungewißheit kam auf, wo ich sie verloren haben mochte ... ich suchte in andern Städten nach ihr, eben noch war ich durch eine Gasse gegangen, die sich in Paris befand, jüdische Schriftzeichen waren auf die Ladenfenster gemalt, Männer im Kaftan, mit breitrandigem Hut und Ohrlocken kamen vorüber (NBII/478).

This is the paternal world, the world of the "Großvater im Kaftan" that Weiss writes about in *Fluchtpunkt* (FP/12). This paternal Jewish world did not enter the text of *Die Ästhetik des Widerstands*; instead, being Jewish is here part of the world of the mother—and that of the narrator, for the dream continues:

> Ich schlug mich durch das Gedränge, doch die Frau war nicht mehr zu sehn ... alles Suchen würde mir nichts nützen, trotzdem lief ich ... auch wenn es zu spät wäre ... würde ich weiterlaufen, zum Bahnhof, von Perron zu Perron, einem Zug nachlaufen ... bis ich einen Waggon fände, dessen Schild meinen Bestimmungsort verkündete, es mußte ein Sinn, ein Ziel vorhanden sein, ich durfte ... nur nicht nachlassen in meiner Anstrengung, es war ja schon

bestimmt, wohin ich sollte, nur hatte ich den Namen der Stadt vergessen
(ÄDWII/77).

We do, of course, know the name of this place where the wagons
will come to a halt. It is Auschwitz,"eine Ortschaft für die ich bestimmt
war, und der ich entkam" (MO/114).

What exactly does this dream achieve? It reconfirms the mother's
identification with the victims of the Shoah and it re-imagines her as
Jewish. It thereby also reconfirms the connection between being Jewish
and femininity. Finally, the scene also positions the narrator on the side
of this feminine Jewishness.

Before drawing further conclusions from this observation of a link
between being Jewishn and femininity, I want to pursue this
constellation of mother and son into volume Three. Far into the narrative
of the parents' flight, we encounter a scene where the narrator addresses
the mother in the hope of making her speak. The story of the parents'
escape emerges slowly from both the father's reconstruction and the
mother's visions, different modes of representation that critics have tried
to capture as the opposition between rational discourse versus mimetic
representation (those are Söllner's terms), or *Vergegenwärtigung* versus
the distancing discourse of historiography (those terms are from Rainer
Rother).[24] I will return to this point but prefer to return now to the
moment when the narrator addresses the mother. Reflecting on his
efforts to help his mother to regain her voice, the narrator suddenly
realizes: "[J]etzt verstand ich plötzlich, warum ich dies erzählte, es
gehörte zu den geheimen Verknüpfungen, die zwischen uns bestanden
und die über all die Jahre hin dazu beigetragen hatten, einander
verstehen zu können" (ÄDWIII/19). This passage refers us back to the
last page of *Fluchtpunkt* and its ecstatic recovery of German. I quote that
passage once again: "Und die Sprache, die sich jetzt einstellte, war die
Sprache, die ich am Anfang meines Lebens gelernt hatte, die natürliche
Sprache, die mein Werkzeug war, die nur noch mir selbst gehörte, und
mit dem Land, in dem ich aufgewachsen war, nichts mehr zu tun hatte"
(FP/196).

Not surprisingly, in *Die Ästhetik des Widerstands* this "natural"
language, the language of origin and of "secret associations," is

connected to the figure of the mother. But the narrator's attempt to recreate this original language fails, his mother remains mute: "Einige Augenblicke lang war das Erinnerungsgewebe, das uns umgab, wahrzunehmen, doch gleich verlor es sich wieder, nichts im Gesicht meiner Mutter deutete darauf hin, daß sie nur ein einziges meiner Worte in sich aufgenommen hätte" (ÄDWIII/20). There is no "natural," no "original" language that links mother and son. Like the mother, the son is mute:

> Im Zug, während der Rückfahrt nach Stockholm, sah ich, aus dem Fenster blickend, dieses Gesicht, groß, grau, abgenutzt von den Bildern, die sich darüber hergemacht hatten, eine steinerne Maske, die Augen blind in der Bruchfläche. Es war das Gesicht der Ge, der Dämonin der Erde, ihre linke Hand, mit den zerborstnen Fingern, ragte auf, die abendlichen Landschaften flogen vorbei, Alkyoneus fiel, von der Schlange in die Brust gebissen, schräg von ihr weg (ÄDWIII/20).

The mother's silence is the cause of the son's death, her refusal to speak strikes him dumb, "verschlägt ihm die Stimme." I am intentionally using the language from "Laokoon," recalling the sentence that introduces the image of what I called Laokoon's younger son: "Für ihn, dem es die Stimme verschlagen hatte, bestand zeitweise nur die Erstarrung" (L/181).

Let's move back to *Die Ästhetik des Widerstands* and its very beginning, that is, to the reading of the Pergamon frieze. The very first figure to acquire a name in this sublime reading is Ge, "die Dämonin der Erde" (ÄDWI/8). Moreover, Ge keeps returning throughout this reading until we arrive at this description:

> Wieder blickten wir hinauf zu ihr, die sich aus dem Boden streckte … in der seitwärts gewandten rohen Fläche des Gesichts war der Ansatz des um Gnade flehenden Munds zu erkennen. Eine Wunde klaffte vom Kinn bis zum Kehlkopf. Alkyoneus, ihr Lieblingssohn, drehte sich, ins Knie sinkend, schräg von ihr weg … Schenkel, Unterleib, Bauch und Brust spannten sich in Konvulsionen. Von der kleinen Wunde … strahlte der Todesschmerz aus (ÄDWI/10).

In *Die Ästhetik des Widerstands* the Laokoon group is replaced by a new image, a completely new constellation: the image of Ge and her "favorite" son—both mute, both dying. Laokoon's youngest son has thus become the son of Ge.

But Ge/the mother does not remain mute, she will speak again thus putting the images that hold her captive into words. Right before she dies, the mother tells the narrator and his father about her experiences in the occupied territories: "lange hatte es gedauert, bis sie ihm gesagt hatte, was ihr zugestoßen war, im Schneegestöber, südlich von Brest, bei Sobibor, sie war mit den andern gestürzt, in die Grube, sie hatte zwischen ihnen gelegen, die Wärme der Körper war um sie gewesen, sie war umgeben gewesen von den zuckenden Armen und Beinen ... dann war es still geworden, sie war hinausgekrochen" (ÄDWIII/124). In *Die Ästhetik des Widerstands*, I would argue, the voice of the Jewish mother makes possible what the narrator at the end of "Meine Ortschaft" cannot achieve: the representation of the slaughter.

The novel stages another moment of witnessing, the story of Graf Seydlitz told by Nyman told by the narrator: "[Seydlitz] rückte an Nyman heran, sein Gesicht war verzerrt, als er ihm beschrieb, was er durch das Guckloch gesehn hatte. Die Menschen stehn drinnen zusammengepfercht, arbeitsuntaugliche alte Männer, Frauen und Kinder. Die Gesichter strecken sich nach oben" (ÄDWIII/119). Nyman's testimony fades, the mother's does not. For what Seydlitz watched from the outside, the mother witnessed from the inside. The mother's knowledge is a bodily knowledge produced in an act of identification. Her voice, this thing located between body and language, a thing that carries the trace of the body, transmits this knowledge to the narrator/the son. What Weiss establishes here is, I would argue, a nexus between writing, body, and voice whereby the body of the Jewish mother functions as the site of authenticity, as the very guarantee of authentic historical knowledge. Thus, the survivor's voice carries the trace of the Jewish body which becomes, in this text, the authentic voice. And, I would argue further, it becomes the very foundation for writing after the Shoah. After all, it is in this context that the narrator starts to reflect once again about the very act of writing, about its relation to the world of dreams, to the world of unconscious fantasy and its multiple, unlimited, possibilities of identification.

However, this new foundation for writing (remember that these extensive reflections on the process of writing occur long after the passages about Brecht) becomes problematic, and the conflict is related to the very act that makes this writing possible, i.e., the act of identification with Jewish victims. For this construction also projects the identification with the Jewish victims as an act of feminine surrender. It is, after all, the mother who engages in this act, not the figure of the father. This writing, in other words, has its origin in a feminine voice, in a feminine body, and in an act of identification with Jewish victims that is—in this particular text—construed as a feminine act.

A reading of Heilmann's last letter, written before his execution at Plötzensee, supports this thesis. One particular aspect of this letter, the part that deals with the figure of Libertas, suggests a curious association of Libertas with Rosa Luxemburg at the very end: "[E]s mag sein, daß Libertas in vielem unserm Anliegen am nächsten kam, denn bei unsern Gesprächen über das künftige Staatswesen hatte sie uns immer wieder aus Rosas Schriften vorgelesen ... und vielleicht hätten wir in ihr eine jener erkennen müssen, für die gilt, daß es Freiheit nicht gebe ohne die Freiheit des anders Denkenden" (ÄDWIII/210). This passage is the result of a process which transforms Libertas from an object of desire to an object of abjection to an object of love, an object of love which is also an object of identification. I will outline this in more detail.

Libertas is first seen in an idealized light—quite literally: "Libertas war rückwärts hineingegangen in das Leuchten" (ÄDWIII/201). While the next sentence expresses Heilmann's desire, the desire is immediately censored:

> Sie trug gern diese langen, dünnen, hemdengleichen Gewänder, die den Hals, viel von den Schultern, der Brust bloß ließen. Ich habe sie nie geküßt. Wir sind doch Moralisten geblieben. Wir hatten von der Freiheit der Sinne gesprochen, hatten geglaubt, daß der Mensch, der für die Revolution lebe, sich ihr mit Körper und Seele hingeben müsse ... und wie ergriffen wir auch immer waren, wir kamen doch nie aus dieser sonderbaren Reinheit heraus (ÄDWIII/201).

Heilmann continues this story of repressed desire: "Wie klein aber wäre alles wieder geworden, da eben doch das Absolute erreicht war, wie hätte die Scham mich überkommen ... wenn ich dem, was mich an die fleischliche Existenz binden wollte, nachgegeben hätte" (ÄDWIII/202). Idealization suddenly turns into abjection. Libertas, the traitor, is now "schmutzig" (ÄDWIII/205), she's sullied. Yet once more the text transforms the object: "Ich sah sie, die kindliche Frau, besudelt, verdreckt, und ihrer Zerstörung erst galt meine wahre Liebe" (ÄDWIII/205). The entire passage makes this process of idealization and abjection readable as male projection. But again, I am not not interested in the more or less explicit psychoanalytic subtext of this passage, rather, I am interested in the logic that transforms Libertas into Rosa, the loved woman into the political text, the woman of flesh and blood into the allegory of a different kind of politics.

Let us return to this rather enigmatic sentence: "Ich sah sie, die kindliche Frau, besudelt, verdreckt, und ihrer Zerstörung erst galt meine wahre Liebe." Poelchau's report on the executions in Plötzensee which follows right after this helps us to decipher the sentence. His report is characterized by an opposition between the pure and the impure, for example: "die von ihren hohen Zielen in tiefste Erniedrigung geworfen werden sollten" (ÄDWIII/211); "daß sie, die nach dem Reinsten dieser Sprache verlangten, von den schmutzigsten Stimmen niedergeschrien worden waren" (ÄDWIII/214); and, finally, "Weil in der Welt, in der auch er ein Gefangener war, alles in Kot, Urin und in dampfenden Lachen von Blut verging" (ÄDWIII/211). Here the abject is the feminine act of surrender, the act of being a victim, the act of dying. Heilmann's final embrace of Libertas signifies the embrace of the act of surrender, the identification with the feminine position. The transformation of Libertas into Rosa, of the victimized body into politics, is a symptom of the strength of the resistance against this identification.

We have encountered the same move in *Rekonvaleszenz*, the move away from the trauma of the German past to the realm of politics, away from the compulsive fantasy of identifying with the dead to the register of politics. Ultimately, it is a move away from what in this text is constructed as Jewishness—the association of Jewishness with feminine surrender—to the realm of politics. For the conflicts around femininity which come to the fore in Heilmann's letter also pertain to the Jewish mother and her identificatory act.

The author as the son of Ge, the author as the son of the Jewish mother, the Jewish author—that is the author of Plötzensee, of the descent into the slaughterhouse. This form of authorship was thematized once before around the figure of Géricault and his intensely identificatory practice: "Mit ihrer Einbildungskraft erzeugten die Maler Situationen, in denen Selbsterlebtes so lange über das gewählte Geschehnis geschoben wurde, bis der Eindruck von Übereinstimmung entstand. Diese Übereinstimmung stellte sich her, wenn der höchste Grad emotionaler Intensität erreicht war" (ÄDWI/347). Géricault is there, on the raft, "zwischen Toten und Verdämmernden" (ÄDWII/22). The raft becomes his world, the Medusa's catastrophe his own catastrophe. As painter he draws the viewer into "eine Preisgabe ohne Rückhalt," forcing him into his own nightmare (ÄDWII/32).

The narrator tells this segment in intense identification with Géricault, but the intense identification ends abruptly: "Plötzlich interessierte es mich nicht mehr, die Rätsel seines Lebens zu lösen" (ADWII/33). Several critics have argued that this statement represents an ideological dismissal of the "Selbsterfahrung des schöpferischen Subjekts, das keinen Zugang zu einer vergewissernden Welterfahrung hat."[25] But this statement overlooks the sudden reappearance of Géricault and the traces of his identificatory art in the Plötzensee segment. Géricault reappears on his way to the morgue: "An diesem Sonntag … stieg, überwältigend, Paris in mir auf. Wieder folgte ich Géricault … in die Morgue … Die Faszination, die der Tod auf ihn ausgeübt hatte, entsprach seinem Trieb, sich mit dem Augenblick zu konfrontieren, an dem alles zu Ende ist. Ich begann zu verstehen, warum er nach diesem Gegenpol zu seiner Aktivität verlangte" (ÄDWII/120). The way this morgue at the very center of civilization is represented makes the associations with the crematoria of Auschitz inescapable. "Wie es drinnen aussah, wußten Meryon und Géricault" (ÄDWII/122). And Plötzensee proves it, the author of *Die Ästhetik des Widerstands* too knows the inside of the slaughterhouse. He knows it as the son of Ge.

I think it would be possible to make an argument that the opposition between the two modes of representation in *Die Ästhetik des Widerstands*—between rational analytic discourse versus mimetic representation, between "vergegenwärtigende Nähe" versus historiographical distance[26]—this opposition could be rethought in terms of an aesthetic of masochism. At this point I can only refer to the masochistic fantasy scenario in Weiss's "Laokoon" speech and to Žižek's insistence on the element of mastery over the staging of the scene.

What happens to this Jewish authorship with its feminine origin? Alkyoneus, the son of Ge, dies. The voice that emerges at the very end of *Die Ästhetik des Widerstands*, the author of the book that will be written, is not the son of Ge. This is the voice of an authorship firmly anchored in the discourse of the communist resistance, a discourse which is, moreover, strongly coded as masculine: "Im Mai, als der Damm geborsten war und alles zerrann, verstand ich, wie utopisch, politisch, unrealistisch ich gedacht hatte. Die Politiker hingegen, in ihrer Beherrschtheit, ihrer Disziplin, befaßten sich mit dem Erreichbaren, dem Möglichen" (ÄDWIII/262).[27] This voice echoes the discourse of the communist functionaries. Yet this author too, eventually loses his voice. When he returns to the Pergamon altar, he encounters a familiar resistance: "Und wenn ich dann Kunde von Heilmann und Coppi erhielte, würde meine Hand auf dem Papier lahm werden" (ÄDWIII/267). As he rereads the Pergamon altar, his eyes rest again on the empty spot left by Herakles. Let me remind you that it was Heilmann who spoke of the necessity to construct an image of one's self. And that Rosa replaced Herakles as the signifier of Heilmann's imaginary identity. But what is missing from the Pergamon frieze at the end of the novel is not only Herakles but also Ge. Ge is dead, as is her son.

III

The title of my essay proposed to trace a certain kind of resistance to Jewish authorship in Weiss's last novel. I proceeded to argue first, that in *Die Ästhetik des Widerstands* Jewish authorship is linked to a female figure, the narrator's mother; second, this authorship grounds a mode of writing that is based on an intense identificatory act; and third, this authorship is contested, made to disappear with the appearance of the novel's post-45 author. In closing, I want to address two additional points. First, making the mother the Jewish figure—and her voice and body the ground for a specific version of Jewish authorship—is, to say the least, a very ambiguous gesture in *Die Ästhetik des Widerstands*. On the one hand, realigning the son with the Jewish mother firmly anchors Jewish authorship; on the other hand, as I have pointed out earlier, the mother's Jewish identity is itself very tenuous. The mother passes as Jewish, the son fantasizes her as Jewish: "Vielleicht war es meine Mutter." Second, as we have seen, this Jewish authorship with its maternal origin is but one form of authorship in this novel, and, beyond that, a very contested form. In the process of writing this last novel, this monumental epic on the German past as his own past, Weiss realized, I think, the extent of his ambivalence toward this other voice, this "Stimme ... die von den rationalen Erwägungen beiseite gedrängt worden war," to repeat a phrase from *Rekonvaleszenz*. The fact of having been persecuted as a Jew always remained a topic for Weiss, the image of Laokoon's younger son never disappeared, but it also always involved a search for an identity other than that of the victim.

This account, which foregrounds the conflicts around the construction of Jewish authorship in Weiss's last novel, inevitably complicates the status of Weiss in the *Yale Companion to Jewish Writing and Thought in German Culture*. Its appropriation of Weiss as the postwar Jewish author is rather problematic.[28] To avoid any misunderstandings, I do not want to engage in some silly debate about whether Weiss is a Jewish author or not. Rather, I am arguing against the attempt to construct a coherent, seamless story about the author Peter Weiss anchored in his Jewish identity. Peter Weiss is not Binjamin Wilkomirski. Moreover, I want to address the issue of the feminization of Jewish authorship. How can we begin to explain its logic? It would be useful to explore Gilman's notion of the feminized Jew as a cultural trope in the context of the post-45 period. This trope certainly is at work within the context of the anti-fascist left, both in East and in West Germany. As Garloff has pointed out, German intellectuals repeatedly confronted Weiss with the opposition of Jewish versus political emigré, voluntary versus forced exile. Not surprisingly, this opposition re-emerges in *Die Ästhetik des Widerstands*. As I have argued, the dichotomy surfaces in a gendered form where politics means masculinity, activity, and ultimately survival, whereas being Jewish means femininity, passivity, and ultimately death. In this system of signification Rosa, the dead Jewish revolutionary, then functions as a symptom, the symptom of fierce resistance.

Notes

1   *Peter Weiss Jahrbuch* 1 (Opladen 1992), p. 7-8. As the *Jahrbuch* demonstrates, the absence of Weiss from the non-academic cultural sphere was, paradoxically, accompanied by an explosion of Weiss scholarship and academic conferences.

2   Heiner Müller, successor to East Germany's Bertolt Brecht, suddenly emerged from an orgy of commemoration at the Berliner Ensemble as the icon of the post Cold-War era, an icon of post-Marxism, and post-modernism celebrated by East and West alike. At the same time, Helmut Kohl and his cultural functionaries from the Christian Democratic party continued to invest considerable time in their efforts to turn Ernst Jünger into the successor of Thomas Mann, the former West Germany's state author. This new configuration did not survive, dissolving as did so many moments in the post-89 attempts to re-capture cultural hegemony.

3   James Young, *Writing and Rewriting the Holocaust. Narrative and Consequences of Interpretation* (Bloomington 1988). Alvin Rosenfeld, *A Double Dying. Reflections on Holocaust Literature* (Bloomington 1980). For an insightful critique of this position, see Robert Cohen, "The Political Aesthetics of Holocaust Literature: Peter Weiss's *The Investigation* and Its Critics." In: *History and Memory* 10.2 (1998), p. 43-67.

4   Sander Gilman and Jack Zipes, eds., *The Yale Companion to Jewish Writing and Thought in German Culture* (New Haven 1997), p. xxiii.

5   Katja Garloff, *Not of This Time, Not of This Place: Diasporic Imagination in Peter Weiss, Nelly Sachs and Paul Celan* (Diss. University of Chicago, 1997), p. 27.

6   Ibid, p. 1.

7   Jochen Vogt, *Peter Weiss* (Reinbek 1987).

8   Peter Weiss, *Fluchtpunkt* (Frankfurt a.M. 1982), p. 196. In the following, I will refer to this text as FP plus page number.

9   Alfons Söllner, *Peter Weiss und die Deutschen: Die Entstehung einer politischen Ästhetik wider die Verdrängung* (Opladen 1988), p. 130.

10 Peter Weiss, *Notizbücher 1960 - 1971* (Frankfurt a.M. 1982), vol. I. p. 389. In the following, I will refer to this text as NBIa plus page number; the second set of *Notizbücher 1971 - 1980* will be referred to as NBII plus page number.

11 Peter Weiss, *Die Ästhetik des Widerstands* (Frankfurt a.M. 1986), vol. III, p. 169. I will refer to this text as ÄDW plus volume and page number.

12 Peter Weiss, "Laokoon oder Über die Grenzen der Sprache," in *Rapporte*

(Frankfurt a.M. 1968), p. 180. In the following, I will refer to this text as L plus page number.

13 *Fluchtpunkt*, Garloff argues, is a text that reveals the fragile status of this new, "pure" language, undermining its claims through what she calls the catastrophic remainder of exile.
Garloff, p. 55-59.

14 Slavoj Žižek, *The Plague of Fantasies* (London 1997), p. 15.

15 Peter Weiss, "Meine Ortschaft," in *Rapporte* (Frankfurt a.M. 1968), p. 124. I will refer to this text as MO plus page number.

16 Karl Heinz Götze, *Poetik des Abgrunds und Kunst des Widerstands: Grundmuster der Bilderwelt von Peter Weiss* (Opladen 1995), p. 185.

17 I would, however, use the word repression cautiously. I am sure that a careful reading of the plays and essays after 1965 would find traces of these same images of the passive, mute survivor/victim and the active, speaking witness.

18 Götze, *Poetik des Abgrunds und Kunst des Widerstands*, p. 185 and 196.

19 Peter Weiss, *Rekonvaleszenz* (Frankfurt a.M. 1991), p. 8. I will refer to this text as R plus page numbers.

20 Götze also correctly observes that they turn from "Lustträume" into "Verfolgungsträume." See *Poetik des Abgrunds und Kunst des Widerstands*, p. 188.

21 What is more pronounced here is the critical stance towards both Germanies, the accent on the common (Nazi) past of both countries (in the West, the practice of "Berufsverbote" recalls that past; in the East, Weiss's experience of being denied entry into the GDR after his *Trotzki* play causes him to reflect on the authoritarian origin of this country). These reflections render Weiss's position in the minefield of the Cold War most accute. In my future work on Weiss I intend to foreground the connection between the question of Weiss's relationship to his Jewishness and his position in Europe's Cold War landscape.

22 Peter Weiss, *Die Besiegten* (Frankfurt a.M. 1985), p. 50.

23 This dream also recurs in the context of the Dehler Prize, NBII/710.

24 Alfons Söllner, *Peter Weiss und die Deutschen*, p. 220; Rainer Rother, *Die Gegenwart der Geschichte: Ein Versuch über Film und zeitgenössische Literatur* (Stuttgart 1990), p. 137.

25 Genia Schulz, "Die Ästhetik des Widerstands," *Variationen des Indirekten* (Stuttgart 1986), p. 85.

26 Söllner, p. 220; Rother, p. 1370.

27 I made this argument in more detail in "Rosa oder die Sehnsucht nach einer

Geschichte ohne Stalin: Zur vergeschlechtlichten Textproduktion in Peter Weiss's *Ästhetik des Widerstands*," *Peter Weiss Jahrbuch* 6 (Opladen 1997), p. 138-63.

28	I should add here that the authors of the two entries on Weiss, Robert Cohen and Robert Holub, both approach the topic more cautiously. Thus Cohen, for instance, writes: "Weiss was never to demonstrate any interest in the Jewish religion, but he eventually developed a deep existential appreciation for his Jewish side, for it had prevented him from becoming a perpetrator and had linked him instead with the victims - of the Holocaust, as well as the atrocities of colonialism, imperialism, and Stalinism." Robert Cohen in the *Yale Companion to Jewish Writing and Thought in German Culture*, p. 722.

Alexander Honold

Deutschlandflug: Der fremde Blick des Peter Weiss

> Nicht analysieren, sondern darstellen.
> Aber in einer verschärften, überdeutlichen Art.
> Eine Art Wirklichkeit geben,
> die in sich schon zerlegt, zergliedert ist.
> (Peter Weiss, *Notizbücher 1960-1971*)

I

Was dem Etablierten das gelegentliche Inkognito, ist dem Außenseiter die Travestie. Spielraum, Schutzkleid, Verstärkung durch ein double. Unter den vielerlei Masken und Haltungen, die der Person des Schreibenden als alter ego dienen, findet sich im Falle von Peter Weiss Abwegiges und Naheliegendes in engster Nachbarschaft. Vertrauliche und intime Offenbarungen stehen neben skurrilen und scheinbar willkürlich herangezogenen Rollenklischees, die von Dante bis zum Briefträger Cheval, von den Bohèmekünstlern des Pariser Montmartre bis zum Geschichtsdrama der Französischen Revolution reichen. Ausfaltungen des Selbst. Zu ihnen gehört jenes frühe Photo im Western-Kostüm, das Weiss einmal scherzhaft als Kinderbild eines Guerilleros deutete, und ebenso das Protokoll bestürzter Ratlosigkeit von 1964, mit dem der Dokumentarist des Frankfurter Auschwitz-Prozesses den Schauplatz der Vernichtung als "Meine Ortschaft" zu identifizieren versuchte.

Aufschlußreich an dieser Kombinatorik des Disparaten ist vor allem Weiss' Neigung, die Ortlosigkeit des eigenen Schreibens teils mit dem Gestus des politischen *coming out,* teils aber auch mit dem Wunschbild des kosmopolitischen Intellektuellen zu camouflieren. Der Unterschied dieser literarischen Selbstversuche zu manchen prätentiösen Schaugefechten der Gegenwart indessen ist unverkennbar, wenn man beispielsweise die erfundene Opfer-Autobiographie Binjamin Wilkormirskis mit der fiktionalen Arbeitervita des Erzählers der *Ästhetik des Widerstands* vergleicht. Weiss maßt sich die Rollen nicht an, er *legt* sie sich *an*, er experimentiert mit den Möglichkeiten, die ein anderes historisches Subjekt ihm als Schreibendem eröffnet, oder, in der retrofaktischen Phantasie, auch als Handelndem hätte eröffnen können. Oft sind es die angelegten Identitäten, die den Ton angeben, wenn ihr Autor sich zu Wort meldet. Geistesgegenwart, die trainiert sein will, bedarf solcher Rollenexperimente; und doch gehen sie bei Weiss über bloße Denkübungen weit hinaus, so daß man in ihnen auch eine Art von künstlerischer Überlebenstechnik vermuten kann.

Unzugehörigkeit und Empfindlichkeit blieben zwei notwendige, aber nicht immer angenehme Begleiter seiner schriftstellerischen Existenz seit den Anfängen der ersten Nachkriegsjahre. Als der Krieg vorbei war, lag alles im Offenen, lockten tausenderlei Lebensentwürfe, und nichts davon war wirklich greifbar. "Ich konnte in Paris leben oder in Stockholm, in London oder New York, und ich trug die Sprache bei mir, im leichtesten Gepäck" (*Fluchtpunkt,* 196). So will es der Roman *Fluchtpunkt,* und so wollte es wohl auch sein autobiographischer Protagonist. Der Alptraum des Migranten scheint in die Sehnsucht des frei ausschweifenden Reisens verwandelt. Es regten sich endlich die ausgestreckten Fühler einer Generation, die mit Krieg und Vertreibung auch ihre Bindungen zurückgelassen hatte. Die zweifache Überschreitung der Schwelle ist das Besondere seiner Lage. Dem *Abschied von den Eltern* war, als erzwungene politische Pubertät dieses jungen deutschen Künstlers, der Abschied mit den Eltern vorausgegangen. Bei aller Euphorie läßt auch die Freiheit von Paris Züge des Schwindelerregenden erkennen, Anwandlungen von Agoraphobie, der Angst vor dem Offenen. "Die Freiheit war absolut, ich konnte mich darin verlieren und ich konnte mich darin wiederfinden, ich konnte alles aufgeben, alle Bestrebungen, alle Zusammengehörigkeit, und ich konnte wieder beginnen zu sprechen" (Ebd.). Von vorn anfangen, überall hin können; die beiden Wunschvorstellungen gehören ebenso zusammen wie das, wogegen sie Front machen: die an Ort und Herkunft gebundene, die festgelegte Geschichte.

Dabei ist das Phantasma des freischwebenden Intellektuellen noch in diesen existentialistisch gefärbten Tagträumen mit jener historischer Erfahrung gesättigt, die es dementiert. Zum selben Jahr des Aufbruchs, zum Sommer 1947 gehört eine weitere Reise. Auch hier entdeckt Weiss im Erlebten, und mehr noch in der Reiseform selbst, ein literarisches Sujet, das er mit einem phantastischen Einfall in Szene setzt. Dieser Einfall liest sich wie eine implizite Replik auf die Vision der Entgrenzung, denn er führt das freie Schweben nicht als Habitus vor, sondern als Extremsportart.[1]

"Unter meinem weißen Flügel hängend gleite ich hinab auf die Steinwelt zu. Ich sinke durch dunkle Wolken und strömenden Regen [...]. Der freie Flug durch den Raum des Vergessens wird jetzt begrenzt von einer zerrissenen Oberfläche, die mir entgegenstürzt, die sich mit schwindelnder Schnelle unter mir erhebt, bis sie hart, hart gegen meine sprungbereiten Füße schlägt. Ich wälze mich zwischen Stein und Stahl, erhebe mich, halb betäubt. Die nächsten Bewegungen sind automatisch: den Fallschirm abschnallen, den Atem beruhigen, mich vertraut machen mit der Umgebung" (*Die Besiegten*, 11). So schildert der mit seinen Eltern 1934 aus Deutschland Geflüchtete die erste Wiederbegegnung mit der ehemaligen Reichshauptstadt Berlin, in der er zur Schule gegangen war. In diese Stadt, "die mich vor langer Zeit verlor", wie er sagt, kommt Weiss 1947 zurück, nicht als Heimkehrer, sondern als ein distanzierter Besucher, der für eine schwedische Zeitung über das besiegte, in Trümmern liegende Deutschland berichtet. Er muß sich also, mehr als das der bloße Abstand der inzwischen vergangenen Jahre erfordert, erst "vertraut machen" mit der Umgebung von einst; denn vertraut ist nichts mehr in dieser zerbombten Welt, und Vertrauen erweckend erst recht nicht. Im Grunde aber geht es, wie der Beobachter dann als Beschreibender feststellt, um das schiere Gegenteil des Vertrautwerdens, um die Schärfung der Unvertrautheit und des Unvertrauens gegenüber Deutschland. "Ich bin fremd hier. Ich kehre nicht heim, ich werde nur gegenübergestellt" (*Die Besiegten*, 13).[2]

Die literarische Transposition seiner Reportagen, die 1948 in Stockholm unter dem Titel *De Besegrade* erschien, verwandelt den "Besucher" (was für ein schwaches, hilfloses Wort!) in einen Fallschirmspringer. Einen, der nicht die Zollgrenze überquert, da er keine Papiere einer amtlich bestätigten Identität und Nationalität vorzuweisen gewillt ist. Aus der Luft kommend, wahrt er bis zu seinem Kontakt mit deutschem Boden den größtmöglichen Abstand. Auf

spektakuläre Weise unterstreicht diese Fiktion des Fallschirmflugs die
Nicht-Verbundenheit des Erzählenden mit jenem Land, das unter ihm
mit rasanter Geschwindigkeit näherrückt. Entsprechend dramatisch gerät
der Einschlag des Schriftstellers in seinem Zielgebiet. Wie er Grund
unter die Füße bekommt: hart und heftig! Keine Ankunft im Alltag,
sondern ein Aufprall in der deutschen Trümmerwirklichkeit. Wenn
Hölderlins Hyperion zu Beginn seines Erinnerungsromans sagen konnte:
"Der liebe Vaterlandsboden giebt mir nun wieder Freude und Leid", so
stattet Weiss den Wiedereintritt in die Erdenschwere des politischen
Terrains mit allen Umständen des Körperlichen und Konkreten aus. Was
für ein bizarres Geburts-Phantasma ist dieses Wälzen "zwischen Stein
und Stahl", wenn wir es mit der wunderbaren Passage am Ende des
Romans *Fluchtpunkt* vergleichen, die den Ankömmling, vom
Menschengetriebe des Bahnhofs in die Straßen und Plätze von Paris
gespuckt, wie ein Neugeborenes in seinem Bastkorb den Strom der Stadt
dahintreiben läßt.

Und doch liegen nur ein paar Monate zwischen jenem großen
Erlebnis der Freiheit, der in *Fluchtpunkt* verklärten Künstlerexistenz des
Pariser Frühsommers, und dem traumwandlerischen Rücksturz in die
deutsche Depression, in ein zum Feindesland mutiertes Berlin. Paris und
Berlin im Jahre 1947, auch dies eine harte Fügung des Disparaten, eine
kaum zu ermessende europäische Ungleichzeitigkeit. Welche
Querverbindungen und Kurzschlüsse muß dies im Beobachter Peter
Weiss ausgelöst haben? Der selbstgewählte, nie wirklich erreichte
Fluchtpunkt des Künstlers, und die unfreiwillig bezogene, unfreiwillig
verlassene Stadt der Jugend und Schulzeit. Paris-Berlin. Auf diese
ungeheuerliche Konstellation trifft vielleicht am ehesten der seltsame,
etwas außer Kurs geratene Begriff der Widerspiegelung zu, wenn damit
nicht eine objektive Tatsache, sondern ein ästhetisches Verfahren
beschrieben wird; ein Verfahren, dessen beträchtliches Potential an
Negativität in dem präpositionalen Index "wider" verborgen liegt.
Spiegelungen zeigen das eine im anderen, erfordern ein polyfokales
Sehen, wie doppeltbelichtete Photographien. Die Straßencafés der
Künstlerszene, der Abendsonnenglanz am Eiffelturm und am Ufer der
Seine; dann die zerstörten Arkaden und ausgebrannten Säle der Berliner
Staatsbibliothek Unter den Linden, "ein Dachskelett mit aufgerissener

Wunde", und doch von "gigantischer Schönheit",[3] wie Weiss in einer der Reportagen verwundert notiert.

Hier, im Zentrum des deutschen Geistes, bleibt der Blick haften. An diesem Ort, vor dem die Nazis im Mai 1933 einen Scheiterhaufen aus Büchern errichtet hatten, sind nun "herabhängende Eisenträger" zu sehen, "leere und zerfetzte Reihen von ringförmig angeordneten Bücherregalen längs der Galerien, Fragmente von Skulpturen und umgestürzte Pfeiler, an den Wänden Reste von Malereien und Ornamenten, die durch die Zerstörung jede Banalität verloren haben [...]. Alles spricht die starke Sprache der Symbole."[4] Soweit die Schilderung des Reporters; wo sie "die starke Sprache der Symbole" am Werk sieht, kann die ästhetisch bearbeitete, die fiktionalisierte Version des Deutschland-Rapports weiter gehen. Sie kann auch die Last, die von diesen Symbolen ausgeht, ihrerseits symbolisch bearbeiten und verändern. Wenn wir versuchen, den Fallschirmflug, diesen traumwandlerischen Auftakt einer literarischen Deutschlandreise, in seiner Bildlichkeit und Bildsprache zu erfassen, dann ist auch in dieser figurativen Umgestaltung des in Berlin Erlebten eine Spur von Paris mit im Spiele. Das Paris Aragons und Bretons. An den surrealistischen Schreibweisen und Wahrnehmungsexperimenten lernt Weiss die *Aisthesis,* die Arbeit an der Erweiterung und Durchdringung des sinnlich Erfahrbaren.

Wie eine Sonde gleitet das Ich an seinem Fallschirm durch eine Welt, in der statt fester Grenzen fließende Übergänge und assoziative Strömungen den Ton angeben. Und doch ist zugleich noch etwas anderes im Spiel, wie man als Weiss-Leser vielleicht erst aus großem Rückblick erkennnen kann, wenn man nämlich in der *Ästhetik des Widerstands* die Episode gelesen hat, in der Lotte Bischoffs *under-cover*-Mission als Agentin des Widerstands im Berlin der Kriegszeit erzählt wird. *Diese* Agentin wird mit einem Schiff nach Deutschland geschleust; aber gab es nicht auch abenteuerliche Pläne, Widerstandskämpfer per Fallschirm im feindlichen Hinterland abzusetzen? Die Assoziation, daß es sich bei dem Deutschlandflug des schwedischen Reporters um eine quasi militärische Operation handeln könnte, ist so leicht nicht abzuweisen. Der Fallschirmspringer muß jedenfalls, ob zu Kriegszeiten oder nicht, mit großer Schnelligkeit und bildhafter Intuition die Gegebenheiten der Topographie und der Infrastruktur erfassen; "wie das feingesponnene Netz von Adern", so registriert der Blick aus der Luft, "glitzern unter mir die weitverzweigten Geleise eines nächtlichen Bahnhofs" (*Die Besiegten*, 11). Bahnanlagen gehören zu den neuralgischen Punkten in Feindesland. An Bahnkotenpunkten kann sich die Vogelflug-Perspektive orientieren; im Luftkrieg gehörten sie zu den vordringlichsten Zielen. Auch der Fallschirmspringer, der zu den Besiegten unterwegs ist, hat es auf einen Bahnhof abgesehen. "Hinter dem Regenvorhang erahne ich die schwarze Masse des Stationsgebäudes. Langsame Züge treiben vorbei mit abgeblendeten Lampen; im Lichtstreifen des Horizonts liegt die zerstörte Stadt der Vergangenheit." In dieser Stadt der Vergangenheit sind das Lebendigste die Wunden des Krieges. Daß bei dem hier phantasierten Deutschlandflug eigentlich ein Szenario der Kriegsjahre zugrundeliegt, verrät sich an einem unscheinbaren Detail, den "abgeblendeten Lampen". Sie sind eine Folge der sogenannten Verdunklung, einer allgemeinen Sicherheitsvorschrift, die während der Jahre des Luftkriegs allnächtlich die Lichter an Häusern, Straßenrändern und Fahrzeugen auf ein Miminum einzuschränken befahl, um den Angriffen kein hellerleuchtetes Ziel zu bieten. In den Nachkriegsjahren war diese Schutzmaßname allerdings hinfällig geworden.

Der Krieg, den Peter Weiss aus schwedischer Perspektive erlebte, ist für diesen Besucher noch nicht zuende. Dieser Deutschlandflug ist zu einer ganzen Reihe ähnlicher Flug-Phantasien zu zählen, die Karl-Heinz Götze als intensives und wiederkehrendes Motiv im Schreiben von Peter Weiss herauspräpariert hat.[5] Doch ist die Figur des Überfluges eben auch, so meine ich, mit einem realen Kontext befrachtet, der sich zeitgeschichtlich aufschlüsseln läßt. Dieser ästhetisch so ausgefallene Beginn der Deutschlandreise von Peter Weiss unternimmt, um es pointiert zu sagen, eine Luft-Boden-Invasion mit den Mitteln des Surrealismus.[6] Die Wunden, die dem Weichbild der Stadt aus der Luft zugefügt wurden—Brecht sprach sarkastisch von einer Radierung Churchills nach Entwürfen Hitlers—diese Spuren sind aus einer virtuellen Vogelflugperspektive auch am genauesten zu bilanzieren. Der Fallschirmspringer-Besuch bei den Besiegten fällt demnach unter jenes Psychodrama, dem die Lektionen des Wiederholens und Durcharbeitens auferlegt sind. Da ist der neuralgische Punkt zu suchen, auf den diese phantastische Operation abzielt.

Die deutsche Zivilbevölkerung erlebte den Kampf der Alliierten gegen den nazistischen Aggressor, wenn man von den letzten Monaten vor Kriegsende absieht, vorwiegend als Luftkrieg; als nächtliches Brummen der Bombengeschwader, als Heulen der Sirenen des Fliegeralarms, als stickige, panische Enge in den Luftschutzbunkern. Vor einigen Jahren erst stellten Schriftsteller und Literaturkritiker (W. G. Sebald, Walter Kempowski, Volker Hage) mit echter oder gespielter Verwunderung die Frage, warum diese Erfahrung, die doch zweifellos elementare Bedrohungsängste ausgelöst hatte und vielfache persönliche Leidenserfahrungen mit sich brachte, warum also dieses mentalitätsgeschichtlich sehr tiefreichende Phänomen so gut wie keine Spuren in der deutschen Literatur hinterlassen hat. Und natürlich lag die suggestiv unterstellte Erklärung nahe, daß die unter dem Besatzerstatut opportune politische Korrektheit eine solche Form der Erinnerungsarbeit nicht zugelassen hätte, bei der die Deutschen als Opfer alliierter Gegengewalt in Erscheinung getreten wären. Wo wäre ein deutsches *War Requiem* in Sicht? Wo ein literarisches Monument für das zerbombte Dresden? Und wenn es sie gäbe: Würden solche Werke nicht jenen Stimmen Auftrieb geben, die immer wieder—wie jüngst Martin Walser in seiner *Friedenspreis*-Rede in der Frankfurter Paulskirche—ein Ende der deutschen Kollektivschuld fordern, ein Ende des geschichtspädagogisch verordneten schlechten Gewissens? Ich glaube nicht; eher im Gegenteil. Je mehr der Krieg vorstellbar ist, desto weniger ist er führbar.

Die Parolen der ersten Nachkriegsjahre waren Trümmerbeseitigung und Wiederaufbau. Man konnte es sich nicht leisten, seine Aufmerksamkeit länger auf die Form der militärischen Niederlage zu richten und auf deren materielle Folgen, die man jeden Tag ohnehin vor Augen hatte. Doch Peter Weiss, oder vielmehr sein fallschirmspringendes alter ego, tut genau dies. Mit einer staunenden, fast naiv erscheinenden Aufmerksamkeit betrachtet er die Schneisen der Zerstörung und die herumliegenden Trümmerstücke. Er sagt: "Die Gegenwart ist erfüllt von Betriebsamkeit, draußen aber liegen die Steine schwer und schweigend über unserer Vergangenheit" (*Die Besiegten*,

112). Da wird nicht 'wiederaufgebaut', sondern Vernarbtes wie-
deraufgerissen, in einer zuweilen recht plakativ aufgetragenen
Bildersprache. "Ich liege am Strand in der Sonne. Meine Hände [...]
dringen ein in den Sand, bis sie Holz oder Stein oder Knochen zu spüren
bekommen; ich grabe das Versteckte aus; ein Kindergerippe und danach
einige Schädel; wo sind ihre Körper?" (*Die Besiegten*, 49). Immer noch,
und gerade auch für die literarischen Mittel des Prosaisten, gilt die
Beobachtung des Reporters: "Alles spricht die starke Sprache der
Symbole."

Der Bericht über die Bibliothek Unter den Linden erwähnt
besonders den gesprengten Fußboden, "unter dem sich die
Kellergewölbe in unterirdischem Dunkel öffnen."[7] Solche
Beobachtungen sind Teil seines Versuchs, "den tiefsten Dimensionen
des Untergangs" nachzuspüren; "nicht der Zerstörung der Städte,
sondern der Zerstörung des Geistes" (*Die Besiegten*, 65). Der da kam,
um "unter den Trümmern" nach "zerschlagenen menschlichen Werten"
zu suchen (*Die Besiegten*, 87), verliert zwar niemals seine Fremdheit in
dieser Stadt, doch schon bald hört er auf, ein unbeteiligter Beobachter zu
sein. "Wo ich mit dem Fallschirm des großen Augenblicks hinabgleite,
sehe ich, wie unlösbar ich mit einem gemeinsamen Schicksal verbunden
bin. Die Trümmer unter mir sind nicht Trümmer eines Landes:hier liegt
unsere ganze Zeit, hier liegt der Steinzeitmensch begraben" (Ebd.).
Lapidar notiert der Berichterstatter: "Besiegt sind die Kinder" (*Die
Besiegten*, 102). Bei einer Kinderpsychologin im Norden Berlins lernt er
ein achtjähriges Mädchen kennen, das nach einem Bombenangriff die
entstellte Leiche seiner jüngeren Schwester gefunden hatte.[8] Die
Erwachsenen erzählten dem Mädchen dann, die kleine Schwester sei nun
ein Engel geworden. "Aber du sahst nur den Todesengel, blutig, voller
Wunden. Nachts schriest du, wenn der Engel zu dir gekommen war in
deinen Träumen. [...] Sie sperrten dich ein, um den Engel auszutreiben,
aber der Engel umschwebte dich und berührte dich mit seinen
unheimlichen Händen. [...] Wir sprachen lange über deine Schwester,
dann gab ich dir Ton und du formtest das Abbild der Toten" (*Die
Besiegten*, 102f.). Da nimmt jemand ernst, was die Träume sagen. Die
surrealen Techniken der Verfremdung werden hier eingesetzt, um an die
psychischen Verschüttungen des Luftkriegs heranzukommen. Um dem

Greifbarkeit und Gestalt zu geben, was verloren ist. Die Reportage *Kinder in Berlin*, die diesen fiktionalisierten Passagen zugrundeliegt, berichtet weiter: "Andere Kinder heilen ihren Schrecken vor den Flugzeugen damit, daß sie dem Flugzeug einen friedlichen Charakter geben; es kommt hier nicht mit Bomben, sondern mit Brot und Schokolade beladen" (*Die Besiegten*, 132). Was aber macht die literarische Bearbeitung aus dieser Beobachtung? "Spielt euren Flugzeugschrecken aus euch heraus", heißt es da, "laßt das Flugzeug niederstürzen auf euer Haus aus Schachteln und Sand [...]. Was hilft es, wenn ich euer Spiel auf friedliche Bahnen lenke" (*Die Besiegten*, 105). Die gestörten Kinder, so erkennt der fremde Beobachter, reagieren im Grunde völlig plausibel auf eine weiterhin gestörte Umgebung. Warum daran rühren, warum auch noch absichtlich zündeln an diesen aufgestauten Gewaltvorstellungen? "Über euren Köpfen hinweg kreisen immer noch Bombenflugzeuge, die Zeitungen und Lautsprecher schreien ihre Verehrung für die immer größeren Flugzeuge hinaus, für die immer größeren Bomben. Spielt im Schatten der Bombenflugzeuge, verirrte, hilflose Kinder!" (*Die Besiegten*, 106). Das ist keine psychotherapeutische Empfehlung, das ist nicht mehr als der Versuch, den hilflosen Schrei dieser Kinder mitzuschreien, ihn zu verstärken, indem das Szenario des Luftkriegs mit ästhetischen Mitteln erneut heraufbeschworen wird.

Das also ist die Mission des schwedischen Fallschirmspringers: die Verfremdung und Verstörung jener Normalität, die sich über die fortdauernde Vergangenheit gelegt hat. "Es ist noch nicht zuende", wird der Besucher in Auschwitz knapp zwei Jahrzehnte später konstatieren.

II

Peter Weiss kehrte nach Berlin zurück als teilnehmender Beobachter eines Schicksals, dem er entkommen war. "Unter den Trümmern suche ich nach mir selbst. Ich erlebte die Folter. Ich erlebte den kollektiven Tod. Wer bin ich? Ich besitze die Freiheit des Heimatlosen" (*Die Besiegten*, 120). Zeigen die Reportagen Weiss als einen "Heimkehrwilligen"? Ich glaube kaum. Die Identifikation mit den Opfern, die Alfons Söllner als zentrales Anliegen der Weiss'schen

Ästhetik wider die Verdrängung herausgearbeitet hat[10], buchstabiert im
Angesicht des geschundenen Leibes die Einsicht: "Ich könnte hier statt
seiner liegen" (*Der Fremde* 47). Der Satz entstammt dem Prosastück
Der Fremde, das Weiss nur kurze Zeit nach dieser Deutschlandreise
niederschrieb. "Ich könnte hier statt seiner liegen." Immer wieder muß
sich politische Solidarität an solchen elementaren Sätzen messen lassen.
Und dennoch ist diese hypothetische Identifikation ein problematisches
Ziel. Empathie hat ihre Grenzen, stellvertretende Fürsprache, und sei sie
noch so gut gemeint, ebenfalls. Der teilnehmende Beobachter ist ein
Konstrukt der Ethnographie, das auf einem unübersehbaren Dilemma
beruht. Stets will der Ethnograph wissen, wie sich die von ihm
erforschten Menschen wirklich verhalten, das heißt dann, wenn sie nicht
beobachtet werden. Er will seine Resultate nicht durch die eigene
Anwesenheit und sein Verhalten beeinflussen, gleichzeitig aber möchte
er die von ihm studierte Kultur so genau kennenlernen, als sei er "einer
von diesen".

Peter Weiss und die Deutschen—so hat Söllner seine Studie genannt,
in bewußter Anspielung auf ein früheres Buch des Politologen Kurt
Sontheimer über Thomas Mann und die Deutschen. Leiden an
Deutschland, das war das große Thema des exilierten Großschriftstellers
Thomas Mann, ein Thema in der Tradition Goethes und Heines. Für
Peter Weiss hatte das Verhältnis zu Deutschland die Form einer
Konfrontation. Es blieb, um das mindeste zu sagen, nicht frei war von
Mißtauen, von gegenseitigem Mißtrauen wohlgemerkt. Er selbst
bezeichnet, wie wir gehört haben, dieses Verhältnis treffend und
illusionslos als eine "Gegenüberstellung". Der kriminalistische
Terminus technicus in diesem frühen Werk verwundert. Er weist darauf
hin, daß hier, mit einem späteren Schlüsselwort des Dramatikers Weiss,
Ermittlungen zu führen sind, in die der Schreibende sich einschaltet.
Aber in welcher Eigenschaft tut er dies? Als Zeuge, als Geschädigter,
gar als ein Nebenkläger? Von all diesen Rollen spielt etwas hinein, sogar
von jener des Komplizen.

Ich möchte vorschlagen, die Umstände dieser Konfrontation als
diejenigen einer ethnographischen Situation[11] zu verstehen; einer
grundlegenden Fremdheit, die Weiss als "Wahrnehmungschance"
(Martin Rector) erlebte und als Grundbedingung seines Schreibens zu

akzeptieren bemüht war. Den Begriff "Ethnographie" betrachte ich dabei nicht als spezialwissenschaftlichen Terminus, sondern als Näherungsvokabel für eine Haltung, die sich dadurch charakterisieren läßt, das sie so ziemlich das Gegenteil der von Kant propagierten ästhetischen Kontemplation praktiziert, also nicht interesseloses Wohlgefallen, sondern "befangene Interessiertheit". Nicht genießende Einfühlung, sondern neugieriges Befremden. Peter Weiss brachte, so meine These, den von ihm beobachteten gesellschaftlichen Mechanismen und Ritualen ein solches ethnographisches Interesse entgegen. Und zwar nicht nur im bezug auf deutsche Angelegenheiten, wenngleich diese sein Hauptthema blieben, bei dem die Gründe für den befremdeten Blick von außen sehr deutlich und sehr konkret waren.

Das Beunruhigende an seiner Perspektive ist ihre fremde Nähe. Positiv formuliert liegt die bewußtmachende Funktion der "Ästhetik wider die Verdrängung" in der Möglichkeit, sich an die Stelle jedes Beteiligten versetzen zu können; also auch in die Rolle des Soldaten, des Machthabers, des Vergewaltigers zu schlüpfen. (Die einzelnen Prosastücke der *Besiegten* sind Beispiele solcher Rollen-Experimente.) Der Impuls zur Identifikation wäre blind ohne das ihn begleitende Befremden; und das bloß moralische Befremden bliebe leer ohne die prinzipielle Möglichkeit, sich mit ästhetischen Mitteln in die denkbar größte Intimität selbst zu den Akteuren und Handlangern der Gewalt zu bringen. Gerade in ihrem Dilemma ist diese Gleichzeitigkeit von fremdem Blick und empathischer Identifikation Ausdruck einer ethnographischen Einstellung. Wie ein Forschungsreisender sah sich dieser Autor den Sitten und Gebräuchen eines fremdartigen Landes gegenübergestellt.

Peter Weiss und die Deutschen—in diesem Verhältnis spielte Fremdheit eine Rolle schon vor dem Einschnitt der Emigration. Vielfach und nicht zu unrecht ist die Besonderheit dieser Schriftsteller-Biographie mit dem Stichwort der "Unzugehörigkeit" beschrieben worden.[12] Und doch ist man immer wieder geneigt, die konkreten Umstände dieser Unzugehörigkeit zu vergessen, etwa die Tatsache, daß Weiss niemals deutscher Staatsbürger war, niemals den Paß eines deutschsprachigen Landes besaß. Da ist ein Jugendlicher im Berlin der frühen dreißiger Jahre, den nicht nur seine künstlerischen Ambitionen zum Sonderling stempeln, sondern auch die bizarren Einsprengsel seiner Familiengeschichte—"als Sohn eines in Ungarn geborenen Vaters jüdischer Herkunft, der mit einem tschechoslowakischen Paß in Berlin eine von elsässischen Vorfahren abstammende, in der Schweiz geborene Schauspielerin heiratete".[13] Lebenslinien, deren verschlungene Wege auch die Auflösungserscheinungen des alten Vielvölkerreiches Österreich-Ungarn nachzeichnen: ein ungeheures Stück Mitteleuropa, das sich nicht reibungslos in die Schablonen der Nationalstaatlichkeit pressen ließ.[14] Vielfältig und plurizentrisch wie diese Herkunftslinien wird dann die Emigrationsgeschichte seiner Familie verlaufen, die über England und die Tschechoslowakei schließlich nach Schweden führt. Man kann diese mäandrierenden Nationalitäten als Ausdruck von "Wurzellosigkeit"[15] verstehen, und kommt damit einer "Motivierung" des Exils gefährlich nahe. Dabei ist es eher eine Überfülle an Wurzeln, auf die Peter Weiss zurückblicken kann, ein rhizomatisches Geflecht, das in die verschiedensten Himmelsrichtungen weist.

Und dann ist es andererseits doch wieder Weiss selber, der die Flucht aus Deutschland nicht als Einbruch des Außergewöhnlichen deutete, sondern als eine stimmige Konsequenz der früh erlebten Desintegration. "Die Emigration war für mich nur die Bestätigung einer Unzugehörigkeit, die ich von frühester Kindheit erfahren hatte" (*Abschied von den Eltern*, 143). Und so wie die Emigration ihn bestätigt hatte in seiner Unzugehörigkeit und in seinem Unverstandensein, so bestätigte er, als er selbst darüber entscheiden konnte, deren Resultat; er blieb in Schweden.

Für Weiss liegt der Fall anders als für jene Emigranten, die Deutschland auf begrenzte Zeit verlassen hatten, weil es vorübergehend unbewohnbar geworden war. In der biographischen Situation ist sein Weg vielleicht mit jenem des in England gebliebenen Lyrikers Erich Fried vergleichbar, der als Jugendlicher aus Wien hatte fliehen müssen. Und was die literarisch-politische Dimension seiner Arbeit betrifft, konnte Weiss am ehesten in der Person des Kollegen Uwe Johnson eine verwandte Skepsis antreffen gegenüber beiden deutschen Nachkriegsstaaten—und ein fast trotziges Beharren, in beiden gehört und gelesen zu werden.

Auch in späteren Jahren hat Weiss vieles, was ihm aus Deutschland widerfuhr, in die Kategorien der Exilerfahrung eingeordnet. Jenen Grenzübertritt in Berlin zum Beispiel, bei dem er stundenlang in den Katakomben des Bahnhofs Friedrichstraße festgehalten wurde. Kultivierte er sein Außenseitertum? In gewissem Sinne, ja. Die erlebte Unzugehörigkeit in den persönlichen Habitus aufzunehmen, bedeutete, auf das erzwungene Schicksal eben nicht nur reagieren, sondern es als Teil seiner selbst begreifen zu können. Für uns Leser aber ist die wichtigere Frage, wie dieses Gefühl der Unzugehörigkeit zur methodischen Haltung und Schreibweise wird.

Wie so viele Jugendliche hatte er unter dem Gefühl gelitten, in seinen Neigungen und Interessen nicht akzeptiert zu werden; er hatte nach Vorbildern und Bündnispartnern gesucht, und er war dabei ungleich erfolgreicher gewesen als andere. Mit dem bewunderten Hermann Hesse wechselte er Briefe, erhielt eine Einladung in die Schweiz, einen Auftrag für eine Buchillustration und einen Ausbildungsplatz an der Prager Kunstakademie.[16] Hesse gab ihm die nötige Starthilfe; und Weiss bewahrte ihm dafür die Dankbarkeit, auch als er längst in ganz anderen ästhetischen und politischen Zusammenhängen arbeitete. An Hesse erinnert auf indirekte Weise auch ein Prosawerk, das Weiss nach dem Berlinbesuch des Jahres 1947 begonnen hatte. *Der Vogelfreie* hieß zunächst dieser Text, der vom langsamen und ängstlichen Eintritt eines Fremden in die große Stadt erzählt. Er wurde, unter dem Titel *Der Fremde,* erst 1980 auf deutsch veröffentlicht. Darin gestaltet Weiss seine Übersiedlung aus dem ländlichen Alingsås, wo die Eltern sich niedergelassen hatten, ins anonyme und bedrohlich wirkende Stockholm. "Das riesenhafte Gebilde umspannt den ganzen überblickbaren Horizont, die Glieder wie zerbrochen wie zerschlagen, wahllos aufgetürmt in der erwachenden fernen Strahlung" (*Der Fremde,* 7). Es ist der alte Mythos vom gesichtslosen Moloch Stadt, in den ein namenloser Habenichts gerät. Daß auch die Berlin-Erfahrung des Sommers 1947 ein auslösendes Moment dieser Geschichte gewesen sein muß, gibt schon der Umstand zu erkennen, daß Peter Weiss nun wieder auf deutsch schreibt: ein Buch, das mit literarischem Ehrgeiz gestaltet ist, und vom Ton angespannter Erwartung getragen. "Hier ist alles ausgehöhlt von ungeheuerlichen Anstrengungen, alles erfüllt von Erwartungen" (*Der Fremde,* 8).

Die hier dargestellte Fremdheit der Großstadt erwecke, so schrieb ein deutscher Lektor in seinem Ablehnungsbrief über die eingereichte Erzählung, den "Eindruck von etwas Gesuchtem".[17] Dieser Lektor war kein anderer als Peter Suhrkamp, und gerade ihn hatte Weiss mit seinem Text tatsächlich gesucht. Nachdem er Suhrkamp während seines Deutschland-Aufenthalts 1947 persönlich kennengelernt hatte, gab es für Weiss wieder einen Adressaten, für den es sich auf deutsch zu schreiben lohnte. Und: Suhrkamp war der Verleger Hermann Hesses, der diese für die Kultur der Bundesrepublik so folgenreiche Verlagsgründung entscheidend unterstützt hatte. Weiss wollte also im Verlag Hermann Hesses erscheinen, woraus bekanntlich erst gut zehn Jahre später etwas wurde. Gerade hatte er als schwedischer Publizist erste, bescheidene Erfolge erzielt, und nun wurde plötzlich die deutsche Sprache in Schweden zu einem Fluchtpunkt für ihn. Die Berichte aus Berlin hatte Weiss noch auf schwedisch verfaßt.

Natürlich verrät das Hin und Her zwischen beiden Sprachen eine gewisse Unsicherheit in den künstlerischen Mitteln und Zielen, aber wahllos sind die Ausdrucksformen dieser kontrastierenden Projekte keinesfalls. Die in Berlin erlebte Fremdheit wird in einem schwedischen Text artikuliert, die Stockholmer Orientierungslosigkeit dagegen findet sich in einer deutschen Erzählung wieder. Beide Welten, zwischen denen sich der Unzugehörige bewegt, scheinen ganz gut ohne ihn auszukommen. Er aber ist die Verunsicherung in Person. Die großen Städte vexieren ihn wie elektrische Spannungspole; sobald er sich nähert, spürt er zunehmend ihre Abstoßungskräfte. Überall. Da geht es nicht darum, den Ort der Zuflucht gegen die Option einer späten Rückkehr auszuspielen Da geht es auch nicht darum, die eine Form der Entfremdung gegen ein anderes, ebenso entfremdetes Leben einzutauschen. Die Stockholmer Gegenwart ist nicht das positive Gegenbild zur Berliner Vergangenheit; nicht einmal die euphorischen Augenblicke in Paris lassen sich zum Entwurf eines anderen Lebens fügen. Diejenigen Orte, von denen die nachhaltigsten Eindrücke der französischen Metropole ausgehen, sind merkwürdigerweise Brücken und Wege am Fluß. Und das berühmte Museum des Louvre selbstverständlich. Das Bild von Paris in *Fluchtpunkt* und noch in der *Ästhetik des Widerstands* ist verbunden mit Wahrnehmungen, die aus der Schwebeform eines virtuellen Kunstraums leben, oder sich von den Schauplätzen des Transitorischen nähren.[18]

Der Fremde ist also kein Emigrant einer spezifischen Bedrohungs- oder Notsituation, die er hinter sich lassen könnte; ebensowenig ist es ein besonderer Ort, der ihn zum Fremden macht. Die gleichnamige Erzählung spielt, obwohl viele Einzelheiten genannt werden, auch nicht in einer wiedererkennbaren Stadt, sondern in der Großstadt schlechthin. Deren Schilderung entspricht dem bekannten Topos des kalten, unmenschlichen Umschlagplatzes der Massen, des abstoßenden Konkurrenzkampfes um die besten Plätze. Die Stadt ist Sinnbild undurchschaubarer gesellschaftlicher Zusammenhänge, die einen wahnsinnig machen könnten. Und doch präsentieren sie sich als das Vernünftigste und Normalste der Welt. Es bedarf des namenlosen Eindringlings, um in ihrer Alltäglichkeit und Normalität das Absurde zu sehen und sich wie neu darüber zu wundern. "Immer tiefer dringe ich ein in diese Stadt, in der die Bewohner auf zwei Beinen gehen und die Vögel nicht vom Himmel fallen, in der die Mauern der Häuser senkrecht aufsteigen" (*Der Fremde*, 31). Hier geschieht nichts anderes als das Selbstverständliche, und genau dies ist am schwierigsten sichtbar zu machen.

Fremdheit als Wahrnehmungschance. Es wäre sicher übertrieben zu behaupten, daß Peter Weiss mit *Der Fremde* das ästhetische Potential einer solchen verfremdenden Wahrnehmung bereits ausgeschöpft habe. Zwar nimmt sich der Suchende vor, ganz Auge und Ohr zu sein, alle Sinne hellwach auf seine Umgebung zu richten, doch sind seine Beobachtungen allzu aufdringlich vom Prozeß der Selbstfindung überlagert. Existentiell gesteiltes Pathos verhindert an vielen Stellen das genaue Hinsehen. Und manchmal ist auch für treffende Beobachtungen nur eine Sprache von verbrauchten Klischees, matten Bildern und abgegriffenen Redewendungen vorhanden. Häufig sind es Metaphern der Eingeschlossenheit, der Vereinzelung und des Gefangenseins, mit denen der Sprechende diese Begrenzung zu reflektieren scheint, aus der er heraus will in eine ganz neue Sprache, deren Laute und Zeichen es erst zu formen gilt. "Da mein ungeheures Bedürfnis, den Gedanken Ausdruck zu verleihen, ganz in sich eingeschlossen wurde", so sagt er an einer Stelle, habe er in sich ein "System von inneren Tönen" ausgebildet

(*Der Fremde*, 97). Helmut Peitsch glaubte an der Texthaltung von *Die Besiegten* eine gewisse Affinität zum Diskurs der Inneren Emigration beobachten zu können.[19] An den Imaginationen des *Fremden* jedenfalls ist, wenn wir von der im deutschen Kontext politisch anders festgelegten Bedeutung dieses Begriffes absehen, in der Tat die Befindlichkeit einer Inneren Emigration zum Ausdruck gebracht, einer Fremdheit, die nach innen zu weisen scheint.

Als *Der Fremde* 1980 doch noch im Suhrkamp-Verlag erscheint, während Peter Weiss am Abschlußband der *Ästhetik des Widerstands* arbeitet, wird dieses Dokument früherer Häutungen unter dem Autoren-Pseudonym *Sinclair* herausgebracht. Wie um diese Phase des schwärmerischen Unverstandenseins auch editorisch mit der gebotenen literaturgeschichtlichen Distanz zu markieren, erscheint auf dem Titel eine Figur, die sich noch einmal mit dem frühen Vorbild Hermann Hesses verbindet. Emil Sinclair ist der Icherzähler aus Hesses *Demian*. In dem innigen Band der Namen Sinclair und Demian verschlingt sich die Geschichte einer idealisierten Jugendfreundschaft, einer Freundschaft unter Gleichaltrigen allerdings, nicht zwischen dem väterlichen Meister und seinem zarten Jünger. Aber der Name Sinclair führt noch weiter zurück. So hatte der Freund und Gefährte Hölderlins geheißen, Isaac Sinclair, der den entlassenen Hofmeister und ortlos gewordenen Dichter Hölderlin aus dem mondänen Frankfurt in das freisinnige Bad Homburg geholt hatte, um mit ihm gemeinsam für eine deutsche Republik zu streiten. Von Hesse zu Hölderlin: die Folge dieser leicht entschlüsselbaren Stichwortgeber des Namens Sinclair ist geeignet, dem existentiellen Pathos der Fremdheit eine geschichtliche Tiefendimension, und damit auch eine politische Wendung zu geben.

Denn Hölderlins Briefroman *Hyperion* war es, der das Pathos der Fremdheit im eigenen Land zum Ausdruck einer scharfen Dissidenz formte, indem er sie in der imaginären Gestalt eines "Eremiten in Griechenland" spiegelte. Nur als einen Fremdling, der dieses Land von außen sah, konnte er seinen Hyperion sagen lassen: "So kam ich unter die Deutschen. Ich foderte nicht viel und war gefaßt, noch weniger zu finden. Demüthig kam ich, wie der heimathlose blinde Oedipus zum Thore von Athen" (MHA I, 754). Später wurde Hölderlins Pathos der Fremdheit als Feier der sozialen Desintegration des Poeten verstanden und affirmiert. Im historischen Kontext aber bot dieser als Fiktion eingesetzte fremde Blick die Möglichkeit, die von Rousseau formulierte Zivilisationskritik auf die Erscheinungen gesellschaftlicher Entfremdung in Deutschland zu beziehen. Nach der Methode von Montesqieus *Lettres Persanes* beschreibt Hölderlin die deutschen Zustände durch den Blick eines jungen Griechen. Die berühmte, sogenannte Scheltrede über die Deutschen betreibt weder nationalen Selbsthaß noch schwärmerischen Utopismus. Ich verstehe diese fiktive Deutschlandreportage des aus Griechenland emigrierten Hyperion als negatives Abziehbild der im 18. Jahrhundert praktizierten Bildungsreise in das klassische Italien. Nicht mehr die idealisierte Antike wird hier als der Ort angesteuert, an dem man etwas lernen kann, sondern gerade der Schauplatz größter Entfremdung: "Es ist ein hartes Wort und dennoch sag' ichs, weil es Wahrheit ist: ich kann kein Volk mir denken, das zerrißner wäre, wie die Deutschen."[20]

III

Wie bedeutsam der politische Hölderlin für Peter Weiss werden sollte, ist bekannt. Das existentielle Thema der Unzugehörigkeit verwandelte sich indessen in ein mehr und mehr kalkuliert eingesetztes ästhetisches Prinzip: die künstlerische Nutzung des fremden Blicks als Form der *Verfremdung*. Diese Entwicklung in der Schreibweise von Peter Weiss wurde angestoßen auch durch die wiederholte Auseinandersetzung mit dem Werk zweier längst kanonisch gewordener Avantgardisten, mit Kafka und Brecht. Kafkas Exkursionen in die Regionen der Sinnlosigkeit und Brechts gestisches Theater förderten das Gespür dafür, wie eng soziale Entfremdung und ästhetisches Befremdetsein miteinander verflochten sind.

Brechts Kritik des aristotelischen Theaters und vor allem der Rezeptionshaltung der Einfühlung, mit der sich der Zuschauer im Dargestellten wiederzuerkennen pflegte, hat in Kafkas Verweigerung einer auktorialen Erzählperspektive und eines rational durchgestalteten Handlungsmusters eine gewisse Entsprechung. Beiden gemeinsam ist nämlich die Einsicht, daß der künstlerische Realismus in der Moderne gerade nicht in der sinnvollen Erklärung der Phänomene sich verwirklicht, sondern in der Haltung eines verwunderten und manchmal fassungslosen Erstaunens.

Der Schlüssel zur Moderne liegt in der Verweigerung des spontan praktizierten, alltäglichen Einverständnisses. Indem sie ihre Welt ethnograpisch einfärben und verfremden, machen Kafka und Brecht die Transparenz des Selbstverständlichen zu einer opaken Größe. Kafkas *Bericht für eine Akademie* schildert den Prozeß der Zivilisation von seiner anderen Seite. Im spektakulären Anpassungsvermögen eines domestizierten Affen reflektiert sich das Staunen über Sitten und Gebräuche des modernen Mitteleuropa. Brechts Begriff des Gestus operiert mit einer Unterbrechung habitualisierter Verhaltensabläufe. Die Körper erstarren, wie zu einer ikonischen Pose; herausgelöst aus ihren Handlungen werden sie unverständlich und dadurch erst wirklich sichtbar. Das "Zeigen des Zeigens" fordert nicht Einfühlung, sondern Distanz, es verstört die langgeübte Identifikationsbereitschaft der Zuschauer.

Diese ästhetischen Prinzipien, so meine ich, sind zumindest indirekt auch Antworten auf die kulturelle Herausforderung durch ethnographische Erfahrungen und Theoriedebatten. "Study ritual, not belief" hatte der Ethnologe Bronislaw Malinoski in den zehner Jahren gefordert. Nicht, was eine Kultur über sich selbst sagt, ist das Entscheidende, sondern welche Institutionen und Verhaltensmuster sie ausbildet. In der Kunstgeschichte und Kultursoziologie der Moderne trug diese methodische Implementierung des fremden Blicks ebenfalls Früchte. Die ikonographische Ausrichtung, die Erwin Panofsky der Kunstgeschichte gab,[21] setzt die Aufkündigung der Sinntransparenz beim Betrachter voraus. Nicht verstehen, sondern sehen. Das nur scheinbar naturwüchsige Band zwischen Körpersprache und Bedeutung wird gelockert. Gesten, Posen und Körpersymptome, die in der mitteleuropäischen Alltagskultur einen genau definierten pragmatischen Aussagewert besitzen, können in anderen Kulturen gar keine oder ganz andere Signalwirkungen haben. Je fremder sie erscheinen, um so deutlicher werden sie als Material herauspräparierbar.

Das Nichtverstehen zwingt uns dazu, um so genauere Beobachter zu sein, denn jede Einzelheit kann möglicherweise wichtig werden. Oder auch nicht. Dann ist die aufgebotene Genauigkeit ganz umsonst, das

Ergebnis enttäuschend. Ein Beispiel: "In die Kniebeuge gehend, drückte der Hausknecht seinen Rücken gegen einen Sack, hob seine Hände über die Schultern, senkte sie hinter die Schultern herab, packte den Sack, straffte die Beine, beugte sich, den Sack auf dem Rücken festhaltend, vor und ging auf die Küchentreppe zu, an der Küchentreppe vorbei und auf die Kellertreppe zu, die Kellertreppe hinab zur Kellertür die er mit dem Fuß aufstieß" (*Schatten*, 95). In diesem Abschnitt aus *Der Schatten des Körpers des Kutschers* spielt Peter Weiss eine Art Rätselspiel. Welchen Sinn hat die dargestellte Handlung, um was für eine Art von Lieferung mag es dabei gehen? Lange läßt der Bericht offen, ob nun— ein wichtiges Indiz—der Hausknecht mit dem Sack den Weg zur Küche oder in den Keller einschlagen wird. Und immer noch zögert der Beschreibende, den naheliegenden Schluß aus seinen Beobachtungen zu ziehen, mit dem er eine halbe Seite später dann doch herausrückt. "Das Geräusch das beim Entladen des Sackes in der Tiefe des Kellers entstand gab meiner Vermutung, daß der Sack Kohlen enthalte, recht" (*Schatten*, 94). Die Deutung 'kommt' aus der Beschreibung wie der Höhepunkt im kunstvoll verzögerten Finale eines Liebesakts (von dem denn auch wenig später tatsächlich die Rede ist, wenngleich nur in der Form eines Schattenspiels).

Was an diesem zugegeben banalen Beispiel in exzellenter Form betrachtet werden kann, ist die künstlerische Strategie, um die Verständlichkeit des Geschilderten herumzuschreiben. Anders als bei den Dramatikern des Absurden wird nicht das Sinnlose ausgestellt, sondern der Sinn möglichst umständlich eingekreist, ganz dicht entlang seiner Ränder (vielleicht liegt darin auch eine Definition des Erotischen...). Stets bleibt nachvollziehbar, worum es sich handelt; und doch gewinnt die Banalität der gezeigten Vorgänge eine zusätzliche, unerwartete Profilierung durch diese penible Umständlichkeit, mit der sie umzingelt werden.

Erst mit dem *Schatten des Körpers des Kutschers* fand Weiss zu einer eigenständigen Ästhetik, so lautet die gängige werkbiographische Periodisierung, die—obwohl auch von äußerlichen Erfolgskriterien beeinflußt—sicher nicht ganz unplausibel ist. Daß sich aber mit diesem Text etwas völlig Neues und Unerhörtes ereignet habe, diese Einschätzung muß freilich relativiert werden. Nach meinem Eindruck liegt die im *Schatten* experimentell erprobte Distanz, dieser mit pedantischer Genauigkeit protokollierte Blick von außen, durchaus in der Entwicklungslinie von *Die Besiegten* und *Der Fremde*. Die Szenerie: eine ländliche Pension, in der das schreibende Ich wie ein Fremdkörper erscheint, und seine seltsame Leidenschaft des Beobachtens und Beschreibens läßt dieses Außenseitertum nur noch krasser hervortreten. Nicht nur in der Großstadt, auch in dieser kleinen Welt gibt es ungeschriebene Gesetze und stillschweigende Verabredungen, mit der sich eine Gemeinschaft als längst verschworener Zirkel gegen neugierige Blicke und Fragen abzuschirmen versteht. Was der Berichterstatter hier zu sehen und zu notieren bekommt, sind Rituale der Ausgrenzung, die signalisieren: all dies läuft ohne dich. Mehr noch: diese unausgesprochene Ausgrenzung adressiert sich gar nicht an ihn, sie zieht ihn noch nicht einmal als Störenden in Betracht.

"Alles ist verkehrt, ich bin hier unzugehörig" (*Der Fremde,* 87); wie *Der Fremde* könnte dies auch der Sprecher im *Schatten des Kutschers* von sich sagen, oder wie jener sich fragen lassen: "Sind Sie berechtigt, sich hier aufzuhalten?" (*Der Fremde,* 83). Was also hat sich in dem knapp fünf Jahre später entstandenen Werk geändert? "Die frühen Werke, bis einschließlich *Der Fremde,* sind geschwätzig", urteilte Stefan Howald. "*Der Schatten des Körpers des Kutschers* grenzt Sprache erstmals ein, als Material wie als Mittel."[22] An diesem etwas unwirsch formulierten Eindruck scheint mir richtig, daß im Vergleich zu den Frühwerken im *Schatten*-Text tatsächlich eine Tendenz der thematischen Beschränkung und stilistischen Strenge zu erkennen ist. Eingegrenzt wird aber nicht die Sprache, sondern zunächst das Gesichtsfeld des Sprechenden. Nur was er selbst wirklich sehen kann, darf erwähnt werden in seinem Protokoll.

Der Beobachter setzt sich zum Ziel, seinen Gesichtskreis möglichst genau zu inventarisieren, und das heißt ohne darüber hinausgehende Spekulationen und Mutmaßungen. Schon der Beginn zeigt dies auf drastische Weise. Akribisch werden sämtliche Beobachtungen aufgezählt, die sich von der Sitzposition eines ländlichen Klohäuschens aus machen lassen. Das ist wenig und auch dies Wenige ist nicht besonders appetitlich: der Schweinekofen, ein Stück der Hauswand mit ihrem abgeblätterten Putz, ein morastiger Fußweg, der zum Abtritt führt und sich auf der anderen Seite in der Ferne des Ackerlandes verliert; schließlich die Einzelheiten und Folgen jener Prozedur, die zu verrichten das Ich des Beobachters sich an diesen Ort zurückgezogen hatte. Und trotz der Buchhalter-Trockenheit, die in dieser Pedanterie liegt, ist die Szene von einem objektiven Humor getränkt, den der Autor vielleicht gar nicht beabsichtigt haben mag. Am Ende der Sequenz heißt es: "Erst jetzt [...] empfinde ich die Kälte an meinem entblößten Gesäß. Die Niederschrift meiner Beobachtungen hat mich davon abgehalten, die Hose hinaufzuziehen; oder auch war es die herabgezogene Hose, das Frösteln, die Selbstvergessenheit die mich hier auf dem Abtritt überkam, die diese besondere Stimmung des Beobachtens in die Wege leitete" (*Schatten*, 9f.).

Auch und vor allem dies hat sich geändert gegenüber den früheren Texten: der Beschreibende stilisiert sich nicht mehr zum Phantasma eines körperlosen Mediums, er ist ein Mensch, wie man so schön sagt, aus Fleisch und Blut, in dieser Szene aber hauptsächlich aus Augen und Arsch. Wenn letzterer hygienisch einigermaßen versorgt ist, dann kommen die Augen dran, denn auch sie müssen "Toilette machen": "in Reichweite neben mir auf dem Tisch habe ich einen Teller mit Salz stehen von dem ich mir zuweilen ein paar Körner in die Augen streue. Die Aufgabe der Salzkörner ist es, meine Tränendrüsen zu reizen, und damit meinen Blick verschwommen zu machen; die entstehenden Tränenfäden, Lichtpünktchen und anschwellenden und zerfließenden Lichtkeile legen sich über das deutlich in meine Netzhaut eingeätzte Abbild des Raumes" (*Schatten*, 18). Selbst die halluzinogenen Überblendungen des Realen werden noch nach ihren physiologischen Bedingungen befragt: Ausscheidungsvorgänge sind es allemal, die das Ich mit seiner Umwelt in Kontakt bringen. Zum Vergleich die Selbstbeschreibung des *Fremden*: "Ein Nichts. Namenlos. Eine Art Seismograph" (*Der Fremde*, 81). Bezeichnenderweise war nun gerade dieses scheinbar so ätherische Ich des Seismographen, der wie eine Sonde durch die Extensionen seiner Wahrnehmung zu gleiten schien, permanent mit sich selbst beschäftigt. Das ungleich fleischlichere Wesen aus dem *Schatten des Kutschers* dagegen schärft mit den Manipulationen an den eigenen Sehorganen auch die Prägnanz seiner Mitwelt.

Die Affekte von Schmerz und Zerstörung, die in *Der Fremde* nur Indizien einer metastasenartig wuchernden allgemeinen Krankheit sind, werden nun als scharfe Klingen geführt, um die Menschen von den Gegenständen, voneinander und von ihren Körperteilen abzutrennen— sie alle stoßen sich hart im Raume, und nichts paßt zusammen: Der Schatten des Körpers des Kutschers ist eben durchaus etwas anderes als der Kutscher selbst. Während die Körper es miteinander treiben, scheinen sie mit den ihnen zugeordneten Personen und Identitäten nur lose verbunden zu sein. Und der Beobachter übt sich in Enthaltsamkeit; er berichtet nur über ein Schattenspiel.

Im *Schatten des Körpers des Kutschers* steckt also ein phänomenologisches Plädoyer: Es lohnt sich, die Synthesis der konventionellen Wahrnehmung aufzuspalten. Die Unterstellung, daß alle diese fragmentierten Bilder, Zeichen und Körper ein Ganzes bilden, sich zu einer zusammengehörigen, sinnvollen Lebenswelt fügen, ist so weitverbreitet wie grundlos. Aber wo kommen wir hin, wenn all dies auseinanderfällt? Die phänomenologische Reduktion kennt nur Eindrücke, keine Zusammenhänge. Das Kaleidoskop des Sichtbaren, von keiner Regie gelenkt.

Der wichtigste Anhaltspunkt in dieser zerstückelten Wahrnehmungswelt ist das Unverständnis des Beobachters selbst; "der Erzählgestus", so drückte es Robert Cohen aus, "ist etwa der eines Marsbewohners, der zu den geschilderten Vorgängen überhaupt keine Beziehung hat, nicht den mindesten Versuch unternimmt, sie zu deuten und sich damit begnügt, sie so genau wie möglich zu beschreiben."[23] Das ist zwar, wie mir scheint, nicht ganz zutreffend, lenkt die Aufmerksamkeit aber dennoch auf den entscheidenden Punkt. Der Beobachtende kann, das läßt sich beispielsweise an der Passage mit den Kohlensäcken zeigen, die beabsichtigte Deutungsabstinenz eben doch nicht durchhalten. Er ist zu gleichen Teilen damit beschäftigt, die Unverständlichkeit des Gesehenen herauszuarbeiten und sie mit immer wieder neuen Mutmaßungen durchdringen zu wollen. So fragt er sich in der erwähnten Szene schließlich, "wie alle die mit Kohlen angefüllten Säcke in der allem Anschein nach nicht einmal vollbeladenen Kutsche Platz gefunden hatten" (*Schatten*, 95), und kann selbst nach drei Tagen und drei Nächten des intensivsten Nachdenkens über dieses faszinierende Problem keine Erklärung finden (*Schatten*, 96). Zum guten Schluß ist es die überraschend plötzliche Rückfahrt des Kutschers nach dem Sex mit der Haushälterin, die dem Beobachter ein Rätsel aufgibt: "Auch dieses, daß das Pferd, nach dem langen Weg den es den größten Teil des Tages mit der Last von Kohlen zurückgelegt hatte, noch in der auf diesen Tag folgenden Nacht den gleichen Weg noch einmal bewältigen sollte, gab mir zu denken" (*Schatten*, 100), resigniert der Sprecher auf der hundertsten Seite im letzten Satz. Hängt vielleicht doch alles mit allem zusammen, Kutscher und Haushälterin, Kohlen und Pferd, der Voyeur und sein Schreiben? Deuten will er schon, dieser "Marsbewohner", doch er weigert sich, zu verstehen.

In einer ethnographischen Beschreibungssituation ist der Inventur des Sichtbaren ein durchaus auf sinnvolle Zusammenhänge gerichtetes Ziel vorgegeben. Gerade weil es nicht möglich ist, sich in 'die anderen' hineinzuversetzen, ist es so aufschlußreich, ihre Handlungsweisen und Gewohnheiten zu studieren. Mit keinem seiner Werke ist Peter Weiss der Haltung des ethnographischen Schreibens näher gekommen als mit dem fragmentarischen *Bericht über Einrichtungen und Gebräuche in den Siedlungen der Grauhäute*, der Anfang 1963 entstand und 1968 in einer Suhrkamp-Anthologie aufgegebener Werke zum ersten Mal veröffentlicht wurde.[24] Der Titel zitiert demonstrativ das Genre der ethnographischen Untersuchung, die ja genau dies zum Gegenstand macht: Institutionen, Gebräuche und Siedlungsformen fremder Völker. Die zwanzigseitige Prosastudie spielt die Möglichkeiten des ethnographischen Diskurses gegen dessen latenten Rassismus aus. Nun geraten endlich nicht mehr die Rothäute ins Visier, an denen sich der exotistische Bedarf an Buntheit lange genug befriedigen konnte. Bei den Grauhäuten allerdings scheint unklar, ob sie nur andersfarbig sind oder gar völlig farblos. Diese "Blankheit" an farblicher Identität wirft ein Licht auf die Tatsache, daß der weiße Mann am wenigsten an sich selbst denkt, wenn er über Rassen spricht. Dem falschen eurozentrischen Universalismus gemäß ist nicht das Spektrum des Regenbogens, der alle Farben in sich bündelt, sondern der matte, nichtssagende Ton einer "schmutzigen Bleichheit" (*Grauhäute*, 126).

Ins Land der Grauhäute also. Mit Montesquieu, Hölderlin und natürlich Kafka hat dieses Schreibexperiment den Impuls gemeinsam, den befremdlichen Blick des Ethnographen nicht auf jene zu richten, die aus europäischer Perspektive weit weg und daher in ihrer Fremdheit kaum wirklich beunruhigend sind. Gegenstand der Exploration ist vielmehr ein Terrain, das dem Autor selbst nur allzu bekannt war. Eine reflexive Ethnographie der eigenen Kultur, die vielleicht sogar speziell auf die Sitten und Gebräuche deutscher Grauhäute gemünzt war. Garloff hat die Vermutung geäußert, der Entwurf dieses Textes sei als Verarbeitung jener Erfahrungen zu verstehen, die Peter Weiss und sein Halbbruder Anfang der sechziger Jahre mit einer Entschädigungsklage vor deutschen Gerichten machen mußten.[25] Zu ihrem Antrag, für das durch den NS-Terror ruinierte väterliche Unternehmen Wiedergutmachungszahlungen zu erhalten, fielen der deutschen Bürokratie immer neue Hinderungsgründe und Verzögerungen ein. Im Kontext der Notizen zu den *Grauhäuten* findet sich die Bemerkung: "Haus der Entschädigungen, Versicherungen—wie man versucht, die Überlebenden zu umgehen, zu betrügen mit Zaubersprüchen— Medizinmänner werden entsandt (Entschädigungsamt)" (*Notizbücher*, 106). Die Eintragung belegt, daß Peter Weiss das Gefühl hatte, von den Rechtsnachfolgern des Deutschen Reiches mit "schmutzigen Riten" abgespeist zu werden. Die modische Konjunktur der Schamanen und Voodoopriester in den kulturwissenschaftlichen Debatten der Gegenwart kann sich auf diese Äußerungen freilich nicht stützen.

Der *Grauhäute*-Text selbst verfolgt ebenfalls die Strategie, nicht die sogenannten Primitiven gegen ihre Entdecker und Ethnographen in Schutz zu nehmen, sondern die atavistischen Formen im Innern der Zivilisation sichtbar zu machen. Insofern hält er an der negativen Semantik des "Primitiven" fest, nicht aber an dessen Projektion auf ferngelegene Regionen. Die beim Stamme der Grauhäute angetroffenen Einrichtungen und Gebräuche erweisen sich als derart vertraut und weitverbreitet, daß sie auf ein bestimmtes Land keineswegs festzulegen sind. Vergessen wir also die Frage: wie deutsch ist es? bei der Begegnung mit diesen seltsamen Menschen.

"Bei der Ankunft bietet sich dem Reisenden zunächst ein einziges, ineinander verschlungenes Gewühl von Lebewesen dar, die in unaufhörlicher Folge von überall hervor- und nach allen Richtungen hinwegströmen" (*Grauhäute*, 119). Der Ethnograph hält sich an die

Phänomene der Oberfläche, an das Straßenleben, den Autoverkehr und das Menschengedränge der großen Kaufhäuser. "Vor ihm auf der Ebene, und an den Steinen der ringsum abzweigenden Schluchten, verschieben sich die Bewohner dieser Siedlung, dicht gedrängt, mit ihrem schlenkernden Gang, ihrer schweren Bekleidung, in Reihen nebeneinander und hintereinander, und auf dem mittleren Teil ihrer glatten gebahnten Wege fließen endlose Züge kleiner Gehäuse in entgegengesetzten Richtungen aneinander vorbei" (*Grauhäute*, 119).

Dieser Ausschnitt genügt bereits, um vom stilistischen Prinzip des Experiments eine Vorstellung zu bekommen. Der Reiz des Textes, der sich nach einer gewissen Gewöhnungszeit freilich auch zu erschöpfen droht, liegt in der Vermeidung vertrauter Namen und identifizierender Bezeichnungen. In erstaunlicher Konsequenz baut Weiss, wobei sicher auch die eigene Exilerfahrung eine Schlüsselrolle spielt, Fremdheit als sprachliches Phänomen und als sprachlich zu inszenierende Haltung auf. Da ist von den Schaufenstern und Konsumtempeln der Grauhäute die Rede und eben gerade nicht die Rede; als heilige Tempelgrotte gilt dem Fremden eine öffentliche Bedürfnisanstalt. Dem Kaufrausch und Konsumismus steht er desto verständnisloser gegenüber, je detaillierter er seine Erscheinungsformen zu beschreiben versucht. "In den unteren Höhlungen der Bauten befinden sich zumeist, hinter spiegelnden Abschirmungen, [...] Anhäufungen der Dinge, die sie zu ihrer Ernährung, Kleidung und Einrichtung benötigen, [...] und locken den Vorübergehenden an" (*Grauhäute*, 120). Der Reisende denkt, auch er müsse vielleicht nur »an den dargebotenen Gegenständen entlanggehen, sich hier und da zu ihnen hinabbeugen, sie befühlen, beklopfen, beriechen, hochheben, drehen, versuchsweise an sich drücken" (*Grauhäute*, 122), um der geheimen Faszination dieser Warenhäuser auf die Spur zu kommen. Um ehrlich zu sein: schon an diesem Unverständnis erkennen wir, daß es sich bei der Figur um eine Fiktion handeln muß.

Den größtmöglichen Grad an Fremdheit aber erreicht Weiss, indem er einen Beobachter imaginiert, der das Auto nicht kennt. Der Grauhäute-Report berichtet aus einer Welt, in der ein Gespräch über Autos das Schweigen über so viel Befremdliches einschließt. Denn berechtigte der Name des Automobils nicht zu den schönsten

Hoffnungen? Gab es den arbeitenden Massen nicht das Versprechen, nun endlich und immer "selbst beweglich" zu sein? Der Blick des Fremden hat sie am Schauplatz ihres Scheiterns erfaßt. "In ihren dahinrollenden Gehäusen, die teils durchsichtig, teils vielfarbig verschalt sind, die vorn runde Augen und breite Mäuler aufweisen, die grollen, brummen, heftig aufschnauben, verharren die Insassen in einer Haltung von Gleichmut oder Müdigkeit, zusammengesunken, einzeln, die Hand an einen Griff geklammert" (*Grauhäute*, 119).

Noch einmal: "Study ritual, not belief", hatte der Ethnograph Malinowski gefordert. Wie sie es machen, und nicht, woran sie zu glauben vorgeben. Das aufgekündigte Einverständnis mit der Ordnung der Dinge und den Zeichen der Menschen, darin liegt der Avantgardismus von Peter Weiss. Die Phänomene müssen opak bleiben, will man den möglicherweise in der Sache selbst liegenden Irrwitz ihres Zusammenhangs durchschauen. Die unheimlichen Vehikel der Grauhäute sieht nur der Blick des Unverständigen. Fremdheit, diese Lehre läßt sich rückblickend wohl schon aus der Deutschlandreise am Fallschirm ziehen, Fremdheit ist weder Zustand noch Schicksal, sondern ein Transportmittel, ein Vehikel ethnographischen Staunens.

Werke von Peter Weiss

"Die Bibliothek in Berlin." In: *Peter Weiss, In Gegensätzen denken. Ein Lesebuch.* Ausgewählt von Rainer Gerlach und Matthias Richter, (Frankfurt a.M. 1986), S. 14-18.
Die Besiegten, (Frankfurt a.M. 1985).
Der Fremde, (Frankfurt a.M. 1980).
Der Schatten des Körpers des Kutschers, (Frankfurt a.M. 1964).
Bericht über Einrichtungen und Gebräuche in den Siedlungen der Grauhäute. In: *Aus aufgegebenen Werken.* Hrsg. von Siegfried Unseld, (Frankfurt a.M. 1968), S. 83-105; wieder abgedruckt in: Peter Weiss, *In Gegensätzen denken*, S. 119-135

Anmerkungen

1   Stefan Howald, dem die Bedeutung des Fallschirmspringers als bildhaft-wörtliche Umsetzung einer freischwebenden Existenz nicht entgangen ist, interpretiert sie, ganz im Gegensatz zur hier vorgeschlagenen Lesart, als Ausdruck einer kulturkonservativen Haltung, die sich "nicht mit der Politik die Hände schmutzig machen will" (Stefan Howald, *Peter Weiss zur Einführung* Hamburg 1994, S. 30). Die im folgenden gezeigten Textbeispiele belegen dagegen die Intention des Berichterstatters, die 'schmutzigen', befremdlichen und traumatischen Züge dieser Erfahrung möglichst scharf und deutlich herauszupräparieren.

2   Im Rückblick erklärt Weiss: "Ich kam als Ausländer, als Fremder, der sich ansah, was aus diesem Land geworden war, mit einer völligen Fremdheit, voller Kühle und Distanz." (Peter Weiss, Der Kampf um meine Existenz als Maler. In: *Der Maler Peter Weiss.* Berlin, 2. Auflage, 1982, S. 11-43, hier S. 38.)

3   Weiss, "Bibliothek in Berlin," S. 14.

4   Weiss, "Bibliothek in Berlin," S. 14f.

5   Karl-Heinz Götze, *Poetik des Abgrunds und Kunst des Widerstands. Grundmuster der Bildwelt von Peter Weiss* (Opladen 1995).

6   Die ästhetische Leistung dieser Figur und insbesondere der militärische background wird nicht gesehen in Söllners Deutung, "daß der Fallschirmspringer nichts weiter ist als die symbolische Inkarnation des literarischen Prinzips, [...] der surrealistischen Vermischung von Traum und Realität." Vom Eigensinn der mit dem Fallschirmsprung gewählten

Annäherung an Deutschland bleibt in dieser Optik lediglich die Ansage eines Stilzitats. (Alfons Söllner, "Kritische Solidarität des Verfolgten mit den Verfolgern. Peter Weiss' 'Die Besiegten' als traumrealistisches Monument der deutschen Situation 1947." In: *Ästhetik, Revolte, Widerstand. Zum literarischen Werk von Peter Weiss.* Hrsg. von Jürgen Garbers u. a. [Lüneburg 1990], S. 9-33, hier S. 18.)

7 Weiss, "Bibliothek in Berlin," S. 14.

8 Vgl. den Artikel "Kinder in Berlin." In: *Die Besiegten,* S. 131.

9 So die These von Söllner, "Kritische Solidarität," S. 13.

10 Alfons Söllner, *Peter Weiss und die Deutschen. Die Entstehung einer politischen Ästhetik wider die Verdrängung* (Opladen 1988).

11 Zu diesem Konzept vgl. Alexander Honold, "Die ethnographische Situation." In: *kultuRRevolution* Nr. 32/33 (1995), S. 29-34.

12 "Wer die literarischen und auch die bildkünstlerischen Werke von Peter Weiss durchgeht, wird auf eine ganze Reihe von Versuchen stoßen, *Unzugehörigkeit* ästhetisch zu artikulieren, reflexiv zu deuten und im Interesse einer gesicherten Lebenspraxis zu überwinden." (Jochen Vogt, *Peter Weiss mit Selbstzeugnissen und Bilddokumenten* [Reinbek 1987], S. 9.) Trotz dieser Betonung des lebenspraktischen und politischen Heimatimpulses erweist sich gerade in dieser Biographie die Unzugehörigkeit als alles überspannendes Leitmotiv. Sie beginnt und endet mit einer Negation, einem Bekenntnis zur Ortlosigkeit: "Ich war nie Deutscher" (S. 7) ist das Eingangszitat von Peter Weiss, und "nirgendwo" ist sein Schlußwort. (S. 138).

13 So die Zusammenfassung bei Martin Rector, "Die Tugend der Not. Fremdheit als Wahrnehmungschance und Identitätsmuster in Peter Weiss' Erzählung 'Der Fremde'." In: *Begegnung mit dem "Fremden". Grenzen – Traditionen – Vergleiche. Akten des VIII. Internationalen Germanisten-Kongresses* (München 1991), Bd. 8, S. 218-224, hier S. 219.

14 Vgl. Robert Cohen, *Peter Weiss in seiner Zeit. Leben und Werk* (Stuttgart 1992), S. 7.

15 Rector, S. 219.

16 "Ich machte das wie viele junge Menschen: Man sucht sich jemand. Ich hatte ja keinen Menschen, keine Freunde und Bekannte" (Weiss, "Der Kampf um meine Existenz als Maler," S. 26).

17 Peter Suhrkamp, Brief an Peter Weiss vom 21.8.1948. In: *Briefe an die Autoren* (Frankfurt a.M. 1963), S. 58.

18 Zur Topographie des Museums als Gedächtnisraum vgl. Alexander Honold, "Das Gedächtnis der Bilder. Zur Ästhetik der Memoria bei Peter Weiss." In:

Die Bilderwelt des Peter Weiss. Hrsg. von Alexander Honold und Ulrich Schreiber (Hamburg 1995), S. 100-113.

19 Helmut Peitsch, "Wo ist die Freiheit? Peter Weiss und das Berlin des Kalten Krieges." In: *Ästhetik, Revolte, Widerstand*, S. 34-56, hier S. 41.

20 Friedrich Hölderlin, *Hyperion oder der Eremit in Griechenland*. In: *Sämtliche Werke und Briefe*. Hrsg. von Michael Knaupp (München 1992), Bd. I, S. 754.

21 Vgl. Karl Mannheim (1922), "Beiträge zur Theorie der Weltanschauungs-Interpretation." In: *Wissenssoziologie. Auswahl aus dem Werk*. Hrsg. von Kurt H. Wolff (Berlin 1964), S. 91-154; Erwin Panofsky (1939), "Ikonographie und Ikonologie." In: *Bildende Kunst als Zeichensystem 1*. Hrsg. von Ekkehard Kaemmerling (Köln 1979), S. 207- 225.

22 Howald, *Peter Weiss*, S. 48

23 Cohen, *Peter Weiss*, S. 76.

24 "Bericht über Einrichtungen und Gebräuche in den Siedlungen der Grauhäute." In: *Aus aufgegebenen Werken*. Hrsg. von Siegfried Unseld (Frankfurt a.M. 1968), S. 83-105; wieder abgedruckt in: *Peter Weiss, In Gegensätzen denken*, S. 119-135.

25 "Peter Weiss' Entry into the German Public Sphere. On Diaspora, Language, and the Uses of Distance." In: *Colloquia Germanica* 30.1 (1997), S. 47-70, S. 55.

Yvonne Spielmann

Theory and Practice of the Avant-garde:
Weiss's Approaches to Film

In the early fifties Peter Weiss became intrigued with film and the idea of film making. In particular he was interested in film's visual expressiveness as an experimental art. In 1952 he joined the Swedish Experimental Film Studio (Svensk Experiment Film Studio) and became the group's most active film maker, engaged in experimental film practices under the influence of Surrealism. Concurrently he wrote about the histories of avant-garde cinema and contemporary independent film making, completing in 1956 the book *Avantgardefilm*. Originally written in Swedish, an abridged German version appeared in a 1963 issue of the journal *Akzente*, but it took another thirty years before the complete, annotated German edition was released in 1995.[1]

Initially Weiss had been trained as a painter, a medium in which he worked for twenty years (with exhibitions in Sweden during the forties and fifties) before concentrating on film and literature. Around 1959/60 he basically abandoned painting and collage to become a writer. In 1952, when conceiving his first major experimental prose, the novel *Der Schatten des Körpers des Kutschers* (written in German but while living in Sweden, his permanent residency after fleeing Germany, and published only in 1959 in Germany with seven collages by the author), Weiss shifted from painting to film in order to expand dynamically the limitations of the static image in painting. "Die Malerei als ein statisches Medium entsprach mir nicht mehr", he later explained, "und ich selbst war so zerfetzt von dieser ganzen Situation, daß ein einziges geschlossenes Bild mir nicht mehr genügte."[2] Retrospectively Weiss described a twofold motivation for exploring another medium, on the one hand as a way to escape the isolating experience of exile and on the other as a result of his artistic need to develop new ideas of visual expression in postwar culture.

Shortly after the end of World War II Weiss came into contact in Paris with Surrealism and experimental film making. Viewing Luis

Buñuel's surrealist film *L'âge d'or* (1930) had a great impact on the artist's conception of collage and cut-up techniques, since he was uncertain about the forms he would choose to visually express ideas. Convinced that fundamentally painting possesses the same expressive means as literature, Weiss nevertheless preferred literature and film when faced with a situation that had become more and more complex. As the above quote suggests, the unity of the surface image in canvas painting was no longer adequate for the artist's approach to formulating incoherence aesthetically. Beyond painting Weiss tried out possibilities of imaging through the use of surrealist collage techniques and by working in film and literature. This allowed him to express better inner feelings of uncertainty, existential doubt, and alienation. On the occasion of the retrospective exhibition of Weiss's paintings in Bochum in 1980 he explained his departure from painting: "Dann, durch die Katastrophe des Faschismus, durch die Katastrophe des Krieges verlor die Welt überhaupt jeden Ansatz einer Heilheit, und dadurch entstand dann auch während der vierziger Jahre die Suche nach neuen Formen der Malerei—die geschlossene realistische, etwas traumhaft magische realistische Welt löste sich auf."[3] In questioning the notion of the image, it is interesting to note that Weiss assigns painting and to some extent also literature to the domain of realism, including its expanded forms, whereas the surrealist impulse automatically leads to film and dynamic features.

Between 1952 and 1956 Weiss directed six short films that interrelate formal elements of Surrealism with contemporary topics such as postwar alienation and personal experiences of isolation through emigration. The surrealist encounter not only heightened the abrasiveness of the personal view, but Surrealism also provided aesthetic strategies to express dislocation and distortion. The visual idea of the series *Studie I-IV* is mainly conceived through *tableaux vivants*, sometimes based on drawings by Weiss that figuratively represent physical and mental processes of motion. These are highlighted in *The Studio of Dr. Faust* (1956), where the modern scientist is seen as fragmented and distorted within a spatial construction of bars. The formal experiments are followed by a series of documentaries that engage social issues, including the investigation into a youth prison in

Enligt lag (In the Name of the Law, 1957), based on Weiss's personal experience of teaching painting in a Stockholm men's prison. Finally, the major feature film *Hägringen* (also known under the title *Le Mirage*, 1959) presents an allegory of modern life that expresses the protagonist's alienation and hopelessness through urban landscape and architectural sites.

With regard to the artist's practice on the whole, Weiss's films span the above-mentioned media specificity in the distinct categories of realism and surrealism, in particular where the body of his cinematic work encompasses the two major tendencies of experimental and documentary film. Furthermore, he extended both features into his literary writing as well, first in the formal language experiments in the early prose of the fifties and then in the documentary theater of the sixties. Evidently Weiss connects the two media, literature/drama and film, through the important role played by the visual in his art. Visual thinking also defines the interrelationship between literature and painting, effecting the structural convergence of visual and textual collage in *Der Schatten des Körpers des Kutschers*, and explains why Weiss continued to treat painterly issues in other media. For Weiss clearly reached the limits of painting because he could not develop further the medium's expressive means: "Die bildnerische Arbeit hörte auf mit Filmen und Collagen, und seit 1960 habe ich mich nur noch als Schriftsteller betätigt".[4] The film medium, when compared to Weiss's previous work as painter and to his later work in literature and drama, represents an intermediate phase of searching for a new visual language:

> In dieser Phase übernahmen meine Filme sehr viel von dem, was im Bild noch statisch war: Der Film war eine Weiterentwicklung des Bildes. [...] In den 50er Jahren war ich nicht mehr der reine Maler, ich selbst nannte mich zwar Maler, machte Ausstellungen, suchte nach immer neuen Mitteln, aber es waren prinzipielle Zweifel da, und nicht nur Zweifel an der Malerei als Medium, sondern Zweifel am Dasein überhaupt, Fragen meine gesamte Existenz betreffend. [...] Wahrscheinlich änderte ich deswegen auch die Formen so oft und suchte immer wieder nach neuen Möglichkeiten, es visuell auszudrücken, im Film, zum Schluß in der Collage, mit der man die zersplitterte Welt sehr eindringlich darstellen kann.[5]

Consequently Weiss developed new forms in film that would articulate the surrealist experience of distortion and express the concept of visual thinking by transforming the painterly collage into moving images.

Hägringen and especially the short films deliberately relate to Surrealism through the predominant patterns of dreamlike reality, incoherent imagery, and the visual style of collage. The lasting influence of surrealist films like *L'âge d'or* can be seen in the acknowledgment of dream structure as another form of reality, a constant feature in Weiss's film making and painting. Furthermore, his cinematic work may be regarded as a striking example of the surrealist heritage in postwar culture generally. Where Weiss cinematically unfolds multiple realities and emphasizes visual thinking together with the assertion of inner vision, he reinforces the essential concern in independent film making imposed by surrealist style, comparable, say, to the films of Gregory Markopoulos. The anticipation of film as expression of inner thought processes relates to the early visionary films of Stan Brakhage, in particular where Weiss's imaginary approach in *The Studio of Dr. Faust* combines expressive and symbolic style. But while film makers of the American avant-garde endeavored to break away from the traditional pictorial framework in order to strengthen film as an singular art form of moving images and as a new medium capable of visualizing unseen realities, Weiss remains close to painting's visual language in his experimental short films by primarily constructing dream tableaus. His film documentaries, however, can be seen as foregrounding and formally preshaping the later experimental work with documentary theater.

Weiss commitment to the avant-garde in the fifties is reflected in his deliberate adaptation of features in the visual arts that were developed in the early avant-garde movements, mainly Surrealism. His post-war reflections on these earlier aesthetic forms reveal the historical difference. Characteristics of avant-garde art practices in the first decades of twentieth century—the use of film or filmic devices, the introduction of fragmented and multiple realities through collage techniques, the aesthetics of shock, and the convergence and expansion of previous arts—defined it as the state-of-the-art. Apparently Weiss's concern, especially with film, was to connect his work to those achievements of the avant-garde and thereby to rescue and keep alive the avant-garde spirit and what he understood as specific filmic artistic practices. These concerns dominate the study *Avantgardefilm,* where Weiss provides an overview of the early film avant-garde that stresses the continuities with postwar film making. Weiss, the film maker, however, in practice focuses his relation to the historical avant-garde film on only two major features: Surrealism as the appropriate point of reference to transgress the coherent image and visually express distortion and alienation, and the shift in media from painting to film.

Like many of the early avant-garde film makers in the twenties, Weiss developed for the cinema painterly techniques of figuration, cut-up, and collage. In this respect he can be compared in particular to painters such as Vikking Eggeling, Hans Richter, and Walter Ruttmann, who had used the film medium intentionally to transgress the temporal-spatial limitations of painting. Unlike these pioneers of the cinematic avant-garde, however, Weiss's early studies in form and motion, e.g., the short films *Studie I-IV*, connect visually to the realm of static imagery, especially where he constructs figurations that depict the nude in the style of *tableaux vivants*. Thus, the individual figures seen partly in movement are defined through a fixed frame, filmed with an immobile camera set against a black background. The single tableau showing different arrangements of nude bodies, sometimes fragmented, are punctuated by fade-ins and fade-outs. These studies dramatize, then, the effects of light and shadow on the body and display the human figure as an object, comparable to a painting. The nude and fragmented body parts are shot in black and white with high contrast lighting and mostly against a dark background. Remarkably this exposure of the human body on display reminds us of surrealist painting, more precisely of painting in a post surrealist style where figuration is shown as deformation or where figures are contrasted rather than connected to a background that is not a habitable space.

The breakaway from surface coherence that results in a separation of figure and background is, of course, the essential concern of the painter Francis Bacon.[6] But while Bacon radicalizes deformation by disrupting the relationship between figures or between figure and setting or finally the isolated body itself, Weiss's approach differs conceptually because he reinforces the underlying concept of an image as tableau. Treating related representational problems, Weiss departs from the disruption of his contemporary Bacon and prefers to depict distortion as a static moment in the frozen tableau of the film image. Thus, whereas Bacon transgresses the limits of canvas through implicit movement and body enlargements that blur the frame, the film maker Weiss uses moving images to confirm the painterly frame in a series of tableaus. Weiss explained the concept of *Studie II* as follows: "Durchgehend wurde die Absicht verfolgt, Körperteile von verschiedenen Personen derart in einem Bild zu arrangieren, daß sie zusammen neue, mehr oder weniger deformierte Gestalten bildeten."[7] Certainly, the use of such devices not only produces spatial density but expresses isolation as well.

Weiss is more interested in film's expressive tension conveyed by the single tableau, another feature clearly related to painting. It seems that maintaining the painterly conceived image is the overriding aesthetic principle in his film making, possibly even stronger than his appropriation of the intriguing surrealist concept of the incoherent image. In the feature film *Hägringen* the black-and-white images primarily support the strong contrast between the human figure and the urban surroundings. As a result, the film's expressive power derives mainly from the visual style rather than narrative elements. Devices such as contrast lighting, key lighting, deep focus, and the preference for tableau images, including immobile framing, shape a film form that corresponds on the level of content to immobility and related motifs of distortion, isolation, and alienation. The tableau character of the images mediates inner feelings of uncertainty rather than change. As a result, stasis rather than mobilization is effected through the dynamics of the moving images. Here film is used to reflect a state of mind that— mediating between the interior and exterior world, between the static and the mobile—reveals the remoteness of the human figure.

Hägringen is especially striking because its refers so clearly to the history of the avant-garde cinema and its influence on Weiss's imagery. The film's form and style is reminiscent, for example, of films by Jean Cocteau and Jean Vigo. As Weiss mentions in *Avantgarde Film*, Jean Cocteau visually expressed for him the way the poet—which in Weiss's view stands for the artist in general—is bound to the past in film through constraints that he must destroy in order to overcome the limits of reality. In the case of Cocteau these constraints are visible in self-reflexive images, and they can be overcome by passing through a mirror and entering another state of reality. In Weiss's films we see another, much earlier phase of this process. Basically Weiss's films deal with the fragmented image as metaphor for these contraints, for example, when the main character in *Hägringen* or the human figure in *Studie I-IV* is alienated from the spatial environment, or when in *The Studio of Dr. Faust* optical distortions suggest multiple realities. Vigo is an equally obvious point of reference. Weiss states in *Avantgarde Film* that Vigo must be seen in relation to Buñuel and to Surrealism insofar as he acknowledges the unity between inner and outer reality, yet he is also to be considered the realist among the surrealists. Cocteau and Vigo, then, can be seen as historical references or as the point of departure for Weiss's films, but this does not necessarily imply that the historical avant-garde's impulse is recreated or even transformed into the state-of-the-art by Peter Weiss.

I suppose it would be difficult to characterize Weiss's films as creating a contemporary form of the avant-garde in the cinema. Rather, he stands in the tradition of the cinematic avant-garde, in other words he develops certain features that seem appropriate for expressing his personal experience of inner and outer exile, that is, alienation. To reiterate, this includes the necessity to abandon the coherent image but to retain a painterly concept of imagery. Thus, unlike the avant-garde of the twenties, which had sought to achieve convergence between previous art forms and thereby expanded the arts and developed new media forms, in the fifties work like that of Peter Weiss pursued possible connections with earlier developments and new aesthetic positions after World War II through experimental film work. But in contrast to the generally successful reappropriation of traditional forms in the postwar arts, especially in painting, it is notable that Weiss engages in a non traditional medium, in avant-garde or experimental film.

Consequently Weiss clearly holds an avant-garde position in the context of restoring cultural norms and forms in the fifties that resulted in the reestablishment of the anti-modern. This is a position defined by the experience of alienation in exile and affects both the content and form of his cinematic work. Not only does Weiss insist on maintaining an avant-garde position that in general has never been acknowledged, but he also defines his own position without the support of a movement because in postwar culture there simply was no avant-garde movement. We may conclude, then, that because of, or despite, the two facets of isolation, Weiss concentrates in his films predominantly on the past in order to deal with representations of loss and he reinforces the visual style of surrealist film in order to create images of the incoherence of the interior and exterior world. If we want to consider Peter Weiss as avant-garde, I suggest it would be more appropriate to discuss the politics of the artist's position rather than the particular merits of his film making.

This said, we should not be at all surprised to see how Weiss conceived his own peculiar style, for when he made the shift from static to dynamic media in order to develop new forms, he made extensive use of cut-up techniques that stem mainly from earlier forms of collage. As mentioned above, the urgency to articulate aesthetically the experience of an incoherent and uncertain external world generally parallels the need to express inner conflict. In fact, Weiss's cinematic work resists a coherent form and style. When viewed together, the films must be situated somewhere between the continuation of avant-garde abstraction and contemporary issues of social criticism. For the most part they depict symbolic dream visions or record and investigate the atmosphere of isolation and remoteness. When these two aspects intersect in black-and-white photography of a feature film like *Hägringen*, the resulting visual effect contrasts the individual human figure with the threatening inhumanity of closure and anonymity.

Weiss's film work holds an intermediate position in his artistic biography which coincides with the last phase of painting (ending in the late fifties) and the beginning of literary writing (starting with *Der Schatten des Körpers des Kutschers*, followed by *Abschied von den Eltern*, released in 1961 in Germany, two years after the publication of the first novel). In the context of shifting media the book *Avantgardefilm* represents another aspect of his work with film in the fifties, one regarded among cognoscenti as one of the few studies in the field. In their encyclopedia of avant-garde, experimental, and underground film

Hans Scheugl and Ernst Schmidt jr. claim that for a long time it was the only attempt to describe the history, the film makers, and the films of the avant-garde.[8] Beginning with the twenties and including the most important precursors, Weiss discusses at length the prominent representatives of avant-garde cinema such as Buñuel, Cocteau, Vigo, and Eisenstein. While Vertov is only briefly mentioned, he does extend the tradition to encompass Carl Theodor Dreyer and experimental film making in the United States during the thirties and forties, thereby introducing alternate developments represented by Maya Deren, Kenneth Anger, and James Broughton. The book concludes with current film practices of the fifties, focusing in particular on France and the "letrist cinema" (Isidore Isoù) and on Sweden (Gösta Werner, Ingmar Bergman, and Weiss himself). The list demonstrates clearly that the study is not a comprehensive survey and certainly does not claim to be read as theory of the avant-garde.

As I already indicated with regard to his film making, Weiss's approach towards cinema initially is meant to position and verify the current state-of-the-art in film. He is particularly interested in experimental film and writes a history of film outside the commercial industry, thereby stressing the political concept of avant-garde. In the book's opening remarks Weiss states that the decline of the original avant-garde movement is widely accepted, but in the following comments he appropriates and expands the term avant-garde as counter concept to that for which it is generally claimed. Essentially Weiss regards film as a universal medium, capable of a new visual language, so that film becomes the medium which allows the avant-garde to express differently a new poetic language via images. Thus, Weiss constructs the history of avant-garde film by privileging those films that strikingly interrelate reality, dream, and fantasy and that formally work on the level of association. Certainly the author is not especially interested in abstract film, for he does not even mention the Futurist contribution to the development of avant-garde film art. Furthermore, Weiss does not determine criteria for what he defines as avant-garde and therefore cannot justify the works he includes or dismisses. More importantly, though, Weiss convincingly argues that the history of film should be regarded from the point of view of the arts, strictly speaking from the position of the artist who shifts from painting to film.

This summary of the book indicates the privileged role of Surrealism in contrast to the devaluation and disregard of the German abstract film, the *cinéma pur*, and self-reflexive film practices, including Vertov, who in Weiss's view was simply obsessed with camera technique. Those approaches are all negatively characterized as "aestheticism," a familiar term for the differentiation of the arts in the nineteenth century and a phenomenon to which the avant-garde responded strongly. Keeping in mind the history and definition of the avant-garde as a politically and aesthetically engaged cultural counter force in the twentieth century, we may better understand what Weiss intended with the following statement about the avant-garde: "Buñuels *Un chien andalou* wandte sich schonungslos gegen den ästhetisierenden Zug des Avantgardefilms, gegen dessen Spiele mit Licht und Schatten, dessen Überbetonung von fotografischen Effekten und technischen Finessen."[9] At stake for Weiss is the conviction that film allows a visual concept of poetics conceived through Surrealism, and his comments throughout the book highlight two major issues: the poetics of cinema as the visual language of film and the interrelationship or shifting relationship between dream and reality, paradigmatically expressed in surrealist film form.

The fact that Weiss was practically engaged in independent film making and a member of the Experiment Film Studio in Stockholm also explains why he draws on specific historical achievements where he can argue the development of cinema poetics. By promoting experimental film making and emphasizing film as art, the study *Avantgarde Film* could contribute to the newly developing debate on the avant-garde in the late fifties that itself was part of a larger postwar discourse on modernism and its continuities and discontinuities. I cautiously say "could" here for two reasons: first, because excerpts from Weiss' s book were published in Germany only in 1963, but second and more important, the postwar debate on modernism and the avant-garde was not really concerned with film and certainly not with the type of film called avant-garde or experimental. Leading critics in the fields of literature, art history, and cultural philosophy have ignored the domain of film in their research on the avant-garde and therefore largely neglect the fact that there is indeed a history of avant-garde film. Most postwar avant-garde theories have been exclusively concerned with literature, the fine arts, in particular painting, and possibly theater, while film as a medium of the avant-garde was slighted. This, however, is only part of the problem because conversely the disregard of film in the general debate on the avant-garde must be compared with film theory that refuses to acknowledge this broader debate at all while blissfully maintaining its own separate discussion on avant-garde cinema. In order to better understand the critique of Peter Weiss's book about the avant-garde film, it is useful to look more closely at two competing debates on the avant-garde.

The avant-garde discussion in literature, the fine arts, and theater is preoccupied with defining the phenomenon within or against concepts of modernism. This dominant approach in avant-garde theory leads to an examination of European avant-garde movements and the resulting developments in the arts. Theories of the avant-garde that reflect this approach do not generally confer upon film an important role. And when film is regarded in the context of literature and the fine arts, the evaluation is not media-specific, so that while its contribution may be considered central to the avant-garde, there is no further detail about what kind of film is meant. Strictly speaking, the issue is not really how film contributes to the avant-garde, but on the contrary the point is to defend the avant-garde quality of literature, the fine arts, and theater that appropriate film and film techniques such as montage. The argument proceeds by claiming that film—because of its advanced techniques of production and distribution—on the whole is to be regarded as avant-garde and then concludes that, since cinematic features are to be identified in literature, fine arts, and theater, these examples prove the avant-garde character of contemporary arts, not of film art.

The debates about the status of the avant-garde in the cinema are removed from this dominant discourse. They reveal the difficulties of distinguishing separate definitions for "avant-garde" and "experiment." In the field of film theory that does discuss issues of experimental film we find two coexisting approaches. The first categorizes the entire domain of experimental and independent cinema as avant-garde by contrasting it to Hollywood and classical narrative cinema. Since these latter are themselves subject to shifting definitions, the actual frame of reference for the avant-garde may be variously contextualized. The second approach is more rigid, equating the term avant-garde with the concept of experiment, so that only the domain of experimental film is considered to be avant-garde. While these two strategies coexist, they are also contradictory, and viewed together, they reflect a conceptual problem in discourse that hinders a reasoned distinction between avant-garde and experimental film. But the problem of naming is more serious and intensifies when film is contextualized with other media.

To distinguish between experimental and avant-garde film within the broader context of debate one must begin with the peculiarity that as soon as experimental film claims to be an integral part of the medium film, another claim immediately asserts that the medium film itself should be regarded as experimental. The logical compromise for this impasse would define the experimental character of experimental film by excluding all features which are not media-specific to film but rather derive from literature or theater. This argument becomes more complicated when we consider parallel developments in literature, the theater, and the fine arts that deliberately employ filmic and cinematic devices such as the interval and montage. The experimental quality of film or filmic techniques in any medium conflicts with the characterization of the experimental qualities in experimental film because it demands, as film theory states, the exclusion of all non filmic elements in favor of the further development of film as film. This approach is symptomatic of early avant-garde practices, when mainly visual artists experimented with film and developed abstract film and pure cinema as the origins of the avant-garde film. Historically it is difficult to differentiate between experimental and avant-garde film. The early phase of film as visual art, however, also provides insight into the experimental film as a development within the medium and not as its sole representative. To conclude, then, in principle the discussion of film avant-garde differs from the avant-garde debate on literature and fine arts that describes the film medium as avant-garde. Therefore the relationship between avant-garde and film cannot be completey described in terms of experimental film and not solely with regard to film debates. At the same time the general discourse on the avant-garde does not sufficiently contribute to understanding media in terms of avant-garde film.

Finally, to discuss the relationship between Peter Weiss's book *Avantgarde Film* and his own films introduces additional problems. There exists no discourse of the avant-garde that is able to cope adequately with such varied phenomena; rather we are confronted with a diversity of strongly competitive approaches. It is truly remarkable that hardly any counter balance has been proposed to the far-reaching exclusion and misrecognition of film in terms of the avant-garde. Moreover, many film histories dedicate only a few pages to the development of avant-garde and experimental film, seen mainly as precursors to the "actual" development of the new medium that the books then proceed to describe. On the whole the domain of avant-garde film is subsidiary to national cinemas and so-called conventional narrative cinema, and strikingly the term "avant-garde" itself is rarely defined. Indeed, even when we consult the major theories of avant-garde film, such as those authored by Peter Adams Sitney, Peter Wollen, or Paul Willemen, we are not presented with a coherent definition of what the avant-garde is and is not.

In his influential study on the American avant-garde film Sitney introduced the term "structural film" to describe recent developments in which the expeirment's characteristics consist of the self-reflexive presentation of the film's structure as the film's form.[10] In general, structural film refers to the concept of "film as film," and with this primary category Sitney can stress certain positions in experimental film and at the same time neglect other major positions in avant-garde film history. For example, Sitney has been widely criticized for not dealing with avant-garde women film makers such as Germaine Dulac and Maya Deren. In contrast, Peter Weiss prominently refers to the latter, since he considers Deren's work to play an important role in the further development of Surrealism, especially when she presents a dream-like scenario and unfolds multiple realities simultaneously in *Meshes of the Afternoon* (1943).

Peter Wollen and Paul Willemen expand the definition of experimental film and merge formal, more precisely, structural elements with narrative. For them the contemporary avant-garde unfolds a "complex way of seeing" and deconstructs preconceived forms in conventional narrative. Willemen states that most films implicate a double strategy, "narrative and setting."[11] Just as Willemen expands the field and under the sign of avant-garde also includes film makers such as Jean-Marie Straub / Danièle Huillet and Jean-Luc Godard, Peter Wollen in his well-known article "The Two Avant-Gardes" calls for a redefinition of the avant-garde encompassing two genealogies.[12] First, there is independent film making that politically and aesthetically opposes dominant and commercial film production and can be identified historically with Sergej M. Eisenstein in the early phase and today with Jean-Luc Godard. Second, avant-garde characterizes the artistic development in film, the historical experiments of painters such as Richter, Ruttmann, and Eggeling that have been conceptually recuperated and extended by later advances of experimental film. As such, the emergence of experimental film as a genre is viewed through the development of early abstract and structural film.

The debates on the cinematic avant-garde took place in the seventies, whereas in the fifties, when Peter Weiss turned to film theory and practice, there were hardly any points of reference. Conversely, the ongoing debates on the continuities and discontinuities of modernism after 1945 as carried on in Germany, France, the USA, and Eastern Europe from the early sixties to the mid eighties had no reason to refer to the work of Peter Weiss on the avant-garde published in 1963 since, as already stated, the discourse mainly concentrated on other media.[13] Moreover, avant-garde film theories only occasionally review Weiss's writings or discuss his films. In *Underground Film* Parker Tyler discusses *Härgingen* (Le Mirage) as a post surrealist approach that uses the medium film to express the instability of dream realities. Based on the surreal imagery, Parker compares Weiss to Gregory Markopoulos, another representative of "consciously subjective" poetic cinema.[14] Finally, Scheugl and Schmidt make clear in their 1974 encyclopedia of avant-garde film that Weiss's films stand in the tradition of the avant-garde without offering new impulses. As pointed out above, the authors acknowledge his writing as a major contribution to the historiography of avant-garde film, however, their examination highlights the singularity of Weiss's approaches towards the avant-garde, in theory and practice. The review reads:

> Der Autor des Buches *Avantgarde Film,* lange Zeit das einzige Werk auf
> diesem Gebiet, gilt gemeinhin als der wichtigste Vertreter der Filmavantgarde
> in Schweden. Seine Filme, vor seinem literarischen Hauptwerk entstanden,
> können indes nur bedingt zur Avantgarde gezählt werden. [...] In ihnen gehen
> Elemente des Surrealismus und eines kalligrafischen Dokumen-tarismus eine
> oft brüchige und eher vage Verbindung ein mit Psychoanalyse und dem
> Pessimismus des schwedischen Nachkriegsfilms, wie er in Filmen von Anders
> Henrikson, Hasse Ekman, Ingmar Bergman und Arne Mattsson zum Ausdruck
> kommt.[15]

Viewed retrospectively, what is then the value of Weiss's work on
the avant-garde in film? To sum up: Weiss's overview of the
avant-garde in film reveals more about his own investigation into the
medium film, in particular regarding his predilection for Surrealism,
while the criteria for evaluating and distinguishing between different
film forms remain secondary. In the first place the book manifests an
intriguing encounter with a medium that, as Weiss discovers and
develops, promises a new visual language that is more expressive than
painting. It is interesting to note that descriptions of individual films in
the book emphasize expressive means that dissolve familiar forms. This
exactly defines the avant-garde's impulse that has historically developed
as an aesthetic and political counter force to existing power and reality
and that Weiss identifies in Luis Buñuel's films. Nevertheless, when
Weiss discusses individual films and describes at length the narrative of
Un chien andalou as if it were a conventional film, it is surprising that
he almost entirely ignores what Buñuel always stressed, that the film is
not meant symbolically but dissolves reality. Curiously enough, Weiss
effortly explains a symbolic level in Buñuel; but maybe this attempt no
longer seems quite so curious when we recall that in the fifties
engagement for an avant-garde that dissolved realities, just like support
for artistic practices that deliberately opposed cultural conventions,
taste, and reason, was by no means self-evident. Thus, the shifting view
of Surrealism may result from the isolated position of the author who is
not embedded in a larger debate.

Furthermore the obvious difficulties in applying Weiss's emphasis on surrealist film to his own films that incorporate such elements but yet do not push surrealist aesthetics further should be seen as part and parcel of the general constraints on experimental film making and of the particular exile experience that created for Weiss a "surrealist feeling." Using surrealist devices, notably *The Studio of Dr. Faust* (1956) expresses alienation and isolation literally by figuring the constraints as spatial limits. Additionally the main character is optically deformed through distorting lenses. This visual expression of the state of mind is physically reinforced through strings in the studio that produce the effect of straining ropes. This example may demonstrate that Weiss's major topic at this same time in film, painting, and literature addressed exile and alienation, not the reawakening of the avant-garde. At the end of *Avantgarde Film* Weiss explains his personal endeavor to express visually instability and to visualize interior and exterior conflict through film. About his own film he writes:

> *Studie II* (1952) von Peter Weiss folgt in seiner Gestaltung unmittelbar einer Serie von zwölf assoziativen Zeichnungen. [...] Das Geschehen liegt vollständig auf einer emotionalen Ebene. Wie Halluzinationen tauchen eine Reihe stark erotisch gefärbter Gefühle in verschiedenen Stadien auf. [...] Das vierte Bild ist Ausdruck eines Unlustgefühls, es schlägt im nächsten Bild um in eine groteske und lächerlicheSzenerie, wie ein Hampelmann hängt man im Dasein, und die wechselnden Gefühle zupfen an den Fäden.[16]

Notes

1   Peter Weiss, *Avantgardefilm* (Stockholm 1956). The German title is *Avantgarde Film*, trans. Beat Mazenauer (Frankfurt a.M. 1995). The French translation was published already in 1989: *Cinéma d'avant-garde*, trans. Catherine de Seynes (Paris 1989).

2   "Der Kampf um meine Existenz als Maler: Peter Weiss im Gespräch mit Peter Roos." In: *Der Maler Peter Weiss: Bilder, Zeichnungen, Collagen, Film.* Peter Spielmann, ed. (Berlin 1982), p. 39.

3   Wolf Schön, "Die Malerei ist statisch: Als aus Bildern Bücher wurden. Ein Gespräch mit Peter Weiss." In: *Peter Weiss im Gespräch.* Rainer Gerlach und Matthias Richter, eds. (Frankfurt a.M. 1986), p. 261.

4   Schön, "Die Malerei ist statisch," p. 259.

5   "Der Kampf um meine Existenz als Maler," p. 40f.

6   For a discussion of Bacon's position on Surrealism, see Dawn Ades, "Web of Images." In: *Francis Bacon,* Dawn Ades and Andrew Forge, eds. (New York 1985), p. 8-23.

7   Weiss, *Avantgarde Film*, p. 141.

8   Hans Scheugl and Ernst Schmidt, Jr., *Eine Subgeschichte des Films. Lexikon des Avantgarde-, Experimental- und Undergroundfilms* (Frankfurt a.M. 1974), vol. II, p. 1082-85.

9   Weiss, *Avantgarde Film*, p. 7.

10 Peter Adams Sitney, *Visionary Film: The American Avant-Garde 1954-1978* (New York 1979).

11 Paul Willemen, "An Avant Garde for the Eighties." In: *Framework* 24 (Spring 1984), p. 69.

12 Peter Wollen, "The Two Avant-Gardes." In: *Studio International* 190.978 (1975), p. 171-75. Reprinted in Peter Wollen, *Readings and Writings: Semiotic Counter-Strategies* (London 1982).

13 For background on these avantgarde debates, see also Yvonne Spielmann, *Eine Pfütze in bezug aufs Mehr. Avantgarde* (Frankfurt a.M. 1991), p. 9ff.

14 Parker Tyler, *Underground Film: A Critical History* (New York 1995), p. 186-87 and 218.

15 Scheugl and Schmidt, *Eine Subgeschichte des Films*, p. 1083.

16 Weiss, *Avantgarde Film*, p. 141.

Klaus L. Berghahn

"Our Auschwitz":
Peter Weiss's *The Investigation* Thirty Years Later

> A living man has come and what happened
> here hides itself from him.[1]

Preface

My reflections on Peter Weiss are tinged with the subjective memories of how I received the message of the Holocaust. As was typical for my generation, I heard nothing about it in high school. The Holocaust was the best kept secret of postwar Germany until the German translation of *The Diary of Anne Frank* was published in 1955. I saw the theater production in 1956 and read the book afterwards, but the full extent of the Holocaust was still shrouded in mystery. This changed at the beginning of the sixties, when I read Hannah Arendt's report *Eichmann in Jerusalem* (1961), when I saw Rolf Hochhuth's play *The Deputy* (1963), and when I followed the heated debate about Pope Pius XII's indifference toward the suffering of the Jews. Finally, Peter Weiss's documentary drama *The Investigation* opened my eyes to the full extent of the Holocaust. In 1978 I saw the television production *Holocaust,* first in the United States and then a year later in Germany, and I was surprised at its impact on the German audience, as if it were the first revelation of the Nazis' extermination campaign against the Jews. Much later Steven Spielberg's film *Schindler's List* renewed interest in the Holocaust for yet another generation, but at the same time it clouded the issue of German guilt by presenting a good German as savior of the Jews.

I want to demonstrate with this abbreviated chronology of Holocaust reception in Germany the simple fact that there were at least four distinctive phases of public discussion. All are connected with artistic representations, which suggests how important literature and film have been in coming to terms with the Nazi past.[2] For me, they are an essential part of my own life experience as a German, perhaps even part of my own identity formation. Thus, my perspective on Weiss's *Investigation* is embedded in historical as well as personal experience, and thus, my observations echo Martin Walser's "Our Auschwitz."[3]

My critical reading of Weiss's *Investigation* has a threefold purpose. First, I wish to counter the claims of many Germans that they knew nothing about the Holocaust until they saw its "most recent" representation, be it the television series *Holocaust* in 1979 or the film *Schindler's List* in 1992. From my perspective Weiss's *Investigation* was a belated turning point in Germany's coming to terms with its Nazi past. Second, I will demonstrate—against all aesthetic, moral, and political criticism of Weiss's documentary drama—that *The Investigation* is one of the best representations of the Holocaust for the stage. Third, I will explore the limits of representing the Holocaust in Weiss's documentary drama and the clash of ideologies of the author and his critics that led to its negative reception in Germany and the United States.

I

Peter Weiss's *Investigation* marks a turning point in the literary as well as political sphere of the Federal Republic of Germany. The year 1965, when it was performed concurrently on fifteen stages in Germany (not to forget the television production, which reached an even wider audience),[4] was also the year that witnessed the conclusion of the Frankfurt Auschwitz trial and that ended the debate on the Statute of Limitations for Nazi crimes in West Germany. There is a reciprocal relationship between these events. Weiss's documentary drama confronted an expanded audience with crimes against humanity committed by the Nazis in Germany's name; at the same time the debate surrounding the play amplified the political discussion about Germany's responsibility for these atrocities. Literature no longer seemed to be merely the "conscience of the nation," as critics in the fifties and early sixties widely considered it to be, but rather it had become an "instrument of political opinion formation and of influencing the public sphere," just as Weiss hoped.[5] The German euphemism *Vergangenheits-bewältigung* (coming to terms with the past) became an educational project for a nation which up to this point had collectively repressed its guilt for what had happened between 1933 and 1945.

Historical markers, such as the one I have just erected, are always too simplistic for explaining the complexities of history. There are, of course, always incubation periods which precede turning points. In our case it is no different. I would venture to say that the transition time lasted from 1961 to 1965. 1961 was not only the year when the Soviets dropped the Iron Curtain by building the Berlin Wall, heating up the Cold War, and leading to stronger anti-communist sentiments in the West; it was also the beginning of the end of the Adenauer Era. With the elections of 1961 the intellectual climate of the Federal Republic was slowly beginning to change. For the first time intellectuals discussed the possibility of a political alternative to Adenauer's government. Martin Walser asked twenty colleagues: *Do We Need A New Government?*[6] Their meager answers aimed at *Gewissensbildung* (conscience raising), but they had as yet nothing to offer that could contribute to political opinion formation. Yes, they were all troubled by Adenauer's authoritarian government; and they had every right to worry, as the *Spiegel* -affair demonstrated one year later. Moreover, disturbing signs of continuity between the Third Reich and the Federal Republic came into public view. Adenauer's personal secretary of the chancellory, Heinrich Globke, had been a commentator of the 1935 racial Nuremberg Laws, a fact that everyone knew, but no one bothered to notice. In 1962 the highest judge of the Federal Republic was exposed as member of the Nazi judicial system, and the President of the Republic had to dismiss him. That same year 143 high judges and prosecutors were forced into early retirement for similar reasons, a special law allowing them to retire with full pensions.[7] Slowly the repressed past was returning with a vengeance, nowhere more obviously than in the Eichmann trial in Jerusalem (1961) and in the Frankfurt trial against Mulka et. al. (1963-65), for they demonstrated that not a small clique of criminals around Hitler had seduced the German people, but that ordinary Germans willingly participated in the slaughter of millions of Jews and other "enemies" of the Third Reich. The "banality of evil," as Hannah Arendt called it, became visible as never before.[8]

Between 1961 and 1965, the theater more than any other political or educational institution confronted the German public with its repressed past. For a short time the theater became once again a moral institution that amplified what the trials in Jerusalem and Frankfurt had exposed through the judicial process. Plays like Rolf Hochhuth's *The Deputy* and Peter Weiss's *The Investigation*, both so-called documentary dramas, provoked public debates which the trials themselves had never been able to stimulate. In both cases, literature reflected and amplified reality so that it influenced public opinion.

To be sure, there were earlier theatrical attempts of coming to terms with the Nazi past, but they either appeased and pleased the audience or they merely provoked tearful pity that dissipated outside the theater. Cases in point are Carl Zuckmayer's *The Devil's General* (1946) and Frances Goodrich's and Albert Hackett's Broadway production based on *The Diary of Anne Frank* (1956). Zuckmayer returned triumphantly from his American exile with a play that portrays a German air force general, Harras, as a tragic hero opposing Hitler, the devil incarnate. By demonizing Hitler and the Third Reich and by presenting a noble general who opposed their policies, the audience could easily identify with the hero and forget about their own involvement in the Nazi past. This was an easy way out for a German audience of the late forties and guaranteed the play's success.

The staging of Anne Frank's diary was a different matter altogether. Here the audience experienced such strong emotional identification with the confinement and observations of young Anne that—according to Adorno—one German lady lamented: "But really, this girl should have been spared."[9] Catharsis resulted from an individual's feeling of pity for the killing of this one nice Jewish girl without understanding the enormity of the genocide. The collectively repressed guilt of the German people for atrocities against the Jews became comprehensible only on an individual level in a gesture of empathy. The silent rejection of German complicity in the murder of the Jews was reflected in the stunned silence at the end of the play. Something dawned on the German audience about the Holocaust, but it found an outlet only in individual pity without breaking through the denial of their responsibility. To recognize the totality of the Holocaust and to demonstrate the German involvement in these crimes against humanity, more was needed than empathy for just one Jewish victim.

A new form of representation was required, one which connected the repressed past with the present. As Martin Walser demanded from his fellow playwrights: "Today a German author has to present exclusively characters who either conceal or express the years from 1933 to 1945. [...] Every sentence by a German author which says nothing about this historical reality conceals something."[10] In his own theatrical attempts he undeniably demonstrated this continuity, but he failed for different a reason: by using rather traditional dramaturgy. *Der schwarze Schwan* (1964) employs the form of a family tragedy, while *Eiche und Angora* (1965) is a dramatic parable. They are well constructed plays, critiquing the denial of the recent past and they are even emotionally provocative, and yet they are unable to recall the horror of the Third Reich adequately. Not even the parable form, propagated and used so successfully by Brecht in *Der aufhaltsame Aufstieg des Arturo Ui*, was capable of such expression, since it distanced the events and made them historically ambivalent.

The best example of a famous play that nevertheless faltered in capturing the essence of the Holocaust was Max Frisch's *Andorra* (1961). By employing two modes of representation, the play invites the audience to identify with Andri, the Jew, while maintaining the recent past at a safe distance—which holds true both for Swiss and German audiences. The Swiss could say that they were threatened by outside forces, the Blacks, clearly recognizable as Fascists, but that they were not responsible for Auschwitz; the Germans on the other hand could identify with the Jewish victim without reflecting on their own responsibility for Auschwitz, since the parable form abstracts from place and history. It displaces the recent past to a fictitious place called Andorra. The strange mixture of identification and distancing is repeated on a more existential level in the character of Andri. As long as the audience can identify in the first part of the play with Andri as the Jewish outsider of Andorra, it feels empathy with the victim of anti-Semitism; in the second half, however, when the townspeople learn that Andri is not a Jew but one of them, the play's emphasis shifts to more universal concerns. Since Andri insists on his "Jewish" identity and is killed in the end as a Jew, his "Jewishness" becomes a matter of existential choice, and the issue of racial anti-Semitism is far removed from the historical events of the Holocaust. The parable form and its technique of estrangement gradually transforms the play into a model for a general rationalization of identity formation as social construct and of anti-Semitism as just another form of prejudice. The far more complex questions—why did the Holocaust happen in Germany? how was it organized and executed?—get lost in the ahistorical parable form. And yet, the final scene marshals all the elements of repressed guilt: The citizens of Andorra pretend that they have seen and heard nothing; they refuse any knowledge about Andri's fate; and Barblin goes mad in mourning for her murdered brother. Perhaps her insanity is Frisch's final word on the incomprehensibility of the Holocaust.

Rolf Hochhuth's *The Deputy* is the most unusual example, since it mixes traditional dramaturgy with documentary commentary and succeeded in provoking a public debate without precedence in the Federal Republic. The rather conventional historical drama à la Schiller would not have provoked such an uproar, had not the subject matter and documentation implicated Pope Pius XII: Why did the Pope keep silent about the genocide of the Jews, which he had known about?[11] The dramatic conflict centers around this question and how the central character, Pater Riccardo, deals with it. This Catholic priest is torn between his helplessness vis-à-vis the SS officers, who organize the deportation of Roman Jews and the acquiescence of Pope Pius XII to Nazi policy. Since he cannot influence the papal authorities to intervene or to protest against this barbarism, he takes it upon himself to act as the deputy of Christ. He accompanies the Roman Jews to Auschwitz, where he is murdered with them. The audience is asked to identify with the hero's inner turmoil and to confront their own responsibility for the deportation of Jews during the Third Reich. However, the Jews are only marginal figures in this historical drama in which all the fear and pity of the classical tragedy are heaped onto the hero Riccardo. Jews appear in only two scenes which ask the audience to identify with their suffering. Act III shows the capture of a prominent Jewish family in Rome, and in the last act they are "mere" victims. This is the most problematic scene, for it aims to represent Auschwitz on stage. Although powerful scenes, they demonstrate the limits of representation of the Holocaust. Hochhuth simplifies the complex history of the Final Solution by presenting it as a classical tragedy in which the struggle of an idealistic priest against the evil of the Third Reich becomes an issue of one individual's moral responsibility and in which Auschwitz, the symbol of the industrialized extermination of Jews, becomes the cathartic locus of the tragedy.[12] In spite of these flaws, Hochhuth's *Deputy* provoked more public debate than either *The Diary of Anne Frank* or *Andorra*. Nevertheless, it failed both to explain the roots of anti-Semitism, which in a Roman Catholic setting could have been age-old anti-Judaism, and to represent Auschwitz on stage.

II

This short historical overview may suffice as a backdrop to one of the most convincing representations of the Holocaust, Peter Weiss's *The Investigation*. Weiss realized from his visit to Auschwitz in 1964 that no visitor could comprehend or imagine what had happened there twenty years earlier. For him, Auschwitz was a place of pilgrimage; it had no connection to the present. The traces of railroad tracks, barracks, rubble, and barbed wire stared at him in silence, and as a museum Auschwitz was merely another horrible place, about which it was too late to do anything. The only connection he could find was the knowledge that "it is a place for which I was destined but which I managed to avoid," and he continued: "I have had no experience of this place, I have no relation to it, except that my name was on the lists of people, who were supposed to be sent there for ever."[13] He had to pay a price, however, for his estrangement from the place and his luck of escaping it: He felt guilty, like most survivors who mourn the loss of loved ones murdered there. Perhaps it was precisely this tension between his experience of estrangement and his personal identification with its victims that catalyzed an artistic response. While watching the Frankfurt Auschwitz trial, he contemplated another artistic possibility, one he considered "dry and emotionless," documentary theater.

As far as I know, this is one of the few places where Weiss reflects

on the limits of representing Auschwitz. What has by now become a commonplace in discussing the Holocaust—that it is impossible to comprehend this catastrophe, or to represent it artistically—seems not to have been a major obstacle for Weiss.[14] He knew, of course, that the bureaucratically organized destruction of life scorns any moral judgment, that the mechanized extermination of life numbs the faculty of reason, and that Auschwitz is beyond human imagination, yet he tried to rationalize the horror nevertheless. Auschwitz may be incomprehensible, but for Weiss it was not beyond representation. He strongly believed that documentary theater and rational analysis could counter any mystification of Auschwitz and could also contribute to our understanding of the present. "We must drop the lofty view/ that the camp world/ is incomprehensible to us."[15] This provocative statement by the Third Witness stands as Weiss's answer to our doubts about the limits of representing the Holocaust.

When Weiss addresses this issue in a short dramaturgical introduction to his play, he states categorically that "any representation of the camp on stage would be impossible." (118) However, this has less to do with the impossibility of representing the Holocaust than with the limits of the theater. Of course, Auschwitz, the concentration camp, cannot be reproduced on stage and any attempt to identify with the victims would be futile. The same holds true for any theatrical re-enactment of the Frankfurt Auschwitz trial, for it would only fictionalize reality, or as Weiss states again in his introduction: "In the production of this play, no attempt should be made to reconstruct the courtroom before which the proceedings of the camp trial took place" (*Ibid*). What he does, however, is to investigate, document, and report what happened in the concentration camp, how and why it happened. His *Investigation* confronts the audience with facts, numbers and names, with testimony of medical experiments, of with torture and murder, with methods of exploitation and of extermination. Weiss leads us through eleven stages of Hell on earth, from the ramp through the camp to the fire ovens. He demonstrates emotionlessly what took place in Auschwitz, analyzes it rationally, and confronts the German audience with "their Auschwitz."

And yet, Weiss knew all too well that facts do not speak for themselves and that documentary drama is not a mere reproduction of

reality, of which it is often accused.[16] He had learned from Brecht that neither facticity nor photorealism says anything about the depicted reality. They do not make it speak, or as Brecht stated: "One has indeed to construct something, something artificial, something formed."[17] It is, therefore, not sufficient merely to document the barbarism of Auschwitz or to let the facts tell the "whole truth" about it, since these are always already insufficient. Some form of art is indeed necessary, but not the kind of dramatic form which relies on plot and character, illusion and identification in order to transform Auschwitz into an emotional experience. Rather, a distancing technique is needed that makes the underlying social causes of reality transparent.

Weiss's first artistic device is the oratorio form. It is well known that Dante's *Divina Commedia*, which he was studying at the time, inspired the structural arrangement of *The Investigation*, using as his model the *Inferno*. Following this example, he divided the material into eleven cantos with three sections each. The proportional arrangement of the dramatis personae (three jurists, nine witnesses, eighteen defendants) employs the Christian symbolism of the holy trinity, standing in stark contrast to the subject matter, the extermination of European Jewry. The play's subtle irony is revealed in the way Weiss plays with this Christian typology and stages the oratorio as a passion play of Jewish suffering. Accordingly the oratorio form, which forgoes traditional scenic devices, costumes, and props, is usually presented as a solemn reading (with a minimum of props), underscoring the estrangement effect of the play.[18]

Montage is the second device Weiss uses.[19] The documentary drama, which is rather undramatic, static, and bare of action, is a collage of quotes, or as Weiss called it: *Konzentrat* (a condensation of evidence). It has by now become a commonplace that documentary drama relies on fact, reports, and quotes, which often lead to the erroneous conclusion that it only reproduces or doubles reality, meaning that the documentary theater is a tautology. Less understood is its montage technique, which distorts, distances, and estranges reality. The documentary material is neither invented nor fictitious and, even more importantly, it is not mediated by a narrator or integrated into the dramatic form. Rather it uses ready-made, found material (reports and quotes) that is then collated into a new pattern, to be analyzed and criticized. In short, the montage distorts existing reality in order to make it recognizable. Cuts, ruptures, and montage, Weiss explained in his "Notes on the Documentary Theater," isolate details of the chaotic material of reality: "By confronting contradictory details, it makes us aware of existing conflicts."[20] The audience is encouraged to be an observer and critic of these contradictions.

The Investigation, Weiss insists, contains no more than a condensation of evidence presented at the trial (118).[21] The documentary material is based—sometimes verbatim—on Bernd Neumann's trial reports for the *Frankfurter Allgemeine Zeitung* and on his own protocols. He compressed, rearranged, and collated it, allocating the quotes to specific players who represent a judge, a prosecutor, defense attorneys, defendants, and witnesses. He retained the names of the eighteen defendants, which is "significant" since they are "distinct figures" who actively participated in the atrocities. At the same time they "stand merely as symbols of a system that implicated in its guilt many others who never appeared in court" (119). The more than four hundred witnesses who had lost their names in the camp are represented by nine "anonymous voices" who testify to the victims' experiences. Consequently there is no courtroom drama, no plot development, and no emotional confrontation, only questions and answers, interrogation and dialogue, report and memory. Auschwitz is triply distanced: what happened in Auschwitz that cannot be represented; what was revealed during the Auschwitz trial by the survivors and was reported by Bernd Neumann; and what was filtered through Weiss's own imagination while watching the trial. As Andreas Huyssen has aptly observed: "Auschwitz is represented through language only."[22] In the survivors' reports it is the language of memory, in the defendants' replies it is the language of denial.[23] Weiss reconstructs the past through the survivors' memory, while attitudes toward the Holocaust are articulated by the defendants. It is precisely this tension between past and present which makes *The Investigation* such a powerful and convincing play.

Yet Weiss seeks not only memory and mourning but also understanding and criticism of a system which produced such well organized and mechanized murder. More than a mere reconstruction of the past through memory—as another prejudice against documentary theater would make us believe—is presented on stage through interrogations and reports. While documentary dramas exits that reproduce the past as realistically as possible and make it emotionally digestible,[24] Weiss's *Investigation* confronts the audience of 1965 with present attitudes toward the Holocaust for which they themselves should accept responsibility and/or show remorse. Auschwitz is brought to the fore through language and memory and it is made accessible through the reactions of witnesses and defendants. By making use of alienation effects, the documentary theater reflects on the past from present perspective, it historizes contradictions of society, and makes them recognizable—setting them up for criticism. "The strength of the documentary theater," as Weiss understood it, is precisely the fact, "that it reconstructs out of the fragments of reality a usable model for explaining present social conditions."[25] *The Investigation* is neither a surrogate for the Auschwitz trial, which is long forgotten, nor just another historical Holocaust drama, but a well-made play, which makes use of the dialectic of past and present in order to construct a model. "*The Investigation* is, therefore, not solely a play about Auschwitz, not even as a precedence, but about our Auschwitz, namely how present conditions are reflected in relation to Auschwitz."[26] What happened in the concentration and extermination camps becomes a provocation for the living and for the society they live in.

Peter Weiss did not exclude himself from this provocation, which cut into his own flesh. When he visited Auschwitz, he realized that he had been destined for this place—and by sheer luck avoided it; when he attended the Auschwitz trial another possibility dawned on him, that he could have been one of the perpetrators himself. He remembered how enthusiastically he had participated in the paramilitary and often sadistic activities of the youth movement before 1933 and how close he had been to becoming a part of this murderous system. "The horror of both possibilities never again left him," as Robert Cohen observed.[27] In the play Weiss demands nothing less than the same painful recognition on the part of the audience. The Third Witness rejects any mystification of Auschwitz as something inconceivable, and he then draws the provocative conclusion that prisoners and guards could have easily exchanged their places:

If they had not been designated prisoners
they could equally well have been guards
We must drop the lofty view
that the camp world
is incomprehensible for us
We all knew the society
that produced a government
capable of creating such camps
The order that prevailed there
was an order whose basic nature
we were familiar with (191).

The prevailing order or the "system", as Weiss called it in the introductory note, is, of course, capitalism, which for him not only explains Nazi barbarity but a familiar continuity between the present and the past. This unbroken continuity between the Third Reich and the Federal Republic is addressed in the play both by the still suffering survivors and the First and Second Witness, who are transitional figures between victims and perpetrators. They stand for many others, also implicated in the atrocities, who were never brought to trial: civil servants, engineers, physicians, scientists, and other ordinary men and women, like "Papa Kaduk", one of the most bestial capos who is now admired by his patients for his gentleness. These handymen of the murderous machine called Auschwitz were integrated into the "new" society of the Federal Republic, where they were prosperous or even occupying leading positions. Their testimonies were meant to trigger an alarming recognition of continuity: In Auschwitz they were railroad specialists, now they are *Bundesbahn* executives. They pretend that they only followed orders, did their duty, and knew nothing of what was going on inside the extermination camp:

> Prosecutor: You heard nothing
> about people being exterminated
> 1st Witness: How could anybody believe a thing like that (121).

Or:

> Judge: What did you see of the camp
> 2nd Witness: Nothing

Judge:	Did you see the chimneys
	at the end of the platform
	or the smoke and the glare
2nd Witness:	Yes
	I saw smoke
Judge:	And what did you think
2nd Witness:	I thought
	those must be bakeries
	I had heard
	they baked bread in there day and night
	After all it was a big camp (123).

The real provocation was, however, that Weiss dragged on stage those former directors of German corporations, those who willingly participated in the systematic exploitation of prisoners and who were now receiving high pensions and living comfortably with their repressed past. By naming Krupp, Siemens, and IG Farben, which at that time "made profits / that annually amounted to billions" and which are now in "a new phase of expansion" (206), the theater became a tribunal for the underlying forces which had made Auschwitz possible and profited from it.[28] The spotlight focused on the capitalistic system as participant in and profiteer of the Holocaust—an implication that West-German industry had avoided for two decades and wished to pass over in silence. In the play these witnesses avoid responsibility, especially since they are not among the defendants, and they make the tired excuses that they had only done their patriotic duty: "We were all concerned with / only one thing / winning the war" (204). They emphatically reject any guilt and call these accusations defamations:

Today
when our nation has worked its way up
after a devastating war
to a leading position in the world
we ought to concern ourselves
with other things
These recriminations
should have fallen
under the Statute of Limitations
a long time ago (296).

With this statement and with the "loud approbation from the Defendants" the play ends. It is precisely against this prevailing sentiment of repression and denial that Weiss wrote *The Investigation*.

As could be expected, many critics reacted with polemics, even slander against Weiss's indictment of the capitalist system, as if the subject matter, the extermination of Jews, Poles, Russians, Gypsies, and other "enemies" of the Nazi state, were of minor importance. Since Weiss had meanwhile given up his "comfortable third position" between capitalism and socialism and had publically opted instead for socialism,[29] *The Investigation* was called a propaganda piece of communist agitation against the Federal Republic.[30] Another critic considered the implication of German corporations to be simply an expression of Weiss's "ideology," as if it had nothing to do with the murder of two million Jews in Auschwitz, claiming as well that "this murderous machine had been a heavy economic burden for the Third Reich".[31] (As if Auschwitz had not been a death factory in itself; as if Auschwitz had been a hindrance in the war effort and not an important element of the total war.) These and other critics objected to nothing less than the political tendency of Weiss's play that offended the bourgeois civility of the theater by implicating major German corporations in the Holocaust and violated its good taste by being tendentious. In short: Weiss had contradicted the bourgeois concept of art, a concept based on autonomy.

This is indeed what he had intended to do, as Weiss affirms in his "Notes on the Documentary Theater." What his critics called propaganda was for him a necessary element of documentary theater: partisanship. Many of the play's themes can no longer be treated "objectively," Weiss insists, "they can only be presented as crimes."[32] What he demands is nothing less than a political theater, which confronts the audience with a repressed past and opens up the present for a critical re-evaluation. *The Investigation* is neither a piece of disinterested art nor a drama in the Aristotelian fashion, but "a form of tribunal", operative art. And yet, Weiss also knew that it is still theater. The documentary theater is no surrogate for reality or political action, "it must be a product of art, if it wants to have any justification."[33]

This is precisely the point I want to stress. The political tendency is embedded in an aesthetic structure, as my observations about the montage technique, the alienation effects, and the model function of *The Investigation* have demonstrated. The montage of authentic material from the Auschwitz trial articulates Weiss's personal interest and political tendency; the alienation effects are suppose to break the numbing emotional experience of the trial as well as the perturbing reports of the witnesses; and the model character of the documented reality allows for a dialectical understanding of the Nazi period, which makes the present transparent in its disturbing continuity.

Yet, despite Weiss's intentions to understand Auschwitz and to criticize the prevailing attitudes toward the Holocaust, there still remains a residue that escapes any attempt to rationalize Auschwitz. As a result, the audience did not hear the underlying message of the play (or at least not until much later). Enduring the relentless reports and descriptions of unbearable suffering, they heard about the extent and brutal details of the Holocaust, which shocked them into silence. There was no applause at the end of the performance. The audience sat numb in their seats for a long while and then filed out quietly. This response is quite different from any catharsis or cleansing of emotions. The audience had been shocked into recognition.

But of what? Certainly not of their complicity in the Holocaust or their collective responsibility for it, although they must have had some feeling of shame for what had been done in Germany's name. Perhaps, they felt even some remorse. The silence, however, marked their recognition of the magnitude and monstrosity of the Holocaust. They had been confronted with detailed reports of survivors who described relentlessly the many forms of destruction of life: by torture and starvation, by shooting and injection, by gas and fire. It was precisely this confrontation with the unbearable horrors and cruelties of Auschwitz that shocked the audience into recognizing the Holocaust's enormity.

The general public could have known about all of this at least since the Eichmann and Auschwitz trials, but the full impact of the Holocaust did not sink in until Weiss staged the terror of Auschwitz. If they were not overwhelmed by this burden of the past, the audience became the judge of what they had just seen. Weiss's *Investigation*, transforming the theater into a tribunal, not only informed the public about one aspect of the Nazi past, which they had repressed or denied, it also stimulated a public debate about this past which went far beyond the theater's threshold. His play truly became an "instrument of political opinion formation," as Weiss had demanded of the documentary theater, and it influenced in no small part the outcome of the parliamentary debate about the Statute of Limitations for Nazi crimes.

III

In spite of the play's tremendous success, the public debates it triggered, and its educational function, the critical reaction in the Federal Republic was anything but enthusiastic. I already mentioned two critics who faulted Weiss for his ideology and called his play mere communist propaganda. Blinded by their own ideology of anti-Communism and/or their aesthetics of autonomous art, they overlooked not only the fact that Weiss's criticism of the capitalistic system comprises only one aspect of the play (roughly one tenth of the text), but, even more importantly, they rejected his dialectical perspective connecting the present with the past. Willingly or not, the critics continued the German politics of denial, although they couched their criticism in aesthetic terms.

A more interesting critique is Ernst Wendt's suspicion that Weiss was fascinated by cruelty or, even more strongly, that "the intensity of his representation of cruelty changes into 'pleasure'."[34] Joachim Kaiser raises a similar point in his criticism of Weiss's "Theater-Auschwitz" by observing that the audience had no respite from the "enormity of horror" and the "magnitude of facts."[35] This is indeed one effect of the play, and it could explain the audience's numbness and silence at the end. Weiss's oratorio is, however, not to be confused with Antonin Artaud's "Theater of Cruelty", as both reviewers seem to suggest.[36] It is a superficial analogy at best and at worst a grave distortion of Weiss's representation of Auschwitz. There are major differences between what an author imagines as cruelty and what happened in Auschwitz, between figments of the imagination and brutal reality. When the Living Theater staged *Death in the Gas Chambers* (1965), they were certainly able to produce raw emotions on stage and horror and fear in the audience, but they could not explain why it happened. They choreographed a dance of death and manipulated audience emotions to the extreme, but it was indeed nothing more than "Auschwitz-Theater," which cannot compete with the reports of Weiss's witnesses. The dance of ecstasy and hysteria lacks any forms of distancing which would allow the audience to reflect on what it sees. This kind of raw emotional experience does not even lead to catharsis, which would entail some sort of emotional cleansing or moral response, and it certainly does not enhance the understanding of Auschwitz, as was the aim of Weiss's representation of cruelty. Weiss's "theater of cruelty," if it can be called that, shocks the audience emotionally, and they leave the theater in silence, but it later also provokes reflections on what they heard and saw.

Aside from these misunderstandings, Kaiser's finer points are directed against the poetics of Weiss's documentary theater. It leaves the sphere of "Kunstwahrheit" (truth in art), which is, of course, the sphere of autonomous art; and it is only a surrogate for truly coming to terms with the past, which could be understood as a direct attack on the documentary drama of the sixties as well as a more general critique of postwar German literature.[37] Wendt draws a much cruder conclusion when he states "that Weiss was obviously more interested in the representation of suffering than in unmasking the perpetrators and the tacit accomplices."[38] By insisting on suffering and cruelty as the main effects of the play, Wendt obviously missed the most important point in Weiss's documentary drama: His insistence on the continuity between Auschwitz and present day German society, and consequently on the ongoing process of repression. These conclusions return us to the focal point of German denial in the disguise of aesthetics.

If the German reception of Weiss's *Investigation* can be characterized—with a few exceptions[39]—as apologetic, regressive, and polemical, the American reaction was altogether different. If the Germans were painfully reminded of a past they would prefer to forget but could not escape, the American audience, fascinated and appalled by the monstrosity of the concentration camps ever since they were discovered in 1945, expected a mimetic representation of crime and punishment, collective guilt and remorse, catharsis or some kind of resolution.[40] Instead they saw a documentary drama in which Auschwitz and the murdered Jews were not even mentioned. In Germany, the documentary drama of the sixties was the most innovative theatrical genre, confronting Germans with the facts, names, and places of their racial war; for many American critics, like Lawrence Langer, the play was nothing more than an journalistic documentation "with a minimum of alterations from the testimony of witnesses at the Auschwitz trial in Frankfurt...," and he concluded that "the result on the stage is singularly undramatic."[41] Many American intellectuals were introduced to the Holocaust by Alain Resnais's film masterpiece *Night and Fog,* which had also used documentary clips, but nothing so factual, so brutal, and so "artless" as Peter Weiss's *Investigation* had confronted them.

Other, more sophisticated arguments developed over time in the United States, dealing with questions of identity and ideology.[42] Eli Wiesel, the moral authority on all matters concerning the Holocaust, apodictically stated: "A prominent European playwright wrote a play about the Auschwitz trials and managed not to mention the word 'Jew' therein."[43] One should add that Weiss also did not mention Auschwitz. While this omission is not so obvious, since text and context clearly delineate Auschwitz, the absence of the word "Jew" is indeed startling. But instead of asking why Weiss, himself a Jew, did not clearly identify the Jews, who made up the vast majority of Auschwitz victims, Wiesel denounces him as if he were a Holocaust denier. The simple truth would be, of course, that Weiss wanted to honor *all* Holocaust victims and that he refused to establish any hierarchy of victims. This explanation, well intended as it may be, will not do.

I forego the somewhat fruitless discussion about whether this omission had anything to do with Weiss's doubts about his own Jewish identity. Instead I summarize the obvious: He identified with the Jewish victims of the concentration camps, he felt guilty like many survivors who were spared, and he defined his own Jewishness by the Holocaust—a typical "Holocaust Jew," as Jean Amery called all Jews who redefined their Jewishness after the trauma of the Holocaust.[44]

Weiss's omission of the word "Jew" is a different matter altogether. In interviews he insisted that he deliberately erased the national and ethnic identity of the victims in order to stress the play's universal message. Universality, a category usually employed in the traditional drama of illusion and identification, is a strange concept in documentary drama, which privileges authenticity and specificity. Its provocation is based on facts, places, and names, indeed it points out the perpetrators and the places of their crimes against humanity. And yet, the victims should have no names, no nationality, and no ethnic identity? It is a contradiction in terms for documentary theater to sacrifice the victims' particularity in the name of universal meaning.

Weiss must have noticed this contradiction, otherwise he would not have identified *one* victim by name or referred repeatedly to the Soviet victims. Lili Tofler, who also has no national or ethnic identity, could be understood as a synecdoche, representing the countless unknown Holocaust victims. But why are the Soviet victims singled out? Is it, as Weiss's American critics love to point out, that he is first and foremost a communist? or as his defenders have suggested that Weiss wanted to make the audience aware as well of the millions of Soviet civilians who were killed in this total war?[45] This has become a major point of contention and irritation for American critics.[46] It would not be, if Weiss had also mentioned the Jews, for then it would have become intelligible to the audience that this was a total war of extermination, especially in the East, for racial reasons. Many scholars have argued that one of the major differences between fascism and National Socialism was the racial plank in the Nazi's political platform. By not naming the Jewish victims, Weiss overlooked or downplayed this most important racial component of the Holocaust. It is the play's gravest fallacy, even if the audience did not notice it, because of the simplified message of universal suffering.[47]

How could this happen to an author who had been so sensitive to the sufferings of the Jewish victims, identified with them, and felt so deeply the guilt of a survivor? This can only be explained by the political tendency of the play, which his American critics were eager to pinpoint as Weiss's "Marxist Credo"[48]: his fixation on the capitalist system and its continuity in the Federal Republic. For Weiss, the concentration camp functioned as a model for the brutal exploitation and extermination of human beings by the Nazi state, which he understood as the most extreme consequence of the capitalist system. He had good reason to pursue this line of thinking, since I.G.Farben, Krupp, and Siemens exploited slave laborers in the vicinity of Auschwitz and since Auschwitz itself was a well organized death factory. It could well be, as Cohen has surmised, that "it was not Weiss's Marxism that produced *The Investigation* but rather his work on the Auschwitz material that intensified his interest in Marxism."[49] To represent Auschwitz he was not satisfied with a mere description of the death camp or reports of the cruelties committed in this place, he was also searching for a convincing model that could explain the Holocaust's social complexity. He found it in the industries surrounding Auschwitz as the most obvious signifier of capitalism. By implicating the German corporations who profited from the exploitation of slave labor, he used a well known Marxist critique of capitalism, the so-called Dimitroff doctrine, which interprets fascism as an extreme form of capitalism. In interviews Weiss repeatedly stated that he wanted "to stigmatize capitalism, which lends itself to profit even from gas chambers."[50]

Before we hastily join Weiss's critics in blaming him for his turn toward doctrinaire Marxism and his rather simplistic ideological criticism of capitalism, let us not forget the time of which we are speaking. It was the time of the cold war and anti-communist propaganda, whose codes can still be detected in the language of Weiss's American critics.[51] At the same time many intellectuals in the West were rediscovering and reconstructing Marxist theory in order to analyze capitalism and fascism—and also to understand Auschwitz. "We will not have come to terms with the past until the causes of what happened then are no longer active. Only because these causes live on does the spell of the past remain unbroken—up to this very day."[52] Adorno's 1959 lecture "What does it mean: Coming to terms with the past?" demonstrates even in its somewhat cryptic language that he too defined fascism's continuity in terms similar to Weiss; and he agreed with his friend Max Horkheimer that the essence of anti-Semitism and an understanding of Auschwitz can only be found in a critical analysis of the society that produces them.[53] If even Adorno and Horkheimer, not to mention other early theorists of fascism, proposed the equation that fascism equals capitalism in its most brutal form, one should be more careful before blaming Weiss for his ideological blinders. Historians established long ago the close cooperation between German corporations and the Nazis.[54] Recent events like the scandals surrounding the "forgotten" Swiss bank accounts of Holocaust victims, the disappearance of records of Nazi gold in Swiss, German, and American banks, or the just settled swindle of German and Italian insurance companies, remind us again to what extent international capital had been involved in the enterprise of the Third Reich.

Nevertheless, in his attempt to make Auschwitz comprehensible by using a one-dimensional Marxist critique of capitalism and by constructing the death camp as an allegory of history, Weiss left himself vulnerable to criticism. With his monocausal explanation of fascism combined with his failure to reflect on anti-Semitism and its history in Germany, he "came dangerously close to depriving the victims of their personal and collective history and identity as Jews, and he just about instrumentalizes Auschwitz in order to advance a questionable interpretation of fascism."[55] Weiss's political rationalization of Auschwitz distracted from its artful representation through memory and language, which is after all the main effect of his oratorio.

For all that, I still insist that Weiss's *Investigation* was a turning point in the literary as well as in the political history of the Federal Republic of Germany. As operative literature his documentary drama provided an impulse for confronting the Nazi past and for coming to terms with it. In the following years the student movement amplified this critical confrontation with the Third Reich's legacy and contributed to educational efforts to disseminate knowledge about the Holocaust in universities and schools. After 1965, no one in Germany could pretend not to know about the Holocaust. In a certain sense Weiss's *Investigation* contributed to a new conscience or to what Adorno called a new categorical imperative: That mankind "should arrange their thoughts and actions so that Auschwitz will not repeat itself, so that nothing similar will happen."[56]

Notes

1 Quoted from Weiss, "Meine Ortschaft" (1965), trans. Christopher Middleton, *German Writing Today* (Baltimore 1967), p. 28.

2 I forego the more recent public debates, such as the historians' debate (1987), the controversies surrounding the German translation of Daniel Goldhagen's book *Hitler's Willing Executioners* (1997), the Wehrmacht exhibition (1997-98), and the ongoing discussions about the Berlin Holocaust Monument, which all demonstrate the burden of the past that cannot be laid to rest.

3 For a similar perspective with different results see Alfons Söllner, "Peter Weiss's *Die Ermittlung* in zeitgeschichtlicher Perspektive." In: *Deutsche Nachkriegslliteratur und der Holocaust*, Stephan Braese et al., eds. (Frankfurt a.M. 1998), p. 99-128. I choose the title of this essay with Martin Walser's "Unser Auschwitz" in mind in order to mark the stark contrast between his famous essay of 1965 and his "Sunday Sermon" about "looking away" from Auschwitz and "repressing" German guilt/shame in his acceptance speech of the German Publishers' Peace Prize at Paul's Church in Frankfurt am Main in October 1998. See Martin Walser, *Erfahrungen beim Verfassen einer Sonntagsrede* (Frankfurt a.M. 1998).

4 In the same year it was also staged in London, New York, Stockholm, Amsterdam, Moscow, Warsaw, and Prague.

5 Peter Weiss, "Notizen zum dokumentarischen Drama" (1968). In: *Rapporte 2* (Frankfurt a.M. 1971), p. 96.

6 Martin Walser, *Die Alternative. Oder brauchen wir eine neue Regierung?* (Hamburg 1965).

7 Werner Stein, *Kulturfahrplan* (Vienna 1974), p. 1310.

8 The reception of her book, *Eichmann in Jerusalem*, was quite different in Germany than in Israel and the United States. Many Jews were offended by her harsh criticism of assimilated Jews and especially of Leo Baeck, who did not resist the Nazis but went so far as to help them round up fellow Jews. For them, her book was and is a provocation, while we missed that completely. For my generation, it was an eye-opener, since it demonstrated for the first time how the extermination of the European Jewry was organized and executed with bureaucratic efficiency and technological know-how and how ordinary civil servants participated in this genocide.

9 Theodor W. Adorno, *Eingriffe* (Frankfurt a.M. 1963), p. 143.

10 Martin Walser, "Vom erwarteten Theater." In: Walser, *Erfahrungen und Leseerfahrungen* (Frankfurt a.M. 1965), p. 64.

11 See *Summa iniuria oder Durfte der Papst schweigen?,* Fritz J. Raddatz, ed. (Hamburg 1963), which documents a selection of the over 3000 responses to the play.

12 Theodor W. Adorno criticized Hochhuth severely for these aesthetic blunders. See his "Offener Brief an Rolf Hochhuth." In: *Noten zur Literatur IV* (Frankfurt a.M. 1974), p. 137-146.

13 Weiss, "Meine Ortschaft," p. 20.

14 Let us recall that this fairly recent debate was triggered by the "linguistic turn" in historiography and by deconstruction in literary theory. See *Probing the Limits of Representation: Nazism and the "Final Solution,"* Saul Friedländer (Cambridge, MA and London 1992), especially Friedländer's introductory essay.

15 Peter Weiss, *Marat/Sade, The Investigation, and The Shadow of the Body of the Coachman,* Robert Cohen, ed. (New York 1998), p. 191. This edition is quoted in the text.

16 For critical positions in this debate on documentary theater (Baumgart, Harich, Kesting, Walser, Handke), see Klaus L. Berghahn, "Operative Ästhetik: Zur Theorie der dokumentarischen Literatur." In: *Deutsche Literatur in der Bundesrepublik seit 1965,* Paul Michael Lützeler und Egon Schwarz, eds. (Frankfurt a.M. 1980), p. 277ff.

17 Bertolt Brecht, *Der Dreigroschenprozeß,* Brecht, *Werke* (Frankfurt a.M. and Berlin 1992), vol. XXI, p. 469.

18 Erika Salloch, *Peter Weiss's "Die Ermittlung": Zur Struktur des Dokumentartheaters* (Frankfurt a.M. 1972), p. 47ff. She reads *The Investigation* from a rather positivistic approach as a "Gegenentwurf" of the *Divina Commedia.*

19 Montage and collage are familiar techniques in avant-garde art forms, yet in literature they are usually overlooked, and in Weiss's play they are not even recognized as such since the material seems to be so "realistic".

20 Peter Weiss, "Notizen zum dokumentarischen Theater." In: *Rapporte II,* p. 97.

21 A detailed comparison of Weiss's play with all documents of the Frankfurt Auschwitz trial, which would go beyond Salloch's study, is yet to be presented. It could demonstrate Weiss's collage technique as well as his use of the Third Witness as protagonist for his own political perspective.

22 Andreas Huyssen, "The Politics of Identification: 'Holocaust' and the West German Drama." In: *New German Critique* 19 (1980), p. 131.

23 Claude Lanzmann uses a similar montage technique and estrangement in his documentary film *Shoah,* which is also solely based on language and

memory. His film shows us the places of destruction, which are now quiet landscapes, museums or monuments; there he interviews survivors, whose memories bring back the past. Past and present intermingle, and the Holocaust becomes present in its absence. Whereas Lanzmann's film and his interrogations seem to be mainly interested in the "how" of the extermination program, leaving the answer as to the "why" up to the audience, Weiss also wants to know why it happened.

24 As for instance Rolf Schneider's *Prozeß in Nürnberg* (1967), which is "simple information," as the author even admits in his preface and which seems to prove the critics of documentary drama right.

25 Peter Weiss, "Notizen zum dokumentarischen Theater," p. 97.

26 Klaus Harro Hilzinger, *Die Dramaturgie des dokumentarischen Theaters* (Tübingen 1976), p. 53. I am very much indebted to this book, which is still the best theoretical treatise on German documentary drama of the sixties.

27 Robert Cohen, "1964—On March 13, in the middle of rehearsals for the premiere of *Marat/Sade*, Peter Weiss attended the Frankfurt Auschwitz trial." In: *Yale Companion to Jewish Writing and Thought in German Culture, 1096-1996*, Sander L. Gilman and Jack Zipes, eds. (New Haven 1987), p. 723.

28 Smaller firms as well, like Degesch (Cyclon B) and Töpfer und Söhne (crematoria), should not be forgotten.

29 Peter Weiss, "10 Arbeitspunkte eines Autors in einer geteilten Welt." In: *Rapporte* 2 (Frankfurt a.M. 1971), p. 14-23.

30 Otto F. Best, *Peter Weiss* (Bern 1971), p. 141.

31 Marianne Kesting, "Völkermord und Ästhetik." In: *Neue Deutsche Hefte* 113 (1967), p. 96.

32 Weiss, "Notizen zum dokumentarischen Theater," p. 99.

33 Weiss, "Notizen zum dokumentarischen Theater," p. 96.

34 Ernst Wendt, "Was wird ermittelt?" In: *Theater heute* 10 (1965): 18. Others used more existential terms to describe Weiss's "fascination with evil." See Salloch, *Peter Weiss's "Die Ermittlung,"* p. 154f.

35 Joachim Kaiser, "Plädoyer gegen das Theater-Auschwitz." In: *Süddeutsche Zeitung* (4 September 1965), and "Theater-Auschwitz." In: *Die Zeit* (2 November 1965).

36 For a historical overview of the representation of cruelty on stage from the 17th century to Artaud and for a refutation of understanding Weiss's play as "Theater of Cruelty, see Ernst Schumacher, "*Die Ermittlung* von Peter Weiss: Über die szenische Darstellbarkeit der Hölle auf Erden." In: *Über Peter Weiss*, ed. Volker Canaris (Frankfurt a.M. 1970), p. 83-87.

37 Or as Jochen Vogt observed, "Denn was haben ihre Autoren, von Heinrich Böll bis Christa Wolf, anderes betrieben als Erinnerungs- und Trauerarbeit - stellvertretend für eine Gesellschaft, die solche Arbeit in ihrer großen Mehrheit und in ihren repräsentativen Institutionen abgelehnt hat." Jochen Vogt, *Peter Weiss* (Hamburg 1987), p. 96.

38 Wendt, "Was wird ermittelt?" p. 18.

39 At least four reviewers should be mentioned: Ernst Schumacher (see note 37), Walter Jens, "*Die Ermittlung* in Westberlin." In: *Die Zeit* (19 October 1965); Martin Esslin in *Die Weltwoche* (29 October 1965), and Gerhard Schoenberner, "*Die Ermittlung* von Peter Weiss: Requiem oder Lehrstück?" In: *Gewerkschaftliche Monatshefte* 12 (1965).

40 A typical expression of this kind of expectation can be found in Sidra DeKoven Ezrahi, *By Words Alone: The Holocaust in Literature* (Chicago 1980), p. 38.

41 Lawrence L. Langer, *The Holocaust and the Literary Imagination* (New Haven 1975), p. 31. Twenty years later he changed his mind and called Weiss's *Investigation* one of the best representations of the Holocaust; see his essay "The Literature of Auschwitz." In: *Admitting the Holocaust: Collected Essays* (New York 1995), p. 97f.

42 For a critical overview of recent literary criticism on *The Investigation* in the United States, see Robert Cohen, "The Political Aesthetics of Holocaust Literature: Peter Weiss's *The Investigation* and Its Critics," *History and Memory* 10.2 (1998), p. 43-67.

43 Eli Wiesel, "The Holocaust as Literary Inspiration," In: *Dimensions of the Holocaust,* Wiesel et al., eds. (Evanston 1990), 19. In an even more denunciatory gesture James Young calls *The Investigation* "judenrein," see James E. Young, *Writing and Rewriting the Holocaust: Narrative and Consequences of Interpretation* (Bloomington 1988), p. 72.

44 See Robert Cohen, "The Political Aesthetics of Holocaust Literature," p. 54f. For further discussion of Weiss's Jewish identity, see Irene Heidelberger-Leonard, "Jüdisches Bewußtsein im Werk von Peter Weiss." In: *Literatur, Ästhetik, Geschichte. Neue Zugänge zu Peter Weiss,* Michael Hoffmann, ed. (St. Ingberg 1992), p. 49-64.

45 Cohen, "The Political Aesthetics of Holocaust Literature," p. 58f.

46 James Young is almost beside himself that Weiss "co-valued political and racial killings," as if it were an issue of first and second-class victims (Young,*Writing and Rewriting the Holocaust,* 75). For a detailed metacritic of Young's book see, Jean-Michel Chaumount, "Der Stellenwert der *Ermittlung* im Gedächtnis von Ausschwitz." In: *Peter Weiss: Neue Fragen*

an alte Texte, Irene Heidelberger-Leonard, ed. (Opladen 1994), p. 77-93.

47 As far as I know, only one West German critic noticed this omission but then drew no conclusion, stating that Weiss presented the crimes of the camp "by abstracting from the race ideology" of the Nazis. See Hilzinger, *Die Dramaturgie des dokumentarischen Theaters*, p. 89. Söllner overlooks (or avoids) this problem altogether and is satisfied with Weiss's view that the nameless witnesses are merely "Sprachrohre." See Söllner, "Peter Weiss's *Die Ermittlung* in zeitgeschichtlicher Perspektive," p. 118.

48 Young, *Writing and Rewriting the Holocaust*, p. 78.

49 Cohen, "The Political Aesthetics of Holocaust Literature," p. 60.

50 Interview with *Stockholms Tidningen*, quoted in *Der Spiegel* 43 (1965), p. 155.

51 See Cohen, "The Political Aesthetics of Holocaust Literature," p. 60.

52 Theodor W. Adorno, "Was bedeutet: Aufarbeitung der Vergangenheit?" In: *Eingriffe* (Frankfurt a.M. 1963), p. 146.

53 See Theodor W. Adorno and Max Horkheimer, "Elemente des Antisemitismus," Adorno and Horkheimer, *Dialektik der Aufklärung* (Frankfurt a.M. 1971), p. 185-230. For Horkheimer, see his essay "Die Juden und Europa." In: *Zeitschrift für Sozialforschung* VII.1-2 (1939), in which he subsumes fascism and anti-Semitism under the broader concept of capitalist crisis: "He who does not wish to speak of capitalism should also be silent about fascism."

54 Raul Hilberg, *The Destruction of the European Jews* (Chicago 1967), p. 590 and 594, and Joseph Borkin, *The Crime and Punishment of I. G. Farben* (New York 1978).

55 Huyssen, "The Politics of Identification," p. 133.

56 Theodor W. Adorno, *Negative Dialektik* (Frankfurt a.M. 1966), p. 356.

Peter Weiss and the Third World

I

Michella E. Lang

Politics and Poetics:
The Reception of *Popanz* in Sweden, Germany, and the United States

Peter Weiss's interest in Angola's efforts to liberate itself from Portugal's colonial constraints arose within the context of larger, international discussions that included a UN council resolution for support of Angolan independence in 1961. American newspapers kept abreast of the political situation in Angola but chose to report a side of the story that foregrounded the United States' benevolent and humanitarian decision to support Angola's self-determination.[1] Likewise, in West Germany the mass media painted such a one-sided and positive picture of Portuguese colonial politics that some critics called the reporting a "Verdrehung der Fakten."[2]

Ironically, this "distortion of the facts" is also what Peter Weiss was accused of by newspapers and theater critics in many Western nations concerning his portrayal of a different side of Angola's story: the documentary drama *Gesang vom Lusitanischen Popanz*. Having no qualms at naming the alleged perpetrators (among them American and West German big businesses), Peter Weiss's text takes on a strongly polemical edge. It problematizes five centuries of Portuguese colonization in Angola by pitting the aggressors against the victims, by shifting between perspectives of exploitation and suffering. The drama can be characterized as a one-sided montage of dates, facts, figures, and highlighted realities collected from various media sources for the audience's investigative and critical eye. In a 1966 interview in the *Tulane Drama Review* Weiss commented on the visual quality of his work and what he expected from an audience:

> From the beginning, everything I have done has been extremely visual, even my novels, and this is essential to the staging of my plays: I have chosen my media so that they were visual, and sometimes I have forced them to be so.... If I want anything from an audience, it's that they listen very carefully and be completely awake, not hypnotized, absolutely alive, answering all the questions in the play.[3]

To be sure, Weiss's *Popanz*, having been written with the cantos of Dante's *Divine Comedy* in mind, is also intended as a highly stylized musical event, which is expressed most distinctly in the three groupings of language used to qualify the characters of the play: rhythmic prose for the oppressors, doggerel for the Angolan leaders, and free verse for the chorus of Africans.[4] With its rich and fast-paced visual and aural effects of experimental theater—including song, pantomime, shadow-play, cabaret, animal fable, sound effects, and dance—Weiss insists upon an attentive audience. And with the play's rigorous political underpinnings supporting an anti-imperialistic, anti-clerical, and anti-capitalistic platform, Weiss insists upon a perceptive and politically conscious audience. *Popanz*, for better or for worse (and there are certainly proponents for both opinions), is a political agenda combined with poetics. The purpose of this paper then is to investigate, through the reception of *Popanz* in Sweden, Germany, and the United States, the effect the play had on its audiences and the extent to which one may or may not be able to determine its success.

Although already socially and politically engaged in the 1950s, the tumultuous 60's lured Weiss even further from his "hiding place"—that safe and protected existence of an artist tucked away in the attics of Sweden analyzing his identity in an absurd society. Weiss now began to make some important personal discoveries about his work, what it meant to him, and what it *could* mean to the world. He took note of the effects of the Cold War: the Cuban missile crisis, the division of Berlin, the armed conflict in Southeast Asia and the exploiting hand of colonialism in Southern Africa, as is evident from his *Notizbücher* during these years. Weiss also became more fully acquainted with Marxist socialism during this period—the consequences of which are pivotal in Weiss' political as well as his literary development. Consequently, it was during this time that Weiss began to make the transition from a more subjective discourse (writing to understand himself, his past and the world he lived in) to a more openly objective discourse (writing *for* and in support of others).

In Weiss's *Notizbücher* there are frequent entries from 1965 onwards concerning the issues of colonization in Central America, Southeast Asia, and the Portuguese colonies of Angola and Mozambique. Indeed, in 1965 third-world struggles, liberation movements, and the exploits of colonizers seem to be on the minds of many West German intellectuals, as Weiss's debate with *Kursbuch* publisher, Hans Magnus Enzensberger, can attest to. In an article published in the second issue of *Kursbuch*, Enzensberger splits the world into two opposing camps: the rich people (among them Europeans, North Americans, and Russians) and the poor people (among them Africans, Indians, and Chinese). He goes on to explain that these two groups are divided so strictly that feelings of solidarity could never unite them. Furthermore, Enzensberger states that the Marxist notion of class struggle did not explain the situation of the great divide, for the richer the rich become and the poorer the poor become, the more quickly and firmly a state of colonialism is instituted.[5] Weiss's response to Enzensberger's article, printed in the sixth issue of *Kursbuch*, not only reasons for rejecting a division of the world into rich and poor countries—preferring to categorize countries as either capitalistic or socialistic—but also argues that the way to unite the peoples of the world is through education: "Indem wir uns soviel Kenntnisse wie möglich verschaffen über die Zustände in den von den 'Reichen' am schwersten bedrängten Ländern, können wir diese Länder in unsere Nähe rücken und unsere Solidarität mit ihnen entwickeln."[6] Weiss then goes on to challenge Enzensberger's moral position as a writer: "Auf welche Seite stellen wir uns? ...Sind wir fähig, unsere Zweifel und unsere Vorsicht aufzugeben und uns zu gefährden, indem wir eindeutig aussprechen: Wir sind solidarisch mit den Unterdrückten, und wir werden als Autoren nach allen Mitteln suchen, um sie in ihrem Kampf (der auch der unsere ist) zu unterstützen?[7] Whereupon Enzensberger retorts:

Wer klopft sich da eigentlich immerfort selbst auf die Schulter? Wer behauptet
im Ernst, er *gefährde sich,* und nimmt den Mund voll mit seinen Mutproben?
Ist der Klassenkampf ein Indianerspiel, die Solidarität ein Federschmuck für
Intellektuelle? ...Peter Weiss ist gegen den Mord, gegen die Ausbeutung, gegen
den Hunger, gegen die Unterdrückung. Er sagt es sich selber, er sagt es allen
anderen vor. Das ist ein begreifliches Bedürfnis. Ihm nachzugeben, schadet
niemandem, nützt niemandem.[8]

Critique of this kind would come more than once and from many
directions for Peter Weiss, especially in regards to his drama *Popanz.*
Critics would not only point to the play's naive and overzealous political
aims but also question Weiss's success with which he was able to meld a
political agenda with poetics.

Gesang vom Lusitanischen Popanz did not have its debut in
Germany, as did Weiss's two previous plays *Marat/Sade* and *Die
Ermittlung,* not that he had not tried to get his play produced in
Germany. In fact, his publishing house Suhrkamp sent copies of the
script to several theaters throughout Germany, but Weiss was appalled
and dismayed at the "Borniertheit und Phantasielosigkeit" with which
the German theaters had suggested the staging of *Popanz.*[9] Meanwhile,
Weiss had become interested in a young Swedish troupe of actors and
actresses, who under the guiding wing of Allan Edwall sought "engaging
and socially critical theater" where they could collaborate as a collective
on the play's production.[10] This suited Weiss quite well, and
subsequently *Popanz* opened in Swedish translation at the small Scala-
Theater of Stockholm in January 1967, under the direction of Etienne
Glaser and Weiss himself. The Stockholm production, labeled as
"Theater der Armen," was kept simple in its staging.[11] Weiss had
utilized recycled materials collected from junk yards and garbage heaps
to construct the Popanz monstrum and had kept the costumes and props
at a minimum. In an interview with Giorgio Polacco, Weiss expressed
his satisfaction with the production of *Popanz* in Stockholm, but also
stated that it did not have "Modellcharakter."[12] He could, for example,
imagine another production of his play that would simulate the lively
and grotesque atmosphere of a "Jahrmarktstheater."[13]

In this same interview Weiss commented on his disappointment in
both West and East Germany for their initial unwillingness to stage

Popanz. He suspected that the real reason the play was not wanted, at least in West Germany, had less to do with theater critics' attitude that it seemed less "colorful and orgiastic" than *Marat/Sade* and more to do with the fact that West Germany was, according to Weiss, a politically "verschlafenes Land."[14] Bitter criticism, however, came from both sides of the demarcation line that *Popanz* was drawing. In February 1967, the Lisbon newspaper *Diario de Noticias* reportedly accused both Weiss *and* Sweden of "politische Unwissenheit, Unhöflichkeit und mangelnde Stärke gegenüber Kommunismus," and went on to call *Popanz* "ein Brechmittel."[15] In Sweden, Stockholm theater critics of major newspapers mostly took issue with the play's artistic form, criticizing its pamphlet-like character, the underscoring music, and the journalistic tone of the verse. In an interview with the liberal newspaper *Dagens Nyheter* Weiss expressed his anxiety and confusion about the Stockholm critics' negative remarks, finding their "mangelnde Verständnis für diese neue Theaterform" contradictory in light of what Weiss considered positive public reaction towards *Popanz*.[16]

In West Germany, on the other hand, theater critics seemed much more expressly concerned with calling into question Weiss's political agenda and the effect of *Popanz* on the German political consciousness. One of the more frequent commentators on Weiss's plays, Henning Rischbieter of *Theater heute*, wrote in his review of the Stockholm production that Weiss's work is not a national literature, but rather a literature that belongs to the world in its proclamation of universal responsibility. And although Rischbieter doubted that "...die Bewohner der Bundesrepublik—ihm nachzufolgen in der Lage sind," West Germany owed it to Weiss (as an act of penitence for having forced him into emigration as a child?) to stage his play *Popanz*:

> Die universale Verantwortlichkeit, die er heute literarisch praktiziert, hat er sich auf einem langen und inständig reflektierten Leidensweg teuer genug erkauft. Wir haben kein Recht, ihn zur Rücksichtsnahme auf deutsche Empfindlichkeiten und (von ihm aus gesehen) Provinzialismen zu verpflichten. Er ist als Kind in die Emigration getrieben worden, das hat ihn der Fremdheit und Undurchdringlichkeit der Welt ausgesetzt.... Wir sind es dem literarischen Rang des Autors, unserer Freiheitlichkeit schuldig, das Stück auch in der Bundesrepublik zur Kenntnis zu nehmen, das heißt: aufzuführen.[17]

In October 1967 *Popanz* premiered at the Schaubühne am Halleschen Ufer in West Berlin under the direction of Karl Paryla. In many ways the West Berlin production was the antithesis of the debut in Stockholm. Paryla used eighteen actors and actresses, a seemingly endless array of props, and costumes that were changed frequently from scene to scene. The audience responded enthusiastically to his interpretation of *Popanz*. However, Rischbieter criticized it as:

> ...ein Erfolg mit falschen Mitteln. Paryla hat um jeden Preis "Theater" gemacht. Er hat sich auf die Härte, die Brüche, den Montage-Charakter des Textes nicht eingelassen. Er gibt eine Massen-Show, aufgeputscht, emotional angeheitzt.... Überspannungen, Attacken, Torturen, wie sie das Living Theatre benutzt, um unerträgliche gesellschaftliche Zustände ebenso unerträglich darzustellen, kommen kaum vor. Dem Publikum wird nichts zugemutet, es wird enthusiasmiert.[18]

Yet an even harsher critique came from the *Frankfurter Allgemeine Zeitung*: "...das laute Spektakel ließ uns kalt. Man fühlte sich als Teilnehmer an der angestrengtesten Totgeburt seit langem...."[19] Again, as Weiss had noticed in Stockholm, critics did not seem to share the public's opinion regarding *Popanz*. In Stockholm they had suggested its aesthetic sterility, and here in West Berlin they were condemning it for its theatrical spectacle. In both cases, they claimed, Weiss's intent to politically provoke and agitate the audience was lost: in Stockholm because of boredom and in West Berlin because of distraction. The question remained then for most theater critics: what did Weiss expect to gain in staging *Popanz* in West Germany? Rischbieter asked: "Betrifft uns Angola? Die Frage bleibt offen."[20]

Shortly after its premiere in West Berlin, *Popanz* made its way to Rostock, where it opened in December 1967 at the Volkstheater under the direction of Hanns Anselm Perten. In East Germany, and especially so at the Volkstheater, Weiss was praised as an important socialist author.[21] In a review published in *Die Weltbühne*, *Popanz* is examined under the terms of world-wide revolt against all forms of colonial oppression and imperialistic exploitation. The author commends Weiss's "historisch-sozialer Bewußtheit" and calls *Popanz* "ein politisch-poetisches Exempel, ... dessen Aussagekraft, dessen gedanklich-emotionelle Wirkung sich tief einprägt."[22] In comparison, it might be suggested that, according to critical reviews of the play, the success of *Popanz* in East Germany rested on Weiss's moral call for universal responsibility and solidarity with the third-world, whereas it is this same moral appellation that disturbed and frustrated especially traditional theater audiences in the West, who may have taken personal offense at Weiss's harsh accusations and finger-pointing.

Likewise, in the United States *Popanz*, which debuted in 1968 at the St. Marks Playhouse in New York, seemed to trouble its audiences. The play was performed by an all black cast—the newly formed Negro Ensemble Company—under the direction of Michael A. Schultz. A review in the *New York Times* hints at the emotional unleashing that *Popanz* seems to have evoked among its white American audiences:

> Certainly here and now it [*Popanz*] acquires a remarkable power because of its relevance to our own Negro ghettos, and neither cast nor audience could deny this. By far the most horrifying moment—for a white man at least—comes when the various industries of Angola and Mozambique are impassively listed on one side of the stage, naming all the great European and Anglo-American corporations that have substantial holdings in them, and at the same time, while women moan and a saxophone wails, someone on the other side of the stage describes the wages of the workers. I felt ashamed, and shame is not something I often feel in the theater.[23]

Contrary then to the critics in West Germany, who predicted that the debut of *Popanz* in the United States would hardly evoke the political enlightenment that Weiss had hoped for, since New York audiences demand something other for their money than "ein solches propaganda-erzieherisches Traktat," critics and audiences alike in the United States seemed to recognize the message of the play.[24] For at least some, *Popanz* proved its influence not only by provoking its audience to feel ashamed of the exploitative activity of American cartels and industries in Southern Africa, but also by inspiring its audience to consider what the play teaches white America about the social treatment of the black individual in their own country—and to feel equally ashamed about this.

It has already been noted at the onset of this paper that Weiss's *Popanz* was criticized by some for what they perceived to be a one-sided misrepresentation of the facts concerning Portuguese colonialism in Angola. In a chapter of his book on Peter Weiss entitled "On the Possibility of Demonstrating 'Objective Absurdity': Pertaining to the Question of 'Documentary Theater,'" Otto Best describes this criticism: "The collage of facts selectively chosen according to a preconceived idea, which in turn uses these facts as proof for its validity, does not promote the trait of the documentary that illuminates reality. Instead, it creates subjectively credulous distortion."[25] The questions that remain then are: how well can documentation reflect reality? Can a document – once it is read, once it is reported upon, once it is discussed—remain objective? And in the same vein: can a political agenda melded with poetics succeed as a drama? Again, according to Best:

> ...the method of the documentary theater must fail on principle when it attempts to capture and to put on the stage collective historical events, contemporary social entities, or socioeconomic attitudes for the purpose of discussion and reflection. Their magnitude does not allow an overall perspective and detachment. Documentary theater defeats itself whenever it abandons the ground of critical rationality, which includes liberalism and tolerance—that is, whenever it sacrifices its purpose of enlightening and clarifying to tendentiousness and propaganda.[26]

If, as Best suggests, *Popanz* must fail because Weiss took liberty in choosing and arranging a particular set of documents to underscore and explain his value system, then it may not be productive to judge its success based solely on its documentary method. Rather, as has been attempted here in examining the reception of its staging in Sweden, Germany, and the United States, one must also consider the social, political, and cultural makeup of the audience, as well as what that audience expected to see on stage—which did not always coincide with Weiss's expectations for *Popanz*. Above all Weiss sought to offer his audience a theater event that would not only show them a different perspective on political issues surrounding Angola, but would present this perspective by implementing, according to Weiss, "eine neue und interessante Form."[27] In an interview with Paul Gray of the Living Theatre in New York Weiss expressed his belief that new theatrical techniques were needed to bring audiences closer to what was happening on stage and thus rejuvenate an antiquated theater:

...the traditional theater... is lost, as petrified as the bourgeois audience which goes to it. But there are new possibilities for a theatre which can take up the reality in and around each human life, and a renaissance is coming for theatre from vastly different and unexpected directions—at one side, the theatre of Happenings, and on the other extreme the theatre of documentation.[28]

Accordingly, Weiss believed, as he would later publish in his 1968 article entitled "The Material and the Models: Notes towards a Definition of Documentary Theater," that the theater should takes sides and attempt above all to be an instrument for forming political opinion. In writing *Popanz*, it was not Weiss's intent to be polite and fair. His play was an assault on Portuguese colonialism, as well as an attack on traditional theater. As a result, some audiences were angered with the play's message, others were supportive of its agenda, and still others found themselves enlightened. Thus, perhaps one should examine the success of *Popanz* less in regards to what various audiences and theater critics may have expected and more in light of what Weiss intended to accomplish with *Popanz*—that is, to agitate the political consciousness of his audience and to contribute to a changing direction in theater.

Notes

1   For an insightful evaluation of the US media's representation of the crisis in Angola see, for example: "Text of Stevenson Speech in Security Council on Angola Issue." In: *New York Times* (March 16, 1961), p. 4; "Excerpts from Senator Brooke's Speech on African Policy." In: *New York Times* (April 30, 1968), p. 15.

2   Manfred Durzak, *Dürrenmatt, Frisch, Weiss: Deutsches Drama der Gegenwart zwischen Kritik und Utopie* (Stuttgart 1972), p. 301.

3   Paul Gray, "A Living World: An interview with Peter Weiss." In: *Tulane Drama Review* 11.1 (T33) (Fall 1966), p. 111.

4   Roger Ellis, *Peter Weiss in Exile: A Critical Study of His Works* (Ann Arbor 1987), p. 63.

5   Hans Magnus Enzensberger, "Europäische Peripherie." In: *Kursbuch* 2 (1965), p. 154-73.

6   Peter Weiss, "Brief an H. M. Enzensberger" (1965). In: Weiss, *Rapporte* 2 (Frankfurt a.M. 1971), p. 35-44. Originally published in "Enzensbergers Illusionen." In: *Kursbuch* 6 (July 1966), p. 165-170.

7   Weiss, "Brief an H. M. Enzensberger," p. 35-44.

8   Enzensberger *Kursbuch* 6 (1966), quoted in Reinhard Baumgart, "In die Moral entwischt? Der Weg des politischen Stückschreibers Peter Weiss." In: *Text + Kritik* 37 (January 1973), p. 8.

9   "Nacht mit Gesten." In: *Der Spiegel* 5 (23 January 1967), p. 84.

10 "Nacht mit Gesten," p. 84.

11 Henning Rischbieter, "Lusitanien - das sind auch wir: Giorgio Strehler inszeniert Weissens *Popanz*," *Theater heute* (May 1969), p. 28.

12 Giorgio Polacco, "Unterentwickelte Länder und revolutionäre Welt: Eine Begegnung mit Peter Weiss," (1969). In: Peter Weiss, *Gesang vom Lusitanischen Popanz*. Mit Materialien (Frankfurt a.M. 1974), p. 87.

13 Polacco, p. 87.

14 Henning Rischbieter, "Peter Weiss dramatisiert Vietnam: Ein Gespräch mit dem Autor nach der Uraufführung seines neuen Stückes *Gesang vom lusitanischen Popanz*." In: *Theater heute* 3 (March 1967), p. 7.

15 Henning Rischbieter, "*Gesang vom lusitanischen Popanz*: Das neue Stück von Peter Weiss und dessen Uraufführung in Stockholm." In: *Theater heute* 3 (March 1967), p. 9.

16 Rischbieter, "*Gesang vom lusitanischen Popanz*," p. 11.

17 Rischbieter, "*Gesang vom lusitanischen Popanz*," p. 9-10.

18 Henning Rischbieter, "Realität, Poesie, Politik. Berliner Festwochen 1967:

Stücke von Beckett, Weiss, Itallie, Hochhuth." In: *Theater heute* 11 (November 1967), p. 10.

19 Günther Cwojdrak, "*Lusitanischer Popanz* in Rostock." In: *Die Weltbühne* 2 (9 January 1968), p. 57.

20 Rischbieter, "Realität, Poesie, Politik," p. 14.

21 Robert Cohen, *Understanding Peter Weiss* (Columbia, SC 1993), p. 122.

22 Cwojdrak, "Lusitanischer Popanz in Rostock," p. 58.

23 Clive Barnes, "Theater: *Lusitanian Bogey* Opens. Peter Weiss Denounces Portugal in Africa." In: *New York Times* (3 January 1968), p. 52.

24 Gerard Willem van Loon, "New York: Neger-Ensemble spielt Weiss-Traktat." In: *Die Bühne* 113 (February 1968), p. 20.

25 Otto Best, *Peter Weiss*, trans. Ursule Molinaro (New York: Frederick Ungar, 1976), p. 102.

26 Best, *Peter Weiss*, p. 103.

27 Sun Axelson, "Gespräch mit Peter Weiss," (May 1967). In: *Peter Weiss im Gespräch*, Rainer Gerlach and Matthias Richter, eds. (Frankfurt a.M. 1986), p. 120.

28 Gray, "A Living World: An interview with Peter Weiss," p. 108.

II

Cordelia Scharpf

Vietnam Discourse: Its Reception in the Two Germanys

Peter Weiss's *Viet Nam Discourse* is a further experiment of documentary theater. Like the *Popanz*, the play is intended to inform its audience about the development in Vietnam during the last two millennia, or to be more exact, until 1964 after the Gulf of Tonkin incident. As Weiss stated in his essay "Materials and Models," his new documentary theater takes sides.[1] Unlike *Popanz*, the new play is about groups: the Vietnamese, the French, the Chinese, the Japanese, and about the Americans. It is about the struggle of the oppressed against the oppressors. The *International Dictionary of Theatre* describes it as "parad[ing] a deliberate dramatic unsubtlety and rely[ing] on ritual movement, pantomime, dance, and acrobatics to compensate for the reduction of complicated historical developments to the essentially banal configuration of oppressors versus oppressed."[2]

It has been thirty years since Peter Weiss's *Viet Nam Discourse* was performed in Germany, both East and West. The most recent works on the play were written by two Korean Germanists examining Weiss's image of and his commitment to the Third World. Earlier scholars such as Warneken, Best, Haiduk, Schmitz, and Ellis analyzed the text and the artistic design of the play.[3] A comprehensive study of the reception of the play has not been attempted. The present paper is based primarily on theater reviews of productions in both Germanies and aims to examine its reception at the time of student unrest and political and social change in West Germany. Weiss finished the manuscript *Viet Nam Discourse* in July 1967. Its world première was scheduled for March 1968 in Frankfurt am Main, followed by performances in Munich in July. Many West German theater directors, however, preferred not to stage the play for various artistic and political reasons.[4] In East Germany productions in Rostock and East Berlin were planned. More performances were planned for that year in Stockholm, Oslo, Havanna, Tokyo, and Milan.[5]

On the eve of the world première the playwright expressed his hope that "the audience ... draws conclusions from it and ... finds out more about what the media have failed to inform it" about Vietnam.[6] The "scholarly-epic" documentary drama was intended for West German audiences,[7] for Weiss felt "[n]owhere else is in more urgent need for enlightenment"than in West Germany.[8] Yet in West Germany the play was not only short-lived but also the focus of controversy in the theater world. My hypotheses for the reasons of the play's failure are fourfold: 1) the staging of *Viet Nam Discourse* was too late to effectively serve the purpose intended for the play; 2) the play did not reach the audience Weiss had in mind; 3) it had structural weaknesses, as Warneken and Haiduk point out, which rendered it difficult to be staged effectively; and 4) the staging was misused as a vehicle for "committed" artists to demonstrate their solidarity with the Vietcong.

I

Weiss's concern for Vietnam began to surface in the *Notizbücher* in spring 1965.[9] A few months later he resolved to write "not for the future, and not for eternity. I will write for now, and for changing the situation now. If I were not able to achieve change, then the whole process of writing is meaningless" (I, 473). He began writing in July 1966, aided by Jürgen Horlemann, who had co-authored a book on the genesis of the Vietnam War. Weiss saw their collaboration as a competition between "encyclopedic knowledge as discipline and poetical debauchery" (II, 527). After taking part in the first Russell Tribunal on Vietnam in Stockholm, he published an article on Vietnam documenting American intervention in the civil war. He compared the extent of Vietnamese civilian casualties to that of Guernica, Lidice, and Maidanek.[10]

By the time *Viet Nam Discourse* was staged in March 1968, the German public had been sensitized to the situation in Vietnam through increasing TV coverage, especially about German physicians and nurses in humanitarian missions who were missing after the Tet Offensive. Student-organized teach-ins and study groups among young workers also began to fill the information gap and to protest against the lack of attention given by politicians. Only a month before the première, an International Vietnam Congress was held in West Berlin. It was followed by a demonstration of 15,000 intellectuals, including Weiss and young people. The municipal government in Berlin in turn organized a counter-demonstration of 80,000 marchers in support of US policy.[11] At the Bundestag US policy in Vietnam was debated for the first time on March 14, 1968. But the federal government's ambivalent position remained unchanged, to the dismay of intellectuals and students.[12]

Weiss had the impression that the coverage of Vietnam by West German media was "more American than in reactionary American newspapers."[13] He thought that the media "undernourished" the German public. In fact, however, there was abundant coverage on Vietnam by the media in 1967 and early 1968. If the play had been staged in early 1966, when the first anti-American protests began, it could have had a more meaningful informational and educational effect on its viewers.

II

Who were the viewers of *Viet Nam Discourse*? What happened at West German performances? In the mid-1960s performances of political plays in major cities were frequently disrupted by young audiences demanding discussions of political issues of the day.[14] Expecting trouble, the theater management took extraordinary precaution to ensure that uninvited viewers did not disrupt the world première at Frankfurt's Städtische Bühne. The theater was filled to its capacity of 900 seats with the city's notables, subscription holders, theater critics, and an unusually large number of young people occupying the upper balconies. The audience was generally well-mannered. When the People's Republic of Vietnam was proclaimed at the end of the first act, university and Gymnasium students chanted Ho-Ho-Ho-Chi-Minh with rhythmic clapping of hands.[15] Another precaution the management took was to be prepared for a discussion after the performance. When the play ended, young audiences members stormed the stage, unfurled the flag of the Vietnamese Liberation Front, encircled Weiss, and demanded a discussion.   Jürgen Habermas moderated it, which, as one reporter observed, was accompanied by a verbal vehemence unusual in Frankfurt.[16]   Reviewing contemporary German theater, Hans Mayer concurred with Habermas's

> ... most pertinent remark on the Frankfurt première: that the general irritation felt during the evening was that theater was being used as a substitute for politics.   Policy toward Vietnam was discussed in the theater because the Bundestag in Bonn refrained from doing what is its legitimate duty.[17]

The students in their political revolt now directed their attention to the traditionally unpolitical theater by using it as a forum of political demonstration and discussion.

The performances of *Viet Nam Discourse* in Munich and Berlin during the ensuing months were preceded by scheduled discussions with political scientists and journalists.[18]   Performances were followed by spontaneously demanded discussions which were not always related to the play and "often led nowhere" in resolving political issues.[19]   The play was scheduled for 32 performances during the 1968/69 season in Frankfurt.[20]   In Munich, the production co-directed by the young and much praised director Peter Stein and political scientist Wolfgang Schwiedrzik was discontinued after three performances.[21]   The directors' demand that collections for the Vietcong in the theater was an integral part of the dramaturgy was rejected by the management of a publicly financed theater.[22]   The Stein/Schwiedrzik production at the Schaubühne in Berlin, a privately financed theater, in January 1969 also lasted three times before the management canceled it due to "lack of artistic quality."[23]   The theater reviews, especially in the conservative Springer newspapers, centered on the question of soliciting donations.[24]   A reviewer observed: "The première was used by young people as a provocative occasion to collect money for weapons for the Vietcong."[25] In Frankfurt, Harry Buckwitz solved the problem by allowing donations to be collected outside the theater.   In an interview Buckwitz emphasized that he intended to have collections after each performance and that the money was not only for "weapons for the Vietcong," but also, as students demanded, for supporting deserted American soldiers. He took the precaution to provide for donations outside the theater, for he was aware of the "bureaucratic hurdle" facing a publicly financed theater.[26]

News reports on performances of *Viet Nam Discourse* in East Germany also mentioned players mingling with audiences after the final curtain to collect donations for Vietnam.[27] In East Germany, youth groups, artists, solidarity committees and citizens' initiative groups collected money and goods to support the People's Republic of Vietnam.[28] By then, the play was used as a vehicle for expressing political solidarity with North Vietnam, thereby fulfilling Weiss's hope for audiences to become politically engaged.

III

The review articles of performances in both Germanies give sufficient descriptions of the set, figures, and speeches to allow a categorization of the productions into three types. The first type of production is characterized by a close reading of Weiss's text and a faithful execution of stage directions as he specified in his unusually detailed instructions for each phase or scene of the play. This is exemplified in the Frankfurt production by Buckwitz. The second type is characterized by modification in varying degrees of text and stage directions to accommodate a certain type of audience or dramaturgy. The production by Hanns Anselm Perten of Rostock and to an extent the staging by Ruth Berghaus at the Berliner Ensemble fall into this category. Finally, the third type is characterized by remodeling the text and stage directions to suit purposes other than those intended by the playwright.

In Frankfurt, Buckwitz and his ensemble began rehearsing the world première of the play on February 5, 1968.[29] Weiss and his wife, who designed the set, frequented the rehearsals (II, 567). The dramaturgy closely followed Weiss's text and stage instructions. The production ran over three hours during which "all scenes, choreographical and musical elements serve to illustrate what is being spoken (thereby doubling), to offer to the eyes what the ears have long perceived."[30] The writer Egon Menz observed the rehearsals at length and reported that the initial tendency of the players was to dramatize the roles, but beginning with the fourth week of rehearsals, the trend reversed itself and many roles were simplified. Weiss and Buckwitz decided to show a documentary film of contemporary Vietnam in a separate room. Menz felt that the film could be used as a third part of the play, allowing the audience to draw its own conclusions.[31] Many critics praised Buckwitz's direction and his young ensemble for staging an extremely difficult play.[32] Günther Rühle found the production uneven, but there were many well-choreographed and well-performed pieces.[33] Joachim Kaiser called the production mediocre and found that Weiss failed to use the stage effectively as "a vehicle of his truth." Instead of a political theater, he continued, the production reminded him of a badly played Chinese Opera.[34] Walter Jens critiqued that the *Discourse* was "not gripping and not very instructive [belehrend]. ... [R]esults were shown, but not the process; theater goers see the conditions, but are not informed about the development." Jens summed up: "The overly schematic accusation here, and the overly schematic glorification there saved the predatory warriors [Raubkrieger] from the worst. The play lacks cunningness and explosiveness."[35]

Perten's production in Rostock was reported as "electrifying" and it was "a politically and artistically impressive theatrical experience."[36] East German theater critic Ernst Schumacher saw the danger of the first act becoming monotonous and the second act being lost amidst recitation of imperialistic statements. He thought players should develop a "collective individuality" for their roles. Contrary to Weiss's and Palmstierna's instruction, colorful vests were added to the white costumes. He reported that Perten was able to present historical phases "not as a constant repetition of the same" but instead "as spiral, as phases of development."[37] In the production by Berghaus in East Berlin, however, Schumacher saw players developing, according to his metaphor, "an individualized collectivity." Berghaus "illuminated" the play by assigning 10 individual players to represent various groups with symbolic postures. The music by Paul Dessau, Berghaus's husband, was melodious and lyrical. Schumacher observed that the few scenes Berghaus chose from the first act resembled a Chinese opera and the second act a gangster spectacle. He concluded that it was an interesting experiment because it tried—in its headstrong way—to grapple with the "weakness inherent in documentary theater." He praised Berghaus for making an effort to fulfill the Berliner Ensemble tradition by finding an adequate form to present a difficult text.[38] On the contrary, Weiss wrote: "[They] completely missed the mark. It was a pain to see it, especially at this theater" (II, 576). Writing for *Neues Deutschland*, Rainer Kerndle found Berghaus trying with "small" but precisely studied details in the performance to show "the dialectics of the social and political course of events." Berghaus tried to reflect the grandeur of events, heroism in political actions, and opportunism of collaborators through realistically played scenes. She did not always succeed, Kerndl said, "[but] the obvious meagerness of the text ... forces [one] to experiment."[39]

If the productions in Rostock and East Berlin represent an experiment for a well-informed socialist audience who needed more than just scenic documentation and information,[40] the productions by Stein and Schwiedrzik in Munich and Berlin represent an entirely different approach. The strongly abbreviated text was barely adequate in conveying the history of Vietnam until 1945. For the second act players with oversized masks representing American oppressors joined Chinese-like and French-like figures, and together they made unbearable noise through megaphones for over ten minutes to the annoyance of the audience. Star actor Wolfgang Neuss appeared as a moderator, interjecting his own commentaries and playing antics.[41] The eighty minute performance was, in Urs Jenny's words: "far from Weiss ... [thereby] declaring the play useless and illusory."[42] Jenny regretted that Weiss's original intention was grossly sacrificed to the point that the production could no longer be called a "discourse."[43] Recalling the Frankfurt staging of the play, which was characterized by "monumental aestheticizing [and] ceremonial sumptuousness" and which elevated the *Viet Nam Discourse* to an oratorio, Jenny could only lament its demise.[44] Weiss was equally dismayed about the fate of his play in Germany when he wrote a year after the Berlin performances: "Where is the director who could stage such a piece faithfully, sober, matter-of-fact, stimulating thinking (don't give a damn about emotions) (and about the Show), adding nothing to [it], which is only external—and where is the ensemble?" (II, 694).

IV

The reasons for the demise of the *Viet Nam Discourse* are not to be found in Weiss's text or in its dramaturgy. The play was staged at a time in West Germany when theater was going through turmoil in an attempt to restructure itself—the younger generation of theater-makers preferred to call it "democratizing" itself. Leading journals on theater abounded with discussion papers, models, and pronouncements of "theater-collectives."[45] It is not the purpose of this paper to elaborate on this development, but one can say that Weiss's *Viet Nam Discourse* was caught in the throes of the process; it was used as a vehicle of confrontation between conservative theater managements and progressive theater directors; and it served as an arena of confrontation between theater directors and members of ensembles, as was the case with Berlin's Schaubühne in January 1969.[46]

In conclusion, by the time *Viet Nam Discourse*, the work of the politically committed writer, was staged by Stein and Schwiedrzik, equally politically committed stage directors, it was no longer a documentary drama and discourse but an agit-prop and "Kasperltheater"—it retained entertainment value. It did not enlighten its audience but instigated it to political action. Botho Strauß commented that "[i]n 1968, this political theater reflects change in our political consciousness."[47] Although Weiss was not satisfied with performances in West Germany and his play arrived too late to reach its intended audience, it nonetheless served to confirm the change that was already underway.

Notes

1   Peter Weiss, "Materials and Models." In: *Theater Quarterly* 1.1 (1971), p. 41-43.

2   John P. Wieczorek, "Peter Weiss," *International Dictionary of Theater - Playwrights*, Mark Hawkins-Dady, ed. (Detroit 1994), p. 1031-1033 (here p. 1032).

3   Hyeong Shik Kim, *Peter Weiss' 'Viet Nam Diskurs': Möglichkeiten und Formen eines Engagements für die Dritte Welt* (New York 1992); Yong-Dae Kim, *Das Dritte-Welt-Bild in deutschsprachigen Dramen der Gegenwart: Eine vergleichende Untersuchung am Beispiel von Stücken Peter Weiss' und Hans Magnus Enzensberger.* (1993); Bernd Jürgen Warneken, "Kritik am *Viet Nam Diskurs*," in *Über Peter Weiss,* Volker Canaris, Hrsg (Frankfurt am Main: Suhrkamp, 1970), 112-130; Otto Best, *Peter Weiss* (New York 1976); Manfred Haiduk, *Der dramatiker Peter Weiss* (Berlin 1977); Ingeborg Schmitz, *Dokumentartheater bei Peter Weiss: Von der 'Ermittlung' zu 'Hölderlin'* (Frankfurt a.M. 1981); Roger Ellis, *Peter Weiss in Exile: A Critical Study of His Works* (Ann Arbor, MI 1986).

4   "Theater. Weiss. Dollars für Ho." In: *Der Spiegel* (25 March 1968), p. 181-82.

5   "Die Vietnam Runde." In: *Frankfurter Allgemeine Zeitung* (28 March 1968), p. 10.

6   Peter Iden, "Vietnam auf der Bühne: Ein Interview mit Peter Weiss und Harry Buckwitz." In: *Die Zeit* (22 March 1968), p. 17.

7   Manfred Müller and Wolfram Schütte, "'Der Kampf geht weiter': FR-Gespräch mit dem Dramatiker Peter Weiss anläßlich der Weltpremiere seines *Vietnam-Diskurses* in Frankfurt," (16 March 1968). In: *Peter Weiss im Gespräch,* Rainer Gerlach and Matthias Richter, eds. (Frankfurt a.M. 1986), p. 136-43 (here p. 138).

8   Claes Sturm, "Peter Weiss fordert Westdeutschland heraus." In: *Dagens Nyheter* (20 March 1968). Reprinted in Gerlach and Richter, *Peter Weiss im Gespräch,* p. 149-53 (here p. 149).

9   Peter Weiss, *Notizbücher 1960-1971* (Frankfurt a.M. 1982), vol. I, p. 371 (early May 1965). Hereafter cited in parentheses.

10 Peter Weiss, "Vietnam!" In: *Rapporte 2* (Frankfurt a.M. 1971), p. 61.

11 Karl A. Otto, *APO: Außerparlamentarische Opposition in Quellen und Dokumenten (1960-1970)* (Köln 1989), p. 206 and p. 431-32. "Berlin." In: *Der Spiegel* 9 (26 February 1968), p. 23-25.

12 "Bonn. Lage der Nation." In: *Der Spiegel* (18 March 1968), p. 31-32; "Beitrag zur atomaren Hi... Martin Walser über die Vietnam-Debatte des Bundestages." In: *Der Spiegel* (18 March 1968), p. 185.

13 Sturm, p. 149.

14 "Theater. Politisierung. Thriller mit Teufel." In: *Der Spiegel* (10 June 1968), p. 113-14.

15 o-k. "Junges Publikum feierte *Vietnam-Diskurs*: Keine Zwischenfälle bei Peter Weiss' Welturaufführung / Diskussion nach der Pause." In: *Frankfurter Rundschau* (24 March 1968), p. 10.

16 Rolf Dornbacher, "Sensationeller Uraufführungserfolg für Weiss-*Diskurs* in Frankfurt. Ho, Ho, Ho-Tschi-Minh." In: *Abendzeitung* (München, 22 March 1968), p. 7.

17 Hans Mayer, "Die Bühne - ein Museum?" Bildung, Besitz und Theater (II). In: *Die Zeit* (27 September 1968), p. 22-23.

18 M.G. "Viet-Nam-Diskussion in den Münchener Kammerspielen." In: *Süddeutsche Zeitung* (4 July 1968), p. 26, and (6/7 July 1968), p. 12.

19 George Salmony, "Peter-Weiss-Premier im Werkraumtheater: Diskurs mit der Narrenpritsche." In: *Abendzeitung* (München, 8 July 1968), p. 11.

20 Klaus Antes and Harald Jung, "AZ-Umfrage bei deutschen Theatern: Spenden für den Vietcong? An sich schon, aber ...." In: *Abendzeitung* (München, 18 July 1968), p. 6.

21 "*Viet Nam Diskurs* abgesetzt." In: *Abendzeitung* (München, 17 July 1968), p. 9.

22 K.B. "Kammerspiel-Direktion verbietet Vietcong-Sammlung: Vorläufig kein Kommentar." In: *Abendzeitung* (München, 9 July 1968), p. 8.

23 Joachim Preuß, "Gespräch mit Jürgen Schitthelm über Absetzung des *Vietnam-Diskurs*." In: Manuscript, Sender Freies Berlin, Theater-Redaktion, Galerie des Theaters, Neue Folge 120. (19 January 1969), p. 8-14.

24 Horst Windelboth, "Nicht mehr als ein Happening zum Gaudi neugieriger Besucher: Turbulente Premiere des *Vietnam-Diskurs* in der Schaubühne" and "Schmutziges Geld." In: *Berliner Morgenpost* (16 January 1969).

25 Rolf Michaelis, "Vereinstheater" Der *Vietnam-Diskurs* in Berlin." In: *Frankfurter Allgemeine Zeitung* (16 January 1969).

26 Antes und Jung, p. 6.

27 "Engagiert." In: *Die Zeit* (5 April 1968); dpa, "*Vietnam-Diskurs* in der DDR." In: *Süddeutsche Zeitung* (2 April 1968), p. 14.

28 "Helft Vietnam!" In: *Berliner Zeitung* (13 March 1968), p. 12; "Stromaggregate für Vietnam: Jugendbrigade spendete 12 000 Mark /

Stahlbauzug aus Dresden für DRV." In: *Berliner Zeitung* (9 May 1968), p. 2.

29   Egon Menz, "Probenbericht vom *Diskurs über Viet Nam*." In: *Theater heute* 4 (April 1968), p. 12-15.

30   Müller and Schütte.

31   Menz, p. 14.

32   Walther Karsch, "Manipulierte Dokumentation: Peter Weiss' *Viet Nam Diskurs* uraufgeführt." In: *Tagesspiegel* (Berlin 22 March 1968), p. 4; Günther Rühle, "Der lange Feldzug des Peter Weiss. *Vietnam Diskurs*: Uraufführung im Frankfurter Schauspielhaus." In: *Frankfurter Allgemeine Zeitung* (22 March 1968), p. 32; Wolfram Schütte, "Abstraktionen: Peter Weiss' *Vietnam Diskurs* in Frankfurt uraufgeführt." In: *Frankfurter Rundschau* (22 March 1968), p. 15.

33   Rühle, p. 32.

34   Joachim Kaiser, "Vietnam oder: Bühne als politische Anstalt. Zur Uraufführung des *Vietnam-Diskurses* von Peter Weiss in Frankfurt." In: *Süddeutsche Zeitung* (22 March 1968), p. 11.

35   Walter Jens, "Fünf Minuten großes politisches Theater: Zur Uraufführung des Viet-Nam-Stücks von Peter Weiss in Frankfurt." In: *Die Zeit* (29 March 1968), p. 18.

36   "*Vietnam-Diskurs* in Der DAR." In: *Süddeutsche Zeitung* (2 April 1968), p. 14.

37   Ernst Schumacher, "*Vietnam-Diskurs* in Rostock: Zur DDR-Erstaufführung des Stückes von Peter Weiss im Volkstheater." In: *Berliner Zeitung* (11 April 1968), p. 6.

38   Schumacher, p. 6.

39   Rainer Kerndl, "Interessante Variante: Zur Aufführung des *Viet Nam Diskurs* von Peter Weiss im Berliner Ensemble." In: *Neues Deutschland* (Berliner Ausgabe, 11 May 1968), p. 14.

40   Schumacher, "*Viet Nam Diskurs*: Diskutables Experiment im Berliner Ensemble."

41   Wolfgang Petzet, *Theater: Die Münchener Kammerspiele 1911-1972* (München 1973), p. 540; Salmomy, ; Urs Jenny, *Süddeutsche Zeitung* (8 July 1968), p. 12; Heinz Ritter, "Revue der Verlegenheit: Diskurs über Vietnam und eine Theaterpremiere." In: *Der Abend* (Berlin 15 January 1969); Claus Menzel, "Kurioser Vietnam-Diskurs in Berlin." In: Manuskript "Kulturelles Wort." In: Hessischer Rundfunk, Frankfurt am Main (16 January 1969); Günther Grack, "Ein unordentlicher Abend: Peter Weiss' *Vietnam-Diskurs* in der Schaubühne." In: *Tagesspiegel* (16 January

1969).

42 Urs Jenny, "Fern von Weiss." In: *Theater heute* 8 (August 1968), p. 37.

43 Urs Jenny, "Ja, die bösen Amerikaner: *Viet Nam Diskurs* von Peter Weiss im Münchener Werkraumtheater." In: *Süddeutsche Zeitung* (8 July 1968), p. 12.

44 Jenny, "Ja, die bösen Amerikaner."

45 *Theater heute* (1968) carried series of articles on this topic.

46 Das Vietnam-Kollektiv des Ensembles der Staatsbühne am Halleschen Ufer, "3. Rückblick auf die Arbeit am *Viet Nam Diskurs* der Schaubühne am Halleschen Ufer, Berlin." In: "Materialien zur Kollektivarbeit im Theater," *Theater heute* 4 (April 1969), p. 24-25. Note: the Schaubühne am Halleschen Ufer was a GmbH, a company with private ownership. It received subsidies from Berlin's Senate but never was a "Staatstheater."

47 Botho Strauß, "3. Chronik: Bilderbuch der Schauspielsaison." In: *Theater heute: Theater 1968 - Das Jahr im Bild* (1968), p. 40.

III

Jennifer Jenkins

Weiss's "Third World": Its Construct and Portrayal in *Engagierte Literatur* of the 1960's

The so-called "Third World" had been of interest to writers and literary scholars prior to the 1960's, as Rüdiger Sareika has illustrated in discussing treatments of colonial aspects of the Franco-Algerian war by writers such as Alfred Andersch.[1] However, whereas in the 1950's countries of the southern hemisphere had for the most part been regarded as interesting owing to their "exoticness," it was the specific climate of political protest during the 1960's with the backdrop of the Vietnam War which served as a breeding ground for political and artistic confrontations with the these contries, referred to collectively as the "Third World", in the Federal Republic of Germany.

The hypocritical role of the USA perceived in the brutal suppression of the popularly supported communist government in North Vietnam had added flames to the fire of protests of a generation of German university students, initiated by the students of the Freie Universität in West Berlin and later continued by a larger group of young citizens in the "APO" or Außerparlamentarische Opposition. These students questioned in general the use of violence in political conflict, as well as the right of one country to impose its ideology upon another. In addition, they criticized the lack of self-examination on the part of their own West German government in the economic restoration of the prosperous, "new," post-World War II West Germany. This spirit of protest was captured and nurtured by several contemporary authors, the most vocal among them in West Germany being Peter Weiss and Hans-Magnus Enzensberger.[2]

How was the "Third World" used in the politically engaged literature of the 1960's? I begin by proposing that it was not solely due to egotistical and Eurocentric concerns that the aforementioned writers turned with literary interest to the "Third World"; they did genuinely hope to effect change in those countries (such as Angola and Vietnam in Weiss's case) in which their works were centered.   However, a "self-interest" can be seen in their good intentions and in the ways progress was encouraged.   Peter Weiss, committed Marxist and member of the Swedish communist party since 1968, was certainly selective in choosing the "Third World" sources with whom he engaged in conversation and/or interviewed, among them the communist leaders in North Vietnam and Fidel Castro in Cuba.   If "common folk" were interviewed, such as the artists and poets in *Notizen zum Kulturellen Leben der Demokratischen Republik Viet Nams*, they were supporters and propagators of communist revolutionary impulses.   It was, then, not necessarily the "Third World" as a whole that interested Weiss, but rather those elements he found there which supported his political beliefs.   Considering the fact that Weiss seems, viewed thus, to be approaching the "Third World" from a standpoint of "what do I want" as opposed to "what do these countries want and/or need," this would seem a rather undemocratic way of going about propagating change (and I say this in the assumption that capitalist systems do not have a monopoly on democracy).   It would seem on the surface almost as if Weiss himself were committing here a form of ideological imperialism. This, however, is not the case, since Weiss was not writing for a Third World audience, and it becomes evident that such works would not have found a receptive audience in the "Third World."

In her essay "Die Rolle der deutschen Literatur im Modernisierungprozeß eines afrikanischen Entwicklungslandes" Edith Ihekweazu informs us that the citizens of these countries do not want a representative of a "First World" country telling them how badly the industrialized nations have it as a result of the modernization that comes, presumably, with capitalism:

> Nichts ist frustrierender für den Bürger eines Entwicklungslandes als der warnende Hinweis auf die Leiden der Industrieländer.... Man will wissen, wie man am schnellsten auf die Bahn der Modernisierung gerät, und ist nicht daran interessiert, welche Leiden und Entsagungen damit verbunden sind: denn diese erscheinen allemal geringer als die gegenwärtigen.[3]

With this in mind, it would perhaps be helpful to consider the limitations of those socially critical literary works of the 1960's which based themselves on constructs of the "Third World," as regards the "usefulness" of this literature for those actually living in "Third World" countries. Put simply, people who have never had electricity or running water in their homes will not be particularly concerned with the purported "loss of innocence" which, we are told, comes with modernization. Ihekweazu also warns against particular tendencies on the part of Western literature, especially as regards Africa, in demonstrating "entwicklungshelferischer Enthusiasmus" and more importantly "naïve Solidarität," presumably by Westerners who themselves have never lived as, or even with, the colonized in colonial lands.[4] This begs the question as to the extent to which well-intentioned "outsiders" can in fact claim solidarity with those who have suffered under colonization.

In writing about a suffering of a different kind, Peter Weiss depicts in *Meine Ortschaft* (1964) his discovery that the sufferings of those who perished at Auschwitz were far removed from his own sphere of experience:

> Ein Lebender ist gekommen, und vor diesem Lebenden verschließt sich, was hier geschah. Der Lebende, der hierherkommt aus einer anderen Welt, besitzt nichts als seine Kenntnisse von Ziffern, von niedergeschriebenen Berichten, von Zeugenaussagen, sie sind Teil seines Lebens, er trägt daran, doch fassen kann, was ihm selbst widerfährt. Nur wenn er selbst von seinem Tisch gestoßen und gefesselt wird, wenn er getreten und gepeitscht wird, weiß er, was dies ist. Nur wenn es neben ihm geschieht, daß man sie zusammentreibt, niederschlägt, in Fuhren lädt, weiß er, was dies ist. Jetzt steht er nur in einer untergegangenen Welt. Hier kann er nichts mehr tun.[5]

Can a similar conclusion be drawn as regards solidarity of relatively privileged "First World" citizens with the "Third World" oppressed? One such conclusion can, up to a point, be arrived at in conjunction with the suffering caused by colonialism by substituting the word "Weißer" for "Lebender" in the above passage:

> Ein Weißer ist gekommen, und vor diesem Weißen verschließt sich, was hier geschah. Der Weiße, der hierherkommt aus einer anderen Welt, besitzt nichts

als seine Kenntnisse von Ziffern, von niedergeschlagenen Berichten, von
Zeugenaussagen, sie sind Teil seines Lebens, er trägt daran, doch fassen kann,
was ihm selbst widerfährt.

This comparison is not as far off as it may seem on the surface, since in
part Weiss's own crisis of identity and his relationship to Auschwitz in
the first place led to his literary-political awakening and then to his
engagement in the plight of "Third World" countries.

If this literature was not directly addressing the "Third World," then
the real function of the "Third World" must be investigated in the works
of those authors in the 1960's who wrote about it. The slowly emerging
examination of Europe's colonialist past by both European scholars as
well as those, such as Frantz Fanon, from formerly colonized countries
certainly can be credited with helping to bring the "Third World" into
the spotlight of leftist academic interest, as well as making it a relevant
subject for literary representation during this time.   However, the
question of the author's individual identity is also a revealing factor in
explaining why this topic moved into the center of leftist literary
discourse during these years. David Bathrick discusses

> ... the relation of the Third World as a locus of a new—in some cases,
> pristine—historical subject to the vital issue of an individual writer's own
> identity: of political and national, but also of psychological and aesthetic
> identity as well... It is for this reason significant that a number of Germany's
> most radical playwrights from the East and West have written key plays about,
> and centered in, the Third World, and that in each instance the implications of
> their choice of subject matter have meant an important political and aesthetic
> "re-locating" for the writer's development as a whole.[6]

Bathrick suggests here that the "Third World" served the specific
purpose of providing a perspective around which German writers could
situate themselves and through which a new locus of self-orientation
could be formed, a development which certainly can be considered
progressive and constructive as far as its implications for the writing of
literature are concerned. By locating themselves outside of the "First
World" capitalistic systems in which they lived and wrote, these authors
were able if not to present necessarily an "outsider's view" of these
economical and political systems, then at least to provide useful

contrasts with which they confronted those societal structures they perceived to be unjust or ineffective.

It is interesting to note that Germans were not the only ones engaged with the "Third World" in this manner. To name just a few representative examples, the Swedish writer Sara Lidman was an active voice in the anti-Vietnam War protests, whose writings focused on depressed areas of her own country as well as Viet Nam. Jan Myrdal, also Swedish, spent time in Afghanistan, India, and China. Both espoused the position of the "tredje ståndpunkt" or "third standpoint," a position of nonalignment and neutrality in Swedish foreign policy between the capitalist and communist poles during the cold war. They also used the "Third World" in their writings as a vehicle for expressing progressive politics. Sara Lidman spent a month in North Vietnam and wrote upon her return "Samtal i Hanoi" (Conversation in Hanoi), which in several obvious ways seems to have been a forerunner to Weiss's *Notizen zum kulturellen Leben der Demokratischen Republik Viet Nams*.[7] As Weiss was not only living in Sweden but also fluent in Swedish and surely no stranger to the literature being produced there at this time, it should come as no surprise that these authors influenced the production of his works centered in the "Third World."

Returning to the question of the role the "Third World" played in European literature of the 1960's, I believe its presence in these works becomes most problematic when we examine more closely some self-centered and even perhaps falsifying uses to which it was put. Edith Ihekweazu writes that European literature has, in its own self-reflection, appropriated and instrumentalized the "Third World" as a "pure" place in contrasting it with the "spoiled" West:

> Die europäische Literatur hat die Rolle übernommen, unglückliches Bewußtsein zu formulieren oder auch auf frühere und glücklichere Bewußtseinszustände zu verweisen, gelegentlich auch auf die einer edlen und unverdorbenen Dritten Welt.[8]

Additionally, Arlene Teraoka, Sara Lennox, and David Bathrick have discussed the ways in which concepts, or more precisely, constructs of the "Third World" were developed and used by leftist authors in West Germany for their own purposes. The constructs "had much more to do with their own political needs than with the realities of particular non-Western countries."[9]   What were these political needs?   Most obvious for writers like Weiss was the need for criticism of the governmental systems in place in Western Europe at the time.   The "Third World" was taken as the basis for such criticism, since these writers saw in it a model with which they could more clearly demonstrate the faults of the existing systems by "alienating" the problems at home (both in the sense of isolating and making them "strange" or "foreign"). Along these lines, David Bathrick states that *Der Gesang vom Lusitanischen Popanz*

> demonstrates an optimism about the coalescence of black and white revolution which tells us more about European intellectuals in the 1960's than it does about the historical realities of Third and First World politics.[10]

This passage certainly reflects Peter Weiss's stance concerning revolutionary ideas, and it was in part his optimism and belief in the possibility of solidarity between the white "First World" oppressed and "Third World" victims of colonialism which formed the cornerstone of the debate between Weiss and Hans Magnus Enzensberger in the 1966 *Kursbuch*.

Kai Köhler has gone a step further in examining the ways in which treatments of the "Third World" were employed by these authors for their own purposes. He suggests that Peter Weiss, for example, has taken his knowledge of a particular Third World country (here, regarding the examination of Vietnamese culture in *Notizen zum kulturellen Leben der Demokratischen Republik Viet Nams*) and not only defends the conscious modification on the part of the Vietnamese of their own history, but he also himself "mythifies" the concept of cultural life there. In discussing the form of the *Notizen*, Köhler writes:

> Mythos, Märchen, Anekdote, politischer Bericht und Gesprächsprotokoll sind stilistisch vereinheitlicht... Die Anordnung der Episoden dient nicht dazu, Kontraste hervorzuheben, sondern ein einheitliches, poetisiertes Bild Vietnams zu evozieren... Die Kultur, der Mythos werden von der Gegenwart aus bestimmt, doch ist diese Gegenwart ihrerseits eine mythisierte.[11]

Further on, he cites entries in Weiss's *Notizbücher*, such as "Der Weg zu einem neuen Internationalismus hat in Viet Nam zunächst über das Nationale zu gehn," and that it was "notwendig, für den nationalen Kampf die Geschichte zu revidieren" the result of a lack of better alternatives.[12]   Peter Weiss presents here an excuse for nationalistic tendencies, which seems to show the limitations of employing the Third World as a model for Western nations, since it can assuredly be assumed that the notion of a "necessary nationalism" would never have been espoused by leftist writers in their quest to change the political system extant in Germany in the 1960's.

With the example of Vietnam, Weiss perhaps unwittingly showed that the "Third World" can not be viewed as the unspoiled, pristine source of solutions to the West's problems, since it had unique limitations of its own.   In functioning as a model, the "Third World" could only suggest alternative courses of action, but it did not allow itself to be molded into an answer to the challenges facing "First World" countries.

Notes

1   Rüdiger Sareika, "Von der Systemkritik zur Ethnopoesie," *Dieser Tag voller Vulkane: Ein Dritte-Welt-Lesebuch*, Christian Schaffernicht ed. (Fischerhude 1983).

2   Arlene Teraoka, *East, West and Others* (Lincoln: University of Nebraska Press, 1996), p. 28.

3   Edith Ihekweazu, "Die Rolle der deutschen Literatur im Modernisierungsprozeß eines afrikanischen Entwicklungslandes." In: *Proceedings of the Symposium Interkulturelle Deutschstudien: Methoden, Möglichkeiten und Modelle*, Takayama/ Japan 1990, Kenichi Mishima and Hikaru Tsuji eds. (Munich 1992), p. 50.

4   Ihekweazu, p. 57.

5   Peter Weiss, *Rapporte* (Frankfurt am Main: Suhrkamp, 1968), 124.

6   David Bathrick, "'The Theater of the White Revolution Is Over': The Third World in the Works of Peter Weiss and Heiner Müller," *Blacks and German Culture* (Monatshefte Occasional Volume Number 4), Reinhold Grimm and Jost Hermand, eds. (Madison, WI 1986), p. 136.

7   Torgny Schunnesson and Lars Wickman, "Varför skriver Sara Lidman inte romaner längre?" In: *Linjer I Nordisk Prosa Sverige 1965-1975*, Kjerstin Norén, ed. (Lund 1977), p. 267-93.

8   Ihekweazu, p. 47.

9   Teraoka , p. 31.

10 Bathrick, p. 141.

11 Kai Köhler, "Mythisierung des Widerstands? Peter Weiss' *Notizen zum kulturellen Leben in der Demokratischen Republik Viet Nam*." In: *Peter Weiss Jahrbuch* 2 (1993), p. 101.

12 Köhler, p. 103.

Robert Cohen

A Dream of Dada and Lenin:
Peter Weiss's *Trotsky in Exile*

Of all of Peter Weiss's works, none has been rejected as vehemently and
purged from the canon as completely as his play of 1970, *Trotsky in
Exile*. Appearing as it did in the year of Lenin's one hundredth birthday,
Trotsky in Exile was declared an anti-communist provocation in the
Soviet Union and the GDR, a distortion and defacement of the historical
truth,[1] and as "objectively counterrevolutionary."[2] Weiss was treated as a
renegade and, in one famous incident, was even denied access to the
GDR, where he had visited many times before, where he had important
friends and interlocutors, and where his previous plays had been staged
with great care. Only with the opening, in 1973, of his following play,
Hölderlin, in the east German city of Rostock, did this period of
estrangement officially come to an end.[3] West German critics denounced
Trotsky in Exile in equally vehement tones, although ostensibly not for
its content. This should, however, not be mistaken for tolerance toward
Weiss's project. The indignation of critics having to sit through endless
intra-communist debates over obscure minutiae of Soviet history
resurfaced in the guise of a rejection of the play's aesthetics. *Trotsky in
Exile*, according to these critics, was nothing but a crude montage of
headlines and front page articles, of facts and figures, of themes and
quotations.[4] Implied in these judgments was the notion that what Lenin
said to Trotsky, what Trotsky did to the sailors of Kronstadt, and what
Stalin did to Trotsky and to the old guard of the Bolsheviks were not fit
subjects for the lofty realm of art. The elimination of his new play from
the public sphere took its toll on Peter Weiss. In June of 1970, he
suffered a heart attack. During the months of his recuperation he
produced a lengthy prose piece containing lucid passages on the public
demolition of *Trotsky in Exile* and shedding light on Weiss's con-
ceptualization of the play. This text was published almost ten years after
Weiss's death, under the title *Rekonvaleszenz* (convalescence).

I do not think that the end of the Cold War marks a radical historical rupture which all of a sudden allows for a dispassionate re-reading of works such as *Trotsky in Exile*. Many of the issues presented in the play, from Stalinist repression to the upheaval and revolts in what is still called, for lack of a more appropriate term, the Third World, from the trauma of Trotsky's personal life to the trauma of the Moscow trials, still arouse passion.[5] What the years which have elapsed since the fall of the Berlin Wall should facilitate, however, is a reading of the play which goes beyond a mere discussion of its historical and factual accuracy, to investigate the ways in which it inscribes itself in the sphere of art rather than historiography.

I

At the end of Scene 7 of *Trotsky in Exile*, Trotsky tells Lenin of his experience of going to the theater for the very first time:

> It was overwhelming. Indescribable. Out of my mind nearly at what was going on. Sat through all the intermissions in case I might miss something. Afterwards they asked me: what did you see? I couldn't say. What had I seen? What had I seen? (52)

This is one of several passages which can be read as a kind of autopoetics of the play. Its tone is set by the staccato phrasing which pervades much of the play's dialogue and tends to defamiliarize the seemingly realistic exchanges. The theatergoer described by Trotsky is in a state of feverish confusion approaching madness, emphasized by his anxious repetition of the question "What had I seen?" As much as to Lenin this question seems to be addressed to the reader or spectator of *Trotsky in Exile*. What, indeed, are we reading or seeing when we read or see Weiss's play?[6]

Trotsky in Exile presents a series of historical tableaux from the life of Lev Davidovich Bronstein, alias Trotsky (1879-1940), from his earliest banishment by the Czar at the turn of the century, through his rise to the highest positions in the Soviet government, first as foreign minister, then as founder of the Red Army, and through his fall, after

Stalin's ascendance to power, to his exile and finally his murder, arranged by the Soviet secret service, in Mexico City, in 1940.[7] But this is not a dramatized biography. Before it even starts the play emits signals, at least to the reader, that its realm is not that of history and that its dramatic mode is far from any traditional notion of realistic representation. The list of cast members includes more than sixty names. Close to forty more appear in the play. In all there are more than one hundred speaking parts. Never mind that there cannot be many commercial theaters capable of casting such a play, at least not if they wish to make a profit. But why include among the cast not only figures such as Inessa Armand, Plekhanov, Parvus, and Shlyapnikov, who might be vaguely familiar to some of the play's readers and viewers, but also the likes of Sermuks, Luzin, Akimov, and so on? Many of these historically authentic but obscure figures have only a few lines of dialogue, anyway. Also, if staged in its entirety, *Trotsky in Exile* would last four to five hours. Weiss rejected any suggestion of cutting his play and insisted it be staged in full.[8] Much of the play's time is taken up by the long political debates deplored by Weiss's critics. What is at work here is an aesthetic concept which underlies much of Weiss's work and which was revealed to a worldwide theatergoing public in the mid-1960s through the title of a play: *The Persecution and Assassination of Jean-Paul Marat as Performed by the Inmates of the Asylum of Charenton under the Direction of Monsieur de Sade.* The length of this title is, of course, excessive, and Weiss followed it four years later with an even longer title: *Discourse on the Progress of the Prolonged War of Liberation in Viet Nam and the Events Leading up to It as Illustration of the Necessity for Armed Resistance against Oppression and on the Attempts of the United States of America to Destroy the Foundations of Revolution.* These titles are only the most obvious manifestations of what might be called Weiss's *aesthetic of excess.*

Excess is what drives Weiss's work, from the titles to the number of cast members to the lengths of his plays (*The Investigation* would take several nights to perform in full). The novel *The Aesthetics of Resistance* is 1000 pages long. Excess also characterizes *ex negativo* the minimalist appearance of a work such as *Leavetaking*, which consists of one single uninterrupted block of text. But the defining aspect of excess in Weiss's work is its excessive depiction of physical pain and suffering, from the elegiac passages on the slaughter of horses, in *Von Insel zu Insel* (From Island to Island, 1944)[9] to the quartering of Damiens in *Marat/Sade*, from the relentless cataloguing of suffering in *The Investigation* to the obsessive description of the execution of members of the resistance group Red Orchestra (Rote Kapelle) in *The Aesthetics of Resistance*. These figurations of excess destabilize and subvert the documentarist, factbased framework of Weiss's texts. They place the reader or viewer in an entirely different mode of experiencing: that of vision and dream, of hallucination and madness.

In *Rekonvaleszenz* this sphere is repeatedly referred to as the "quarters of the night" (R 458). Reflecting on the defeat he had suffered with *Trotsky in Exile*, Weiss here reminds himself that his entire work is rooted in this dark sphere, which he now attempts to revalidate in the face of the total politicization to which the play on Trotsky had fallen victim. He relates a dream (R 355-57) in which he visits an exhibition of surrealist works and is confronted with the achievements as well as with the decline of this movement. While acknowledging in *Rekonvaleszenz* that Surrealism has long since faded away, Weiss at the same time emphasizes the impact of André Breton, Luis Buñuel, and Antonin Artaud, and tries to recuperate some of their key concepts, such as the irrational, the anarchic, the spontaneous, the fantasmatic, and the hallucinatory.

All these elements are, of course, fundamental to Weiss's own work which is essentially located in the European avant-garde, from Expressionism and Dadaism to Surrealism (and its revival in the 1960s, Fluxus). These movements had increasingly come under attack in the Soviet Union when, in the 1930s, a dogmatic concept of Socialist Realism stifled artistic experimentation. They remained marginalized even in the post-Stalinist era. In *Trotsky in Exile*, Weiss stages a kind of rescue mission for the historical avant-garde. He has Lenin, who in 1916 lived in Zurich, and some of the other Bolsheviks, debate with Richard Huelsenbeck, Emmy Hennings, Hugo Ball, Tristan Tzara, and Marcel Janco, who at that time were launching the Dadaist movement at the Cabaret Voltaire, just a few hundred feet from Lenin's apartment. The vanishing point of this debate B which in reality never took place B is Weiss's utopian project of an alliance between the political and the aesthetic avant-gardes. This scene in *Trotsky in Exile* did not, for Weiss, exhaust the potentialities of an encounter between the two avant-gardes. Weiss staged it again in *The Aesthetics of Resistance*, where it attracted wide attention.[10]

Now, looking back during his convalescence on his more recent work, Weiss perceives the surrealist and avant-gardist concepts as the "missing dimension" (R 356). In a gesture of autocritique he notes that he himself has of late denounced the irrational in art and that, as a consequence, some of his work has become dreary. He gives, however, no indication of which of his texts he has in mind. To the contrary, Weiss seems bent on validating every one of them, most of all *Trotsky in Exile*, which to its critics appears as the very model of a drearily rationalist piece.

Weiss's art has always pursued the surrealist tradition of dissolving and at times violently shattering the boundaries of the rational, of crossing over into a sphere of heightened awareness, of expanded consciousness, and of conjuring up dreamlike feverish states bordering on madness and illness.[11] In some of Weiss's works the protagonists induce these states by artificial means, as for example in *The Shadow of the Body of the Coachman*, where the narrator sprinkles salt in his eyes in order to produce visions and hallucinations.[12] More often a heightened state of awareness is induced by illness, as in the various boyhood illnesses of the narrator in the autobiographical novel *Leavetaking*. The topos of illness as suggestive of a state of expanded perception and even revolutionary zeal literally moves center stage with *Marat/Sade*. Marat in his bathtub, feverish, his skin burning and repeatedly cooled by Simonne's wet cloth, is the emblem of the play. Marat's illness is the somatic allegory for a state of mind constantly verging on madness, a madness compounded by the madness which surrounds Marat at Charenton, as well as by the madness which is engulfing the revolution. The play's equating revolution with illness and madness is, of course, devoid of any denunciatory gesture. On the contrary, in true surrealist fashion illness and madness appear as liberating forces and as a kind of precondition for emancipatory and revolutionary action. There is, in Marat's feverish enunciations, no distinguishing between personal agony and revolutionary ecstasy. His cry "my head's on fire" is followed by the sublime statement: "*I am the Revolution.*"[13]

It is within this unfathomable realm between madness and lucidity, between illness and revolutionary fervor, where consciousness is at the same time reduced and expanded, that *Trotsky in Exile* unfolds. There are markers pointing to this realm early on. Trotsky evokes the state the revolutionary conspirators were in during their meeting in Brussels in 1903: "Worn out. Sweating. Half out of our minds" (25). In a discussion with fellow prisoners in 1907, Trotsky hints at an exhaustion bordering on loss of consciousness: "We give expression to the violence which engulfs us. Then hardly remember what we said" (38).[14] The dimension opened up by these statements becomes manifest with the appearance of Lenin. A stage direction reads: "LENIN presses both hands to his temples" (21). It is a gesture which refers back to Marat, whose head is "on fire" and who wears a bandage around his temples.[15] Lenin repeats the gesture throughout *Trotsky in Exile*. It becomes a vaguely unsettling signal: There is something wrong with Lenin, and, more generally, there is something wrong with what is being represented on stage. East German critics inferred from the play's insistence on Lenin's illness a bias against Lenin.[16] This overlooks not only the fact that Trotsky, too, is shown repeatedly to be ill (87, 98), but also the play's numerous other references to, or rather, its obsession with, illness, both in its psychic and somatic manifestations.

The topos of illness with its overtones of feverishness and madness runs through Weiss's work all the way to *The Aesthetics of Resistance*. The narrator of the novel, during his first visit to Brecht's appartment, where the Spanish civil war is being discussed, leafs through a book on Brueghel. Brueghel's nightmarish creatures and grotesque phantasmagorias seem to him an adequate expression of the horrendous reality of war which, until now he had held to be beyond expression. He remembers that while he worked in a military hospital in Spain it was the wounded and feverish, hallucinating and near death who were able to conjure up the same type of hellish images and who thus had access to a realm of understanding and truth closed to the healthy.[17] Near the end of the novel occurs the final meeting of the resistance group Red Orchestra. It is recorded through one of its youngest members, Coppi. He arrives at the meeting utterly exhausted from running through the streets of Berlin. Sensing that the members of the organization are about to be apprehended and that a horrifying end awaits them, Coppi is in a state near fainting, drifting in and out of a stupor.[18] His state is very nearly identical with that of the wounded in Spain; it is also similar to that of the participants in the Brussels meeting, in *Trotsky in Exile*, whom Trotsky described as "Worn out. Sweating. Half out of our minds." And as in Weiss's other scenes of physical and mental exhaustion and illness, this state allows access, in this case for Coppi, to a plane of understanding and insight inaccessible to the healthy.

Beyond its centrality to his art, illness is also the sphere where the distinction between Weiss's life and work tends to dissolve. As the earlier reference to *Leavetaking* suggests, illness played an important part in Weiss's own life. It also played an increasing role in the way he produced his work. He appears to have been almost unable to undertake a project without being in a state of feverish exhaustion or actually falling ill. This is true for *The Investigation* (NB II, 876) as much as for *Trotsky in Exile*, during the writing of which Weiss noted a "churning sense of illness" (NB I, 618), and it is true for *The Aesthetics of Resistance* and particularly for the period during which he wrote its final volume (NB II, 748). What may be impossible to determine is the chronology. Did the work on these traumatic topics provoke Weiss's illnesses or did the heightened sensibility produced by his illnesses allow Weiss to undertake these projects? Unlike Brecht, and in total contrast to a key component of Brechtian estrangement, Weiss, especially in his later work, proceeded from identification with his figures. This manifested itself most strikingly when, while working on a passage about Lenin in *The Aesthetics of Resistance*, he ended up with the same illness which had plagued Lenin (the shingles, already hinted at in *Trotsky in Exile*).[19] On the other hand, Weiss ascribed to Trotsky the same "difficulty in breathing" (98) he himself was experiencing during the writing of the play (NB I, 618). In a disturbing process of substitution,

Weiss experienced the physical and mental traumas of his protagonists while they experienced his. The dramatist and his figures were joined in a space defined by exhaustion, hallucination, dreamlike states, and illness, but also of hightened creativity and of access to an expanded sphere of knowledge. So that, far from being a denunciatory gesture on Weiss's part, Lenin's illness, just like Trotsky's, suggests the kind of expanded consciousness promoted by the Surrealists as a precondition for revolutionary action.

The difference between Trotsky and Lenin, in *Trotsky in Exile*, arises over the way they react to their illnesses. When Trotsky asks Lenin how he can stand the constant pain of his inflamed body, Lenin answers: "It is not important." To which Trotsky replies: "Not important? The body. Feel it all the time. Stomach. Intestines. Heart. Kidneys. These functions often claim my attention for days on end. Growing old. The beginning of death" (52). Quite unexpectedly Trotsky reveals an obsession with the body that is entirely Peter Weiss's. I have emphasized elsewhere Weiss's obsession with the body, his many excessive depictions of physical pain and suffering, of torture, mutilation, and death.[20] At the center of Weiss's aesthetic of excess, this focus on the body relentlessly confronts readers and spectators with the realization that, in the words of Weiss's Marquis de Sade, "this is a world of bodies".[21] It is an obsession Weiss shares with the Surrealists, from Artaud to Buñuel. But World War II added for Weiss a new dimension to this obsession. It is formulated in Adorno's dictum that after Auschwitz metaphysics, the sphere of the mind, is reduced to the pondering of its material other, "the somatic [...] stratum," the "wretched physical existence." This, as much as any surrealist concept, drives the relentless descriptions of pain and suffering in *The Investigation*.[22] It is also behind what Stanton Garner has called "a prominent signature of post-Brechtian political drama," namely "the almost obsessive interest in the body as a political unit." In contemporary drama, for which Garner considers Weiss to be a prime representative, the body is "tortured, disciplined, confined, penetrated, maimed, extinguished".[23] This goes to the essence of Weiss's work. The body is the site where catastrophic politics and ideologies play themselves out, where the ultimate truth about them is revealed. So it is for Nazi ideology (*The Investigation*), colonialism (*Song of the Lusitanian Bogey*) and imperialism (*Viet Nam Discourse*) and so it is for the Stalinist system, in *Trotsky in Exile*.

Which takes us back to the question Trotsky invites the spectator of the play to ask: "What had I seen?"

II

Trotsky in Exile is generally perceived as employing the strategies of the West German Documentary Theater of the 1960s. The two plays which preceded it, *Song of the Lusitanian Bogey* and *Viet Nam Discourse* had established Peter Weiss as the leading representative of this genre, while with his essay of March 1969, "Notes Towards a Definition of Documentary Theater," he had also become the foremost theoretician among its practitioners.[24] The characteristics of the Documentary Theater cannot be inferred simply from its name, for while its works are based on authentic sources and testimonies it also avails itself of the whole gamut of dramatic means available to traditional theater.[25] *Trotsky in Exile* adheres to the Documentary Theater to the extent that it presents factually established events, places, dates, and names, and that much of its dialogue is lifted from historical sources. But as with other plays of this genre, *Trotsky in Exile*'s adherence to facts tends to overshadow the many signals which point toward a realm other than that of historiographic documentation.

The opening stage directions indicate that the play takes place in a space devoid of any identifiable attributes (11), and, as the ending reveals, in a moment suspended in time, just before Trotsky's death. In this imaginary time-space, various stations in Trotsky's life unfold in the manner of flashbacks and in a generally chronological order. The repeated return to the time-space, however, tends to dissolve the chronology, which is never firmly established in the first place. In the second act of the two act play, the distinction between the time-space, from which Trotsky looks at his life, and the flashbacks, dissolves. The dialogue now provides no more than a subtle hint for the orientation of the reader or spectator. Whenever Trotsky and Lenin slide into the imaginary time-space where their dialogue unfolds, they switch from the more formal "Sie" to the familiar "Du."[26] In translation even this subtle shift is lost.

The play's unstable sense of place and time mirrors Trotsky's own perception. At times he seems disoriented in space, unsure of his geographic location (97). In yet another dialogue with autopoetic overtones, he also appears disoriented in time:

> Time. I thought of that even as a child. Saw it once as something like the large rock by our doorstep. Chronology. Counting. Time is formless. Has no shape till you begin to count. (52)[27]

But there is very little counting or accounting of time in the play. While the dates and the locations of the historical scenes are given, time itself remains essentially "formless." Also, scenic arrangements, as well as individual gestures and phrases are repeated throughout the play, further strengthening the sense of fractured time, of a broken mechanism which resists rational analysis.

Stalinism as a broken mechanism: this metaphor is suggested by the structure of *Trotsky in Exile*, as scenes representing the ascent of the Bolsheviks and the victorious revolution alternate with scenes which represent the decline of the Soviet state into Stalinism and terror. Weiss's confounding juxtaposition of scenes B a collage rather than a montage B subverts any narrow notion of causality.[28] Renouncing the historiographic norms of cogent presentation of historical facts, *Trotsky in Exile* appears as a meditation on the possibilities, conditions, and roots of failure of the revolution. In this it is more in line with *Marat/Sade* and *Hölderlin*, than with the documentary plays which precede it.

The concept of meditation denotes a region beyond the strictly rational and intellectual. In *Trotsky in Exile*, as in many of Weiss's works, this realm extends beyond the written text and the stage to the reader and spectator who are invited to identify with Trotsky, to enter his fragmented and formless time-space, and even his feverish and hallucinatory states bordering on delirium B in short, to watch *Trotsky in Exile* the same way Trotsky had watched his first play: "Out of my mind nearly at what was going on." Adopting such a state, readers and spectators may not be able to pedantically follow or even understand every obscure detail of the political arguments. Rather they immerse themselves in the play in a way such that it is both more and less than an intellectual experience. Weiss's Soviet critic, deploring the "endless, dreary debates" of *Trotsky in Exile* since, in his words, "they could only tire and exhaust" the spectators,[29] grasps, if negatively, Weiss's aesthetic project. Exhausted, tired, drifting in and out of consciousness in a dreamlike state: thus might indeed be described the ideal spectator suggested by the play.

For the reality of *Trotsky in Exile* is the reality of a dream, of a nightmare. This, too, is true for much of Weiss's work since his early prewar paintings. In the 1950s, during his period as a filmmaker, Weiss developed a special affinity for the work of Luis Buñuel. In writing about some of Buñuel's early documentary films Weiss noted that Buñuel used reality as a "primary material" which he then compressed "until it reached the density of a hallucination, of a dream."[30] The same can be said of *Trotsky in Exile*; it, too, seems to have been compressed to the density of a dream. This aspect was largely overlooked in the ideological debates which accompanied the play's disastrous opening. In its aftermath Weiss insisted repeatedly that *Trotsky in Exile* was "a monumental *dream* of the revolution."[31] The dreamlike or nightmarish qualities which permeate the play manifest themselves not only in illness, exhaustion, and madness, and in the dissolution of time and space. There are instances when the play enters a nonrational realm, as when the dialogue between Trotsky and Lenin passes through the moment of Lenin's death and continues on the other side, with Trotsky saying to Lenin: "But when you died..." (86). The height of nightmarish compression, however, is reached during the Moscow trials (Scene 13), when all certainties of a familiar reality break down. Trotsky, shirt in hand, in exile in Norway, intervenes in the trials in Moscow, some of which have not even taken place yet; Pyatakov, defending himself in Moscow, claims to have visited Trotsky in Norway, which Trotsky, still in Norway, repudiates; the prosecutor picks up on Trotsky's arguments; and finally the accused are taken away to be shot and Zinoviev intones the Sh'ma Israel; while Trotsky still stands, shirt in hand, but now it is several years later and he is four thousand miles away in Mexico City.

If the reality of *Trotsky in Exile* is that of a dream or nightmare, whose dream or nightmare is it? That of Peter Weiss? of Trotsky? of the spectator and reader? Though the dreamlike space the play inhabits is the creation of the dramatist, it can be realized only with the participation of the reader or spectator. But while they participate in its realization, both the author and the reader or spectator remain outside the reality of the text or stage. The structure of the play hints strongly at who is the subject of the dream that is Trotsky *in Exile*. From the opening tableau, through the presentation of events from Trotsky's point of view (which the play maintains throughout), to the final moments, *Trotsky in Exile* takes place inside Trotsky's head. This also seems to be what Weiss intended. In an interview in 1971 he noted that the historical events in his play should be staged "the way they are mirrored in the fantasy of the protagonist."[32]

There is, if not a lighter, at times an almost clownishly absurd side to Trotsky's nightmare. The stage direction for the meeting of the Russian conspirators in Brussels reads as follows: "During the discussion there is constant unrest: some scratch themselves, stand up, wave their arms, kick their legs, throw books in corners. Now and again a participant wanders about like a sleep walker" (25). Through their textual presentation these trivial activities take on an air of significance. They appear as though observed from a great distance or by someone from a distant culture, if not from a different planet. Since they remain unexplained, they seem absurd. They conjure up an atmosphere Weiss created years earlier in *The Shadow of the Body of the Coachman*. In the famous final passage of this text, the sexual intercourse between the coachman and the housekeeper is registered as a shadow play, to the significance of which the narrator has no clue. *The Shadow of the Body of the Coachman* pursues the kind of grotesque satire of the bourgeoisie, central to the surrealist project and notably to Buñuel. At the same time it also explores absurdist themes and motifs more characteristic of Beckett. But along with revealing his affinity for the author of *Waiting for Godot* Weiss is already marking their differences.[33] In his later turn toward Marxism and with his plays about Angola and Vietnam, Weiss emphatically moves away from Beckett's absurdist world view.

Therefore it is easy to miss the oblique reference to Beckett in *Trotsky in Exile*. At the beginning of the second act, exiled on the Turkish island of Prinkipo, Trotsky sits in a chair at the front of the stage. The stage direction reads: "He is looking through a telescope, describing with it a semi-circle to the front" (70). Preoccupied with the catastrophic developments in the Soviet Union and Germany, Trotsky finds the idyllic Agaean seascape he observes through the telescope "appalling." In his next station in exile, near the eastern French city of Grenoble, Trotsky is again introduced looking through a telescope. This time he looks at the world in extreme close-up, observing every crack in the rocks, with which he associates "liquidation,"[34] a term which refers to the elimination of perceived enemies by Stalin's secret service. Trotsky's play with the telescope has been interpreted as a reference to Brecht's *Galilei*.[35] But, as the next scene shows, there is a more obvious reference to a very different work. As Trotsky, whose exile has by now taken him to Norway, again looks through the telescope, the following exchange occurs:

> NATALIA. Here's nothing to see but the barn and the fence. Why don't you turn your chair round? The fjord's over there.
> TROTSKY *gets up.* NATALIA *helps him turn the chair sideways. He sits down again.*
> TROTSKY. Can you tell the difference between a lovely view and a less lovely one? (97)

This exchange might have been lifted almost verbatim from Beckett's *Endgame*. But it is much more than an enigmatic and absurdist physical gesture which is being cited in *Trotsky in Exile*. Just as Beckett's Hamm, looking through his telescope, sees only "Zero ... zero ... and zero," so Trotsky, in Norway, registers "an absolute void."[36] Pressed by Clov to be more precise, Hamm eventually comes up with a definitive characterization of the world he observes through his telescope: it is "corpsed."[37] It is this apocalyptic vision, folded into Beckett's absurdist gesture, which Weiss cites in his play. The two dramatists are united in a gaze which, in a world after Auschwitz, can see only catastrophes, from Hiroshima to Angola and Vietnam, and which, in *Trotsky in Exile*, comes to rest on the catastrophe of Stalinism.

III

To paraphrase one more time Trotsky's question: What are we seeing or reading, when we see or read *Trotsky in Exile*?

My own reading thus far has focused almost exclusively on the nonrational aspects of the play. It is an attempt not so much to validate the nonrational elements as opposed to the rational ones but to show how the play undermines this opposition.

Still, there is a rational and deadly serious political, historical, and ideological discourse unfolding in *Trotsky in Exile*. Those interested in this discourse have tended to focus on the arguments between Trotsky and Lenin in order to determine on whose side the play comes down. They generally conclude that it favors Trotsky and distorts Lenin's contribution to the revolution. How could it be otherwise, if indeed *Trotsky in Exile* is a materialization of Trotsky's memories, visions, and nightmares? Also, there are some obvious ideological affinities between Weiss and the historical Trotsky. They mostly have to do with Trotsky's internationalism. In the play, this internationalism takes on a contemporary ring as Trotsky and a group of students debate political events in Asia and Africa in ways which seem closer to Weiss's own preoccupation with Vietnam, Angola, and South Africa than to the issues of the 1930s (Scene 12). Still, Weiss was not a Trotskyite, and his play about Trotsky is not a Trotskyite play.[38] There is a rather different agenda driving Weiss's effort on behalf of Trotsky.

The scandal for Weiss as a Marxist did not consist in the fact that in the socialist countries Trotsky's views were rejected and distorted, or that Trotsky was denounced and defamed. The real scandal, the scandal which demeaned and subverted the whole socialist project, lay in the fact that the object of these denunciations didn't even exist. Of Trotsky's achievements and failures, and of his enormous impact on the first years of the Soviet State no evidentiary trace could be found. The founder of the Red Army had disappeared, and his name, even his face had been erased from the records: from historical documents, from books, even from photographs and films. One particular such instance came to embody for Weiss the effect of this erasure since it concerned a great fellow artist. In Scene 10 a visitor to Prinkipo tells Trotsky: "The name of Trotsky is being scratched from the records of the revolution. In Eisenstein's film about the October rising you're not even mentioned" (73). The reference is to Sergej Eisenstein's film of 1927, *October* (also known as *Ten Days That Shook the World*). Weiss's interest in Eisenstein dates back to the 1950s. During his period as a filmmaker Weiss wrote a slim volume, *Avantgarde Film*, which contains a short chapter on Eisenstein's unfinished film about Mexico.[39] In the first half of 1969, during the work on *Trotsky in Exile*, there is renewed intense interest in the Soviet director. Weiss's notebooks contain numerous entries on Eisenstein, his films, his unfinished projects, his aesthetic theories, and his clashes with repressive cultural institutions, as well as notes on his private life, including his homosexuality (NB I, 633-42). Some of these entries are in the first person singular, suggesting that Weiss was already experimenting with literary forms into which he might shape this material. For his film *October*, Weiss notes, Eisenstein had been ordered to eliminate all footage showing Trotsky's participation in the Revolution. This absurd demand had turned the great director into a "clown" (NB I, 634). The fate of Eisenstein's film remains a key item in Weiss's critique of Stalinist and post-Stalinist historiography, turning up once again in his reply to the Soviet critic who denounced *Trotsky in Exile*.[40] It this eradication from the record not only of Trotsky, but also of the true extent of Stalinist terror, which the play addresses.

There is in *Trotsky in Exile* a trope which recurs insistently. About the revolution of 1905, Trotsky says: "Historians can record that [...]" (37). During the hectic hours of October 1917, there are repeated demands of "Put in the minutes: ..." (64, 65). The full meaning of this trope is brought out by Lenin. After praising Trotsky's contribution to the revolution Lenin adds:

I state this for the record.[41] There are no official records of these days. Only scribbled notes and verbal orders. None of us has time to write history [...] Those who follow us will report incompletely, perhaps misrepresent. I put on record that Comrade Trotsky planned every step of the rebellion (59).

This is the language of testimony, of bearing witness. In their book, *Testimony: Crises of Witnessing in Literature, Psychoanalysis, and History*, Shoshana Felman and Dori Laub point out that testimony has become central and omnipresent, "a privileged contemporary mode of transmission and communication."[42] The language from the legal sphere, of courtrooms and trials, of historical records and documents, has, according to Felman and Laub, invaded a wide range of discourses. They analyze this development in the context of Holocaust testimonials. In the sphere of literature the German Documentary Theater, and *The Investigation* in particular, would seem to be prime examples of this shift. Much of Weiss's work, in fact, shows the characteristics of literature as testimony. The tone of many of his early texts is one of bearing witness to trauma and suffering, most often from his own childhood. With *Marat/Sade* and *The Investigation*, and with his turn toward Marxism, Weiss moves away from solipsistic introspection. His works now bear witness to traumatic events in history, from the Holocaust to the struggles in Africa and Vietnam. With *Trotsky in Exile* the gesture of witnessing is brought to the trauma of Stalinism.

Weiss's play aimed to reinscribe Trotsky's existence and traumatic fate, as well as the traumatic facts of the Moscow trials, into the record. As long as there was no record of them in the socialist countries, these events did not exist. There were, of course, the novels and testimonials by former communists such as Gustav Regler, Arthur Koestler, and Manès Sperber. But these, as well as much of the historiographical work in the capitalist countries, were shaped by the Cold War and carried hardly any weight in the Eastern bloc countries. Also, the official silence in the socialist countries notwithstanding, many facts about Trotsky and about the Moscow trials were known, but they had never entered the public discourse, had never been the subject of open debate. Weiss's play, the work of a fellow Marxist and a communist, was intended to finally stir public debate.

Laub, a psychoanalyst working with Holocaust survivors, calls the Holocaust "an event without a witness," not just because the Nazis tried to exterminate every witness to their crime, but because "the inherently incomprehensible *and* deceptive psychological structure of the event precluded its own witnessing, even by its very victims."[43] While the Moscow trials must have in many ways, if for different reasons, appeared equally incomprehensible to their victims, the Soviet government handled these trials far differently from the way the Nazis treated the Holocaust.[44] The Moscow trials were public, the transcripts were published. There is also this crucial difference: while there was no conceivable reason for Nazi action against the Jews, the Soviet Union was, during the second half of the 1930s, confronted with Nazi Germany's murderous hatred of communism. The Soviet Government had every reason to suspect that the Nazis had infiltrated the Communist party and other major institutions of the USSR in order to weaken Soviet war preparations. This eminently reasonable suspicion conferred upon the trials a sheen of logic even in the eyes of its victims, and may have prevented a public telling of these traumatic events for decades.

Reflecting on the aporetic situation of the Holocaust survivor, between the impossibility and the necessity of telling of the traumatic event, Laub states: "The 'not telling' of the story serves as a perpetuation of its tyranny. The events become more and more distorted in their silent retention and pervasively invade and contaminate the survivor's daily life. The longer the story remains untold, the more distorted it becomes in the survivor's conception of it, so much so that the survivor doubts the reality of the actual events."[45] Of course the psychoanalytic model, with its focus on the individual, cannot simply be applied to the "not telling" of the trauma of Stalinist repression by a whole society. Psychoanalysis is no substitute for historical analysis. Its usefulness for an interpretation of *Trotsky in Exile*, however, stems precisely from the fact that the play does not stage the trauma of Stalinism primarily in a discursive manner, but rather in a way which engages the readers' or spectators' fantasies, dreams, and nightmares. It is to this realm of the unconscious that Laub is referring when he notes that traumatic events take place "outside the parameters of 'normal' reality, such as causality, sequence, place, and time," and that "the trauma is thus an event that has no beginning, no ending, no before, no during and no after."[46] This is an almost uncanny description of the fragmented structure and dreamlike atmosphere of *Trotsky in Exile*. And just like the therapeutic process described by Laub, Weiss's play is not designed, or at least not primarily designed, to "explain" the trauma but rather to repeat it, to articulate and externalize it so it can be publicly acknowledged as real, as having indeed occurred. The play invites and facilitates the therapeutic process by focusing on the psychological and irrational aspects of the trials, the relentless humiliation of the accused, their willingness to implicate themselves, their lovers, their friends, and their families, and to admit to the most farfetched and absurd crimes in ways which defy one's capacity for understanding. Having been repressed for so long, their story had very nearly entered the realm of fiction and fantasy. In its public telling, *Trotsky in Exile* reasserts "the hegemony of reality" (Laub).[47]

This same gesture of bearing witness pervades other themes of *Trotsky in Exile*, most notably its references to Jewish issues. The Jewish question is introduced innocently enough. When, during his stay in the Tsarist penal colony of Verkholensk, Trotsky is repeatedly addressed as "Bronstein" (16, 18) this seems to reflect nothing more than the historic fact that at the time he had not yet changed his name to Trotsky. In the course of the play, Trotsky never hides or denies his Jewishness. His position of rejecting Jewish demands of autonomy, of a "self-contained Jewish culture," and, of course, of Zionism (25-26), is representative of the prevailing Marxist position, which goes back to Marx himself.[48] Trotsky is unwavering in his belief that Jewish issues, like the issues of other national or religious minorities, should be subsumed under the class struggle and will be resolved in a socialist society (25-26). He does not abandon this conviction even when confronted by a Jewish student who has escaped from Nazi Germany (88-89). Much as it provokes debate on these issues, the focus of the play as regards Judaism lies elsewhere. Along with references to White-Russian (60) and Nazi-German anti-Semitism (70) there are repeated hints of Bolshevik and Soviet anti-Semitism (38, 89). Weiss makes this point much more emphatically in *Rekonvaleszenz*, where he speaks openly of "anti-Semitic tendencies" in the USSR in the present (R 417). But as with Trotsky and the Moscow trials the focus of the play is not so much on analyzing Soviet anti-Semitism as on openly acknowledging its existence. For the reality of Soviet anti-Semitism, though it, too, was widely known, had hardly entered public discourse. The extreme discomfort surrounding this issue is transmitted through the play's appeal to the unconscious, to hidden and unacknowledged fears and prejudices, for instance when Trotsky refers to himself as "still somehow the poor Jewboy Lev Bronstein" (62).[49] The most unsettling moment, however, occurs when the play itself becomes a witness to witnessing. As he is taken away to be executed, Zinoviev, who was one of Lenin's closest collaborators and whose real name is Radomilsky, invokes the Jewish prayer of Sh'ma Israel, "Hear, O Israel" (112), asking God to bear witness to the awful fate which has befallen him.

Analyzed in this way, using some of the concepts developed through psychoanalytic work with Holocaust survivors, *Trotsky in Exile* appears as a therapeutic rather than a historical re-enactment of the trauma of Stalinism. That would of course not be entirely surprising given Weiss's own extensive experience with psychotherapy[50] and his enduring interest in psychoanalysis stimulated by Marxist psychotherapist Max Hodann whom Weiss memorialized in several of his works, most notably in *The Aesthetics of Resistance*. In reflecting back upon the failure of *Trotsky in Exile* in *Rekonvaleszenz*, Weiss repeatedly resorts to the vocabulary of psychoanalysis. The silence surrounding Trotsky and Stalinism in the Socialist countries is characterized as a "repression," its result as a "collective psychosis" (R 357). *Trotsky in Exile* was meant to be the therapy for this psychosis.

Even after he had written his play about the catastrophe of Stalinism, Weiss continued to believe that a democratic socialist society would eventually come to exist (R 476). One which would acknowledge, publicly debate, and thus be able to avoid the awful excesses of the past. One which would finally bring Trotsky's exile to an end.

Notes

In referring to Weiss's works the following abbreviations are used:
NB I - *Notizbücher 1960-1971* (Frankfurt a.M. 1982).
NB II - *Notizbücher 1971-1980* (Frankfurt a.M., 2nd ed., 1982).
R - *Rekonvaleszenz*. In Weiss, *Werke in sechs Bänden* (Frankfurt a.M. 1991), Vol. 2, p. 345-546.

1   Soviet critic B and translator of some of Weiss's works B Lew Ginsburg, "'Selbstdarstellung' und Selbstentlarvung des Peter Weiss." In: *Über Peter Weiss,* Volker Canaris, ed. (Frankfurt a.M., 4th ed., 1976), p. 136 ff.
2   Anneliese Grosse and Brigitte Thurm, "Gesellschaftliche Irrelevanz und manipulierbare Subjektivität." In: *Weimarer Beiträge*, 16.2 (1970), p. 151-181, here p. 175.
3   Robert Cohen, *Understanding Peter Weiss* (South Carolina 1993), p. 131.
4   Marcel Reich-Ranicki, "Die zerredete Revolution. Peter Weiss: 'Trotzki im Exil'" [1970]. In: idem, *Lauter Verrisse. Erweiterte Neuausgabe* (Stuttgart 1984), p. 97-101, here p. 99; and Henning Rischbieter, *Peter Weiss* (Hannover, 2nd ed., 1974), p. 95-96.
5   As the intense debates over Stéphane Courtois's revisionist *Le livre noir du communisme* of 1997 have shown; see *"Roter Holocaust"? Kritik des Schwarzbuchs des Kommunismus*. Jens Mecklenburg and Wolfgang Wipperman, eds. (Hamburg 1998).
6   Peter Weiss, *Trotsky in Exile*, trans. Geoffrey Skelton (New York 1972). References to this work in the text are by page number only.
7   For a general introduction to *Trotsky in Exile*, see Cohen, *Understanding Peter Weiss*, p. 122-31. For an informative early assessment of the play, see east German Weiss specialist Manfred Haiduk, *Der Dramatiker Peter Weiss* (East-Berlin 1977).
8   *Peter Weiss im Gespräch,* Rainer Gerlach and Matthias Richter, eds. (Frankfurt a.M. 1986), p. 187.
9   Peter Weiss, *Von Insel zu Insel*, trans. from the Swedish by Heiner Gimmler. In: idem, *Werke in sechs Bänden*, vol. I, p. 7-52, here p. 27.
10 For a discussion of this scene in *Trotsky in Exile*, see Hans Mayer, "Peter Weiss und die zweifache Praxis der Veränderung. Marat - Trotzki - Hölderlin" [1972], in idem, *vereinzelt Niederschläge* (Pfullingen 1973), p. 244-252; for a discussion of the same encounter in *The Aesthetics of Resistance,* see Christian Fritsch, "Engramme aus der Spiegelgasse.

Möglichkeiten und Grenzen der kulturrevolutionären Utopie." In: *Die "Ästhetik des Widerstands" lesen,* Karl-Heinz Götze and Klaus R. Scherpe, eds. (Berlin 1981), p. 121-133; and Andreas Huyssen, *Memory, Myth, and the Dream of Reason: Peter Weiss's 'The Aesthetics of Resistance,"* University of Wisconsin-Milwaukee, Center for Twentieth Century Studies, Working Paper No. 1, Fall 1986.

11 For a concise introduction to the surrealist movement, see Dietrich Mathy, "Europäischer Surrealismus oder: Die konvulsivische Schönheit." In: *Die literarische Moderne in Europa,* Hans Joachim Piechotta et al., eds. (Opladen 1994), p. 123-45.

12 Peter Weiss, *The Shadow of the Body of the Coachman.* In: *Peter Weiss: Marat/Sade, The Investigation, and The Shadow of the Body of the Coachman,* Robert Cohen, ed. (New York 1998), p. 1-39, here p. 6.

13 Peter Weiss, *Marat/Sade.* In: *Peter Weiss: Marat/Sade, The Investigation, and The Shadow of the Body of the Coachman,* Cohen, ed., p. 41-114, here p. 51-52 (original emphasis).

14 Skelton translates, "We give expression to the violence we come on."

15 Weiss, *Marat/Sade,* p. 42.

16 Grosse/Thurm, p. 177.

17 Peter Weiss, *Die Ästhetik des Widerstands,* 3 vols. in one (Frankfurt a.M., 2nd ed., 1986), vol. II, p. 149-50.

18 Ibid., vol. III, p. 190 ff.

19 Ibid., vol. II, p. 60. On Weiss's acquiring Lenin's illness, see Robert Cohen, *Versuche über Weiss' "Ästhetik des Widerstands"* (Bern 1989), p. 54.

20 Cohen, *Understanding Peter Weiss,* p. 69 ff, etc.

21 Weiss, *Marat/Sade,* p. 105.

22 Theodor W. Adorno, *Negative Dialectics* [*Negative Dialektik,* 1966], trans. E.B. Ashton (New York 1987), p. 365-66. On the concept of the suffering body in *The Investigation,* see Robert Cohen, "The Political Aesthetics of Holocaust Literature: Peter Weiss's 'The Investigation' and its Critics," *History & Memory* 10.2 (1998), p. 43-67, here p. 47 ff.

23 Stanton B. Garner Jr., "Post-Brechtian Anatomies: Weiss, Bond and the Politics of Embodiement," *Theater Journal,* 42.2 (1990), p. 145-64, here p. 146-47.

24 Peter Weiss, "The Material and the Models. Notes Towards a Definition of Documentary Theater" ["Notizen zum dokumentarischen Theater," 1968], trans. Heinz Bernard. *Theatre quarterly* 1.1 (1971), p. 41-43; also translated as "Notes on the Contemporary Theater," trans. Joel Agee. In: *Essays on*

German Theater, Margaret Herzfeld-Sander, ed. (New York 1985), p. 294-301.

25   Cohen, "The Political Aesthetics of Holocaust Literature," p. 50-53.

26   Peter Weiss, *Trotzki im Exil. Stück in 2 Akten.* In: idem, *Stücke II/2* (Frankfurt a.M. 1977), p. 417-517, here p. 437, 455, 463-64, 484.

27   I have slightly modified the translation.

28   Sigrid Lange, "Biographie und Epoche. Peter Weiss' 'Marat/Sade', 'Trotzki im Exil' und 'Hölderlin' aus der Sicht der 'Ästhetik des Widerstands'." In: *Ästhetik Revolte Widerstand. Zum literarischen Werk von Peter Weiss,* Jürgen Garbers et al., eds. (Lüneburg/Jena 1990), p. 138.

29   Ginsburg, p. 137.

30   Peter Weiss, *Avantgarde Film* (Frankfurt a.M. 1995), p. 55.

31   In an interview from 1971; see Gerlach/Richter, p. 187 (emphasis added).

32   Ibid.

33   Cohen, *Understanding Peter Weiss*, p. 35, 36.

34   The German original has "Liquidation." Skelton translates "reckoning," p. 87.

35   Garner, p. 153.

36   "Absolute Leere." Skelton translates: "Nothing but empty space," p. 97.

37   Samuel Beckett, *Endgame* [1957]. In: idem, *The Complete Dramatic Works* (London 1986), p. 89-134, here p. 106.

38   This according to Ernest Mandel, whom Weiss consulted during his work on the play, and one of the leading Trotskyite theorists of the time. Ernest Mandel, "Trotzki im Exil." In: Canaris, p. 131-35, here p. 135.

39   Weiss, *Avantgarde Film*, p. 76-78.

40   Peter Weiss, "Offener Brief an Lew Ginsburg." In: Canaris, p. 141-50, here p. 150.

41   "Ich halte fest [...]" Skelton translates: "I state this categorically."

42   Shoshana Felman and Dori Laub, *Testimony: Crises of Witnessing in Literature, Psychoanalysis, and History* (New York 1992), p. 6.

43   Laub. In: Felman/Laub, p. 80.

44   With this parallel I do not wish suggest any overal congruence between the Holocaust and the Moscow trials (and the Stalinist system for which they stand). While comparisons are unavoidable, each of these two events needs to be investigated as *sui generis*.

45   Laub, p. 79.

46   Ibid., p. 69.

47   Ibid.

48 For a condensed historical overview of Marxist attitudes toward anti-Semitism and the Jewish question, see Detlev Claussen, "Antisemitismus." In: *Historisch-kritisches Wörterbuch des Marxismus*, Wolfgang Fritz Haug, ed., vol. I (Berlin 1994), p. 356-64.

49 Skelton has: "Somewhere in me there's still that poor young Jewish lad Lev Bronstein." This makes the staccato tone as well as the negative connotations of the German original disappear.

50 On Weiss's own psychotherapy, as well as on his relationship with Hodann, see Cohen, *Understanding Peter Weiss*, p. 15-16.

Jochen Vogt

Ugolino trifft Medusa:
Nochmals über das "Hadesbild" in der *Ästhetik des Widerstands*

> "Gut, ich erreiche ein Extrem. Ein Schiffbrüchiger, der
> auf einem Wrack treibt, indem er auf die Spitze des
> Mastbaums klettert, der schon zermürbt ist. Aber er hat
> die Chance, von dort zu seiner Rettung ein Signal zu geben."
> Walter Benjamin an Gershom Scholem, 17.4.1931

Bilder und Beschreibungen des Schreckens und des Schmerzes, der Ausübung von Gewalt und der Deformation leidender Körper durchziehen das bildkünstlerische und literarische Werk von Peter Weiss von Anfang bis Ende. Sie sind mehr als ein roter Faden, sie bilden seine grundlegende Textur. Ein anfangs besonders glühender—und später umso tiefer enttäuschter Verehrer des Künstlers, Karlheinz Bohrer, hat dies als erster im Begriff der "Tortur" festgehalten. Fast ebenso früh, vor fast dreißig Jahren, hat Reinhold Grimm auf das unverwechselbare "Bilderdenken" des Autors Weiss hingewiesen.[1] An beide Beobachtungen möchte ich, im Blick auf ein besonders herausragendes "Schreckens-Bild", das ominöse *Floß der Medusa*, anknüpfen. Nicht weiter eingehen will ich hingegen auf die kontroverse Diskussion über das Verhältnis von "Wort" und "Bild", oder von Literatur und Malerei (bzw. Film), bei Weiss, die er mit ebenso apodiktischen wie ambivalenten Formulierungen in seiner *Laokoon*-Rede von 1965 selbst provoziert hatte. Mir scheint es ausreichend, das Unstrittige festzuhalten: daß es bei Weiss—*erstens*—eine lebenslang produktive Spannung zwischen Bild- und Sprachmedium gibt: "Das Bild liegt tiefer als die Worte. ... Worte bezweifeln die Bilder ...." Und daß—*zweitens*— aller Medienkonkurrenz ein anthropologisches *factum brutum* vorausgeht: "Bilder begnügen sich mit dem Schmerz. Worte wollen vom Ursprung des Schmerzes wissen."[2] Wir dürfen also im weiteren von Alexander Honolds Annahme ausgehen, "daß die beiden Medien Schrift

und Bild für Weiss eine gemeinsame Grundlage haben, die in der
Körperlichkeit, vor allem in der Erfahrung des schmerzverzerrten,
angespannten und aufbegehrenden Leibes zu suchen ist."[3]

"Bilder" erscheinen in Weiss' literarischen Werken mindestens in
zweifacher Gestalt: als elementare *visuelle Vorstellungsbilder*, also
Traum- oder Erinnerungsbilder, die dann in *sprachlichen Bildern*
(Metaphern) oder auch bildkünstlerisch, beispielsweise in Weiss'
Collagen, materialisiert werden; denken wir nur an das erwähnte,
durchgängige Bildfeld der *körperlichen Tortur*. "Bilder" spielen aber
auch als historisch überlieferte Artefakte eine wichtige Rolle: als
Grafiken, Gemälde, Foto- oder Filmaufnahmen, Skulpturen, die Weiss
im Rahmen essayistischer oder narrativer Prosa beschreibt, erörtert und
"erzählt". Dieses Verfahren ist, wie bekannt, besonders für die *Ästhetik
des Widerstands* stilbildend, ja werkkonstitutiv; und ich will
exemplarisch zeigen, wie vielschichtig und anspielungsreich Weiss—auf
der Höhe seiner Prosakunst—ein kunsthistorisch ebenso skandalöses wie
(inzwischen) kanonisches Gemälde in sein Erzählwerk integriert—und
wie intensiv und kenntnisreich er sich dafür in den Schreckenskammern
der europäischen Kultur ausgerüstet hat.

Daß die Bilder der gefährlichen Seefahrt und des Schiffbruchs seit
der Antike zum elementar-literarischen Fundus unserer Kultur gehören,
haben wir von Dolf Sternberger, Ernst Robert Curtius und vor allem
Hans Blumenberg gelernt.[4] Solche Bilder finden sich, analog zu den
häufigen Flugphantasien,[5] auch schon im Frühwerk von Peter Weiss.
Nicht nur unter dem sprechenden Titel *Von Insel zu Insel* gibt es da
immer wieder Szenen des Ausgesetztseins, aber auch des wohligen
Dahingleitens, die zwischen Verlorenheitsangst und Auflösungs-
phantasien oszillieren und bisweilen idyllischen Charakter annehmen. In
Abschied von den Eltern wird der Schiffbruch hingegen, als Sprach-Bild
im engeren Sinne, zur metaphorischen Deutung des Geschehens, also
zur Leserlenkung, verwendet. In einer Berliner Klinik ist die geliebte
Schwester des Ich-Erzählers, wenige Tage vor der Emigration der
Familie 1934, an den Folgen eines Unfalls verstorben: "In völliger
Erschöpfung lag meine Mutter zurückgelehnt im offenen Auto, als wir
langsam durch die Straßen nachhause fuhren. Nachhause. Es gab kein
nachhause mehr. Die Fahrt ins Ungewisse hatte begonnen. Wie
Schiffbrüchige in einem Boot trieben wir durch das sanft rauschende

Meer der Stadt. ... Dies war der Anfang von der Auflösung unserer Familie." Die unverkennbar allegorische Funktion des sprachlichen Bildes wird noch überboten durch die entsprechende Illustration, die sich fast ganz von der eigentlichen Handlungsebene (Autofahrt) löst und—in surrealistischer Tradition—exklusiv die übertragene, sinnstiftende Ebene (Schiffbruch) ausgestaltet.[6]

Dies sei erwähnt, weil im Kontrast leicht zu sehen ist, um wieviel komplexer nun die Verarbeitung des Schreckensbildes vom Schiffbruch in der *Ästhetik des Widerstands* ausfällt. Es geht dabei um zwei—in der Forschung häufig kommentierte[7]—Passagen, die den ersten und den zweiten Band des dreiteiligen Werkes narrativ und thematisch verklammern und schon dadurch, aber auch durch ihren Umfang und die Intensität der Darstellung aus dem Fluß der Erzählung herausragen.[8]

Am Ende des ersten Bandes, 1938 während des endgültigen Rückzugs der Internationalen Brigaden aus dem Spanischen Bürgerkrieg und kurz vor dem Einmarsch der Nationalsozialisten in die Tschechoslowakei, betrachten die Ich-Figur und sein verwundeter Freund Ayschman Reproduktionen von Picassos *Guernica*, verschiedener Gemälde von Goya, Delacroix und anderen,—und eben auch *Das Floß der Medusa* von Théodore Géricault. Überdeutlich ist diese Episode im Handlungsverlauf als Zäsur, als *Zwischen-Zeit* angelegt, als erste Gelegenheit zur reflexiven und affektiven Bearbeitung des Erfahrenen, also der politischen, militärischen und persönlichen Katastrophe. Die Ich-Figur wird diese Betrachtung wenig später, nach der Ankunft in Paris, in tiefster persönlicher und politischer Desorientierung, für sich allein fortsetzen und dabei auch vor das Original von Géricaults Bild treten, das hundertzwanzig Jahre zuvor, im "Pariser Salon" von 1819, zum Skandalon geworden war.

Was war damals geschehen? Das Gemälde hatte seine Betrachter nicht nur durch sein gigantisches Format (7 mal 5 Meter) und seine düstere Expressivität verstört, sondern v.a. das politische Establishment provoziert—und zwar durch seinen Gegenstand, der unmittelbar die politischen Konflikte und Frontstellungen in der restaurierten Monarchie der Bourbonen betraf. Ich referiere mit den Worten von Weiss, der sich seinerseits auf die historischen Quellen stützt:[9]

Am zweiten Juli Achtzehnhundert Sechzehn war, durch Unfähigkeit des
Kommandanten und Fahrlässigkeit der Marinebehörden, die Medusa, das
Flagschiff eines französischen Flottenverbandes auf dem Weg nach Senegal, in
der Nähe von Cap Blanc auf Grund gelaufen. Von den etwa dreihundert
Kolonialsoldaten und Siedlern an Bord konnten die Rettungsboote kaum die
Hälfte fassen. Der Kapitän, die höheren Offiziere und einflußreiche Passagiere
nahmen mit Gewalt Besitz von den Booten. Auf einem Floß, notdürftig aus
Bohlen und Maststücken erbaut, drängten sich die übrigen Schiffbrüchigen
zusammen. Die Rettungsboote sollten das Floß ziehn, beim aufkommenden
Sturm aber wurden die Taue gekappt, das Floß trieb ab, und von den
hundertfünfzig Menschen, die dort, verhungernd, verdurstend gegeneinander
kämpften, waren nach zwölf Tagen noch fünfzehn am Leben. ... Der vom
Maler geschilderte Augenblick, da der Mast der rettenden Fregatte am
Horizont auftauchte, ... weckte eine Empfindung von Schwindel. Nicht auf das
ferne Schiff zu, sondern an ihm vorbei glitt das Floß, und diese Wahrnehmung
erfuhr eine weitere Beunruhigung durch den Anblick der Woge, die, von
niemandem auf dem Fahrzeug beachtet, sich turmhoch vor dem leeren Bug
erhob, um auf die Übriggebliebnen niederzuschlagen
(I, 344).

Wie hier schon angedeutet, wird im Verlauf von Géricaults
langwierigem Arbeitsprozeß aus dem aktuell motivierten
Historiengemälde ein "Drama der Elemente", eine Art Allegorie (die
übrigens auch formgeschichtlich mit barocken Zügen arbeitet und den
tonangebenden Klassizismus subversiv unterläuft.) Die allegorische
Gestaltung, sagt der maßgebliche Géricault-Experte Lorenz Eitner,
ermöglicht ihrerseits immer neue Annäherungen und Aktualisierungen,
"bietet wechselnden Ideologien und Weltsichten einen Halt und
überdauert sie alle."[10] Die erzählerische Transformation und Integration
des Bildes durch Peter Weiss, diese These möchte ich belegen, *vollzieht*
nun die allegorische Applikation *nach*, aber sie *überwindet* sie auch. Mit
spezifisch erzählerischen Mitteln wird das Bedeutungspotential des
Gemäldes nicht dupliziert oder gar reduziert, sondern *entfaltet* und
potenziert. Um dies zu zeigen, will ich zunächst eine im engeren Sinne
narratologische Analyse vornehmen und sodann, gewissermaßen quer
dazu, einige ikonographische Hinweise aufgreifen und illustrieren.
    Zunächst also: Wie übersetzt Weiss das Gemälde in seinen Roman?
Ganz banal, aber auch ganz grundsätzlich: indem er es in mehrfacher
Hinsicht *narrativisiert*. Er beschreibt es nicht, er *erzählt* es.[11] Und zwar
mit sprachlichen Verfahren, die wir—grob gesagt—dem Repertoire der

klassischen Moderne zurechnen dürfen. Entscheidend für seine Erzählweise hier wie in der gesamten *Ästhetik* erweist sich, daß ein relativ starker, quasi-auktorialer Ich-Erzähler im Rückblick mehrere Handlungsebenen oder "Diegesen" verknüpft oder sogar verschmilzt. Damit wird eine *assoziative* Schreibweise ermöglicht, aber niemals völlig freigesetzt, sondern immer auch *kontrolliert*, an den konventionellen Erzählplan oder das "ideologische Projekt" (Genia Schulz) der *Ästhetik des Widerstands* rückgebunden. Möglicherweise liegt hier, neben den beträchtlichen erzählerischen Möglichkeiten, auch eine der ernsthaften konzeptionellen Schwächen des Werkes. Wie auch immer: Ereignisse und Handlungen, die innerhalb des Romans auf unterschiedlichen logischen und historischen Ebenen liegen, werden bei Weiss nicht, wie in vielen konventionellen oder auch postmodernen Erzählwerken als *Meta-Diegesen* ineinander geschachtelt, sondern zu einer einzigen *Mega-Diegese* verschmolzen.[12] In der Episode vom *Floß der Medusa* sind grundsätzlich *drei Ebenen* zu unterscheiden, die teilweise in sich noch differenziert werden könnten: *Erstens* der historische Schiffbruch 1816 samt Vor- und Nachgeschichte, der sozusagen aus dem im Gemälde stillgestellten 'letzten Augenblick' heraus entwickelt oder *re-diegetisiert* wird; *zweitens* die Rezeption des Gemäldes durch verschiedene Betrachter zu verschiedenen Zeiten (von denen die Salonbesucher 1819 und die Ich-Figur 1938 am wichtigsten sind); und *drittens* die Produktionsgeschichte des Werkes bzw. die Lebensgeschichte seines Schöpfers 1816 bis 1819 (mit Vor- und Rückgriffen), die von der Ich-Figur recherchiert wurde und vom Ich-Erzähler dokumentiert wird.

Diese verschiedenen Ebenen (oder Diegesen) werden durch einige narrative Techniken miteinander *verknüpft*, die zumeist syntaktischer, teilweise auch semantischer Art sind und ihrer Wirkung nach als *Montage- oder Überblendungseffekte* charakterisiert werden können. Es entsteht also eine in sich sehr variable, syntagmatisch oft in Phasen gegliederte und vom Ich-Erzähler stets gut kontrollierte Mega-Diegese. Ihr wird schließlich ein Erfahrungs- und Lernprozeß der Ich-Figur unterlegt, der sie über kurz oder lang in den politischen Kampf zurückkehren läßt. Inwiefern dieser Prozeß wirklich Resultat der am Schreckensbild gemachten ästhetischen Erfahrung ist oder sich konzeptionellen Zwängen der Romankomposition bzw. jenes "ideologischen Projekts" von Weiss verdankt, wäre noch gesondert zu überprüfen.

Aber werfen wir jetzt einen genaueren Blick auf die beiden Textpassagen (I,330-360, besonders 343ff.; II,7-33). Die *erste* läßt sich nach den dominierenden Zeitebenen und erkennbaren Erzählphasen in ihrem Ablauf etwa so schematisieren: *Erstens* die historische Rezeption des Gemäldes im Salon von 1819, *zweitens* die Ereignisse um den Schiffbruch 1816, *drittens* wieder Rezeption 1819, *viertens* eigentliche Bildbeschreibung und, davon recht gut abtrennbar, *fünftens* die Deutung durch die Betrachter 1938, wobei der Bildinhalt quasi aus dem Jahr 1816 in deren Gegenwart gehoben wird.

All dies, auch die vergleichsweise konventionelle Beschreibung im vierten Abschnitt, steht nun aber im historischen Präteritum, nicht im referierenden Präsens. Dies ist als *erstes* spezifisches Erzählverfahren festzuhalten. Das Bild scheint genauso zu "geschehen" wie die Geschichte, die es darstellt, seine Ausstellung in Paris und seine Betrachtung durch die Freunde. Dieses *assimilierende Präteritum* bringt alles auf die gleiche Ebene; dies aber ist Voraussetzung für die ständige Engführung von historischen Ereignissen, ästhetischen Sinnkonstruktionen und aktueller, politisch oder persönlich geprägter Befindlichkeit. Die Kunst gewinnt bei ernsthafter Auseinandersetzung Leben, weil die Nöte, die sie zum Ausdruck bringt, alles andere als abgegolten sind.

Verstärkt wird diese Wirkung durch ein *zweites* Verfahren, die mehr oder weniger explizite *Metaphorisierung des Erzählertexts*; beispielsweise schon in der ersten Erwähnung von Géricaults Bild. Da werden die revolutionären Ereignisse von 1830/31 erwähnt, und dann heißt es: "Zwölf Jahre früher war das Floß der Medusa in die akademischen Kunsträume eingebrochen" (I, 343). Das oszilliert zwischen eigentlichem und metaphorischen Sprachgebrauch (beim Verbum "eingebrochen"), sowie zwischen dem Titel des Gemäldes und dem Realgegenstand, den es abbildet ("Floß der Medusa") und suggeriert damit ein ähnliches Überschwemmungsbild, wie es die alte Collage zu *Abschied von den Eltern* zeigt. Man sieht die Flutwelle "buchstäblich" in den Museumssaal hineinstürzen... Zwei Seiten später gipfelt dann die Betrachtung des Bildes selbst in einer allegorischen Doppel-Übertragung:

Aus der vereinzelten Katastrophe war das Sinnbild eines Lebenszustandes geworden. Voller Verachtung den Angepaßten den Rücken zukehrend, stellten die auf dem Floß Treibenden Versprengte dar einer ausgelieferten Generation, die von ihrer Jugend her noch den Sturz der Bastille kannte. Sie lehnten und hingen aneinander, alles Widerstreitende, das sie auf dem Schiff zusammengeführt haben mochte, war vergangen, vergessen war das Ringen, der Hunger, der Durst, das Sterben auf hoher See, zwischen ihnen war eine Einheit enstsanden, gestützt von der Hand eines jeden, gemeinsam würden sie jetzt untergehn oder gemeinsam überleben, und daß der Winkende, der Stärkste von ihnen, ein Afrikaner war, vielleicht zum Verkauf als Sklave auf die Medusa verladen, ließ den Gedanken aufkommen an die Befreiung aller Unterdrückten (I,345).

Die allegorische Auslegung des Schiffbruchs auf die politische Situation von 1819 wird explizit durchgeführt und vom Erzähler ausdrücklich— und mit dem barocken *terminus technicus*—als solche deklariert: "Aus der vereinzelten Katastrophe war das *Sinnbild* eines Lebenszustandes geworden" (ebda., meine Hervorhebung). Zugleich aber drängt sich eine—sprachlich *nicht* realisierte, sozusagen elliptische—Auslegung auf die Situation der Betrachter und ihrer Genossen im Jahr 1938 auf. Viele Befunde können ohne weiteres auf sie "übertragen" werden: auch sie sind "Versprengte einer ausgelieferten Generation", verbunden in einer von "Widerstreit" stets gefährdeten "Einheit", in historischer Perspektive kämpfend für die "Befreiung aller Unterdrückten". Andere *termini* müßten lediglich metaphorisch verstanden (Spanien als eine Art "Floß") oder historisch supponiert werden (statt "Sturz der Bastille" vielleicht "Sturm aufs Winterpalais"), um auf die aktuelle Situation der Betrachter applizierbar zu sein. Die Betrachtung des Schreckensbildes mündet jedenfalls in eine dem Verfahren nach *allegorische*, dem Inhalt nach *kollektiv-politische Aktualisierung*.

Daß die jungen Männer sich in diesem "Sinnbild" selbst erkennen, wird an dieser Stelle *nicht gesagt*; es wird in einem Erkenntnisschock mit existenzieller Wucht *erfahren*: "Ayschmann war plötzlich blaß geworden, er sank vornüber, das Buch fiel ihm aus der Hand" (ebda.). Und es wird den Lesern *intertextuell* signalisiert, weil ja hier unüberhörbar aus einem anderen, dem Schreckensbuch schlechthin zitiert wird, und zwar aus eben der Episode, die das erzählende Ich zwei Jahre zuvor auf einem Berliner Friedhof mit Coppi und Heilmann gelesen und diskutiert hatte; also aus der Paolo-und-Francesca-Episode im Fünften Gesang von Dantes *Inferno*: *Quel giorno più non vi leggemo avante* (An diesem Tage lasen wir nicht weiter); und *E caddi come corpo morto cade* (Und ich fiel nieder wie ein toter Körper).[13]

Abb. 1: Théodore Géricault: Das Floß der Medusa, 1819 (Ausschnitt: Vater und Sohn)

Die *zweite* "Medusa"-Passage, zu Beginn des Zweiten Bandes, ist umfangreicher, auch diegetisch noch komplizierter und in syntagmatischer Hinsicht auffällig gegliedert. Ich unterscheide, unterhalb der Narrationsebene, vier diegetische Niveaus: *erstens* Aktionen der Ich-Figur, 1939 in Paris, dabei besonders seine Lektüre des Dokumentarberichts von Savigny und Corréard und seine Besuche im Louvre; *zweitens* die historische Rezeption um 1819; *drittens* Géricaults Lebens- und Werkgeschichte vor und nach 1816/19, darin besonders seine Lektüre des Berichts von 1818; *viertens* wieder die historischen Ereignisse um den Schiffbruch von 1816.

Die primäre Diegese mit den Handlungen der Ich-Figur ist ihrerseits in *fünf Phasen* gegliedert. Man könnte sie fast, in Abwandlung der konventionellen Dramentheorie, als fünf Akte verstehen. *Exposition:* die nächtliche Lektüre in Paris; *Steigerung:* der Gang zum Louvre am nächsten Morgen; *Antiklimax:* die Besichtigung des sich verschließenden Bildes; *erneuter Spannungsaufbau:* die Recherche nach den Lebensspuren Géricaults beim erneuten Gang durch Paris; *(nichtkatastrophische) Auflösung:* die erneute Besichtigung des Bildes und Abwendung von ihm.

Zunächst wird dabei die allegorisch-aktualisierende Rezeption aus der ersten Passage noch weitergeführt. In der ersten Nacht in Paris stößt die Ich-Figur "zufällig" auf den auch von Géricault benutzten Bericht der Überlebenden Corréard und Savigny, der ihn buchstäblich bis in den Schlaf verfolgt:

> Noch wollten sich die Versammelten nicht für verlassen halten. Die Küste war zu sehn, und ... die Schiffbrüchigen nahmen an, daß die Boote zu ihnen zurückkehren ... würden. Doch die Nacht brach ein, ohne daß *sie* Hilfe erhalten hätten. Mächtige Fluten überrollten *uns*. Bald vor, bald zurückgeschleudert, um jeden Atemzug ringend, die Schreie der über Bord Gespülten vernehmend, ersehnten *wir* den Anbruch des Tags" (II,13—meine Hervorhebungen).

Der abrupte und unkommentierte *Pronominalwechsel* (das *dritte* spezifische Erzählverfahren, das Weiss verwendet)—dieser Wechsel vom "sie" zum "uns/wir" montiert gewissermaßen zwei Diegesen in eine und darf als syntaktisch-technisches Pendant zu der "halluzinatorischen Identifikation" gesehen werden, die nun mehr und mehr zum Charakteristikum der Ich-Figur wie auch der Géricault-Figur wird. Die allegorisch-politische, die *applizierende* Deutung wird also zunächst affektiv intensiviert, dann aber dadurch relativiert, ja überholt, daß die lesende Ich-Figur sich zunehmend in den—hundertzwanzig Jahre zuvor den gleichen Bericht lesenden—Maler Géricault *einfühlt*, der sich seinerseits in die Diegese dieses Berichts *hineinphantasiert*: "Mehr und mehr wurde das Floß zu seiner eignen Welt" (II,16). Es gibt also ein Dreieck von *imaginären Identifikationen*, die vom Erzähler aber auch weiterhin koordiniert und "überwacht" werden; das strukturell und konzeptionell neue Moment ist dabei der Bezug des Ich auf die Subjektivität Géricaults.

Die Bild-Rezeption des Protagonisten vertieft sich also einerseits, einer alten hermeneutischen Maxime gemäß, als Nachkonstruktion des

Produktionsprozesses, und das heißt auch: durch Einbezug immer neuer Kontexte. Das bedeutet aber andererseits, im Blick auf das in der *Ästhetik des Widerstands* bisher entwickelte Konzept von Kunst und Kunstdeutung, eine erhebliche Akzentverschiebung. Bei der Behandlung des *Pergamon-Frieses*, um das wichtigste Gegenstück zu nennen, steht die *kollektive* Deutungsarbeit, die mimetische und formsemantische Funktion des Kunstwerks, und allenfalls die Abhängigkeit der Produktion von historisch-materiellen Faktoren im Vordergrund. Beim *Floß der Medusa* hingegen erschließen sich in der *individuellen* Betrachtung eines bürgerlichen Kunstwerks die künstlerische Subjektivität, die Privatmythologie und die Beziehungsdramen des Künstlers, ja die "kranken und depressiven Aspekte" seines Schaffens als Wurzelgrund seiner Kreativität.[14]

Das erfährt die Ich-Figur zunächst negativ, als ihr Weg zum Louvre und vor das "Hadesbild"—so heißt es in den *Notizbüchern* von Weiss[15]—mit einer Enttäuschung über das "Erloschensein des Gemäldes" endet, das nur noch "ein Gefühl der Ausweglosigkeit" zu vermitteln scheint (II,21). Notgedrungen macht der Betrachter sich auf zur Erkundung der Lebensspuren und -räume des Malers in Paris. Und erst nachdem er dabei dessen "persönliche Katastrophe", seine Obsessionen und selbstzerstörerischen Phantasien ausgelotet und projektiv nachvollzogen, fast möchte ich sagen: kathartisch ausgeschwitzt hat, da wagt er es, einen Tag später (und auf den Tag genau ein Jahr nach der ersten Betrachtung des Pergamon-Frieses!), sich dem Original und seiner düsteren Aura nochmals zu stellen. Diese Aura liegt ja nicht zuletzt darin begründet, daß das Gemälde *aufgrund* seiner "Düsternis" (chemisch gesprochen: des ungewöhnlich hohen Bitumen-Anteils in seinen Farben), einem ständigen Verdunkelungs- und letztlich *Auslöschungsprozeß* ausgesetzt war und ist: Ein kunsthistorisches Kuriosium, dessen allegorisches Potential Peter Weiss sich ebenso wenig entgehen ließ wie sein postmoderner Konkurrent Julian Barnes.[16]

An dieser Stelle erlischt dann aber auch das Interesse des Betrachters an Géricault und seinem Hadesbild, und zwar ziemlich plötzlich bzw. nicht ohne narrative Gewaltsamkeit. Ohne größere Umstände läßt der Erzähler es in der imaginären Asservatenkammer der europäischen Kunst verschwinden, irgendwo zwischen Caravaggio und van Gogh, und wendet sich wieder der Politik zu.

Dazu muß er die Sphäre der bürgerlichen Kunst verlassen, in der die persönliche Katastrophe jenseits des Formwillens konstitutiv ist. Der Zweck der Kunstbetrachtung ist erfüllt, indem sie eine politische Identitätskrise aufhebt: parallel zur Beschäftigung mit Géricaults *Floß der Medusa* entsteht beim Ich der Wunsch, in die kommunistische Partei gerade zu einem Zeitpunkt einzutreten, in dem diese—auch für das Ich ersichtlich—moralisch und politisch diskreditiert ist und die Austritte sich häufen.[17]

In dieser Schlußwendung sehe ich in handwerklicher Hinsicht, ähnlich wie Genia Schulz in ideologischer, eine Schwachstelle des Werks bzw. eine konzeptionelle Verlegenheit des Autors. Nach der sehr exponierten Stellung des Géricault-Blocks, nach seiner inneren Dramatik, auch nach dem halluzinatorischen Spiel der Identifikationen, das er freigesetzt hat, ist im Grunde nur noch erzählerische *Deeskalation* möglich. Und schließlich ist es, wie schon erwähnt, nach dem Gesamtplan der *Ästhetik* unabdingbar, daß der Zögling auf den rechten bzw. linken Bildungsweg zurückgeführt wird. Man stelle sich vor, er wäre, wie der eine oder andere bewunderte Kollege aus der *lost generation*, in Clichy gelandet....[18]

Anders als der Maler, der sich der "endgültigen Fassung" seines Bildes auf dem Weg der "Konzentration" und thematischen Reduktion nähert, arbeitet der Erzähler nach dem Prinzip der *auktorialen Supplementierung*. Er erzählt eben nicht nur die historischen Abläufe und das *chef d'oeuvre* selbst, er diegetisiert auch die Skizzen, Entwürfe und thematisch verwandten Nebenwerke, die den psychischen und kreativen Prozeß des Malers in seiner Komplexität und Radikalität erst nachvollziehbar machen. Dies will ich zum Schluß an einem thematisch zentralen Bild- und Textdetail verdeutlichen, auf das schon verschiedentlich, besonders von Waltraud Wiethölter, hingewiesen wurde.[19]

Wir wissen, daß Géricault die bezeugten Szenen der niedergeschlagenen Meuterei, aber auch des späteren Kannibalismus zunächst skizziert, im Laufe seines Arbeitsprozesses aber aus der Werkkonzeption getilgt hat. Die Überlebenden Corréard und Savigny berichten ja recht detailgenau über abgenagte Knochen und zum Dörren aufgehängte Fleischportionen. Géricault dürfte aber sowohl mit seinem einschlägigen Entwurf unzufrieden gewesen sein als auch gewußt haben, daß einem *solchen* Bild der Salon definitiv verschlossen bleiben würde. Und letztlich paßte das auch nicht zu seiner gestalterischen Absicht der unterschwelligen (und insofern auch klassizistischen) Heroisierung.— Dieser Intention hat Géricault letztlich eine ganze Menge "Realismus" geopfert, so daß man mit einigem Recht und *common sense* gefragt hat: Warum sind diese Menschen nach zwei Wochen Hunger und Schrecken so wohlgenährt? Und die Männer so *frisch rasiert?*[20]

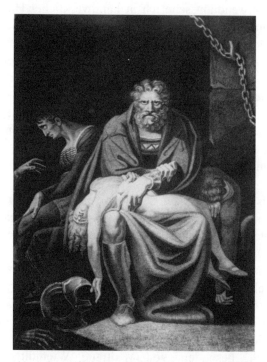

Abb. 2: Johann Heinrich Füssli: Ugolino im Kerker, 1806

Was also malt Géricault *statt* der Kannibalismus-Szene? Er rückt, an kompositorisch wie rezeptionsästhetisch zentraler Stelle, da wo der Fuß des Betrachters das Floß zu berühren scheint (wie Delacroix gesagt hat), die sogenannte Vater-und-Sohn-Szene in den Blick, die er zwar in einer ganzen Serie von Skizzen vorbereitet hatte, für die es aber (anders als für die meisten Figuren), keine realhistorischen Vorbilder gibt. Sie scheinen aus einer ganz anderen *horror story* auf das Floß verschlagen; tatsächlich kommen sie diesmal aus dem neunten Kreis von Dantes Hölle, wenn auch auf einem kleinen Umweg. Der Maler Johann Heinrich Füssli, ein Generationsgenosse Goethes, hatte trotz seines eidgenössisch-gemütlichen Namens ein ausgeprägtes *faible* für die dunklen Seiten der Weltliteratur und hat Homer, die Nibelungen, Dante, Shakespeare und manch anderes illustriert, was gut und gruselig war. In England, wo er unter dem Namen Henry Fuseli Karriere machte, erklärte er seinem jungen Kollegen William Blake die *Divina Commedia* (so wie sie ihm selbst einst der alte Johann Jacob Bodmer erklärt hatte) und malte 1806, zehn Jahre vor dem Schiffbruch der *Medusa*, den toskanischen Grafen Ugolino. Im 33. *Canto* von Dantes *Inferno*, also ganz unten, muß dieser seine Sünden- und Leidensgeschichte offenbaren: Als Verräter im Labyrinth der italienischen Innenpolitik wird er mit vier Söhnen und Enkeln im März 1289 im Hungerturm von Pisa zu Tode gebracht; über ihm, der als allerletzter stirbt, schwebt der massive Verdacht der Anthropophagie: *Poscia, più che il dolor, potè il digiuno* (dann war der Hunger stärker als die Trauer).[21]

Dem europäischen Lesepublikum außerhalb Italiens war Anfang des 19. Jahrhunderts die Ugolino-Episode so bekannt wie sonst nur noch die von Paolo und Francesca. Relativ bekannt und in Moses Haughtons Druck von 1809 verbreitet war auch Füsslis Bild[22]—so daß, um es kurz zu machen, das Sensationsbedürfnis von Géricaults Pariser Zeitgenossen, die ja von der Presse über das Geschehen auf dem Floß gut informiert waren, durch seine metonymische Zitation auf recht subtile Weise zugleich enttäuscht und befriedigt wurde.

Aber was hat Peter Weiss damit zu tun? Die entsprechende Passage aus der *Ästhetik des Widerstands* lautet so:

Je geringer die Anzahl der Menschen auf dem Floß wurde, desto näher kam der Maler der Konzentration, die er für die endgültige Fassung seines Bildes benötigte. Nach der Entladung des Kampfs erfuhr der Wunsch, das Leben so lange wie möglich auszuhalten, eine fremdartige Verwandlung. Die ersten begannen damit, die umherliegenden Leichname mit ihren Messern zu zerteilen. Einige verschlangen das rohe Fleisch auf der Stelle, andre ließen es in der Sonne dörren, um es auf diese Art schmackhafter zu machen, und wer es jetzt noch nicht über sich brachte, die neue Kost zu sich zu nehmen, der wurde am folgenden Tag doch vom Hunger dazu gezwungen. Auf die Turbulenz folgte die Zeitspanne der völligen Abgeschiedenheit. In dem Herausgerissensein aus allen Zusammenhängen erkannte der Maler seine eigene Situation wieder. Er versuchte, sich vorzustellen, wie dies war, das Hineinschlagen der Zähne in den Hals, den Schenkel eines verendeten Menschen, und während er den Biß des Ugolino in das Fleisch seiner Söhne zeichnete, lernte er, sich damit abzufinden, so wie sie es auf dem Floß, nach einem Stoßgebet, getan hatten. Die nackten, auf dem Floß zusammengekauerten Gestalten befanden sich in einer Welt, die von Fieber und Wahn deformiert war, die noch Lebenden wuchsen mit den Toten zusammen, indem sie diese sich einverleibten. Dahintreibend auf dem Plankengefüge, im wolkengleichen Gewässer, fühlte Géricault das Eindringen der Hand in die aufgeschnittne Brust, den Griff um das Herz desjenigen, den er am Tag zuvor zum Abschied umarmt hatte. Nach einer Woche waren ihrer noch dreißig auf dem Floß (II,15f.).

Abb. 3: Théodore Géricault: Ugolino und seine Kinder im Kerker, 1815/16

Es war Weiss also wichtig, die ikonographische Anspielung, das *Bildzitat*, in seine Erzählung hinüberzuretten. Dies leistet der Name "Ugolino" als Signal und Symbol für "the unpaintable horror of cannibalism".[23] Weiss stellt die Verbindung aber nicht, wie Géricault, über Füssli her, sondern über *Géricault selbst*. Erzählerisch handelt es sich hier um die Überblendung von drei Diegesen. Der Ich-Erzähler fühlt sich (1) in den arbeitenden Géricault ein, der die Ugolino-Episode zeichnet (2) und dabei in "halluzinatorischer Identifikation" (3) den Kannibalismus auf dem Floß miterlebt.

Abb. 4: Théodore Géricault: Ugolino, 1815/16

Damit ist die Grenze aller Hermeneutik erreicht: Einfühlung und Einverleibung sind nicht mehr zu unterscheiden. Daß dies nur mit kaum legitimierbarer erzählerischer "Auktorialität" geht, wollen wir großzügig übergehen. Interessanter ist schon, daß die beiden Ugolino-Zeichnungen Géricaults bisher fast ganz unbeachtet geblieben sind. Die eine, mit dem Titel *Ugolino* ist eine eher untypische Umrißzeichnung einer männlichen

Figur; die andere—*Ugolino und seine Kinder im Kerker* eine mit Öl
lavierte Federzeichnung, die sich schon eher der Inspiration durch
Füsslis Bild verdanken könnte. Entstanden sind sie nach Eitner 1815/16,
nach Bazin während Géricaults Italienreise 1816/17, in jedem Fall aber,
bevor das *Medusa*-Projekt Kontur gewann.

Welche Schlüsse dürfen wir daraus ziehen? *Erstens,* daß Peter Weiss
für die *Ästhetik* genau recherchiert hat (denn die beiden *Ugolino*-
Zeichnungen sind, wie gesagt, wenig bekannt); aber vielleicht doch nicht
genau genug. Denn Ugolino beißt auf dem Blatt, das ihn mit seinen
Söhnen zeigt, keineswegs in deren "Fleisch", sondern allenfalls in den
eigenen Unterarm; auf dem anderen knabbert er, gewissermaßen
"autophagisch", an seinem Daumen. Im übrigen scheint es fraglich, ob
Weiss den *Ugolino mit seinen Kindern im Kerker* gesehen hat.[24]
Zweitens: Weiss baut die Ugolino-Anspielung also gegen die
Chronologie und mit imaginiertem bzw. retuschiertem Bildinhalt hier
ein, wo und weil er sie thematisch benötigt, um nicht nur die
Kannibalismus-Thematik, sondern *drittens* wieder einen intertextuellen
Verweis auf Dantes *Inferno* anzubringen. Denn die *Divina Commedia,*
und besonders ihr erster Teil, das zeigen solche Details und das ist in
den letzten Jahren in der Weiss-Forschung immer deutlicher geworden,
ist der wichtigste—sowohl punktuell wie strukturell herbeigezogene—
Prätext für die meisten Projekte von Weiss' seit 1965 (gerade auch die
nicht abgeschlossenen), und eben—mit ganz besonderem Gewicht, auch
für die *Ästhetik des Widerstands.*[25]

In unserem engeren Kontext darf aber nicht unerwähnt bleiben, daß
sich die Ich-Figur der Ästhetik erst nach einem langen, ausführlich
geschilderten Weg durch Paris vor dem Floß der Medusa, dem "Hades-
Bild" einfindet,—nach einem Weg, der durch allerlei danteske
Konnotationen als Abstieg ins Inferno modelliert ist (eine Struktur
übrigens, die sich später in Stockholm und in radikalisierter Form in
Berlin wiederholt). Daran läßt sich ein letzter Hinweis anschließen, der
uns zeigen kann, wie Peter Weiss bemüht ist, seinen Roman nach Dantes
Vorbild als Raum der *memoria,* als eine "literarische
Gedächtnisarchitektur" auszugestalten[26]—und welche Rolle dabei die
"Bilder", in der ganzen Vieldeutigkeit des Wortes, spielen.

Vielleicht sollte man sich noch einmal in Erinnerung rufen, daß das
"*Floß* der Medusa" nur zufällig und ohne alle semantische Relevanz

"Floß der *Medusa*" hieß. Jenes Schiff hätte ja ebensogut *Antigone* oder *Marie Antoinette* (oder auch *La douceur de vivre*) heißen können—aber da es nun einmal *Medusa* hieß, ist eine unterschwellige Semantisierung unvermeidlich. Medusa ist jedenfalls in all ihren mythologischen oder künstlerischen Varianten—als "hideous monster" oder als "beautiful *femme fatale*" wie die antike *Medusa Rondanini*,[27] eine Kopie des

Abb. 5: Medusa Rondanini, 440 v. Chr.

Schmucks von Athenas Schild bzw. "Schuppenpanzer" (vgl. I,10), oder auch Carvaggios berühmtes Medusenhaupt—sie ist konnotiert mit tödlicher Bedrohung, Geschlechterkampf, (Selbst-)Zerstörung, Schrecken und Untergang. Insofern ist *Medusa* ein "passender" Name für das Todesschiff (so wie auch hundert Jahre später die *Titanic* einen hat). Das hat den Religionsphilosophen Klaus Heinrich 1981 zu der Frage geführt: "Was hat das 'Floß der Medusa' mit der Medusa zu tun? Auf den ersten Blick nichts, auf den zweiten und dritten und vierten dann doch etwas..." Heinrich "liest" das Gemälde von Géricault (ohne jeden Bezug auf Weiss) als Dokument einer *Faszinationsgeschichte*: "In dem, was fasziniert durch die reale Geschichte hindurch, sind unerledigte Konflikte, nicht ausgetragene Spannungen, ist das nichtgelöste Problem jeweils präsent." Heinrich analysiert weiterhin die berühmte Doppeldiagonale der Bildkomposition, die auch Weiss zitiert; sie baut nach rechts einen *"Hoffnungs-Turm"* auf, eine dynamisch aufwärts strebende *"demonstrative* Männerwelt"; und nach links unten eine *"Verzweiflungsgruppe"*, die auf verschlüsselte Weise "auch in dieses Floß *Geschlechterspannung* hineinträgt, nämlich: eine *weibliche* Welt".[28] Diese zunächst überraschende These stützt Heinrich, wie nach ihm ausführlicher Waltraud Wiethölter,[29] mit der ikonographischen Affinität dieser Gruppe zur Mutter-Sohn-Konstellation der *pietà*, zur mittelalterlichen Fortuna, und zu Dürers *Melencolia I*. Besonderes Gewicht kommt dabei der *"Rätselfigur"* zu, die wir bisher Ugolino nannten und der "ein wildes Haargekräusel den Kopf umfangen läßt; das ist ein richtiger *Medusenkopf*" in antiker oder Renaissance-Gestaltung.[30] Heinrich spricht, wohlgemerkt, über Géricaults Bild, nicht über Weiss und seinen Roman.[31] (Er scheint die 1981 vorliegenden beiden ersten Bände der *Ästhetik des Widerstands* nicht zur Kenntnis genommen zu haben.)

Uns aber drängt sich die Schlußfolgerung auf, daß der Erzähler Weiss sich bemüht hat, die ikonographischen Anspielungen und Verknüpfungen aus Géricaults Bild in seinen narrativen Text hinüberzuretten.[32] Die *Melencolia*-Figur wird im dritten Band des Romans von Hodann (also einer Ersatz-Vaterfigur) beschrieben und mit dem Schicksal der Mutter des Erzählers verknüpft: "So habe meine Mutter verharrt, wie von Dürer gezeichnet, unter der Waage, der Sanduhr, der Tafel mit den unverständlichen Ziffern, mit aufgestütztem Haupt, vor sich hindämmernd, unnahbar" (III,132). Der *Medusa*-Mythos wird auf den ersten Seiten des Romans erwähnt, in Zusammenhang mit Picassos *Guernica* diskutiert (I, 339) und, wenn auch indirekt, in Verbindung gebracht mit der Erdgöttin Ge (Gäa), deren Haupt von "Wellen des aufgelösten Haars umflossen" ist (II,10). Die Mutterfigur am Pergamonfries wiederum wird vom Erzähler später, ebenso ausdrücklich wie halluzinatorisch, mit seiner todesnahen Mutter identifiziert:

Einige Augenblicke lang war das Erinnerungsgewebe, das uns umgab, wahrzunehmen, doch gleich verlor es sich wieder, nichts im Gesicht meiner Mutter deutete darauf hin, daß sie auch nur ein einziges meiner Worte in sich aufgenommen hätte. Im Zug, während der Rückfahrt nach Stockholm, sah ich, aus dem Fenster blickend, dieses Gesicht, groß, grau, abgenutzt von den Bildern, die sich darüber hergemacht hatten, eine steinerne Maske, die Augen blind in der Bruchfläche. Es war das Gesicht der Ge, der Dämonin der Erde, ihre linke Hand, mit den zerborstenen Fingern, ragte auf, die abendlichen Landschaften flogen vorbei, Alkyoneus fiel, von der Schlange in die Brust gebissen, schräg von ihr weg (III,20).

Abb. 6: Pergamonfries: Athena, mit Medusenhaupt geschmückt, besiegt Gäa, 2. Jh v. Chr.

Ich breche den Hinweis auf diese, auch im dritten Band noch weitergeführten Figuren- und Bild-Verknüpfungen ab und komme zu einem minimalistischen Fazit: Die Rätselfigur alias Ugolino alias Medusa erweist sich bereits im Gemälde als Schnittpunkt, in dem sich eine paternalistische und eine maternalistische Linie kreuzen; auf analoge Weise sucht Weiss im Roman ein "Erinnerungsgewebe" (III,20) aufzuziehen, das den politisch-diskursiven Roman faszinationsgeschichtlich bzw. mythologisch fundiert (und uns auch davor schützen sollte, ihn eindimensional allegorisch oder aktualisierend zu lesen). Im Zentrum dieser faszinationsgeschichtlichen Schicht, als "unausgetragener Konflikt", wie Heinrich sagt, ist zweifellos die Geschlechterspannung zu sehen. Peter Weiss (ich neige ein wenig zu altmodisch-biographischen Erklärungen) bringt sie, und zwar sehr massiv, aus seiner eigenen Psychohistorie und Werkgeschichte mit, aber (was wichtiger ist), er hat sie ja auch in der Oberflächenhandlung der *Ästhetik* solide verankert. Die Spannung zwischen der Vaterfigur des Erzählers (dem rationale Erklärungen, artikulierter Protest und politischer Widerstand zugerechnet werden) und der Mutter (die für Einfühlung in die Opfer, überwältigtes Verstummen und mitleidenden Untergang steht) ist vielfach bemerkt und als Kontrast von maskulinem und femininem Diskurs kommentiert worden.[33] Auf vielschichtige und subtile Weise spiegelt die narrative Verarbeitung des Bildes vom Floß der *Medusa* auch diese Problemschicht des Romans,—spiegelt sie gewissermaßen in verschiedene Partien des Romans zurück. Um dieses Spiegelkabinett, das "Arsenal der Bilder" (II,19) in all seinen Facetten wahrnehmen zu können, dies bleibt die rezeptionsästhetische—und typisch Weiss'sche—Zumutung der *Ästhetik des Widerstands*, müssen wir nicht nur den Roman, sondern (ganz wie dessen Figuren) auch die Bilder lesen, von denen er handelt.

Anmerkungen

Aus der *Ästhetik des Widerstands* zitiere ich nach der Erstausgabe (Frankfurt a.M. 1975, 1978, 1981) mit den üblichen Bandziffern I, II und III.

1   Karlheinz Bohrer, "Die Tortur - Peter Weiss' Weg ins Engagement - Die Geschichte des Individualisten" (1970). In: *Peter Weiss.* Hrsg. von Rainer Gerlach (Frankfurt a.M. 1984), S. 182ff. Reinhold Grimm, "Blanckenburgs *Fluchtpunkt* oder Peter Weiss und der deutsche Bildungsroman." In: *Basis* 2 (1971), S. 234ff.

2   Peter Weiss, "Laokoon oder Über die Grenzen der Sprache," Weiss, *Rapporte* (Frankfurt a.M. 1968), S. 182. Vgl. zur Diskussion u.a. Martin Rector, "Laokoon oder der vergebliche Kampf gegen die Bilder. Medienwechsel und Politisierung bei Peter Weiss" sowie Michael Hofmann, "Der ältere Sohn des Laokoon. Bilder und Worte in Peter Weiss' Lessingpreisrede und in der *Ästhetik des Widerstands,*" beide in *Peter Weiss Jahrbuch* 1 (1992), S. 24ff. bzw. S. 42ff.

3   Alexander Honold, "Das Gedächtnis der Bilder. Zur Ästhetik der Memoria bei Peter Weiss." In: *Die Bilderwelt des Peter Weiss.* Hrsg. von Alexander Honold und Ulrich Schreiber (Hamburg 1995), S. 106.

4   Dolf Sternberger, "Hohe See und Schiffbruch. Verwandlungen einer Allegorie." In: *Die Neue Rundschau* (1935), Bd. II, S. 185ff; Ernst Robert Curtius, *Europäische Literatur und lateinisches Mittelalter*, 5. Aufl. (Bern und München 1965), S. 138ff; Hans Blumenberg, *Schiffbruch mit Zuschauer. Paradigma einer Daseinsmetapher* (Frankfurt a.M. 1979). Kunstgeschichtlich weiterhin Eduard Hüttinger, "Der Schiffbruch." In: *Beiträge zur Motivkunde des 19. Jahrhunderts* (München 1970), S. 211ff.

5   Vgl. den Beitrag von Alexander Honold in diesem Band.

6   Peter Weiss, *Abschied von den Eltern*, 13. Aufl. (Frankfurt a.M. 1979), S. 81. Die Collage ist u.a. abgedruckt bei Jochen Vogt, *Peter Weiss mit Selbstzeugnissen und Bilddokumenten* (Reinbek 1987), S. 24f.

7   Ich nenne hier ohne Anspruch auf Vollständigkeit einige methodisch divergierende Arbeiten, die in den achtziger Jahren entstanden sind: Jost Hermand, "*Das Floß der Medusa.* Über Versuche, den Untergang zu überleben." In: *Die "Ästhetik des Widerstands" lesen. Über Peter Weiss.* Hrsg. von Karl-Heinz Götze und Klaus R. Scherpe (Berlin 1981), S. 112ff; Klaus Herding, "Arbeit am Bild als Widerstandsleistung." In: *Die Ästhetik des Widerstands.* Hrsg. von Alexander Stephan (Frankfurt a.M. 1983), S. 246ff; Genia Schulz, *"Die Ästhetik des Widerstands". Versionen des Indirekten in Peter Weiss' Roman* (Stuttgart 1986), bes. S. 64ff; Michael

Hofmann, *Ästhetische Erfahrung in der historischen Krise. Eine Untersuchung zum Kunst- und Literaturverständnis in Peter Weiss' Roman "Die Ästhetik des Widerstands"* (Bonn 1990), S. 79ff; Roberto Rizzi, "'Ihr, die ihr vor diesem Bild steht ..., seid die Verlornen, denen, die ihr verlassen habt, gehört die Hoffnung". Weiss, Géricault und *Das Floß der Medusa.*" In: *Ästhetik-Revolte-Widerstand. Ergänzungsband.* Hrsg. von Internationale Peter Weiss Gesellschaft (Luzern und Mannenberg 1990), S. 211ff; Rainer Rother, *Die Gegenwart der Geschichte. Ein Versuch über Film und zeitgenössische Literatur* (Stuttgart 1990), bes. S. 125ff.

8   Es scheint, als wäre die Géricault-Passage ursprünglich als Abschluß des Romanprojekts, dann als Mittelachse einer zweibändigen Konzeption geplant gewesen. Aber auch in der jetzigen Komposition steht sie noch sehr herausgehoben zwischen der geschichtshermeneutischen Entzifferung des Pergamon-Frieses am Romanbeginn und der produktionsästhetischen Diskussion von Brechts Engelbrekt-Projekt im zweiten Band. Wir absolviern also, fast wie in Hegels *Ästhetik*, einen geschichts- und kunstphilosophischen Kursus, der von Architektur und Skulptur über die Malerei bis zur Literatur führt, ehe dann im dritten Band die Kunst an ihr Ende gelangt...

9   Hauptquelle ist der buchstarke Bericht der beiden Überlebenden A. Corréard und H.Savigny, "Relation complète du naufrage de la frégate la Méduse faisant partie de l'expedition du Sénégal en 1816", der 1968 neu ediert und von Weiss offensichtlich benutzt wurde. Ein Reprint der "zeitgenössischen Übersetzung" (II, 9), die der Autor Weiss seiner Ich-Figur in die Hände spielt, erschien hingegen erst nach Abschluß der *Ästhetik des Widerstands* (*Schiffbruch der Fregatte Medusa ...*, Nördlingen 1987).

10   Lorenz Eitner, *Géricault. His Life and Work* (London 1983), S. 197. Die Géricault-Adaption von Weiss würdigt Eitner als "a word-picture of the 'Raft' and its human cargo, 'Versprengte einer verlorenen Generation', that so excites one of the novel's characters as to bring on a faint" (S. 347, Anm. 178).

11   Vgl. das aufschlußreiche Kapitel über Géricault und Weiss in Bernard Dieterle, *Erzählte Bilder. Zum narrativen Umgang mit Gemälden* (Marburg 1988), S. 141ff., dem ich einige Anregungen verdanke.

12   Mein terminologischer Vorschlag in Anlehnung an Gérard Genette, *Die Erzählung*. Hrsg. und mit einem Nachwort von Jochen Vogt (München 1994), S. 162ff. Für eine narratologische Expertise danke ich Steffen Richter.

13   *Inferno* V, vol.138, p. 142. Vgl. Dante Alighieri, *Die Göttliche Komödie*

italienisch und deutsch. Übersetzt und kommentiert von Hermann Gmelin (München 1988), Bd. I, S. 68f.

14 Genia Schulz, *"Die Ästhetik des Widerstands"*, S. 76ff.

15 Peter Weiss, *Notizbücher 1971-1980* (Frankfurt a.M. 1981), Bd. I, S. 236.

16 Julian Barnes, *Eine Geschichte der Welt in 10 1/2 Kapiteln.* Aus dem Englischen von Gertraude Krueger, 5. Aufl. (München 1996), Kapitel 5: Schiffbruch. Die Lektüre sei allen Weiss-Leser(inne)n zur gelegentlichen Entkrampfung empfohlen. Weitere, mehr oder weniger postmoderne Verarbeitungen des Stoffes: Francois Weyergans, *Le radeau de la Méduse* (Paris 1983); Alessandro Baricco, *Oceano mare* (Mailand 1993).

17 Genia Schulz, *"Die Ästhetik des Widerstands"*, S. 88.

18 Von Henry Miller ist bekanntlich am Ende von *Fluchtpunkt* die Rede (und wie!).

19 Ihrer detailreichen, insgesamt zu wenig beachteten Studie verdanke ich entscheidende Hinweise: Waltraud Wiethölter, "Mnemosyne oder Die Höllenfahrt der Erinnerung. Zur Ikono-Graphie von Peter Weiss' *Ästhetik des Widerstands.*" In: *Zur Ästhetik der Moderne.* Für Richard Brinkmann zum 70. Geburtstag. Hrsg. von Gerhart von Graevenitz u.a. (Tübingen 1992), S. 217ff.

20 Vgl. Julian Barnes, *Eine Geschichte der Welt in 10 1/2 Kapiteln*, 162, sowie Germain Bazin, *Théodore Géricault. Etude critique, documents et catalogue raisonné*, 6 Bde. (Paris 1987-1994), hier Bd. VI. *Génie et folie. Le radeau de la Méduse et les Monomanes*, S. 55. Vgl. schließlich Eitners Chrakteristik: "The Raft of the Medusa combined two sides of Géricault's art, its realist tendencies ans its monumental, heroic aspirations. ... It remains one of the very few works in modern art which raises an actual event to the level of grand style and timeless significance." In *Géricault.* Ausstellungskatalog (Los Angeles, Detroit, Philadelphia 1971f.), S. 23.

21 *Inferno* XXXIII, 74. Vgl. Gmelin, Bd. I: S. 394f.

22 Leicht auffindbare Abbildung bei Nana Badenberg, "Die *Ästhetik* und ihre Kunstwerke. Eine Inventur." In: *Die Bilderwelt des Peter Weiss*, S. 114ff. Grundlegend: Gert Schiff, *Johann Heinrich Füssli 1741-1825*, 2 Bde. (Zürich und München 1973), Bd. I: S. 100ff., bes. S. 102f.; Abb. in Bd. II: S. 1200. Zum Stand der Füssli-Forschung jetzt Matthias Vogel, "Der Maler als Feuergeist und kühler Stratege. Neue Forschungsergebnisse zu Johann Heinrich Füssli." In: *Neue Zürcher Zeitung*, Nr. 19 (1998), S. 54.

23 Lorenz Eitner, *Géricaults "Raft of the Medusa"* (London 1972), S. 45: "Some years earlier als Füssli, Géricault himself had drawn an 'Ugolino in Prison', of rather similar appearance, and there can be little doubt that to his mind the image of the brooding Count did not simply represent starvation,

but symbolized the unpaintable horror of cannibalism."

24 Reproduktionen in Germain Bazin, *Théodore Géricault*, Bd. IV: *Le voyage en Italie* (1990), S. 187f., Katalognummer 1334 und 1335. *Ugolino und seine Kinder im Kerker* ist eine atmosphärisch dichte, mit Öl lavierte Federzeichnung auf einem herausgetrennten Albumblatt, dessen Rückseite Skizzen einer Koitusszene trägt (vgl. Katalognummern 1318, S.181, und 1035, S.176). Die Kerkerszene kommentiert Bazin: "En voyant la belle composition de Bayonne, on peut regretter que l'artiste n'en ait fait un tableau. C'eût été une oeuvre puissante et pathétique. Mais le destin de Géricault était de rêver son oeuvre plutôt que de la réaliser" (Bd. IV: S. 30). Das Blatt befindet sich seit langem im Musée Bonnat in Bayonne (Inv. 735 ro); 1979 war es im Louvre ausgestellt; der zweite Band der *Ästhetik* erschien 1978.

25 Klaus R. Scherpe, "Die *Ästhetik des Widerstands* als *Divina Commedia*. Peter Weiss' künstlerische Vergegenständlichung der Geschichte." In: *Peter Weiss. Werk und Wirkung*. Hrsg. von Rudolf Wolff (Bonn 1987), S. 88ff.; Kurt Oesterle, "Dante und das Mega-Ich. Literarische Formen politischer und ästhetischer Subjektivität bei Peter Weiss." In: *Literaturmagazin* 27 (1991): "Widerstand der Ästhetik? Im Anschluß an Peter Weiss", S. 45ff.; Jens Birkemeyer, *Bilder des Schreckens. Dantes Spuren und die Mythosrezeption in Peter Weiss' Roman "Die Ästhetik des Widerstands"* (Wiesbaden 1994). Weiterhin die Aufsätze von Peter Kuon, Christine Ivanovic, Michael Hofmann, und Martin Rector in *Peter Weiss Jahrbuch* 6 (1997).

26 Vgl. Waltraud Wiethölter, "Mnemosyne oder die Höllenfahrt der Erinnerung," S. 218, vgl. S. 228 u. 256.

27 Martin Robertson, *A History of Greek Art* (Cambridge 1975), Bd. I, S. 313.

28 Klaus Heinrich, "Das Floß der Medusa." In: Heinrich, *Floß der Medusa. 3 Studien zur Faszinationsgeschichte mit mehreren Beilagen und einem Anhang* (Basel und Frankfurt a.M. 1995), S. 15f.

29 Vgl. Waltraud Wiethölter, "Mnemosyne oder Höllenfahrt der Erinnerung," S. 247ff. und Abbildungsteil.

30 Klaus Heinrich, "Das Floß der Medusa," S. 16.

31 Jenseits der Werkgrenze, aber im Gedächtnisraum der Weiss-Leserschaft drängt sich natürlich auch das Schreckensbild der collagierten Medusen-Maschinen-Mutter aus *Abschied von den Eltern* auf (Abdruck u.a. bei Jochen Vogt, *Peter Weiss*, S. 72).

32 Zu den Varianten und der Verknüpfung der Mutterfigur(en) vgl. auch den frühen, nach wie vor lesenswerten Aufsatz von Carol Poore, "Mother Earth, Melancholia, and Mnemosyne: Women in Peter Weiss' *Die Ästhetik des*

Widerstands." In: *The German Quarterly* 85.1 (1985), S. 68ff.

33   Vgl. den Beitrag von Julia Hell in diesem Band.

List of Contributors

Klaus L. Berghahn is the Max and Frieda Weinstein-Bascom Professor of German and Jewish Studies at the UW-Madison.

Robert Cohen is Adjunct Associate Professor of German at the New York University.

Katja Garloff is Assistant Professor of German and Humanities at Reed College.

Julia Hell is Professor of German at the University of Michigan-Ann Arbor.

Jost Hermand is the William F. Vilas Professor of German Culture at the UW-Madison.

Alexander Honold is a Research Fellow at the Kulturwissenschaftliches Institut in Essen.

Jennifer Jenkins is a graduate student at the UW-Madison.

Michaella Lang is a graduate student at the UW-Madison.

Cordelia Scharpf is a graduate student at the UW-Madison.

Marc Silberman is Professor of German at the UW-Madison.

Yvonne Spielmann is Privatdozentin at the University of Siegen.

Jochen Vogt is Professor of German at the University of Essen.

German Life and Civilization

German Life and Civilization provides contributions to a critical understanding of Central European cultural history from medieval times to the present. Culture is here defined in the broadest sense, comprising expressions of high culture in such areas as literature, music, pictorial arts, and intellectual trends as well as political and sociohistorical developments and the texture of everyday life. Both the cultural mainstream and oppositional or minority viewpoints lie within the purview of the series. While it is based on specialized investigations of particular topics, the series aims to foster progressive scholarship that aspires to a synthetic view of culture by crossing traditional disciplinary boundaries.

Interested colleagues are encouraged to send a brief summary of their work to the general editor of the series:

Jost Hermand
Department of German
University of Wisconsin
Madison, Wisconsin 53706

To order other books in this series, please contact our Customer Service Department at:

800-770-LANG (within the U.S.)
(212) 647-7706 (outside the U.S.)
212) 647-7707 FAX

Or browse online by series at:

WWW.PETERLANG.COM